GENA SHOWALTER

"Showalter delivers yet again!"
—*RT Book Reviews* on *Wicked Nights*

"One of the premier authors of paranormal romance."
—#1 *New York Times* bestselling author Kresley Cole

"Gena Showalter knows how to keep readers glued to the pages
and smiling the whole time."
—*New York Times* bestselling author Lara Adrian on *The Darkest Surrender*

Praise for

KAIT BALLENGER

"Nonstop action, pulse-pounding suspense, and red-hot romance...
Kait Ballenger's Execution Underground series delivers in spades!"
—*New York Times* bestselling author Jaime Rush

"Action and romance in one mesmerizing story.
A phenomenal start to the Execution Underground series.
Shadow Hunter will leave you breathless and demanding more."
—Cecy Robson, author of *Sealed with a Curse*

"Taut with action, suspense, and romance that sizzles,
Shadow Hunter is an evocative prelude to what's certain to be
an exciting new series! Fans of J.R. Ward are going to love the sexy warriors
of Kait Ballenger's Execution Underground."
—Kate SeRine, author of *Red* and *The Better to See You*

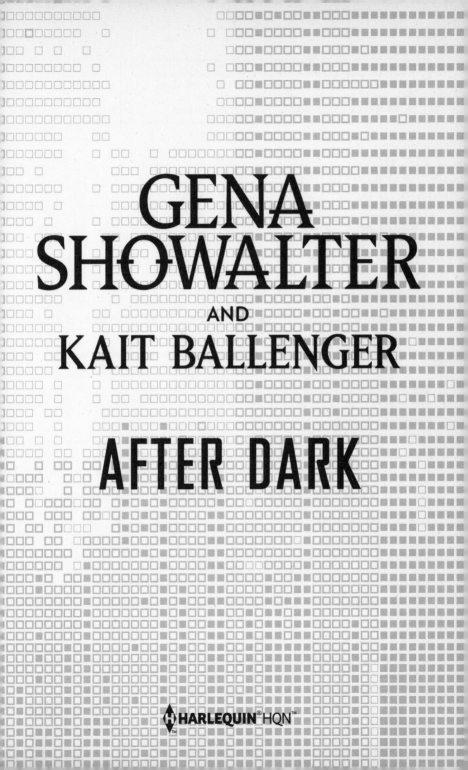

GENA SHOWALTER

AND

KAIT BALLENGER

AFTER DARK

HARLEQUIN® HQN™

Recycling programs
for this product may
not exist in your area.

ISBN-13: 978-0-373-77825-6

AFTER DARK

Printed in U.S.A.

CONTENTS

THE DARKEST ANGEL   7

SHADOW HUNTER   139

THE DARKEST ANGEL

GENA SHOWALTER

A huge THANK YOU (yes, I'm shouting joyfully) to my editor
Emily Ohanjanians, an amazing woman. I'm blessed to work with her!

And to all my wonderful readers! A joyfully shouted THANK YOU to you,
as well, for taking a chance on me, no matter what I write
or what direction I go, and always being willing to come along for the ride.
I hope you enjoy the view!

CHAPTER 1

From high in the heavens, Lysander spotted his prey. *At last.
Finally, I will end this.* His jaw clenched and his skin pulled
tight. With tension. With relief. Determined, he jumped from
the cloud he stood upon, falling quickly... Wind whipping
through his hair...

When he neared ground, he allowed his wings, long and
feathered and golden, to unfold from his back and catch in
the current, slowing his progress.

He was a soldier for Germanus, the leader of the Sent
Ones—winged warriors, like angels, but...not. Sent Ones
were far more, and Lysander was more than most. He was one
of the Elite Seven. With as many millennia as he'd lived, he'd
come to learn that each of the Elite Seven had one temptation.
One potential downfall. Like Eve with her apple. When they
found this...thing, this abomination, they happily destroyed
it before it could destroy them.

Lysander had finally found his.

Bianka Skyhawk.

She was the daughter of a Harpy and a phoenix shape-
shifter. She was a thief, a liar and a killer who found joy in
the vilest of tasks. Worse, the blood of demons—his great-

est enemy—flowed through her veins. Which meant *Bianka* was his enemy.

He lived to destroy his enemies.

However, he could only act against them when given permission from Germanus, who had to gain permission from the Most High—the absolute, final authority in the heavens. The Most High loved humans and wanted them protected. Wanted them trained to fight evil, not destroyed by it. But Bianka wasn't exactly human, was she?

Bianka was more like him, and she had cursed him with a taste for what the mortals referred to as "desire."

Something had to be done.

He'd seen her for the first time several weeks ago, long black hair flowing down her back, amber eyes bright and lips bloodred. Watching her, unable to turn away, a single question had drifted through his mind: Was her pearllike skin as soft as it appeared?

Forget desire. He'd never wondered such a thing about *anyone* before. He'd never cared. But the question was becoming an obsession, discovering the truth a need. And it had to end. Now. This day.

He landed just in front of her, but she couldn't see him. No one could. He existed on another plane, invisible to mortal and immortal alike. He could scream, and she would not hear him. He could walk through her, and she would not feel him. For that matter, she would not smell or sense him in any way.

Until it was too late.

He could have formed a fiery sword from air and cleaved her head from her body, but didn't. As he'd already realized and accepted, he could not kill her. Yet. But he could not allow her to roam unfettered, tempting him, a plague to his good sense, either. Which meant he would have to settle for imprisoning her in his home in the sky.

That didn't have to be a terrible ordeal for him, however. He could use their time together to show her the right way to live. And the right way was, of course, his way. What's more, if she did not conform, if she *did* finally commit that unpardonable sin, he would be there, at last able to rid himself of her influence.

Do it. Take her.

He reached out. But just before he could wrap his arms around her and fly her away, he realized she was no longer alone. He scowled, his arms falling to his sides. He did not want a witness to his deeds.

"Best day ever," Bianka shouted skyward, splaying her arms and twirling. Two champagne bottles were clutched in her hands and those bottles flew from her grip, slamming into the ice mountains of Alaska surrounding her. She stopped, swayed, laughed. "Oopsie."

His scowl deepened. A perfect opportunity lost, he realized. Clearly, she was intoxicated. She wouldn't have fought him. Would have assumed he was a hallucination or that they were playing a game. Having watched her these past few weeks, he knew how much she liked to play games.

"Waster," her sister, the intruder, grumbled. Though they were twins, Bianka and Kaia looked nothing alike. Kaia had red hair and gray eyes flecked with gold. She was shorter than Bianka, her beauty more delicate. "I had to stalk a collector for days—days!—to steal that. Seriously. You just busted Dom Pérignon White Gold Jeroboam."

"I'll make it up to you." Mist wafted from Bianka's mouth. "They sell Boone's Farm in town."

There was a pause, a sigh. "That's only acceptable if you also steal me some cheese tots. I used to highjack them from

Sabin every day, and now that we've left Budapest, I'm in withdrawal."

Lysander tried to pay attention to the conversation, he really did. But being this close to Bianka was, as always, ruining his concentration. Only her skin was similar to her sister's, reflecting all the colors of a newly sprung rainbow. So why didn't he wonder if *Kaia's* skin was as soft as it appeared?

Because she is not your temptation. You know this.

There, atop a peak of Devil's Thumb, he watched as Bianka plopped to her bottom. Frigid mist continued to waft around her, making her look as if she were part of a dream. Or a Sent One's nightmare.

"But you know," Kaia added, "stealing Boone's Farm in town doesn't help me now. I'm only partially buzzed and was hoping to be totally and completely smashed by the time the sun set."

"You should be thanking me, then. You got smashed last night. And the night before. And the night before that."

Kaia shrugged. "So?"

"So, your life is in a rut. You steal liquor, climb a mountain while drinking and dive off when drunk."

"Well, then yours is in a rut, too, since you've been with me each of those nights." The redhead frowned. "Still. Maybe you're right. Maybe we need a change." She gazed around the majestic summit. "So what new and exciting thing do you want to do now?"

"Complain. Can you believe Gwennie is getting married?" Bianka asked. "And to Sabin, keeper of the demon of Doubt, of all people. Or demons. Whatever."

Gwennie. Gwendolyn. Their youngest sister.

"I know. It's weird." A still-frowning Kaia eased down beside her. "Would you rather be a bridesmaid or be hit by a bus?"

"The bus. No question. That, I'd recover from."

"Agreed."

Bianka did not like weddings? Odd. Most females *craved* them. Still. *No need for the bus,* Lysander wanted to tell her. *You will not be attending your sister's wedding.*

"So which of us will be her maid of honor, do you think?" Kaia asked.

"Not it," Bianka said, just as Kaia opened her mouth to say the same.

"Cheater!"

Bianka laughed with genuine amusement. "Your duties shouldn't be too bad. Gwennie's the nicest of the Skyhawks, after all."

"Nice when she's not protecting Sabin, that is." Kaia shuddered. "I swear, threaten the man with a little bodily harm, and she's ready to claw your eyes out."

"Think we'll ever fall in love like that?" As curious as Bianka sounded, there was also a hint of sadness in her voice.

Why sadness? Did she want to fall in love? Or was she thinking of a particular man she yearned for? Lysander had not yet seen her interact with a male she desired.

Kaia waved a deceptively delicate hand through the air. "We've been alive for centuries without falling. Clearly, it's just not meant to be. But I, for one, am glad about that. Men become a liability when you try and make them permanent."

"Yeah," was the reply. "But a fun liability."

"True. And I haven't had fun in a long time," Kaia said with a pout.

"Me, either. Except with myself, but I don't suppose that counts."

"It does the way I do it."

They shared another laugh.

Fun. Sex, Lysander realized, now having no trouble keeping

up with their conversation. They were discussing sex. Something he'd never tried. Not even with himself. He'd never wanted to try, either. Still didn't. Not even with Bianka and her amazing (soft?) skin.

As long as he'd been alive—a span of time far greater than their few hundred years—he'd seen many humans caught up in the act. It looked…messy. As un-fun as something could be. Yet humans betrayed their friends and family to do it. They even willingly, happily gave up hard-earned money in exchange for it. When not taking part themselves, they became obsessed with it, watching others do it on a television or computer screen.

"We should have nailed one of the Lords when we were in Buda," Kaia said thoughtfully. "Paris is hawt."

She could only be referring to the Lords of the Underworld. Immortal warriors possessed by the demons once locked inside Pandora's box. As Lysander had observed them throughout the centuries, ensuring they obeyed heavenly laws, he knew that Paris was host to Promiscuity, forced to bed a new person every day or weaken and die.

"Paris is hot, yes, but I liked Amun." Bianka stretched to her back, mist again whipping around her. "He doesn't speak, which makes him the perfect man in my opinion."

Amun, the host of the demon of Secrets. So. Bianka liked him, did she? Lysander pictured the warrior. Tall, though Lysander was taller. Muscled, though Lysander was more so. Dark where Lysander was light. He was actually relieved to know the Harpy preferred a different type of male than himself.

That wouldn't change her fate, but it did lessen Lysander's burden. He hadn't been sure what he would have done if she'd *asked* him to touch her. That she wouldn't was most definitely a relief.

"What about Aeron?" Kaia asked. "All those tattoos…" A moan slipped from her as she shivered. "I could trace every single one of them with my tongue."

Aeron, host of Wrath. One of only two Lords with wings, Aeron's were black and gossamer. He had tattoos all over his body, and looked every inch the demon he was. What's more, he had recently broken a spiritual covenant. Therefore, Aeron would be dead before the upcoming nuptials.

Lysander's charge, Olivia, had been ordered to slay the warrior. So far she had resisted the decree. The girl was too soft-hearted for her own good. Eventually, though, she would do her duty. Otherwise, she would be kicked to earth, immortal no longer, and that was not a fate Lysander would allow.

Of all the Sent Ones he'd trained, she was by far his favorite. As gentle as she was, a man couldn't help but want to make her happy. She was trustworthy, loyal and all that was pure; she was the type of female who should have tempted him. A female he might have been able to accept in a romantic way. Wild Bianka…no. Never.

"However will I choose between my two favorite Lords, B?" Another sigh returned Lysander's focus to the Harpies.

Bianka rolled her eyes. "Just sample them both. Not like you haven't enjoyed a twofer before."

Kaia laughed, though the amusement didn't quite reach her voice. Like Bianka, there was a twinge of sadness to the sound. "True."

Lysander's mouth curled in mild distaste. Two different partners in one day. Or at the same time. Had Bianka done that, too? Probably.

"What about you?" Kaia asked. "You gonna hook up with Amun at the wedding?"

There was a long, heavy pause. Then Bianka shrugged. "Maybe. Probably."

He should leave and return when she was alone. The more he learned about her, the more he disliked her. Soon he would simply snatch her up, no matter who watched, revealing his presence, his intentions, just to save this world from her dark influence.

He flapped his wings once, twice, lifting into the air.

"You know what I want more than anything else in the world?" she asked, rolling to her side and facing her sister. Facing Lysander directly, as well. Her eyes were wide, amber irises luminous. Beams of sunlight seemed to soak into that glorious skin, and he found himself pausing.

Kaia stretched out beside her. "To co-host *Good Morning America?*"

"Well, yeah, but that's not what I meant."

"Then I'm stumped."

"Well…" Bianka nibbled on her bottom lip. Opened her mouth. Closed her mouth. Scowled. "I'll tell you, but you can't tell anyone."

The redhead pretended to twist a lock over her lips.

"I'm serious, K. Tell anyone, and I'll deny it then hunt you down and chop off your head."

Would she truly? Lysander wondered. Again, probably. He could not imagine hurting his Olivia, whom he loved like a sister. Maybe because she was not one of the Elite Seven, but was a joy-bringer, the weakest of the Sent Ones.

There were three factions in the skies. The Elite Seven, the warriors and the joy-bringers. Their status was reflected in both their different duties and the color of their wings. Each of the Seven possessed golden wings, like his own. Warriors possessed white wings merely threaded with gold, and the joy-bringers' white wings bore no gold at all.

Olivia had been a joy-bringer all the centuries of her existence. Something she was quite happy with. That was why everyone, including Olivia, had experienced such shock when golden down had begun to grow in her feathers.

Not Lysander, however. He'd petitioned the Heavenly High Council, and they'd agreed. It had needed to be done. She was too fascinated by the demon-possessed warrior Aeron. Too... infatuated. Ridding her of such an attraction was imperative. As he well knew.

His hand clenched into a fist. He blamed himself for Olivia's circumstances. He had sent her to watch the Lords. To study them. He should have gone himself, but he'd hoped to avoid Bianka.

"Well, don't just lie there. Tell me what you want to do more than anything else in the world," Kaia exclaimed.

Bianka uttered another sigh. "I want to sleep with a man."

Kaia's brow scrunched in confusion. "Uh, hello. Wasn't that what we were just discussing?"

"No, dummy. I mean, I want to sleep. As in, conk out. As in, snores so loud he contemplates kicking me out—before realizing he can't live without me."

A moment passed in silence as Kaia absorbed the announcement. "What! That's forbidden. Stupid. Dangerous."

Harpies lived by two rules, he knew. They could only eat what they stole or earned, and they could not sleep in the presence of another. The first was because of a curse on all Harpy-kind, and the second because Harpies were suspicious and untrusting by nature.

Lysander's head tilted to the side as he found himself imagining holding Bianka in his arms as she drifted into slumber. That fall of dark curls would tumble over his arm and chest. Her warmth would seep into his body. Her leg would rub over his.

He could never allow it, of course, but that didn't diminish the power of the vision. To hold her, protect her, comfort her would be…nice.

Would her skin be as soft as it appeared?

His teeth ground together. There was that ridiculous question again. *I do not care. It does not matter.*

"Forget I said anything," Bianka grumbled, flopping to her back and staring up at the bright sky.

"I can't. Your words are singed into my ears. Do you know what happened to our ancestors when they were stupid enough to fall asl—"

"Yes, okay. Yes." She pushed to her feet. The faux fur coat she wore was bloodred, same as her lips, and a vivid contrast to the white ice around her. Her boots were black and climbed to her knees. She wore skintight pants, also black. She looked wicked and beautiful.

Would her skin be as soft as it appeared?

Before he realized what he was doing, he was standing in front of her, reaching out, fingers tingling. *What are you doing? Stop!* He froze. Backed several steps away.

Sweet heaven. How close he'd come to giving in to the temptation of her.

He could not wait any longer. Could not wait until she was alone. He had to act now. His reaction to her was growing stronger. Any more, and he *would* touch her. And if he liked touching her, he might want to do more. That was how temptation worked. You gave in to one thing, then yearned for another. And another. Soon, you were lost.

"Enough heavy talk. Let's get back to our boring routine and jump," Bianka said, stalking to the edge of the peak. "You know the rules. Girl who breaks the least amount of bones wins. If you die, you lose. For, like, ever." She gazed down.

So did Lysander. There were crests and dips along the way,

ice bounders with sharp, deadly ridges and thousands of feet of air. Such a jump would have killed a mortal, no question. The Harpy merely joked about the possibility, as if it were of no consequence. Did she think herself invulnerable?

Kaia lumbered to her feet and swayed from the liquor still pouring through her. "Fine, but don't think this is the last of our conversation about sleeping habits and stupid girls who—"

Bianka dove.

Lysander expected the action, but was still surprised by it. He followed her down. She spread her arms, closed her eyes, grinning foolishly. That grin…affected him. Clearly she reveled in the freedom of soaring. Something he often did, as well. But she would not have the end she desired.

Seconds before she slammed into a boulder, Lysander allowed himself to materialize in her plane. He grabbed her, arms catching under hers, wings unfolding, slowing them. Her legs slapped against him, jarring him, but he didn't release his hold.

A gasp escaped her, and her eyelids popped open. When she spotted him, amber eyes clashing with the dark of his, that gasp became a growl.

Most would have asked who he was or demanded he go away. Not Bianka.

"Big mistake, Stranger Danger," she snapped. "One you'll pay for."

As many battles as he'd fought over the years and as many opponents as he'd slain, he didn't have to see to know she had just unsheathed a blade from a hidden slit in her coat. And judging by the smug smile that appeared, the deranged woman clearly thought she could stab him. As if he wasn't faster. Stronger. Better. The last thought caused his chest to ache, but he wasn't sure why.

"It is you who made the mistake, Harpy. But do not worry.

I have every intention of rectifying that." Before she could ensure that her weapon met its intended target, he whisked her into another plane, into his home—where she would stay. Forever.

CHAPTER 2

Bianka Skyhawk gaped at her new surroundings. One moment she'd been tumbling toward an icy valley, intent on escaping her sister's line of questioning, as well as winning their break-the-least-amount-of-bones game, and the next she'd been in the arms of a gorgeous blond. Which wasn't necessarily a good thing. She'd tried to stab him, and he'd blocked her. Freaking blocked her. No one should be able to block a Harpy's deathblow.

Now she was standing inside a cloud-slash-palace. A palace that was bigger than any home she'd ever seen. A palace that was warm and sweetly scented, with an almost tangible sense of peace wafting through the air.

The walls were wisps of white and smoke, and as she watched, murals formed, seemingly alive, winged creatures, both angelic and demonic, soaring through a morning sky. They reminded her of Danika's paintings. Danika—the All-Seeing Eye who could glimpse into both heaven and hell. The floors, though comprised of that same ethereal substance, allowing a view of the land and people below, were somehow solid.

Angelic. Cloud. The lowest level of heaven? Dread flooded her as she spun to face the male who had grabbed her. "Angelic" described him perfectly. From the top of his pale head to the strength in that leanly muscled, sun-kissed body, to the golden wings stretching from his back. Even the white robe that fell to his ankles and the sandals wrapped around his feet gave him a saintly aura.

Was he an angel, then? Or a Sent One? Her heart skipped a beat. He wasn't human, that was for sure. No human male could ever hope to compare to such blinding perfection. But hello baby, those eyes...they were dark and hard and almost, well, empty.

His eyes don't matter. Angels and Sent Ones were demon assassins, and she was as close to a demon as a girl could get. After all, her ancestors hailed from the depths of hell. Long ago, fallen angels had mated with humans, and the children born from those unions had later mated with other humans, and her race was one of the results.

Unsure of what to do, Bianka strode around her blond; he remained in place, even when she was at his back, as if he had nothing to fear from her. Maybe he didn't. Obviously he had powers. One, he'd blocked her—she just couldn't get over that fact—and two, he'd somehow removed her coat and all her weapons without touching her.

"Are you an angel?" she asked when she was once again in front of him.

"No. I'm a Sent One."

Poor guy, she thought with a shudder. Clearly he had no idea the crappy hand he'd been dealt. If she had to choose between being a Sent One and a dog, she'd choose the dog. They, at least, were respectable.

She'd never been this close to a Sent One before. Seen one, yes. Or rather, seen what she'd thought was one of the winged warriors of the skies but had later learned was a demon in disguise. Either way, she hadn't liked the guy, her youngest sister's father. He considered himself a god and everyone else beneath him.

"Did you bring me here to kill me?" she asked. Not that he'd have any luck. He would find that she was not an easy target. Many immortals had tried to finish her off over the years, but none had succeeded. Obviously.

He sighed, warm breath trekking over her cheeks. She had accidentally-on-purpose closed some of the distance between them; he smelled of the icecaps she so loved. Fresh and crisp with just a hint of earthy spice.

When he realized that only a whisper separated them, his lips, too full for a man but somehow perfect for him, pressed into a mulish line. Though she didn't see him move, he was suddenly a few more inches away from her. Huh. Interesting. Had he increased the distance on purpose?

Curious, she stepped toward him.

He backed away.

He had. Why? Was he scared of her?

Just to be contrary, as she often was, she stepped toward him again. Again, he stepped away. So. The big bad Sent One didn't want to be within striking distance. She almost grinned.

"Well," she prompted. "Did you?"

"No. I did not bring you here to kill you." His voice was rich, sultry, a sin all its own. And yet, there was a layer of absolute truth to it, and she suspected she would have believed anything he said. As if whatever he said was simply fated, meant to be. Unchangeable. "I want you to emulate my life. I want you to learn from me."

"Why?" What would he do if she touched him? The tiny gossamer wings on her own back fluttered at the thought. Her T-shirt was designed especially for her kind, the material loose to keep from pinning those wings as she jolted into super-speed. "Wait. Don't answer. Let's make out first." A lie, but he didn't need to know that.

"Bianka," he said, his patience clearly waning. "This is not a game. Do not make me bind you to my bed."

"Ohh, now that I like. Sounds kinky." She darted around him, running her fingertips over his cheek, his neck. "You're as soft as a baby."

He sucked in a breath, stiffened. "Bianka."

"But better equipped."

"Bianka!"

She patted his butt. "Yes?"

"You will cease that immediately!"

"Make me." She laughed, the amused, carefree sound echoing between them.

Scowling, he reached out and latched on to her upper arm. There wasn't time to evade him; shockingly, he was faster than she was. He jerked her in front of him, and dark, narrowed eyes stared down at her.

"There will be no touching. Do you understand?"

"Do you?" Her gaze flicked to his hand, still clutching her arm. "At the moment, you're the one touching me."

Like hers, his gaze fell to where they were connected. He licked his lips, and his grip tightened just the way she liked. Then he released her as if she were on fire and once again increased the distance between them.

"Do you understand?" His tone was hard and flat.

What was the problem? He should be begging to touch her. She was a desirable Harpy, thank you very much. Her body was a work of art and her face total perfection. But for his benefit, she said, "Yeah, I understand. That doesn't mean I'll obey." Her skin tingled, craving the return of his. *Bad girl. Bad, bad girl. He's a stupid warrior, more brawn than brains, and therefore not an appropriate plaything. Wait.* Surely that thought hadn't come from her. She loved men with more brawn than brains, right?

A moment passed as he absorbed her words. "Are you not frightened of me?" His wings folded into his back, arcing over his shoulders.

"No," she said, raising a brow and doing her best to appear unaffected. "Should I be?"

"Yes."

Well, then, he'd have to somehow grow the fiery claws of her father's people. That was the only thing that scared her. Having been scratched as a child, having felt the acid-burn of fire spread through her entire body, having spent days writhing in agonizing, seemingly endless pain, she would do anything to avoid such an experience again.

"Well, I'm still not. And now you're starting to bore me." She anchored her hands on her hips, glaring up at him. "I asked you a question but you never answered it. Why do you want me to be like you? So much so, that you brought me into the skies?"

A muscle ticked below one of his eyes. "Because I am good and you are evil."

Another laugh escaped her. He frowned, and her laughter increased until tears were running from her eyes. When she quieted, she said, "Good job. You staved off the boredom."

His frown deepened. "I was not teasing you. I mean to keep you here forever and train you to be respectable."

"Golly gee—is that right? Is that what you'd say? How adorable are you? 'I mean to keep you here forever and train you,'" she said in her best impersonation of him. There was no reason to fight about her eventual escape. She'd prove him wrong just as soon as she decided to leave. Right now, she was too intrigued. With her surroundings, she assured herself, and not the Sent One. The skies were not a place she'd ever thought to visit.

His chin lifted a notch, but his eyes remained expressionless. "I am serious."

"I'm sure you are. But you'll find that you can't keep me anywhere I don't want to be. And me? Respectable? Funny!"

"We shall see."

His confidence might have unnerved her had she been less confident in her own abilities. As a Harpy, she could lift a semi as if it were no more significant than a pebble, could move faster than the human eye could see and had no problem slaying an unwelcome host.

"Be honest," she said. "You saw me and wanted a piece, right?"

For the briefest of moments, horror blanketed his face. "No," he croaked out, then cleared his throat and said more smoothly, "No."

Jerk! Why such horror at the thought of being with her? *She* was the one who should be horrified. He was clearly a do-gooder, more so than she'd realized. *I am good and you are evil,* he'd said. Ugh.

"So tell me again why you want to change me. Didn't anyone ever tell you that you shouldn't mess with perfection?"

That muscle started ticking below his eye again. "You are a menace."

"Whatever, dude." She liked to steal—so what. She could kill without blinking—again, so what. It wasn't like she worked for the IRS or anything. "Where's my sister, Kaia? She's as much a menace as I am, I'm sure. So why don't you want to change her?"

"She is still in Alaska, wondering if you are buried inside an ice cave. And you are my only project at the moment."

Project? Oh, that burned more than all his other insults

put together. But she did like the thought of Kaia searching high and low but finding no sign of her, almost like they were playing a game of hide-and-seek. Bianka would totally, finally win.

"You appear...excited," he said, head tilting to the side. "Why? Does her concern not disturb you?"

Yep. A certified do-gooder. "It's not like I'll be here long." She peeked over his shoulder; more of that wisping white greeted her. "Got anything to drink here?"

"No."

"Eat?"

"No."

"Wear?"

"No."

Slowly the corners of her lips lifted. "I guess that means you like to go naked. Awesome."

His cheeks reddened. "Enough. You are trying to bait me and I do not like it."

"Then you shouldn't have brought me here." Hey, wait a minute. He'd never really told her why he'd chosen her as his *project,* she realized. "Be honest. Do you need my help with something?" After all, she, like many of her fellow Harpies, was a mercenary, paid to find and retrieve. Her motto: if it's unethical and illegal and you've got the cash, I'm your girl! "I mean, I know you didn't just bring me here to save the world from my naughty influence. Otherwise, millions of other people would be here with me."

He crossed his arms over his massive chest.

She sighed. Knowing men as she did, she knew he was done answering that type of question. Oh, well. She could have convinced him otherwise by annoying him until he caved, but she didn't want to put the work in.

"So what do you do for fun around here?" she asked.

"I destroy demons."

Like you, she finished for him. But he'd already said he had no intention of killing her, and she believed him—how could she not? That voice… "So you don't want to hurt me, you don't want to touch me, but you do want me to live here forever."

"Yes."

"I'd be an idiot to refuse such an offer." That she sounded sincere was a miracle. "We'll pretend to be married and spend the nights locked in each other's arms, kissing and touching, our bodies—"

"Stop. Just stop." And, drumroll please, that muscle began ticking under his eye again.

This time, there was no fighting her grin. It spread wide and proud. That tic was a sign of anger, surely. But what would it take to make that anger actually seep into his irises? What would it take to break even a fraction of his iron control?

"Show me around," she said. "If I'm going to live here, I need to know where my walk-in closet is." During the tour, she could accidentally-on-purpose brush against him. Over and over again. "Do we have cable?"

"No. And I cannot give you a tour. I have duties. Important duties."

"Yeah, you do. My pleasure. That should be priority one."

Teeth grinding together, he turned on his heel and strode away. "You will find it difficult to get into trouble here, so I suggest you do not even try." His voice echoed behind him.

Please. She could get into trouble with nothing but a toothpick and a spoon. "If you leave, I'll rearrange everything." Not that there was any furniture to be seen.

Silence.

"I'll get bored and take off."

"Try."

It was a response, at least. "So you're seriously going to leave me? Just like that?" She snapped her fingers.

"Yes." Another response, though he didn't stop walking.

"What about that bed you were going to chain me to? Where is it?"

Uh-oh, back to silence.

"You didn't even tell me your name," she called, irritated despite herself. How could he abandon her like that? He should hunger for more of her. "Well? I deserve to know the name of the man I'll be cursing."

Finally, he stopped. Still, a long while passed in silence and she thought he meant to ignore her. Again. Then he said, "My name is Lysander," and stepped from the cloud, disappearing from view.

CHAPTER 3

Lysander watched as two newly recruited warrior Sent Ones—Sent Ones under his training and command—finally subdued a demonic minion charged with influencing a human to commit evil. The creaure had whispered in a human female's ear, stirring her up with fear in an attempt to open a doorway to her mind so he could slip inside and live. The creature was scaled from head to hoof and little horns protruded from its shoulders and back. Its eyes were bright red, like crystallized blood.

The fight had lasted half an hour, and both Sent Ones were now bleeding, panting. Demons were notorious for their biting and scratching.

Lysander should have been able to critique the men and tell them what they had done wrong. That way, they would do a better job next time. But as they'd struggled with the fiend, his mind had drifted to Bianka. What was she doing? Was she resigned to her fate yet? He'd given her several days alone to calm and accept.

"What now?" one of his trainees asked. Beacon was his name.

"You letsss me go, you letsss me go," the demon said pleadingly, its forked tongue giving it a lisp. "I behave. I do good. Ssswear."

Lies. As a minion, it was one of the weaker demons and

quite low on the chain of power. Oh, yes. Even demons had a hierarchy, one they strictly followed, and a fact that never failed to baffle him. But the war between good and evil demanded no less as chaos could never win.

"Execute it," Lysander commanded. "No longer shall it reign in terror."

The minion began to struggle again. "You going to lisssten to him when you obviousssly ssstronger and better than him? He make you do all hard work. He do nothing hissself. Lazy, if you asssk me. Kill *him*."

"We do not ask you," Lysander said.

Both Sent Ones raised their hands and fiery swords appeared.

"Pleassse," the demon screeched. "No. Don't do thisss."

They didn't hesitate. They struck.

The scaled head rolled, yet the warriors did not dematerialize their swords. They kept the tips poised on the motionless body until it caught flame. When nothing but ash remained, they looked to Lysander for instruction.

"Excellent job." He nodded in satisfaction. "You have improved since your last killing, and I am proud of you. But you will train with Raphael until further notice," he said. Raphael was strong, intelligent and one of the best trackers in the lower heavens.

Raphael would not be distracted by a Harpy he had no hopes of possessing.

Possessing? Lysander's jaw clenched tightly. He was not some vile demon. He possessed nothing. Ever. And when he finished with Bianka, she would be glad of that. There would be no more games, no more racing around him, caressing him and laughing. The clenching in his jaw stopped, but his shoulders sagged. In disappointment? Couldn't be.

Perhaps *he* needed a few days to calm and accept.

★ ★ ★

He'd left her alone for a week, the sun rising and setting beyond the clouds. And each day, Bianka grew madder—and madder. And madder. Worse, she grew weaker. Harpies could only eat what they stole (or earned, but there was no way to earn a single morsel here). And no, that wasn't a rule she could overlook. It was a curse. A curse her people had endured for centuries. Reviled as Harpies were, the Greeks—the former leaders of a lower realm of the skies and offspring of fallen angels and humans in a much higher concentrate than Bianka's people—had banded together and decreed that no Harpy could enjoy a meal freely given or one the females had prepared themeselves. If they did, they sickened terribly. The Greeks' hope? Destruction.

Instead, they'd merely ensured Harpies learned how to steal from birth. To survive, she would do just about anything.

Lysander would learn that firsthand. She would make sure of it.

Had he planned this to torture her?

In this palace, Bianka had only to speak of something and it would materialize before her. An apple—bright and red and juicy. Baked turkey—succulent and plump. But she couldn't eat them, and it was killing her. Liter—freaking—ally.

At first, Bianka had tried to escape. Several times. Unlike Lysander the Cruel, she couldn't jump from the clouds. The floor expanded wherever she stepped and remained as hard as marble. All she could do was move from ethereal room to ethereal room, watching the murals play out battle scenes. Once she'd thought she'd even spied Lysander.

Of course, she'd said, "Rock," and a nice-size stone had appeared in her hand. She'd chucked it at him, but the stupid thing had fallen to earth rather than hit him.

Where was he? What was he doing? Did he mean to kill

her like this, despite his earlier denial? Slowly and painfully? At least the hunger pains had finally left her. Now she was merely consumed by a sensation of trembling emptiness.

She wanted to stab him the moment she saw him. Then set him on fire. Then scatter his ashes in a pasture where lots of animals roamed. He deserved to be smothered by several nice steaming piles. Of course, if he waited much longer, *she* would be the one burned and scattered. She couldn't even drink a glass of water.

Besides, fighting him wasn't the way to punish him. That, she'd realized the first day here. He didn't like to be touched. Therefore, touching him was the way to punish him. And touch him she would. Anywhere, everywhere. Until he begged her to stop. No. Until he begged her to continue.

She would make him *like* it, and then take it away.

If she lasted.

Right now, she could barely hold herself up. In fact, why was she even trying?

"Bed," she muttered weakly, and a large four-poster appeared just in front of her. She hadn't slept since she'd gotten here. Usually she crashed in trees, but she wouldn't have had the strength to climb one even if the cloud had been filled with them. She collapsed on the plush mattress, velvet coverlet soft against her skin. Sleep. She'd sleep for a little while.

Finally Lysander could stand it no more. Nine days. He'd lasted nine days. Nine days of thinking about the female constantly, wondering what she was doing, what she was thinking. If her skin was as soft as it looked.

He could tolerate it no longer. He would check on her, that was all, and see for himself how—and what—she was doing. Then he would leave her again. Until he got himself under control. Until he stopped thinking about her. Stopped wanting to be near her. Her training had to begin sometime.

His wings glided up and down as he soared to his cloud. His heartbeat was a bit…odd. Faster than normal, even bumping against his ribs. Also, his blood was like fire in his veins. He didn't know what was wrong. Sent Ones only sickened when they were infected with demon poison, and as Lysander had not been bitten by a demon—had not even fought one in weeks—he knew that was not the problem.

Blame could probably be laid at Bianka's door, he thought with a scowl.

First thing he noticed upon entering was the food littering the floor. From fruits to meats to bags of chips. All were uneaten, even unopened.

Scowl melting into a frown, he folded his wings into his back and stalked forward. He found Bianka inside one of the rooms, lying atop a bed. She wore the same clothing she'd been clad in when he'd first taken her—red shirt, tights that molded to her perfect curves—but had discarded her boots. Her hair was tangled around her, and her skin worryingly pale. There was no sparkle to it, no pearllike gleam. Bruises now formed half-moons under her eyes.

Part of him had expected to find her fuming—and out for his head. The other part of him had hoped to find her compliant. Not once had he thought to find her like *this*.

She thrashed, the covers bunched around her. His frown deepened.

"Hamburger," she croaked.

A juicy burger appeared on the floor a few inches from the bed, all the extras—lettuce, tomato slices, pickles and cheese—decorating the edges of the plate. The manifestation didn't surprise him. That was the beauty of these angelic homes. Whatever was desired—within reason, of course—was provided.

All this food, and she hadn't taken a single bite. Why would she request— It wasn't stolen, he realized, and for the first time in his endless existence, he was angry with himself. And scared. For her. He hated the emotion, but there it was. She hadn't eaten in these past nine days because she couldn't. She was truly starving to death.

Though he wanted her out of his head, out of his life, he hadn't wanted her to suffer. Yet suffer she had. Unbearably. Now she was too weak to steal anything. And if he force-fed her, she would vomit, hurting more than she already was. Suddenly he wanted to roar.

"Blade," he said, and within a single blink, a sharp-tipped blade rested in his hand. He stalked to the side of the bed. He was trembling.

"Fries. Chocolate shake." Her voice was soft, barely audible.

Lysander slashed one of his wrists. Blood instantly spilled from the wound, and he stretched out his arm, forcing each drop to fall into her mouth. Blood was not food for Harpies; it was medicine. Therefore her body could accept it. He'd never freely given his blood to another living being and wasn't sure he liked the thought of something of his flowing inside this woman's veins. In fact, the thought actually caused his heartbeat to start slamming against his ribs again. But there was no other way.

At first, she didn't act as if she noticed. Then her tongue emerged, licking at the liquid before it could reach her lips. Then her eyes opened, amber irises bright, and she grabbed on to his arm, jerking it to her mouth. Her sharp teeth sank into his skin as she sucked.

Another odd sensation, he thought. Having a woman drink from him. There was heat and wetness and a sting, yet it was not unpleasant. It actually lanced a pang of...something un-nameable straight to his stomach and between his legs.

"Drink all you need," he told her. His body would not run out. Every drop was replaced the moment it left him.

Her gaze narrowed on him. The more she swallowed, the more fury he saw banked there. Soon her fingers were tightening around his wrist, her nails cutting deep. If she expected some sort of reaction from him, she would not get it. He'd been alive too long and endured far too many injuries to be affected by something so minor. Except for that pang between his legs... *What* was that?

Finally, though, she released him. He wasn't sure if that gladdened him or filled him with disappointment.

Gladdened, of course, he told himself.

A trickle of red flowed from the corner of her mouth, and she licked it away. The sight of that pink tongue caused another lance to shoot through him.

Definitely disap—uh, gladdened.

"You dirty rat," she growled through her panting. "You sick, dirty, torturing rat."

He moved out of striking distance. Not to protect himself, but to protect her. If she were to attack him, he would have to subdue her. And if he subdued her, he might hurt her. And accidentally brush against her. *Blood...heating...*

"It was never my intent to harm you," he said. And now, even his voice was trembling. Odd.

"And that makes what you did okay?" She jerked to a sitting position, all that dark hair spilling around her shoulders. The pearllike sheen was slowly returning to her skin. "You left me here, unable to eat. Dying!"

"I know." Was that skin as soft as it looked? He gulped. "And I am sorry." Her anger should have overjoyed him. As he'd hoped, she would no longer laugh up at him, her face lit with the force of her amusement. She would no longer race around him, petting him. Yes, he should have been over-joyed. Instead, the disappointment he'd just denied experiencing raced through him. Disappointment mixed with shame.

She was more a temptation than he had realized.

"You know?" she gasped out. "You know that I can only consume what I steal or earn and yet you failed to make arrangements for me?"

"Yes," he admitted, hating himself for the first time in his existence.

"What's more, you left me here. With no way home."

His nod was stiff. "I have since made restitution by saving your life. But as I said, I am sorry."

"Oh, well, you're sorry," she said, throwing up her arms. "That makes everything better. That makes almost dying acceptable." She didn't wait for his reply. She kicked her legs over the bed and stood. Her skin was at full glow now. "Now you listen up. First, you're going to find a way to feed me. Then, you're going to tell me how to get off this stupid cloud. Otherwise I will make your life a hell you've never experienced before. Actually, I will, anyway. That way, you'll never forget what happens when you mess with a Harpy."

He believed her. Already she affected him more than anyone else ever had. That was hell enough. Proof: his mouth was actually watering to taste her, his hands itching to touch her. Rather than reveal these new developments, however, he said, "You are powerless here. How would you hurt me?"

"Powerless?" She laughed. "I don't think so." One step, two, she approached him.

He held his ground. He would not retreat. Not this time. *Assert your authority.* "You cannot leave unless I allow it. The cloud belongs to me and place my will above yours. Therefore, there is no exit for you. You would be wise to curry my favor."

She sucked in a breath, paused. "So you still mean to keep me here forever? Even though I have a wedding to attend?" She sounded surprised.

"When did I ever give you the impression that I meant otherwise? Besides, I heard you tell your sister you didn't want to go to that wedding."

"No, I said I didn't want to be a bridesmaid. But I love my baby sis, so I'll do it. With a smile." Bianka ran her tongue over her straight white teeth. "But let's talk about you. You like to eavesdrop, huh? That sounds a little naughty for a goody-goody angel."

He'd never been naughty before. The goody-goody, though... Was that how she saw him? Rather than as the righteous soldier he was? "In war, I do what I must to win."

"Let me get this straight." Her eyes narrowed as she crossed her arms over her middle. Stubbornness radiated from her. "We were at war before I even met you?"

"Correct." A war he would win. But what would he do if he failed to set her on the right path? He would have to destroy her, of course, but for him to legally be allowed to destroy her, he reminded himself, she would first have to commit an unpardonable crime. Though she'd lived a long time, she had never crossed that line. There was a solution, of course, but one he found distasteful. He would never stoop to the level of the demons and try to trick her into warring against the Most High or even Germanus—the only way to ensure her death happened now rather than later. When it came to heavenly laws, breaking one meant death, but that death didn't always manifest right away. This would. Other Sent Ones would come after her and treat her just as they treated the demons. And yet, he...didn't like the idea.

Maybe because it was too messy, he told himself. He liked things neat and orderly.

Perhaps he would simply leave Bianka here, alone for the rest of eternity. That way, she could live but would be unable to cause trouble. He would visit her every few weeks—perhaps months—but never remain long enough for her to corrupt him.

A sudden blow to the cheek sent his head whipping to the side. He frowned, straightened and rubbed the now-stinging spot. Bianka was exactly as she'd been before, standing in front of him. Only now she was smiling.

"You hit me," he said, his astonishment clear.

"How sweet of you to notice."

"Why did you do that?" To be honest, he should not have been surprised. Harpies were as violent by nature as their inhuman counterparts the demons. Why couldn't she have looked like a demon, though? Why did she have to be so lovely? "I saved you, gave you my blood. I even explained why you could not leave, just as you asked. I did not have to do any of those things."

"Do I really need to repeat your crimes?"

"No." They were not crimes! But perhaps it was best to change the subject. "Allow me to feed you," he said. He walked to the plate holding the hamburger and picked it up. The scent of spiced meat wafted to his nose, and his mouth curled in distaste.

Though he didn't want to, though his stomach rolled, he took a bite. He wanted to gag, but managed to swallow. Normally he only ate fruits, nuts and vegetables. "This," he said with much disgust, "is mine." Careful not to touch her, he placed the food in her hands. "You are not to eat it."

By staking the verbal claim, the meal did indeed become his. He watched understanding light her eyes.

"Oh, cool." She didn't hesitate to rip into the burger, every crumb gone in seconds. Next he sipped the chocolate shake.

The sugar was almost obscene in his mouth, and he did gag. "Mine," he repeated faintly, giving it to her, as well. "But next time, please request a healthier meal."

She flipped him off as she gulped back the ice cream. "More."

He bypassed the French fries. No way was he going to defile his body with one of those greasy abominations. He found an apple, a pear, but had to request a stalk of broccoli himself. After claiming them, he took a bite of each and handed them over. Much better.

Bianka devoured them. Well, except for the broccoli. That, she threw at him. "I'm a carnivore, moron."

She hardly had to remind him when the unpleasant taste of the burger lingered on his tongue. Still, he chose to overlook her mockery. "All of the food produced in this home is mine. Mine and mine alone. You are to leave it alone."

"That'd be great if I were actually staying," she muttered while stuffing the fries in her mouth.

He sighed. She would accept her fate soon enough. She would have to.

The more she ate, the more radiant her skin became. Magnificent, he thought, reaching out before he could stop himself.

She grabbed his fingers and twisted just before contact. "Nope. I don't like you, so you don't get to handle the goods."

He experienced a sharp pain, but merely blinked over at her. "My apologies," he said stiffly. Thank the Most High she'd stopped him. No telling what he would have done to her had he actually touched her. Behaved like a slobbering human? He shuddered.

She shrugged and released him. "Now for my second order. Let me go home." As she spoke, she assumed a battle stance. Legs braced apart, hands fisted at her sides.

He mirrored her movements, refusing to admit, even to himself, that her bravery heated his traitorous blood another degree. "You cannot hurt me, Harpy. Fighting me would be pointless."

Slowly her lips curled into a devilish grin. "Who said I was going to try and hurt you?"

Before Lysander could blink, she closed the distance between them and pressed against him, arms winding around his neck and tugging his head down. Their lips met and her tongue thrust into his mouth. Automatically, he stiffened. He had seen humans kiss more times than he could count, but he'd never longed to try the act for himself.

Like sex and trickery, it seemed messy—in every way imaginable—and unnecessary. But as her tongue rolled against his, as her hands caressed a path down his spine, his body warmed—far more than it had when he'd simply thought of being here with her—and the tingle he'd noticed earlier bloomed once more. Only this time, that tingle grew and spread. Like the shaft between his legs. Rising…thickening…

He'd wanted to taste her and now he was. She was delicious, like the apple she'd just eaten, only sweeter, headier, like his favorite wine. He should make her stop. This was too much. But the wetness of her mouth wasn't messy in the least. It was electrifying.

More, a little voice said in his head.

"Yes," she rasped, as if he'd spoken aloud.

When she rubbed her lower body against his, every sensation intensified. His hands fisted at his sides. He couldn't touch her. Shouldn't touch her. Should stop this as she'd stopped him, as he'd already tried to convince himself.

A moan escaped her. Her fingers tangled in his hair. His scalp, an area he'd never considered sensitive before, ached, soaking up every bit of attention. And when she rubbed against him again, *he* almost moaned.

Her hands fell to his chest and a fingertip brushed one of his nipples. He did moan; he did grab her. His fingers gripped her hips, holding her still even though he wanted to force her to rub against him some more. The lack of motion didn't slow her kiss. She continued to dance their tongues together, leisurely, as if she could drink from him forever. And wanted to.

He should stop this, he told himself yet again.

Yes. Yes, he would. He tried to push her tongue out of his mouth. The pressure created another sensation, this one new and stronger than any other. His entire body felt aflame. He started pushing at her tongue for an entirely different reason, twining them together, tasting her again, licking her, sucking her.

"Mmm, yeah. That's the way," she praised.

Her voice was a drug, luring him in deeper, making him crave more. More, more, more. The temptation was too much, and he had to—

Temptation.

The word echoed through his mind, a sword sharp enough to cut bone. She was a temptation. She was *his* temptation. And he was allowing her to lead him astray.

He wrenched away from her, and his arms fell to his sides, heavy as boulders. He was panting, sweating, things he had not done even in the midst of battle. Angry as he was—at her, at himself—his gaze drank in the sight of her. Her skin was flushed, glowing more than ever. Her lips were red and swollen. And he had caused that reaction. Sparks of pride took him by surprise.

"You should not have done that," he growled.

Slowly she grinned. "Well, you should have stopped me."

"I wanted to stop you."

"But you didn't," she said, that grin growing.

His teeth ground together. "Do not do it again."

One of her brows arched in smug challenge. "Keep me here against my will, and I'll do that and more. Much, much more. In fact…" She ripped her shirt over her head and tossed it aside, revealing breasts covered by pink lace.

Breathing became impossible.

"Want to touch them?" she asked huskily, cupping them with her hands. "I'll let you. I won't even make you beg."

Sweet mercy. His mind latched on to the word *mercy* and held on. Yes, he needed her to have mercy on him. Her breasts were plump and mouth-watering. Lickable. And if he did lick them, would they taste as her mouth had? Like that heady wine? *Blood…heating…again…*

He didn't care what kind of coward his next action made him. It was either jump from the cloud or replace her hands with his own.

He jumped.

CHAPTER 4

Lysander left Bianka alone for another week—jerk!—but she didn't mind. Not this time. She had plenty to keep her occupied. Like her plan to drive him utterly insane with lust. So insane he'd regret bringing her here. Regret keeping her here. Regret even being alive.

That, or fall so in love with her that he yearned to grant her every desire. If that was the case—and it was a total possibility since she was *insanely* hot—she would convince him to take her home, and then she would finally get to stab him in the heart.

Perfect. Easy. With her breasts, it was almost too easy, really.

To set the stage for his downfall, she decorated his home like a bordello. Red velvet lounges now waited next to every door—just in case he was too overcome with desire for her to make it to one of the beds now perched in every corner. Naked portraits—of her—hung on the misty walls. A decorating style she'd picked up from her friend Anya, who just happened to be the goddess of Anarchy.

As Lysander had promised, Bianka had only to speak what she wanted—within reason—to receive it. Apparently furniture and pretty pictures were within reason. She chuckled. She could hardly wait to see him again. To finally begin.

He wouldn't stand a chance. Not just because of her (magnificent) breasts and hotness—hey, no reason to act as if she didn't know—but because he had no experience. She had been his first kiss; she knew it beyond any doubt. He'd been stiff at first, unsure. Hesitant. At no point had he known what to do with his hands.

That hadn't stopped her from enjoying herself, however. His taste...decadent. Sinful. Like crisp clean skies mixed with turbulent night storms. And his body, oh, his body. Utter perfection with hard muscles she'd wanted to squeeze. And lick. She wasn't picky.

His hair was so silky she could have run her fingers through it forever. His shaft had been so long and thick she could have rubbed herself to orgasm. His skin was so warm and smooth she could have pressed against him and slept, just as she'd dreamed about doing before she'd met him. Even though sleeping with a man was a dangerous crime her race never committed.

Stupid girl! The warrior wasn't to be trusted, especially since he clearly had nefarious plans for her—though he still refused to tell her exactly what those plans were. Teaching her to act like him had to be a misdirection of the truth. It was just too silly to contemplate. But his plans didn't matter, she supposed, since he would soon be at her mercy. Not that she had any.

Bianka strode to the closet she'd created and flipped through the lingerie hanging there. Blue, red, black. Lace, leather, satin. Several costumes: naughty nurse, corrupt policewoman, devil, angel. Which should she choose today?

He already thought her evil. Perhaps she should wear the see-through white lace. His very own innocent bride. Oh, yes. That was the one. She laughed as she dressed.

"Mirror, please," she said, and a full-length mirror appeared in front of her. The gown fell to her ankles, but there was a slit between her legs. A slit that stopped at the apex of her thighs. Too bad she wasn't wearing any panties.

Spaghetti straps held the material in place on her shoulders and dipped into a deep vee between her breasts. Her nipples, pink and hard, played peek-a-boo with the swooping make-me-a-woman pattern.

She left her hair loose, flowing like black velvet down her back. Her gold eyes sparkled, flecks of gray finally evident, like in Kaia's. Her cheeks were flushed like a rose, her skin devoid of the makeup she usually wore to dull its shimmer.

Bianka traced her fingertips along her collarbone and chuckled again. She'd summoned a shower and washed off every trace of that makeup. If Lysander had found himself attracted to her before—and he had, the size of his hard-on was proof of that—he would be unable to resist her now. She was nothing short of radiant.

A Harpy's skin was like a weapon. A sensual weapon. Its jewellike sheen drew men in, made them slobbering, drooling fools. Touching it became all they could think about, all they lived for.

That got old after a while, though, which was why she'd begun wearing full body makeup. For Lysander, though, she would make an exception. He deserved what he got. After all, he wasn't just making Bianka suffer. He was making her sisters suffer. Maybe.

Was Kaia still looking for her? Still worried or perhaps thinking this was a game as Bianka had first supposed? Had Kaia called their other sisters and were the girls now searching the world over for a sign of her, as they'd done when Gwennie went missing? Probably not, she thought with a sigh. They knew her, knew her strength and her determination. If they suspected she'd been taken, they would have confidence in her ability to free herself. Still.

Lysander was such a turd.

And most likely a virgin. Eager, excited, she rubbed her hands together. Most men kissed the women they bedded. And if she had been his first kiss, well, it stood to reason he'd never bedded anyone. Her eagerness faded a bit. But that begged the question, why hadn't he bedded anyone?

Was he a young immortal? Had he not found anyone he desired? Did Sent Ones not often experience sexual need? She didn't know much about them. Fine, she didn't know anything about them. Did they consider sex wrong? Maybe. That would explain why he hadn't wanted to touch her, too.

Okay, so it made more sense that he simply hadn't experienced sexual need before.

He'd definitely experienced it during their kiss, though. She went back to rubbing her hands together.

"*What* are you wearing? Or better yet, not wearing?"

Heart skidding to a stop, Bianka whipped around. As if her thoughts had summoned him, Lysander stood in the room's doorway. Mist enveloped him and for a moment she feared he was nothing more than a fantasy.

"Well?" he demanded.

In her fantasies, he would not be angry. He would be overcome with desire. So…he was here, and he was real. And he was peering at her breasts in open-mouthed astonishment.

Astonishment was better than anger. She almost grinned.

"Don't you like it?" she asked, smoothing her palms over her hips. *Let the games begin.*

"I—I—"

Like it, she finished for him. With the amount of truth that always layered his voice, he probably couldn't utter a single lie.

"Your skin…it's different. I mean, I saw the pearlesque tones before, but now…it's…"

"Amazing." She twirled, her gown dancing at her ankles. "I know."

"You know?" His tongue traced his teeth as the anger she'd first suspected glazed his features. "Cover her," he barked.

A moment later, a white robe draped her from shoulders to feet.

She scowled. "Return my teddy." The robe disappeared, leaving her in the white lace. "Try that again," she told him, "and I'll just walk around naked. You know, like I am in the portraits."

"Portraits?" Brow furrowing, he gazed about the room. When he spotted one of the pictures of her, sans clothing, reclining against a giant silver boulder, he hissed in a breath.

Exactly the reaction she'd been hoping for. "I hope you don't mind, but I turned this quaint little cloud into a love nest so I'd feel more at home. And again, if you remove anything, my redesign will be a thousand times worse."

"What are you trying to do to me?" he growled, facing her. His eyes were narrowed, his lips thinned, his teeth bared.

She fluttered her lashes at him, all innocence. "I'm afraid I don't know what you mean."

"Bianka."

It was a warning, she knew, but she didn't heed it. "I think it's my turn to ask the questions. So where do you go when you leave me?"

"That is not your concern."

Was he panting a little? "Let's see if I can make it my concern, shall we?" She sauntered to the bed and eased onto the edge. Naughty, shameless girl that she was, she spread her legs, giving him the peek of a lifetime. "For every question you answer, I'll put something on," she said in a sing-song voice. "Deal?"

He spun, but not before she saw the shock and desire that

played over his harshly gorgeous face. "I do my duty. Hunt and kill demons. Guard humans. Now cover yourself."

"I didn't say what item of clothing I'd don, now did I?" She gave herself a once-over. "One shoe, please. White leather, high heel, open toe. Ties up the calf." The shoe materialized on her foot, and she laughed. "Perfect."

"A trickster," Lysander muttered. "I should have known."

"How did I trick you? Did you ask for specifics? No, because you were secretly hoping I wouldn't cover myself at all."

"That is not true," he said, but for once, she did not hear that layer of honesty in his voice. Interesting. When he lied, or perhaps when he was unsure about what he was saying, his tone was as normal as hers.

That meant she would always know when he lied. Did things get any better than that?

This was going to be even easier than she'd anticipated. "Next question. Do you think about me while you're gone?"

Silence. Thick, heavy.

Wait. She could hear him breathing. In, out, harsh, shallow. He *was* panting.

"I'll take that as a yes," she said, grinning. "But since you really didn't answer, I don't have to add the other shoe."

Again, he didn't reply. Thankfully, he didn't leave, either.

"Onward and upward. Are Sent Ones allowed to dally?"

"Yes, but they rarely want to," he rasped.

So she'd been right. He didn't have firsthand knowledge of desire. What he was now feeling had to be confusing him, then. Was that why he'd brought her here? Because he'd seen her and wanted her, but hadn't known how to handle what he was feeling? The thought was almost…flattering. In a stalkerish kind of way, of course. That didn't change her plans, however. She would seduce him—and then she would slice his heart in two. A symbolic gesture, really. An inside joke between them. Well, for herself. He might not get it.

Still, she couldn't deny that she liked the idea of being his first. None of the women after her would compare, of course, and that— Hey, wait. Once he tasted the bliss of the flesh, he would want more. Bianka would have escaped him and stabbed him—and he would have recovered because he was an immortal—by then. He could go to any other female he desired.

He would kiss and touch that female.

"I'm waiting," he snapped.

"For?" she snapped back. Her hands were clenched, her nails cutting her palms. He could be with anyone; it wouldn't bother her. They were enemies. Someone else could deal with his Neanderthal tendencies. But oh, she might just kill the next woman who warmed his bed out of spite. Not jealousy.

"I answered one of your questions. You must add a garment to your body. Panties would be nice."

She sighed. "I'd like the other shoe to appear, please." A moment later, her other foot was covered. "Back to business. Did you return so that I'd kiss you again?"

"No!"

"Too bad. I wanted to taste you again. I wanted to touch you again. Maybe let you touch me this time. I've been aching since you left me. Had to bring myself to climax twice just to cool the fever. But don't worry, I imagined it was you. I imagined stripping you, licking you, sucking you into my mouth. Mmm, I'm so—"

"Stop!" he croaked out, spinning to face her. "Stop."

His eyes, which she'd once thought were black and emotionless, were now bright as a morning sky, his pupils blown with the intensity of his desire. But rather than stalk to her, grab her and smash his body into hers, he held out his hand, fingers splayed. A fiery sword formed from the air, yellow-gold flames flickering all around it.

"Stop," he commanded again. "I do not want to hurt you, but I will if you persist with this foolishness."

That layer of truth had returned to his voice.

Far from intimidating her, his forcefulness excited her. *I thought you didn't like his Neanderthal tendencies.*

Oh, shut up.

Bianka leaned back, resting her weight against her elbows. "Does Lysandy like to play rough? Should I be wearing black leather? Or is this a game of bad cop, naughty criminal? Should I strip for my body-cavity search?"

He stalked to the edge of the bed, his thick legs encasing her smaller ones, pressing her knees together. He was hard as a rock, his robe jutting forward. Those golden flames still flickering around the sword both highlighted his face and cast shadows, giving him a menacing aura.

Just then, he was both angel and demon. A mix of good and evil. Savior and executioner.

Her wings fluttered frantically, readying for battle—even as her skin tingled for pleasure. She could be across the room before he moved even a fraction of an inch. Still. She had trouble catching her breath; it was like ice in her lungs. And yet her blood was hot as his sword. This mix of emotions was odd.

"You are worse than I anticipated," he snarled.

If this progressed the way she hoped, he would be very happy about that one day. But she said, "Then let me go. You'll never have to see me again."

"And that will purge you from my mind? That will stop the wondering and the craving? No, it will only make them worse. You will give yourself to others, kiss them the way you kissed me, rub against them the way you rubbed against me, and I will want to kill them when they will have done nothing wrong."

What a confession! And she'd thought her blood hot before... "Then take me," she suggested huskily. She traced her tongue over her lips, slow and measured. His gaze followed. "It'll feel sooo good, I promise."

"And discover if you are as soft and wet as you appear? Spend the rest of eternity in bed with you, a slave to my body? No, that, too, will only make my cravings worse."

Oh, warrior. You shouldn't have admitted that. A slave to his body? If that was his fear, he more than craved her. He was falling. Hard. And now that she knew how much he wanted her...he was as good as hers. "If you're going to kill me," she said, swirling a fingertip around her navel, "kill me with pleasure."

He stopped breathing.

She sat up, closing the rest of the distance between them. Still he didn't strike. She flattened her palms on his chest. His nipples were as beaded as hers. He closed his eyes, as if the sight of her, looking up at him through the thick shield of her lashes, was too much to bear.

"I'll let you in on a little secret," she whispered. "I'm softer and wetter than I appear."

Was that a moan?

And if so, had it come from him? Or her? Touching him like this was affecting her, too. All this strength at her fingertips was heady. Knowing this gorgeous warrior wanted her—her, and no other—was even headier. But knowing she was the very first to tempt him, and so strongly, was the ultimate aphrodisiac.

"Bianka." Oh, yes. A moan.

"But if you'd like, we can just lie next to each other." Said the spider to the fly. "We don't have to touch. We don't have to kiss. We'll lie there and think about all the things we dislike about each other and maybe build up an immunity. Maybe we'll stop *wanting* to touch and to kiss."

Never had she told such a blatant lie, and she'd told some big ones over the centuries. Part of her expected him to call her on it. The other part of her expected him to grasp on to the silly suggestion like a lifeline. Use it as an excuse to finally take what he wanted. Because if he did this, simply lay next to her, one temptation would lead to another. He wouldn't be thinking about the things he disliked about her—he would be thinking about the things he could be doing to her body. He would feel her heat, smell her arousal. He'd want—need— more from her. And she'd be right there, ready and willing to give it to him.

She fisted his robe and gently tugged him toward her. "It's worth a try, don't you think? *Anything's* worth a try to make this madness stop."

When they were nose to nose, his breath trickling over her face, his gaze fastened on her lips, she began to ease backward. He followed, offering no resistance.

"Want to know one of the things I dislike about you?" she asked softly. "You know, to help get us started."

He nodded, as if he were too entranced to speak.

She decided to push a little faster than anticipated. He already seemed ready for more. "That you're not on top of me." Just a little more persuasion, and that would be remedied. Just a little... "How amazing would it feel to be that close?"

"Lysander," an unfamiliar female voice suddenly called. "Are you here?"

Girl was going to die! Bianka scowled.

Lysander straightened, jerking away from her as if she had just sprouted horns. He stepped back, disengaging from her completely. But he was trembling, and not from anger.

"Ignore her," she said. "We have important business to attend to."

"Lysander?" the woman called again.

Bloody nuisance. Couldn't she take a hint and leave?

His expression cleared, melted to steel. "Not another word from you," he barked, backing away. "You tried to lure me into bed with you. I don't think you meant to make me dislike you at all. I think you meant to—" A low snarl erupted from his throat. "You are not to try such a thing with me again. If you do, I will finally cleave your head from your body."

Well, this battle was clearly over. Not one to give up, however, she tried a different strategy. "So you're going to leave again? Coward! Well, go ahead. Leave me helpless and bored. But you know what? When I'm bored, bad things happen. And next time you come back here, I just might throw myself at you. My hands will be all over you. You won't be able to pry me off!"

"Lysander," the girl called again.

He ground his teeth. "Return to your *cloud*," he threw over his shoulder. "I will meet you there."

He was going to meet another girl? At her cloud? Alone, private? Oh, no, no, no. Bianka hadn't worked him into a frenzy so that someone else could reap the reward.

Before she could inform him of that, however, he said, "Give Bianka whatever she wants." Talking to his own cloud, apparently. "Anything but escape and more of those…outfits." His gaze intensified on her. "That should stave off the boredom. But I only agree to this on the condition that you vow to keep your hands to yourself."

Anything she wanted? She didn't allow herself to grin, the girl forgotten in the face of this victory. "Done."

"And so it is," he said, then spun and stalked from the room. His wings expanded in a rush, and he disappeared before she could follow. But then, there was no need to follow him. Not now.

He had no idea that he'd just ensured his own downfall. *Whatever she wants,* he'd said. She laughed. She didn't need to touch him or wear lingerie to win their next battle. She just needed his return.

Because then, *he* would become *her* prisoner.

CHAPTER 5

He'd almost given in.

Lysander could not believe how quickly he'd almost given in to Bianka. One sultry glance from her, one invitation, and he'd forgotten his purpose. It was shameful. And yet, it was not shame that he felt. It was more of that strange disappointment—disappointment that he'd been interrupted!

Standing before Bianka, breathing in her wicked scent, feeling the heat of her body, all he'd been able to recall was the decadent taste of her. He'd wanted more. Wanted to finally touch her skin. Skin that had glowed with health, reflecting all those rainbow shards. She'd wanted that, too, he was sure of it. The more aroused she'd become, the brighter those colors had glowed.

Unless that was a trick? What did he truly know of women and desire?

She was worse than a demon, he thought. She'd known exactly how to entrance him. Those naked photos had nearly dropped him to his knees. Never had he seen anything so lovely. Her breasts, high and plump. Her stomach, flat. Her navel, perfectly dipped. Her thighs, firm and smooth. Then, being asked to lie beside her and think of what he disliked about her…both had been temptations, and both had been irresistible.

He'd known his resolve was crumbling and had wanted to rebuild it. And how better to rebuild than to ponder all the things he disliked about the woman? But if he had lain next to her, he would not have thought of what he disliked—things he couldn't seem to recall then or now. He might have even thought about what he *liked* about her.

She was brilliant. She'd had him.

He'd never desired a taste of the forbidden. Had never secretly liked bad behavior. Yet Bianka excited him in a way he could not have predicted. So, what did he like most about her at the moment? That she was willing to do anything, say anything, to tempt him. He liked that she had no inhibitions. He liked that she gazed up at him with longing in those beautiful eyes.

How would she look at him if he actually kissed her again? Kissed more than her mouth? How would she look at him if he actually touched her? Caressed that skin? He suddenly found himself wanting to watch mortals and immortals alike more intently, gauging their reactions to each other. Man and woman, desire to desire.

Just the thought of doing so caused his body to react the way it had done with Bianka. Hardening, tightening. Burning, craving. His eyes widened. That, too, had never happened before. He was letting her win, he realized, even though there was distance between them. He was letting his one temptation destroy him, bit by bit.

Something had to be done about Bianka, since his current plan was clearly failing.

"Lysander?"

His charge's voice drew him from his dark musings. "Yes, sweet?"

Olivia's head tilted to the side, her burnished curls bouncing. They stood inside her cloud, flowers of every kind scattered across the floor, on the walls, even dripping from the ceiling.

Her eyes, as blue as the sky, regarded him intently. "You haven't been listening to me, have you?"

"No," he admitted. Truth had always been his most cherished companion. That would not change now. "My apologies."

"You are forgiven," she said with a grin as sweet as her flowers.

With her, it was that easy. Always. No matter how big or small the crime, Olivia couldn't hold a grudge. Perhaps that was why she was so treasured among their people. Everyone loved her.

What would other Sent Ones think of Bianka?

No doubt they would be horrified by her. *He* was horrified.

I thought you were not going to lie? Even to yourself. He scowled. Unlike the forgiving Olivia, he suspected Bianka would hold a grudge for a lifetime—and somehow take that grudge beyond the grave.

For some reason, his scowl faded and his lips twitched at the thought. *Why* would that amuse him? Grudges were born of anger, and anger could be such an ugly thing. Except, perhaps, on Bianka. Would she erupt with the same amount of unrelenting passion she brought to the bedroom? Probably. Would she want to be kissed from her anger, as well?

The thought of kissing her until she was happy again did *not* delight him.

Usually he dealt with other people's anger the way he dealt with everything else. With total unconcern. It was not his job to make people feel a certain way. They were responsible for their own emotions, just as he was responsible for his. Not that he experienced many. Over the years, he'd simply seen too much to be bothered. Until Bianka.

"Lysander?"

Olivia's voice once more jerked him from his mind. His hands fisted. He'd locked Bianka away, yet she was still managing to change him. Oh, yes. His current plan was failing.

Why couldn't he have desired someone like sweet Olivia? It would have made his endless life much easier. As he'd told Bianka, desire wasn't impossible, but not many of their kind ever experienced it. Those that did only wanted other Sent Ones and often wed their chosen partner.

"—you go again," Olivia said.

He blinked, hands fisting all the tighter. "Again, I apologize. I will be more diligent the rest of our conversation." He would make sure of it.

She offered him another grin, though this one lacked her usual ease. "I only asked what was bothering you." She folded her wings around herself and plucked at the feathers, carefully avoiding the strands of gold. "You're so unlike yourself."

That made two of them. Something was troubling her; sadness had never layered her voice before, yet now it did. Determined to help her, he summoned two chairs, one for him and one for her, and they sat across from each other. Her robe plumed around her as she released her wings and twined her fingers together in her lap. Leaning forward, he rested his weight on his elbows.

"Let us talk about you first. How goes your mission?" he asked. Only that could be the cause. Olivia found joy in all things. That's why she was so good at her job. Or rather, her former job. Because of him, she was now something she didn't want to be. A warrior. But it was for the best, and he did not regret the decision to change her station. Like him, she'd become too fascinated with someone she shouldn't.

Better to end that now, before the fascination ruined her.

She licked her lips and looked away from him. "That's actually what I wanted to speak with you about." A tremor shook her. "I don't think I can do it, Lysander." The words emerged as a tortured whisper. "I don't think I can kill Aeron."

"Why?" he asked, though he knew what she would say. But unlike Bianka, Aeron had stepped past the point of no return. For every natural action, there was a spiritual reaction, and as he had knowingly escorted a demon out of hell, his actions had produced a death sentence—for himself.

If Olivia failed to destroy the demon-possessed male, another Sent One would be tasked with doing so—and Olivia would be punished for her refusal. She would be cast out of the heavens, her immortality stripped, her wings ripped from her back.

"He hasn't hurt anyone since his blood-curse was removed," she said, and he heard the underlying beseeching.

"He helped one of Lucifer's minions escape hell."

"Yes, Aeron did that, and there is no excuse for him. But he can return her."

"That doesn't change the fact that Aeron helped the creature escape."

Olivia's shoulders sagged, though she in no way appeared defeated. Determination gleamed in her eyes. "I know. But he's so…nice."

Lysander barked out a laugh. He just couldn't help himself. "We are speaking of a Lord of the Underworld, yes? The one whose entire body is tattooed with violent bloody images no less? That is the male you call *nice?*"

"Not all of the etchings are violent," she mumbled, offended for some reason. "Two are butterflies."

For her to have found the butterflies amid the skeletal faces decorating the man's body meant she'd studied him intently.

Lysander sighed. "Have you...felt anything for him?" Physically?

"What do you mean?" she asked, but rosy color bloomed on her cheeks.

She had, then. "Never mind." He scrubbed a hand down his suddenly tired face. "Do you like your home, Olivia?"

She blanched at that, as if she knew the direction he was headed. "Of course."

"Do you like your wings? Do you like your lack of pain, no matter the injury sustained? Do you like the robe you wear? A robe that cleans itself and you?"

"Yes," she replied softly. She gazed down at her hands. "You know I do."

"And you know that you will lose all of that and more if you fail to do your duty." The words were harsh, meant for himself as much as for her.

Tears sprang into her eyes. "I just hoped you could convince the council to rescind their order to execute him."

"I will not even try." Honest, he reminded himself. He had to be honest. Which he preferred. Or had. "Rules are put into place for a reason, whether we agree with those reasons or not. I have been around a long time, have seen the world—ours, theirs—plunged into darkness and chaos. And do you know what? That darkness and chaos always sprang from one broken rule. Just one. Because when one is broken, another soon follows. Then another. It becomes a vicious cycle."

A moment passed as she absorbed his words. Then she sighed, nodded. "Very well." Words of acceptance uttered in a tone that was anything but.

"You will do your duty?" What he was really asking: Will you slay Aeron, keeper of Wrath, whether you want to or not? Lysander wasn't asking more of her than he had done himself. He wasn't asking what he *wouldn't* do himself.

Another nod. One of those tears slid down her cheek.

He reached out and captured the glistening drop with the tip of his finger. "Your compassion is admirable, and it's an admirable thing, it is, but I do wish you had none right now."

She waved his words away. Perhaps because she knew there was nothing she could do to change, or perhaps because Lysander could use some of that compassion right now. "So who was the woman in your home? The one in the portraits?"

He…blushed? Yes, that was the heat spreading over his cheeks. "My…" How should he explain Bianka? How could he, without lying?

"Lover?" she finished for him.

His cheeks flushed with more of that heat. "No." Maybe. No! "She is my captive." There. Truthful without giving away any details. "And now," he said, standing. If she could end a subject, so could he. "I must return to her before she causes any more trouble." He must deal with her. Once and for all.

Olivia remained in place long after Lysander left. Had that blushing, uncertain, distracted man truly been her mentor? She'd known him for centuries, and he'd always been unflappable. Even in the heat of battle.

The woman was responsible, she was sure. Lysander had never kept one in his cloud before. Did he feel for her what Olivia felt for Aeron?

Aeron.

Just thinking his name sent a shiver down her spine, filling her with a need to see him. And just like that, she was on her feet, her wings outstretched.

"I wish to leave," she said, and the floor softened, turning to mist. Down she fell, wings flapping gracefully. She was careful to avoid eye contact with the other Sent Ones flying through the sky as she headed into Budapest. They knew her destination; they even knew what she did there.

Some watched her with pity, some with concern—as Lysander had. Some watched her with antipathy. By avoiding their gazes, she ensured no one would stop her and try and talk sense into her. She ensured she wouldn't have to lie. Something she hated to do. Lies tasted disgustingly bitter.

Long ago, during her training, Lysander had commanded her to tell a lie. She would never forget the vile flood of acid in her mouth the moment she'd obeyed. Never again did she wish to experience such a thing. But to be with Aeron…maybe.

His dark menacing fortress was perched high on a mountain and finally came into view. Her heart rate increased exponentially. Because she existed on another plane, she was able to drift through the stone walls as if they were not even there. Soon she was standing inside Aeron's bedroom.

He was polishing a gun. His little demon friend, Legion, the one he'd helped escape from hell, was darting and writhing around him, a pink boa twirling with her.

"Dance with me," the creature beseeched.

That was dancing? That kind of heaving was what humans did as they were dying.

"I can't. I've got to patrol the town tonight, searching for Hunters."

Hunters, sworn enemy of the Lords. They hoped to find Pandora's box and draw the demons out of the immortal warriors, killing each man. The Lords, in turn, hoped to find Pandora's box and destroy it—the same way they hoped to destroy the Hunters.

"Me hate Huntersss," Legion said, "but we needsss practice for Doubtie'sss wedding."

"I won't be dancing at Sabin's wedding, therefore practice isn't necessary."

Legion stilled, frowned. "But we dance at the wedding. Like a couple." Her thin lips curved downward. Was she… pouting? "Pleassse. We ssstill got time to practice. Dark not come for hoursss."

"As soon as I finish cleaning my weapons, I have to run an errand for Paris." Paris, Olivia knew, was keeper of Promiscuity and had to bed a new woman every day or he would weaken and die. But Paris was depressed and not taking proper care of himself, so Aeron, who felt responsible for the warrior, procured females for him. "We'll dance another time, I promise." Aeron didn't glance up from his task. "But we'll do it here, in the privacy of my room."

I want to dance with him, too, Olivia thought. What was it like, pressing your body against someone else's? Someone strong and hot and sinfully beautiful?

"But, Aeron…"

"I'm sorry, sweetheart. I do these things because they're necessary to keep you safe."

Olivia tucked her wings into her back. Aeron needed to take time for himself. He was always on the go, fighting Hunters, traveling the world in search of Pandora's box and aiding his friends. As much as she watched him, she knew he rarely rested and never did anything simply for the joy of it.

She reached out, meaning to ghost a hand through Aeron's hair. But suddenly the scaled, fanged creature screeched, "No, no, no," clearly sensing Olivia's presence. In a blink, Legion was gone.

Stiffening, Aeron growled low in his throat. "I told you not to return."

Though he couldn't see Olivia, he, too, always seemed to know when she arrived. And he hated her for scaring his friend away. But she couldn't help it. Sent Ones were demon assassins and the minion must sense the menace in her.

"Leave," he commanded.

"No," she replied, but he couldn't hear her.

He returned the clip to his weapon and set it beside his bed. Scowling, he stood. His violet eyes narrowed as he searched the bedroom for any hint of her. Sadly, it was a hint he would never find.

Olivia studied him. His hair was cropped to his scalp, dark little spikes barely visible. He was so tall he dwarfed her, his shoulders so wide they could have enveloped her. With the tattoos decorating his skin, he was the fiercest creature she'd ever beheld. Maybe that was why he drew her so intensely. He was passion and danger, willing to do anything to save the ones he loved.

Most immortals put their own needs above everyone else's. Aeron put everyone else's above his own. That he did so never failed to shock her. And she was supposed to destroy him? She was supposed to end his life?

"I'm told you're some type of angel," he said.

How had he known what— The demon, she realized. Legion might not be able to see her, either, but as she'd already realized, the little demon knew danger when she encountered it. Plus, whenever Legion left him, she returned to hell. Fiery walls that could no longer confine her but could welcome her any time she wished. Olivia's lack of success had to be a great source of amusement to that region's inhabitants.

"If that's true, you should know that won't stop me from cutting you down if you dare try and harm Legion."

Once again, he was thinking of another's welfare rather than his own. He didn't know that Olivia didn't need to bother with Legion. That once Aeron was dead, Legion's bond to him would wither and she would again be chained to hell.

Olivia closed the distance between them, her steps tentative. She stopped only when she was a whisper away. His nostrils flared as if he knew what she'd done, but he didn't move. Wishful thinking on her part, she knew. Unless she fell, he would never see her, never smell her, never hear her.

She reached up and cupped his jaw with her hands. How she wished she could feel him. Unlike Lysander, who was of the Elite, she could not materialize into this plane. Only her weapon would. A weapon she would forge from air, its heavenly flames far hotter than those in hell. A weapon that would remove Aeron's head from his body in a mere blink of time.

"I'm told you're female," he added, his tone hard, harsh. As always. "But that won't stop me from cutting you down, either. Because, and here's something you need to know, when I want something, I don't let anything stand in the way of my getting it."

Olivia shivered, but not for the reasons Aeron probably hoped. Such determination...

I should leave before I aggravate him even more. With a sigh, she spread her wings and leaped, out of the fortress and into the sky.

CHAPTER 6

"You, cloud, belong to me," Bianka said. That was not an attempt to escape, nor another sexy outfit, therefore it was acceptable. "Lysander gave you to me, so as long as I don't touch him, I get what I want. And I want you to obey me, not him. Therefore, you have to heed my commands rather than his. If I tell you to do something and he tells you not to, you still have to do it. *That's* what I want."

And oh, baby, this was going to be fun.

The more she thought about it, the happier she was that she couldn't touch Lysander again. Really. Seducing—or rather, trying to seduce—him had been a mistake. She'd basically ended up seducing herself. His heat…his scent…his strength… *Give. Me. More.*

Now, all she could think about was getting his weight back on top of her. About how she wanted to teach him where she liked to be touched. Once he'd gotten the hang of kissing, he'd teased and tantalized her mouth with the skill of a master. It would be the same with lovemaking.

She would lick each and every one of his muscles. She would hear him moan over and over again as *he* licked *her*.

How could she want those things from her enemy? How could she forget, even for a moment, how he'd locked her away? Maybe because he was a challenge. A sexy, tempting, frustrating challenge.

Didn't matter, though. She was done playing the role of sweet needy prisoner. She still couldn't kill him; she'd be stuck here for eternity. Which meant she'd have to make him want to get rid of her. And now, as master of this cloud, she would have no problem doing so.

She could hardly wait to begin. If he stuck to past behavior, he'd be gone for a week. He'd return to "check on" her. Operation Cry Like A Baby could begin. Tomorrow she'd plan the specifics and set the stage. A few ideas were already percolating. Like tying him to a chair in front of a stripper pole. Like enforcing Naked Tuesdays.

Chuckling, she propped herself against the bed's headboard, yawned and closed her eyes.

"I'd like to hold a bowl of Lysander's grapes," she said, and felt a cool porcelain bowl instantly press atop her stomach. Without opening her eyes, she popped one of the fruits into her mouth, chewed. Wow, she was tired. She hadn't rested properly since she'd gotten here—or even before.

She couldn't. There were no trees to climb, no leaves to hide in. And even if she summoned one, Lysander could easily find her if he returned early—

Wait. No. No, he wouldn't. Not if she summoned hundreds of them. And if he dismissed all the trees, she would fall, which would awaken her. He would not be able to take her unaware.

Chuckling again, Bianka pried her eyelids apart. She polished off the grapes, scooted from the bed and stood. "Replace the furniture with trees. Hundreds of big, thick, green trees."

In the snap of her fingers, the cloud resembled a forest. Ivy twined around stumps and dew dripped from leaves. Flowers of every color bloomed, petals floating from them and dancing to the ground. She gaped at the beauty. Nothing on earth compared.

If only her sisters could see this.

Her sisters. Winning a game or not, she missed them more with every second that passed. Lysander would pay for that, too.

She yawned again. When she attempted to climb the nearest oak, her lingerie snagged on the bark. She straightened, scowled—reminded once again of the way her dark angel had stalked to her, leaned into her, hot breath trekking over her skin.

"I want to wear a camo tank and army fatigues." The moment she was dressed, she scaled to the highest bough, fluttering wings giving her speed and agility, and reclined on a fat branch, peering up into a lovely star-sprinkled sky. "I'd like a bottle of Lysander's wine, please."

Her fingers were clutching a flagon of dry red a second later. She would have preferred a cheap white, but whatever. Hard times called for sacrifices, and she drained the bottle in record time.

Just as she summoned a second, she heard Lysander shout, "Bianka!"

She blinked in confusion. Either she'd been up here longer than she'd thought or she was hallucinating.

Why couldn't she have imagined a Lord of the Underworld? she wondered disgustedly. Oh, oh. How cool would it be if Lysander oil-wrestled a Lord? They'd be wearing loincloths, of course, and smiles. But nothing else.

And she could totally have that! This was her cloud, after all. She and Lysander were now playing by her rules. And, because she was in charge, he couldn't rescind his command that she be obeyed without her permission.

At least, she prayed that was the way this would work.

"Remove the trees," she heard him snap.

She waited, unable to breathe, but the trees remained. He couldn't! Grinning, she jolted upright and clapped. She'd been right, then. This cloud belonged to her.

"Remove. The. Trees."

Again, they remained.

"Bianka!" he snarled. "Show yourself."

Anticipation flooded her as she jumped down. A quick scan of her surroundings revealed that he wasn't nearby. "Take me to him."

She blinked and found herself standing in front of him. He'd been shoving his way through the foliage and when he spotted her, he stopped. He clutched that sword of fire.

She backed away, remaining out of reach. No touching. She wouldn't forget. "That for me?" she asked, motioning to the weapon with a tilt of her chin. She'd never been so excited in her life and even the sight of that weapon didn't dampen the emotion.

A vein bulged in his temples.

She'd take that for a yes. "Naughty boy." He'd come to kill her, she thought, swaying a little. That was something else to punish him for. "You're back early."

His gaze raked her newest outfit, his pupils dilated and his nostrils flared. His mouth, however, curled in distaste. "And you are drunk."

"How dare you accuse me of such a thing!" She tried for a harsh expression, but ruined it when she laughed. "I'm just tipsy."

"What did you do to my cloud?" He crossed his arms over his chest, the picture of stubborn male. "Why won't the trees disappear?"

"First, you're wrong. This is no longer your cloud. Second, the trees will only leave if I tell them to leave. Which I am.

Leave, pretty trees, leave." Another laugh. "Oh, my stars— that's an expression you should love!—I said leave to a tree. I'm a poet and I didn't know it." Instantly, there was nothing surrounding her and Lysander but glorious white mist. "Third, you're not going anywhere without my permission. Did you hear that, cloud? He stays. Fourth, you're wearing too many clothes. I want you in a loincloth, minus the weapon."

His sword was suddenly gone. His eyes widened as his robe disappeared and a flesh-colored loincloth appeared. Bianka tried not to gape. And she'd thought the forest gorgeous. Wow. Just...wow. His body was a work of art. He possessed more muscles than she'd realized. His biceps were perfectly proportioned. Rope after rope lined his stomach. And his thighs were ridged, his skin sun-kissed.

"This cloud is mine, and I demand the return of my robe." His voice was so low, so harsh, it scraped against her eardrums.

The sweet sound of victory, she thought. He remained exactly as she'd requested. Laughing, she twirled, arms splayed wide. "Isn't this fabulous?"

He stalked toward her, menace in every step.

"No, no, no." She danced out of reach. "We can't have that. I want you in a large tub of oil."

And just like that, he was trapped inside a tub. Clear oil rose to his calves, and he stared down in horror.

"How do you like having your will overlooked?" she taunted.

His gaze lifted, met hers, narrowed. "I will not fight you in this."

"Silly man. Of course you won't. You'll fight..." She tapped her chin with a fingernail. "Let's see, let's see. Amun? No. He won't speak and I'd like to hear some cursing. Strider? As keeper of Defeat, he'd ensure you lost to prevent himself from feeling pain, but that would be an intense battle and I'm just wanting something to amuse me. You know, something light and sexy. I mean, since I can't touch you, I want a Lord to do it for me."

Lysander popped his jaw. "Do not do this, Bianka. You will not like the consequences."

"Now that's just sad," she said. "I've been here two weeks, but you don't know me at all. Of course I'll like the consequences." Torin, keeper of Disease? Watching him fight Torin would be fun, 'cause then he'd catch that black plague. Or would he? Could Sent Ones get sick? She sighed. "Paris will have to do, I guess. He's handsy, so that works in my favor."

"Don't you dare—"

"Cloud, place Paris, keeper of Promiscuity, into the tub with Lysander."

When Paris appeared a moment later, she clapped. Paris was tall and just as muscled as Lysander. Only he had black hair streaked with brown and gold, his eyes were electric-blue and his face perfect enough to make her weep from its beauty. Too bad he didn't stir her body the way Lysander did. Making out with him in front of the angel would have been fun.

"Bianka?" Paris looked from her to the Sent One, the Sent One to her. "Where am I? Is this some ambrosia-induced hallucination? What the hell is going on?"

"For one thing, you're overdressed. You should only be wearing a loincloth like Lysander."

His T-shirt and jeans were instantly replaced with said loincloth.

Best. Day. Ever. "Paris, I'd like you to meet Lysander, the Sent One who abducted me and has been holding me prisoner up here in the skies."

Instantly Paris morphed from confusion to fury. "Return my weapons and I'll kill him for you."

"You are such a sweetie," she said, flattening a hand over her heart. "Why is it we haven't slept together yet?"

Lysander snarled low in his throat.

"What?" she asked him, all innocence. "He wants to save me. You want to subjugate me for the rest of my long life. But anyway, let me finish the introductions. Lysander, I'd like you to meet—"

"I know who he is. Promiscuity." Disgust layered Lysander's voice. "He must bed a new woman every day or he weakens."

Another grin lifted the corners of her lips, this one smug. "Actually, he can bed men, too. His demon's not picky. I do hope you'll keep that in mind while you guys are rubbing up against each other."

Lysander took a menacing step toward her.

"What's going on?" Paris demanded again, glowering now. Bianka knew he was picky even if his demon wasn't.

"Oh, didn't I tell you? Lysander gave me control of his home, so now I get whatever I want and I want you guys to wrestle. And when you're done, you'll find Kaia and tell her what's happened, that I'm trapped with a stubborn skybarron—how funny is that word!—and can't leave. Well, I can't leave until he gets so sick of me he allows the cloud to release me."

"Or until I kill you," he snapped.

She laughed. "Or until Paris kills *you*. But I hope you guys will play nice for a little while, at least. Do you have any idea how sexy you both are right now? And if you want to kiss or something while rolling around, don't let me stop you."

"Uh, Bianka," Paris began, beginning to look uncomfortable. "Kaia's in Budapest. She's helping Gwen with the wedding, and thinks you're hiding to get out of your maid of honor duties."

"I am not maid of honor, blast it!" But at least Kaia wasn't worried. *The hooker,* she thought with affection.

"That's not what she says. Anyway, I don't mind fighting another dude to amuse you, but seriously, he's a Sent One. I need to return to—"

"No need to thank me." She held out her hands. "A bowl of Lysander's popcorn, please." The bowl appeared, the scent of butter wafting to her nose. "Now then. Let's get this party started. Ding, ding," she said, and settled down to watch the battle.

CHAPTER 7

Lysander could not believe what he was being forced to do. He was angry, horrified and, yes, contrite. Hadn't he done something similar to Bianka? Granted, he hadn't stripped her down. Hadn't pitted her against another female.

There was the tightening in his groin again.

What was wrong with him?

"I will set you free," he told Bianka. And sweet mercy, she looked beautiful. More tempting than when she'd worn that little bit of nothing. Now she wore a green-and-black tank that bared her golden arms. Were those arms as soft as they appeared? *Don't think like that.* Her shirt stopped just above her navel, making his mouth water, his tongue yearn to dip inside. *What did I just say? Don't think like that.* Her pants were the same dark shades and hung low on her hips.

He'd come here to fight her, to finally force her hand, and judging by that outfit, she'd been ready for combat. That... excited him. Not because their bodies would have been in close proximity—really—and not because he could have finally gotten his hands on her—again, really—but because, if she injured him, he would have the right to end her life. Finally.

But he'd come here and she'd taught him a quick yet unforgettable lesson instead. He'd been wrong to whisk her to his home and hold her captive. Temptation or not. She might be his enemy in ways she didn't understand, but he never should have put his will above hers. He should have allowed her to live her life as she saw fit.

That's one of the reasons he existed in the first place. To protect free will.

When this wrestling match ended, he would free her as he'd promised. He would watch her, though. Closely. And when she made a mistake, he would strike her down. And she would. Make a mistake, that is. As a Harpy, she wouldn't be able to help herself. He wished it hadn't come to that. He wished she could have been happy here with him, learning his ways.

The thought of losing her did not sadden him. He would not miss her. She'd placed him in a vat of oil to wrestle with another man, and he was angry, that was all.

There was suddenly a bitter taste in his mouth.

"Bianka," he prompted. "Have you no response?"

"Yes, you will set me free," she finally said with a radiant grin. She twirled a strand of that dark-as-night hair around her finger. "After. Now, I do believe I rang the starting bell."

Her words were slightly slurred from the wine she'd consumed. A drunken menace, that's what she was. And he would not miss her, he told himself again.

The bitterness intensified.

A hard weight slammed into him and sent him propelling to his back. His wings caught on the sides of the pool as oil washed over him from head to toe, weighing him down. He grunted, and some of the stuff—cherry-flavored—seeped into his mouth.

"Don't forget to use tongue if you kiss," Bianka called helpfully.

"You don't lock women away," Paris growled down at him,

a flash of scales suddenly visible under his skin. Eyes red and bright. Demon eyes. "No matter how irritating they are."

"Your friends did something similar to their women, did they not? Besides, the girl isn't your concern." Lysander shoved, sending the warrior hurtling to *his* back. He attempted to use his wings to lift himself, but their movements were slow and sluggish so all he could do was stand.

Oil dripped down his face, momentarily shielding his vision. Paris shot to his feet, as well, hands fisted, body glistening.

"So. Much. Fun," Bianka sang happily.

"Enough," Lysander told her. "This is unnecessary. You have made your point. I'm willing to set you free."

"You're right," she said. "It's unnecessary to fight without music!" Once again she tapped her chin with a nail, expression thoughtful. "I know! We need some rock in this crib."

A song Lysander had never heard before was playing through the cloud a second later. Like a siren rising from the sea, Bianka began swaying her hips seductively.

Lysander's jaw clenched so painfully the bones would probably snap out of place at any moment. Clearly there would be no reasoning with Bianka. That meant he had to reason with Paris. But who would ever have thought he'd have to bargain with a demon?

"Paris," he began—just as a fist connected with his face.

His head whipped back. His feet slipped on the slick floor and he tumbled to his side. More of the cherry flavor filled his mouth.

Paris straddled his shoulders, punched him again. Lysander's lip split. Before a single drop of blood could form, however, the wound healed.

He frowned. He now had the right to slay the man, but he couldn't bring himself to do it. He did not blame Paris for this battle; he blamed Bianka. She had forced them into this situation.

Another punch. "Are you the one who's been watching Aeron?" Paris demanded.

"Hey, now," Bianka called. No longer did she sound so carefree. "Paris, you are not to use your fists. That's boxing, not wrestling."

Lysander remained silent, not understanding the difference. A fight was a fight.

Another punch. "Are you?" Paris growled.

"Paris! Did you hear me?" Now she sounded angry. "Use your fists like that again and I'll cut off your head."

She'd do it, too, Lysander thought, and wondered why she was so upset. Could she, perhaps, care for his health? His eyes widened. Was *that* why she preferred the less intensive wrestling to the more violent boxing? Would she want to do the same to him if he were to punch the Lord? And what would it mean if she did?

How would he feel about that?

"Are you?" Paris repeated.

"No," he finally said. "I'm not." He worked his legs up, planted his feet on Paris's chest and pressed. But rather than send the warrior flying, his foot slipped and connected with Paris's jaw, then ear, knocking the man's head back.

"Use your hands, Sent One," Bianka suggested. "Choke him! He deserves it for breaking my rules."

"Bianka," Paris snapped. He lost his footing and tumbled to his butt. "I thought you wanted me to destroy him, not the other way around."

She blinked over at them, brow furrowed. "I do. I just don't want you to hurt him. That's my job."

Paris tangled a hand through his soaked hair. "Sorry, darling, but if this continues, I'm going to unleash a world of hurt on your frenemy. Nothing you say will be able to stop me. Clearly, he doesn't have your best interests at heart."

Darling? Had the demon-possessed immortal just called Bianka *darling?* Something dark and dangerous flooded Lysander—*mine* echoed through his head—and before he realized what he was doing, he was on top of the warrior, a sword of fire in his hand, raised, descending...about to meet flesh.

A firm hand around his wrist stopped him. Warm smooth skin. His wild gaze whipped to the side. There was Bianka, inside the tub, oil glistening off her. How fast she'd moved.

"You can't kill him," she said determinedly.

"Because you want him, too," he snarled. A statement, not a question. Rage, so much rage. He didn't know where it was coming from or how to stop the flow.

She blinked again, as if the thought had never entered her mind, and that, miraculously, cooled his temper. "No. Because then you would be like me and therefore perfect," she said. "That wouldn't be fair to the world."

"Stop talking and fight," Paris commanded. A fist connected with Lysander's jaw, tossing him to the side and out of Bianka's reach. He maintained his grip on the sword and even when it dipped into the oil, it didn't lose a single flame. In fact, the oil heated.

Great. Now he was hot-tubbing, as the humans would say.

"What'd you do that for, you big dummy?" Bianka didn't wait for Paris's reply but launched herself at him. Rather than scratch him or pull his hair, she punched him. Over and over again. "He wasn't going to hurt you."

Paris took the beating without retaliating.

That saved his life.

Lysander grabbed the Harpy around the waist and hefted her into the hard line of his body. Soaked as they both were, he had a difficult time maintaining his grip. She was panting, arms flailing for the demon-possessed warrior, but she didn't try to pull away.

"I'll teach you to defy me, you rotten piece of crap," she growled.

Paris rolled his eyes.

"Send him away," Lysander commanded.

"Not until after I—"

He splayed his fingers, spanning much of her waist. He both rejoiced and cursed that he couldn't feel the texture of Bianka's skin through the oil. "I want to be alone with you."

"You—what?"

"Alone. With you."

With no hesitation, she said, "Go home, Paris. Your work here is done. Thanks for trying to rescue me. That's the only reason you're still alive. Oh, and don't forget to tell my sisters I'm fine."

The sputtering Lord disappeared.

Lysander released her, and she spun around to face him. She was now grinning.

"So you want to be alone with me, do you?"

He ran his tongue over his teeth. "Was that fun for you?"

"Yes."

And she wasn't ashamed to admit it, he realized. Captivating baggage. "Return the cloud to me and I will take you home."

"Wait. What?" Her grin slowly faded. "I thought you wanted to be alone with me."

"I do. So that we can conclude our business."

Disappointment, regret, anger and relief played over her features. One step, two, she closed the distance between them. "Well, I'm not giving you the cloud. That would be stupid."

"You have my word that once you return it to me, I will take you home. I know you hear the truth in my claim."

"Oh." Her shoulders sagged a little. "So we really would be rid of each other. That's great, then."

Did she still not believe him? Or... No, surely not. "Do you want to stay here?"

"Of course not!" She sucked her bottom lip into her mouth, and her eyes closed for a moment, an expression of pleasure consuming her features. "Mmm, cherries."

Blood...heating...

Her lashes lifted and her gaze locked on him. Determination replaced all the other emotions, yet her voice dipped sexily. "But I know something that tastes even better."

So did he. Her. A tremor slid the length of his spine. "Do not do this, Bianka. You will fail." He hoped.

"One kiss," she beseeched, "and the cloud is yours."

His eyes narrowed. Hot, so hot. "You cannot be trusted to keep your word."

"That's true. But I want out of this hellhole, so I'll keep it this time. Promise."

Hold your ground. But that was hard to do while his heart was pounding like a hammer against a nail. "If you wanted out, you would not insist on being kissed."

Her gaze narrowed, as well. "It's not like I'm asking for something you haven't already given me."

"Why do you want it?" He regretted the question immediately. He was prolonging the conversation rather than putting an end to it.

Her chin lifted. "It's a goodbye kiss, moron, but never mind. The cloud is yours. I'll go home and kiss Paris hello. That'll be more fun, anyway."

There would be no kissing Paris! Lysander had his tongue sliding into her mouth before he could convince himself otherwise. His arms even wound around her waist, pulling her closer to him—so close their chests rubbed each time they breathed. Her nipples were hard, deliciously abrading.

"Out of the oil," she murmured. "Clean."

He was still in the loincloth, but his skin was suddenly free of the oil, his feet on soft yet firm mist. The cloud might belong to him once more, but she could still make reasonable demands.

Bianka tilted her head and took his possession deeper. Their tongues dueled and rolled and their teeth scraped. Her hands were all over him, no part of him forbidden to her.

Goodbye, she had said.

This was it, then. His last chance to touch her skin. To finally know. Yes, he planned to see her again, to watch her from afar, to wait for his chance to rid himself of her permanently, but never again would he allow himself to get this close to her. And he had to know.

So he did it.

He glided his hands forward, tracing from her lower back to her stomach. There, he flattened his palms, and her muscles quivered. She was softer than he'd realized. Softer than anything else he'd ever touched.

He moaned. *Have to touch more.* Up he lifted, remaining under her shirt. Warm, smooth, as he'd already known. Still soft, so sweetly soft. Her breasts overflowed, and his mouth watered for a taste of them. Soon, he told himself. Then shook his head. This was it; the last time they would be together. Goodbye, pretty breasts. He kneaded them.

More soft perfection.

Trembling now, he reached her collarbone. Her shoulders. She shivered. Still so wonderfully soft. More, more, more, he had to have more. Had to touch all of her.

"Lysander," she gasped out. She dropped to her knees, working at the loincloth before he realized what she was doing.

His shaft sprang free, and his hands settled atop her shoulders to push her away. But once he touched that soft skin, he was once again lost to the sensation. Perfection, this was perfection.

"Going to kiss you now. A different kind of kiss." Warm wet heat settled over the hard length of him. Another moan escaped him. Up, down that wicked mouth rode him. The pleasure…it was too much, not enough, everything and nothing. In that moment, it was necessary to his survival. His every breath hinged on what she would do next. There would be no pushing her away.

She twirled her tongue over the plump head; her fingers played with his testicles. Soon he was arching his hips, thrusting deep into her mouth. He couldn't stop moaning, groaning, the gasping breaths leaving him in a constant stream.

"Bianka," he growled. "Bianka."

"That's the way, baby. Give Bianka everything."

"Yes, yes." Everything. He would give her everything.

The sensation was building, his skin tightening, his muscles locking down on his bones. And then something exploded inside him. Something hot and wanton. His entire body jerked. Seed jetted from him, and she swallowed every drop.

Finally she pulled away from him, but his body wouldn't stop shaking. His knees were weak, his limbs nearly uncontrollable. That was pleasure, he realized, dazed. That was passion. That was what human men were willing to die to possess. That was what turned normally sane men into slaves. *Like I am now.* He was Bianka's slave.

Fool! *You knew this would happen.* Fight. It was only as she stood and smiled at him tenderly—and he wanted to tug her into his arms and hold on forever—that a measure of sanity stole back into his mind. Yes. Fight. How could he have allowed her to do that?

How could he still want her?

How could he want to do that to her in return?

How could he ever let her go?

"Bianka," he said. He needed a moment to catch his breath. No. He needed to think about what had happened and how they should proceed. No. He tangled a hand in his hair. What should he do?

"Don't say anything." Her smile disappeared as if it had never been. "The cloud is yours." Her voice trembled with... fear? Couldn't be. She hadn't showed a moment of fear since he'd first abducted her. But she even backed away from him. "Now take me home. Please."

He opened his mouth to reply. What he would say, he didn't know. He only knew he did not like seeing her like that.

"Take me home," she croaked.

He'd never gone back on his word, and he wouldn't start now. He nodded stiffly, grabbed her hand and flew her back to the ice mountain in Alaska, exactly as he'd found her. Red coat, tall boots. Sensual in a way he hadn't understood then.

He maintained his grip on her until the last possible second—until she slipped away from him, taking her warmth and the sweet softness of her skin with her.

"I don't want to see you again." Mist wafted around her as she turned her back on him. "Okay?"

She...what? After what had happened between them, *she* was dismissing *him?* No, a voice roared inside his head. "Behave, and you will not," he gritted out. A lie? The bitter taste in his mouth had returned.

"Good." Without meeting his gaze, she twisted and blew him a kiss as if she hadn't a care in the world. "I'd say you were an excellent host, but then, you don't want me to lie, do you?" With that, she strolled away from him, dark hair blowing in the wind.

CHAPTER 8

First thing Bianka did after bathing, dressing, eating a bag of stolen chips she had hidden in her kitchen, painting her nails, listening to her iPod for half an hour and taking a nap in her secret basement was call Kaia. Not that she had dreaded the call and wanted to put it off or anything. All of those other activities had been necessary. Really.

Plus, it wasn't like her sister was worried about her anymore. Paris would already have told her what was going on. But Bianka didn't want to discuss Lysander. Didn't even want to think about him and the havoc he was causing her emotions— and her body and her thoughts and her common sense.

After making out with him a little, she'd wanted to freaking stay with him, curl up in his arms, make love and sleep. And that was unacceptable.

The moment her sister answered, she said, "No need to throw me a Welcome Home party. I'm not sticking around for long." *Do not ask me about the Sent One. Do not ask me about the Sent One.*

"Bianka?" her twin asked groggily.

"You were expecting someone else to call in the middle of the night?" It was 6:00 a.m. here in Alaska. Having traveled between the two places multiple times since Gwen had gotten involved with Sabin, she knew that meant it was 3:00 a.m. there in Budapest.

"Yeah," Kaia said. "I was."

Seriously? "Who?"

"Lots of people. Gwennie, who has become the ultimate bridezilla. Sabin, who is doing his best to soothe the beast but whines to me like I care." She rambled on as if Bianka had never been abducted and she'd never been worried. Sure, she'd thought Bianka was merely shirking her duties, but was a little worry too much to ask for? "Anya, who has decided she deserves a wedding, too. Only bigger and better than Gwen's. William, who wants to sleep with me and doesn't know how to take no for an answer. He's not possessed by a demon so he's not my type. Shall I go on?"

"Yes."

"Shut up."

She imagined Kaia high in a treetop, clutching her cell to her ear, grinning and trying not to fall. "So really, you were *sleeping?* While I was missing, my life in terrible danger? Some loving sister you are."

"Please. You were on vacay, and we both know it. So don't give me a hard time. I had an…exciting day."

"Doing who?" she asked dryly. Only two weeks had passed since she'd last seen Kaia, but suddenly a wave of homesickness—or rather, sistersickness—flooded her. She loved this woman more than she loved herself. And that was a lot!

Kaia chuckled. "I wish it was because of a *who*. I'm waiting for two of the Lords to fight over me. Then I'll comfort them both. So far, no luck."

"Idiots."

"I know! But I mentioned Gwen has become the bride from

hell, right? They're afraid I'll act just like her, so no one's will-ing to take a real chance on me."

"Bride from hell, how?"

"Her dress didn't fit right. Her napkins weren't the right color. No one has the flowers she wants. Whaa, whaa, whaa."

That didn't sound like the usually calm Gwen. "Distract her. Tell her the Hunters captured me and performed a hand-botomy on me like they did on Gideon." Gideon, keeper of Lies. A sexy warrior who dyed his hair as blue as his eyes and had a wicked sense of humor.

The thought of seducing him didn't delight her as it once might have. Stupid Sent One. *Do not think about him.*

"She wouldn't care if you were chopped up into little pieces. You're too much like me and apparently we take nothing se-riously so we deserve what we get," Kaia said. "She's driving me freaking insane! And to top off my mountain-o-crap, I was totally losing our game of hide-and-seek. So anyway, why'd you decide to rescue yourself? I'm telling you, you have a bet-ter chance of survival in the clouds than here with Gwen."

"Survival schmival. It wasn't fun anymore." A lie. Things had just started to heat up the way she'd wanted. But how could she have known that would scare her so badly?

"Good going, by the way. Allowing yourself to be taken into the clouds where I couldn't get to you. Brilliant."

"I know, *right?*"

"So was it terrible? Being spirited away by a sexy winged warrior?"

She twirled a strand of hair around her finger and pictured Lysander's glorious face. The desire he'd leveled at her while she'd sucked him dry had been miraculous. *You don't want to talk about him, remember?* "Yes. It was terrible." Terribly won-derful.

"You bringing him to Buda for the wedding?"

The words were sneered, clearly a joke, but Bianka found herself shouting, "No!" before she could stop herself. A Harpy dating someone like Lysander? Unacceptable!

And anyway, allowing the demon-possessed Lords of the Underworld to surround a warrior straight from the skies would be stupid. Not that she feared for Lysander. Guy could handle himself, no problem. The way he formed a sword of fire from nothing but air was proof of that. But if something were to happen to Gwennie's precious Sabin, like, oh, decapitation, the festivities would be somewhat dimmed.

"I'll be there, though," she added in a calmer tone. "I kinda have to, you know. Since I'm the maid of honor and all."

"Oh, no, no, no. I am, remember?"

She grinned slowly. "You told me you'd rather be hit by a bus than be a bridesmaid."

"Yeah, but I want to have a bigger part than you, so...here I am, in Budapest, helping little Gwennie plan the ceremony. Not that she's taking my suggestions. Would it kill her to at least *consider* making everyone come naked?"

They shared a laugh.

"Well, you and I can attend naked," Bianka said. "It'll certainly liven things up."

"Done!"

There was a pause.

Kaia pushed out a breath. "So you're fine?" she asked, a twinge of concern finally appearing in her voice.

"Yeah." And she was. Or would be. Soon, she hoped. All she had to do was figure out what to do about Lysander. Not that he'd tried to stick around, the jerk. He hadn't been able to get away from her fast enough. Sure, she'd pushed him away. But dude could have fought for her attention after what she'd done for him.

"You're gonna make the Sent One pay for taking you without permission, right? Who am I kidding? Of course you are. If you wait till after the wedding, I can help. Please, please let me help. I have a few ideas and I think you'll like them. Picture this. It's midnight, your warrior is strapped to your bed, and we each rip off one of his wings."

Nice. But because she didn't know whether Lysander was watching and listening or not—was he? It was possible, and just the thought had her skin heating—she said, "Don't worry about it. I'm done with him."

"Wait, what?" Kaia gasped out. "You can't be done with him. He abducted you. Held you prisoner. Yeah, he oil-wrestled Paris and I'm ticked I didn't get to see, but that doesn't excuse his behavior. If you let him off without punishment, he'll think it's okay. He'll think you're weak. He'll come after you again."

Yes. Yes, he would, she thought, suddenly trying not to grin. "No, he won't," she lied. *Are you listening, Lysander, baby?*

"Bianka, tell me you don't like him. Tell me you aren't lusting for a guy from the skies."

Abruptly her smile faded. This was exactly the line of questioning she'd hoped to avoid. "I'm not lusting for a guy from the skies." Another lie.

Another pause. "I don't believe you."

"Too bad."

"Mom thought Gwen's dad was some kind of an angel and she's regretted sleeping with him all these years. They're too good. Too…different from us. Angel types and Harpies are not meant to mix. Tell me you know that."

"Of course I know it. Now, I've gotta go. Tell the bridezilla to go easy on you. Love you and see you soon," she replied and hung up before Kaia could say anything else.

Despite her fear of what Lysander made her feel, Bianka wasn't done with him. Not even close. But she'd been on his turf before and therefore at a disadvantage. If he wasn't here, she needed to get him here. Willingly.

She'd told him to leave her alone, she thought, and that could be a problem. Except...

With a whoop, she jumped up and spun around. That wouldn't be a problem at all. That was actually a blessing and she was smarter than she'd realized. By telling him to stay away from her, she'd surely become the forbidden fruit. Of course he was here, watching her.

Men never could do what they were told. Not even Sent Ones.

So. Easy.

Even better, she'd given him a little taste of what it was like to be with her. He would crave more. But also, she hadn't allowed him to pleasure her. His pride would not allow her to remain in this unsatisfied state for long, while he had enjoyed such sweet completion.

And if that wasn't the case, he wasn't the virile warrior she thought he was and he therefore wouldn't deserve her.

How long till he made an actual appearance? They'd only been apart half a day, but she already missed him.

Missed him. Ugh. She'd never missed a man before. Especially one who wanted to change her. One who despised what she was. One who could only be labeled *enemy.*

You have to avoid him. You want to sleep in his arms. You were protective of him while he fought Paris. He angered you but you didn't kill him. And now you're missing him? You know what this means, don't you?

Her eyes widened, and her excitement drained. Someone save her stat. She should have realized...should at least have suspected. Especially when she'd protected him, defended him.

Lysander, a goody-goody, was her consort.

Her knees gave out and she flopped onto the floor. As long

as she'd been alive, she'd never thought to find one. Because, well, a consort was a meant-to-be husband. Some nights she'd dreamed of finding hers, yes, but she hadn't thought it would actually happen.

Her consort. Wow.

Her family was going to flip. Not because Lysander had abducted her—they'd come to respect that—but because of what he was. More than that, she didn't trust Lysander, would never trust him, and so could never do any actual sleeping with him.

Sex, though, she could allow. Often. Yes, yes, she could make this work, she thought, brightening. She could lure him to the dark side without letting her family know she was spending time with him. Humiliation averted!

Decided, she nodded. Lysander would be hers. In secret. And there was no better time to begin. If he was watching as she suspected, there was only one way to get him to reveal himself.

She dressed in a lacy red halter and her favorite skinny jeans and drove into town. Only reason she owned a car was because it made her appear more human. Flying kind of gave her away. Though her arms and navel were exposed, the frigid wind didn't bother her. Chilled her, yes, but that she could deal with. She wanted Lysander to see as much of her as possible.

She parked in front of The Moose Lodge, a local diner, and strode to the front door. Because it was so early and so cold, no one was nearby. A few street lamps illuminated her, but she wasn't worried. She unlocked the door—she'd stolen the key from the owner months ago—and disabled the alarm.

Inside, she claimed a pecan pie from the glassed refrigerator, grabbed a fork and dug in while walking to her favorite booth. She'd done this a thousand times before.

Come out, come out, wherever you are. He wouldn't have just left her to her evil ways without thinking to protect the world from her. Right? She wished she could feel him, at least sense him in some way. His scent perhaps, that wild, night-sky scent. But as she breathed deeply, she smelled only pecans and sugar. Still. She hadn't sensed him when he'd snatched her from mid-free fall, so it stood to reason she wouldn't sense him now.

Once the pie was polished off, the pan discarded and her fork licked clean, she filled a cup with Dr. Pepper. She placed a few quarters in the old jukebox and soon an erratic beat was echoing from the walls. Bianka danced around one of the tables, thrusting her hips forward and back, arching, sliding around, hands roving over her entire body.

For a moment, only a brief, sultry moment, she thought she felt hot hands replace her own, exploring her breasts, her stomach. Thought she felt soft feathered wings envelop her, closing her in. She stilled, heart drumming in her chest. So badly she wanted to say his name, but she didn't want to scare him away. So…what should she do? How should she—

The feeling of being surrounded evaporated completely.

Stubborn man.

Teeth grinding, not knowing what else to do, she exited the diner the same way she'd entered. Through the front door, as if she hadn't a care. That door slammed behind her, the force of it nearly shaking the walls.

"You should lock up after yourself."

He was here; he'd been watching. She'd known it! Trying not to grin, she spun around to face Lysander. The sight of him stole her breath. He was as beautiful as she remembered. His pale hair whipped in the wind, little snow crystals flying around him. His golden wings were extended and glowing. But his dark eyes were not blank, as when she'd first met him. They were as turbulent as an ocean—just as they'd been when she'd left him.

"I thought I told you to stay away from me," she said, doing her best to sound angry rather than aroused.

He frowned. "And I told you to behave. Yet here you are, full of stolen pie."

"What do you want me to do? Return it?"

"Don't be crass. I want you to pay for it."

"Moment I do, I'll start to vomit." She crossed her arms over her middle. *Close the distance. Kiss me.* "That would ruin my lipstick, so I have to decline."

He, too, crossed his arms over his middle. "You can also earn your food."

"Yeah, but where's the fun in that?"

A moment passed in silence. Then, "Do you have no morals?" he gritted out.

"No." *No sexual boundaries, either. So freaking kiss me already!* "I don't."

He popped his jaw in frustration and disappeared.

Bianka's arms dropped to her sides and she gazed around in astonishment. He'd left? Left? Without touching her? Without kissing her? She stomped to her car.

Lysander watched as Bianka drove away. He was hard as a rock, had been that way since she'd paraded around her cabin naked, had lingered in a bubble bath and then changed into that wicked shirt. His shaft was desperate for her.

Why couldn't she be like him? Why couldn't she abhor sin? Why did she have to embrace it?

And why was the fact that she did these things—steal, curse, lie—still exciting him?

Because that was the way of things, he supposed, and had been since the beginning of time. Temptation seeped past your defenses, changed you, made you long for things you shouldn't.

There had to be a way to end this madness. He couldn't

destroy her, he'd already proven that. But what if he could change *her*? He hadn't truly tried before, so it *could* work. And if she embraced his way of life, they could be together. He could have her. Have more of her kisses, touch more of her body.

Yes, he thought. Yes. He would help her become a woman he could be proud to walk beside. A woman he could happily claim as his own. A woman who would not be his downfall.

CHAPTER 9

As Lysander had never had a…girlfriend, as the humans would say, he had no idea how to train one. He knew only how to train his soldiers. Without emotion, maintaining distance and taking nothing personally. His soldiers, however, *wanted* to learn. They were eager, his every word welcomed. Bianka would resist him at every turn. That much he knew.

So. The first day, he followed her, simply observing. Planning.

She, of course, stole every meal, even snacks, drank too much at a bar, danced too closely with a man she obviously did not know, then broke that man's nose when he cupped her bottom. Lysander wanted to do damage of his own, but restrained himself. Barely. At bedtime, Bianka merely paced the confines of her cabin, cursing his name. Not for a minute did she rest.

How lovely she was, dark hair streaming down her back. Red lips pursed. Skin glowing like a rainbow in the moonlight. So badly he wanted to touch her, to surround her with his wings, making them the only two people alive, and simply enjoy her.

Soon, he promised himself.

She'd given him release, yet he had not done the same for

her. The more he thought about that—and think about it he did, all the time—the more that did not sit well with him. The more he thought about it, in fact, the more embarrassed he was.

He didn't know how to touch her to bring her release, but he was willing to try, to learn. First, though, he had to train her as planned. How, though? he wondered again. She seemed to respond well to his kisses—his chest puffed up with pride at that. He'd never rewarded his soldiers for a job well done, but perhaps he could do so for Bianka. Reward her with a kiss every time she pleased him.

A failproof plan. He hoped.

The second day, he was practically humming with anticipation. When she entered a clothing store and stuffed a beaded scarf into her purse, he materialized in front of her, ready to begin.

She stilled, gaze lifting and meeting his. Rather than bow her head in contrition, she grinned. "Fancy meeting you here."

"Put that back," he told her. "You do not need to steal clothing to survive."

She crossed her arms over her middle, a stubborn stance he knew well. "Yeah, but it's fun."

A human woman who stood off to the side eyed Bianka strangely. "Uh, can I help you?"

Bianka never looked away from him. "Nope. I'm fine."

"She cannot see me," Lysander told her. "Only you can."

"So I look insane for talking with you?"

He nodded.

She laughed, surprising him. And even though her amusement was misplaced, he loved the sound of her laughter. It was magical, like the strum of a harp. He loved the way her mirth softened her expression and lit her magnificent skin.

Have to touch her, he thought, suddenly dazed. He took a

step closer, intending to do just that. *Have to experience that softness again.* And in doing so, she could begin to know the delights of his rewards.

She gulped. "Wh-what are you—"

"Are you sure I can't help you?" the woman asked, cutting her off.

Bianka remained in place, trembling, but tossed her a glare. "I'm sure. Now shut it before I sew your lips together."

The woman backed away, spun and raced to help someone else.

Lysander froze.

"You may continue," Bianka said to him.

How could he reward her for such rudeness? That would defeat the purpose of her training. "Do you not care what people think of you?" he asked, head tilting to the side.

Her eyes narrowed, and she stopped trembling. "No. Why should I? In a few years, these people will be dead but I'll still be alive and kicking." As she spoke, she stuffed another scarf in her purse.

Now she was simply taunting him. "Put it back, and I'll give you a kiss," he gritted out.

"Wh-what?"

Stuttering again. He was affecting her. "You heard me." He would not repeat the words. Having said them, all he wanted to do was mesh their lips together, thrust his tongue into her mouth and taste her. Hear her moan. Feel her clutch at him.

"You would willingly kiss me?" she rasped.

Willingly. Desperately. He nodded.

She licked her lips, leaving a sheen of moisture behind. The sight of that pink tongue sent blood rushing into his shaft. His hands clenched at his sides. Anything to keep from grabbing her and jerking her against him.

"I—I—" She shook her head, as if clearing her thoughts.

Her eyes narrowed again, those long dark lashes fusing together. "Why would you do that? You, who have tried to resist me at every turn?"

"Because."

"Why?"

"Just put the scarves back." *So the kissing can begin.*

She arched a brow. "Are you trying to bribe me? Because you should know, that won't work with me."

Rather than answer—and lie—he remained silent, chin jutting in the air. Blood…heating.

Still watching him, she reached out, palmed a belt and stuffed it in her purse, as well. "So what do you plan to do to me if I keep stealing? Give me a severe tongue-lashing? Too bad. I *don't* accept."

Fire slid the length of his spine even as his anger spiked. He closed the distance until the warmth of her breath was fanning over his neck and chest. "You could not get enough of me in the skies, yet now that you are here, you want nothing to do with me. Tell me. Was your every word and action up there a lie?"

"Of course my every word and action was a lie. That's what I do. I thought you knew that."

So…did she desire him or not? Two days ago she'd told her sister Kaia that she wanted nothing to do with him. At the time, he'd thought she was merely saying that for Kaia's benefit. Now, he wasn't so sure.

"You could be lying now," he said. At least, that's what he hoped. And who would have thought he'd ever wish for a lie?

Excitement sparked in her eyes and spread to the rest of her features. She patted his cheek, then flattened her palm on his chest. "You're learning, warrior."

He sucked in a breath. So hot. So soft.

"Here's a proposition for you. Steal something from this store and *I'll* kiss *you.*"

Wait. Her words from a moment ago drifted through his head. *You're learning, warrior. He* was learning? "No," he croaked out. He would not do such a thing. Not even for her. "These people need the money their goods provide. Do you care nothing for their welfare?"

A flash of guilt joined the excitement. "No," she said.

Another lie? Probably. That guilt…it gave him hope. "Why do you need to steal like this, anyway?"

"Foreplay," she said with a shrug.

Blood…heating…again.

"Ma'am, I need you to come with me."

At the unexpected intrusion, they both stiffened. Bianka's gaze pulled from his; together they eyed the policeman now standing beside her.

She frowned. "Can't you see that I'm in the middle of a conversation?"

"Doesn't matter if you're talking to God Himself." The grim-faced officer latched on to her wrist. "I need you to come with me."

"I don't think so, Lysander," she said, clearly expecting him to do something.

Instinct demanded he save her. He wanted her safe and happy, but this would be good for her. "I told you to put the items back."

Her jaw dropped as the officer led her away. And, if Lysander wasn't mistaken, there was pride in her gaze.

Arrested for shoplifting, Bianka thought with disgust. Again. Her third time that year. Lysander had watched the policeman usher her in back, empty her purse and cuff her. All without a word. His disapproval had said plenty, though.

She hadn't let it upset her. He'd stood his ground, and she admired that. Was turned on by it. This wouldn't be an easy victory, as she'd assumed. Besides, for the first time in their relationship, he'd offered to kiss her. *Willingly* kiss her.

But only if she replaced her stolen goods, she reminded herself darkly. Didn't take a genius to figure out that he wanted to change her. To condition her to his way of life.

It was exactly what she wanted to do to him. Which meant he wanted her as desperately as she wanted him.

It also meant it was time to take this game to the next level. She, however, would not be the one to cave. The six hours she'd spent behind bars had given her time to think. To form a strategy.

She was whistling as she meandered down the station steps. Lysander had finally posted her bail, but he hadn't hung around to speak with her. Well, he hadn't needed to. She knew he was following her.

At home, she showered, lingering under the hot spray, soaping herself more slowly than necessary and caressing her breasts and playing between her legs. Unfortunately, he never appeared. But no matter.

Just in case her shower hadn't gotten him in the mood, she read a few passages from her favorite romance novel. And just in case *that* hadn't gotten him in the mood, she decorated her navel with her favorite dangling diamond, dressed in a skintight tank and skirt and knee-high boots, and drove to the closest strip club.

"I only have a few days left. Then I'm traveling to Budapest for Gwen's wedding and you are not invited. Do you hear me? Try and come and I'll make your life hell. So, if you want a go at me, now's the time," she said as she got out of the car.

Again, he didn't appear.

She almost screeched in frustration. So far, her strategy sucked. What was he doing?

The night was cold yet the inside of the club was hot and stuffy, the seats packed with men. Onstage, a redhead—clearly not a natural redhead—swung around a pole. The lights were dimmed, and smoke clung to the air.

"You gonna dance, darling?" someone asked Bianka.

"Nope. Got better things to do." She did, however, steal the stranger's wallet, sneak a beer from the bar and settle into a table in the back corner. Alone. "Enjoy," she whispered to Lysander, toasting him with the bottle.

"Have you no shame?" he suddenly growled from behind her.

Finally! Every muscle in her body relaxed, even as her blood heated with awareness. But she didn't turn to face him. He would have seen the triumph in her eyes. "You have enough shame for both of us."

He snorted. "That does not seem to be the case."

"Really? Well, then, let's loosen you up. Do you want a lap dance?" She held up the cash she'd taken. "I'm sure the red-head onstage would love to rub against you."

His big hands settled on her shoulders, squeezing.

"Or maybe you'd like a beer?"

"I would indeed," the stranger she'd stolen from said, now in front of her table. He reached into his back pocket. Frowned. "Hey, my wallet's gone." His gaze settled on the small brown leather case resting on her tabletop. His frown deepened. "That looks like mine."

"How odd," she said innocently. "So do you want me to buy you a beer or not?"

Lysander's grip tightened. "Give him back his wallet and I'll kiss you."

Her breath caught in her throat. Oh, she wanted his kiss.

More than she'd ever wanted anything. His lips were soft, his taste decadent. And if she allowed him to kiss her, well, she knew she could convince him to do other things.

But she said, "Steal his watch and I'll kiss you."

"What are you talking about?" the guy asked, brow furrowed. "Steal whose watch?"

She rolled her eyes, wishing she could shoo him away.

Lysander leaned down and cupped her breasts. A tremor moved through her, her nipples beading, reaching for him. Sweet heaven. Her stomach quivered, jealous of her breasts, wanting the touch lower.

"Give him back the wallet."

Suddenly she wanted to do just that. Anything for more of Lysander and this sultry side of him. She didn't need the money, anyway. Wait. *What are you doing? Caving?* She straightened her spine. "No, I—"

"I'll kiss you all over your body," Lysander added.

Oh… Hell. He'd decided to take their game to the next level, as well.

But…she couldn't lose. If she did, he would control her with sex. He would expect her to be good like him. There would be no more stealing, no more cursing, no more *fun*. Well, except when they were in bed—but would he expect her to be good there, too?

Life would become boring and sinless, everything a Harpy was taught to fight against.

She stood to shaky legs and turned, finally facing him. His hands fell away from her. She tried not to moan in disappointment. His expression was blank.

She blanked hers, as well, reached out and cupped *him*. Though he showed no emotion, he couldn't hide his hardness. "Steal something, anything at all, and I'll kiss *you* all over."

Her voice dipped huskily. "Remember last time? You came in my mouth, and I loved every moment of it."

His nostrils flared.

"Yes!" the guy behind her exclaimed. "Give me five minutes and I'll have stolen something."

"You aren't trainable, are you?" Lysander asked stiffly.

"No," she said, but suddenly she didn't feel like smiling. There'd been resignation in his tone. Had she pushed him too far again? Was he going to leave her? Never return? "That doesn't mean you should stop trying, though."

"Wait. Trying what?" the stranger asked, confused.

Seriously, when would he leave?

"Lysander," she prompted.

"That's not my name."

"Get lost," she growled.

Lysander's gaze lifted, narrowed on the human. Then Bianka heard footsteps. Her warrior hadn't said anything, hadn't revealed himself, but had somehow managed to make the human leave. He had powers she hadn't known about, then. Why was that even more exciting?

"If you won't give the wallet back and I won't steal anything, where does that leave us?" he asked.

"At war. I don't know about you, but I do my best fighting in bed," she said, and then threw her arms around his neck.

CHAPTER 10

Wind whipped through Bianka's hair, and she knew that Lysander was flying her somewhere with those majestic wings. She had her eyes closed, too busy enjoying him—finally!—to care where he took her. His tongue made love to hers. His hands clutched her hips, fingers digging sharply. Then she was tipping over, a cool, soft mattress pressing into her back. His weight pinned her deliciously.

And it shouldn't have been delicious. This was not a position she allowed. Ever. It caged her wings, and her wings were the source of her strength. Without them, she was almost as weak as a human. But this was Lysander, honest to a fault, and she'd wanted him forever, it seemed. And as wary as he'd been about this sort of thing, she was afraid any type of rebuke would send him flying away.

Besides, he could do anything he wanted to her like this…

"No one is to enter," he said roughly.

Moaning, she wound her legs around his waist, tilted her head to receive his newest kiss and enjoyed a deeper thrust of his tongue. White lightning, the man was a fast learner. Very fast. He was now an expert at kissing. The best she'd ever had. By the time she finished with him, he'd be an expert at *everything* carnal.

His erection, hard and long and thick, rode the apex of her thighs. She could feel every inch of him through the softness of his robe. His arms enveloped her, and when she opened her eyes—they were inside his cloud, she realized—she saw his golden wings were spread, forming a blanket over them.

She tangled her hands in his hair and pulled from the kiss. "Are you going to get into trouble for this?" she asked, panting. Wait. What? Where had that thought come from?

His eyes narrowed. "Do you care?"

"No," she lied, forcing a grin. No, no, no. That wasn't a lie. "But that adds a little extra danger, don't you think?" There. Better. That was more like her normal self. She didn't like his goodness, didn't want to preserve it and keep him safe.

Did she?

"Well, I will not get into the kind of trouble you mean." He flattened his palms at her temples, boxing her in and taking the bulk of his own weight. "If that is the only reason you are here, you can leave."

How fierce he appeared. "So sensitive, warrior." She hooked her fingers at the neck of his robe and tugged. The material ripped easily. But as she held it, it began to weave itself back together. Frowning, she ripped again, harder this time, until there was a big enough gap to shove the clothing from his shoulders and off his arms. "I was only teasing."

His chest was magnificent. A work of art. Muscled and sunkissed and devoid of any hair. She lifted her head and licked the pulse at the base of his neck, then traced his collarbone, then circled one of his nipples. "Do you like?"

"Hot. Wet," he rasped, lids squeezed tight.

"Yeah, but do you like?"

"Yes."

She sucked a peak until he gasped, then kissed away the sting. A tremor of pleasure rocked him, which caused a lance of pride to work through her. "Why do you desire me? Why do you care if I'm good or not?"

A pause. A tortured, "Your skin…"

Every muscle in her body stiffened, and she glared up at him. "So any Harpy will do?" She tried to hide her insult, but didn't quite manage it. The thought of another Harpy—hell, any other woman, immortal or not—enjoying him roused her most vicious instincts. Her nails lengthened, and her teeth sharpened. A red haze dotted her line of vision. *Mine,* she thought. She would kill anyone who touched him. "We all have this skin, you know?" The words were guttural, scraping her throat.

His lashes separated as his eyes opened. His pupils were dilated, his expression tightening with…an emotion she didn't recognize. "Yes, but only yours tempts me. Why is that?"

"Oh," was all she could first think to say, her anger draining completely. But she needed to respond, had to think of something light, easy. "To answer your question, you want me because I'm made of awesome. And guess what? I will make you so happy you said that, warrior."

"No. I will make *you* happy." He ripped her shirt just as she had done his robe. She wasn't wearing a bra, and her breasts sprang free. Another tremor moved through him as he lowered his head.

He licked and sucked one nipple, as she had done to him, then the other, feasting. Savoring. Soon she was arching and writhing against him, craving his mouth elsewhere. Her skin was sensitized, her body desperate for release. Yet she didn't want to rush him. She was still afraid of scaring him away. But if he didn't hurry, didn't touch her between her legs, she was going to die.

"Lysander," she said on a trembling breath.

His wings brushed both her arms, up and down, tickling,

caressing, raising goose bumps on her flesh. Oh, that was good. So good.

He lifted from her completely.

"Wh-what are you doing? I wasn't going to tell you to leave," she screeched, bracing her weight on her elbows.

"I do not want anything between us." He shoved the robe down his legs until he was gloriously naked. Moisture gleamed at the head of his penis, and her mouth watered. Reaching out, he gripped her boots and tore them off. Her jeans quickly followed. She, of course, was not wearing any panties.

His gaze drank her in, and she knew what he saw. Her flushed, glowing skin. The aching juncture between her legs. Her rose-tinted nipples.

"I want to touch and taste every inch," he said and just kind of fell on her, as if his will to resist had abandoned him completely.

"Touch and taste every inch next time." Please let there be a next time. She tried to hook her legs around his waist again. "I need release *now*."

He grabbed her by the knees and spread her. Her head fell back, her hair tangling around her, and he kissed a path to her breasts, then to her stomach. He lingered at her navel until she was moaning.

"Lysander," she said again. Fine. She'd jump on this grenade if she had to; if he wanted to taste, he could taste. "More. I need more."

Rather than give it to her, he stilled. "I…took care of myself before following you this day," he admitted, cheeks pinkening. "I thought that would give me resistance against you."

Her eyes widened, shock pouring through her. "You pleasured yourself?"

A stiff nod.

"Did you think of me?"

Another nod.

"Oh, baby. That's good. I can picture it, and I love what I see." His hand on his shaft, stroking up and down, eyes closed, features tight with arousal, body straining toward release. Wings spread as he fell to his knees, the pleasure too much. Her, naked in his mind. "What did you think about doing?"

Another pause. A hesitant response. "Licking. Between your legs. Tasting you, as I said."

She arched her back, hands skimming down her middle to her thighs. Although he already held her open, she pushed her legs farther apart. "Then do it. Lick me. I want it so bad. Want your tongue on me. See how wet I am?"

He hissed in a breath. "Yes. Yes." Leaning down, he started at her ankles and kissed his way up, lingering at the back of her knees, at the crease of her legs.

"Please," she said, so on edge she was ready to scream. "Please. Do it."

"Yes," he whispered again. "Yes." Finally he settled over her, mouth poised, ready. His tongue flicked out. Then, sweet contact.

She expected the touch, but nothing could have prepared her for the perfection of it. She did scream, shivered. Begged for more. "Yes, yes, yes. Please, please, please."

At first, he merely lapped at her, humming his approval at her taste. *Thank you, thank you, thank you.* If he hadn't liked her in that way, she wasn't sure what she would have done. In that moment, she wanted—needed—to be everything *he* wanted—needed. She wanted him to crave every part of her, as she craved every part of him.

Even his goodness?

Yes, she thought, finally admitting it. Yes. Just then, she had no defenses; she'd been stripped to her soul. His goodness somehow balanced her out. She'd fought against it—and still had no plans to change—but they were two extremes and actually complemented each other, each giving the other what he or she lacked. In her case, the knowledge that some things were worth taking seriously. In his, that it wasn't a crime to have fun.

"Bianka," he moaned. "Tell me how…what…"

"More. Don't stop."

Soon his tongue was darting in and out of her, mimicking the act of sex. She grasped at the sheets, fisting them. She writhed, meeting his every thrust. She screamed again, moaned and begged some more.

Finally, she splintered apart. Bit down on her bottom lip until she tasted blood. White lights danced over her eyes—from her skin, she realized. Her skin was so bright it was almost blinding, glowing like a lamp, something that had never happened before.

Then Lysander was looming above her. "You are not fertile," he rasped. Sweat beaded him.

That gave her fuzzy mind pause. "I know." Her words were as labored as his. Harpies were only fertile once a year and this wasn't her time. "But how do you know that?"

"Sense it. Always know that kind of thing. So…are you ready?" he asked, and she could hear the uncertainty in his voice.

He must not know proper etiquette, the darling virgin. He would learn. With her, there was no etiquette. Doing what felt good was the only thing that drove her.

"Not yet." She flattened her hands on his shoulders and pushed him to his back, careful of his wings. He didn't protest or fight her as she straddled his waist and gripped his length by the base. Her wings fluttered in joy at their freedom. "Better?"

He licked his lips, nodded. *His* wings lifted, enveloped her, caressing her. Her head fell, the long length of her hair tickling his thighs. He trembled.

Would he regret this? she suddenly wondered. She didn't want him to hate her for supposedly ruining him.

"Are *you* ready?" she asked. "There's no taking it back once it's done." If he wasn't ready, well, she would...wait, she realized. Yes, she would wait until he *was* ready. Only he would do. No other. Her body only wanted him.

"Do not stop," he commanded, mimicking her.

A grin bloomed. "I'll be careful with you," she assured him. "I won't hurt you."

His fingers circled her hips and lifted her until she was poised at his tip. "The only thing that could hurt me is if you leave me like this."

"No chance of that," she said, and sank all the way to the hilt.

He arched up to meet her, feeding her his length, his eyes squeezing shut, his teeth nearly chewing their way through his bottom lip. He stretched her perfectly, hit her in just the right spot, and she found herself desperate for release once more. But she paused, his enjoyment more important than her own. For whatever reason.

"Tell me when you're ready for me to—"

"Move!" he shouted, hips thrusting so high he raised her knees from the mattress.

Groaning at the pleasure, she moved, up and down, slipping and sliding over his erection. He was wild beneath her, as if he'd kept his passion bottled up all these years and it had suddenly exploded from him, unstoppable.

Soon, even that wasn't enough for him. He began hammering inside her, and she loved it. Loved his intensity. All she could do was hold on for the ride, slamming down on him, gasping. Her nails dug into his chest, her moans blended with his. And when her second orgasm hit, Lysander was right there with her, roaring, muscles stiffening.

He grabbed her by the neck and jerked her down, meshing their lips together. Their teeth scraped as he primitively, savagely kissed her. It was a kiss that stripped her once more to her soul, left her raw, agonized. Reeling.

He was indeed her consort, she thought, dazed. There was no denying it now. He was it for her. Her one and only. Necessary. She laughed, and was surprised by how carefree it sounded. Tamed by great sex. It figured. After this, no other man would do. Ever. She knew it, sensed it.

She collapsed atop him, panting, sweating. Scared. Suddenly vulnerable. How did he feel about her? He didn't approve of her, yet he had gifted her with his virginity. Surely that meant he liked her, just as she was. Surely that meant he wanted her around.

His heart thundered in his chest, and she grinned. Surely.

"Bianka," he said shakily.

She yawned, more replete than she'd ever been. *My consort.* Her eyelids closed, her lashes suddenly too heavy to hold up. Fatigue washed through her, so intense she couldn't fight it.

"Talk…later," she replied, and drifted into the most peaceful sleep of her life.

CHAPTER 11

For hours Lysander held Bianka in the crook of his arm while she slept, marveling—this was what she'd craved most in the world and *he* had given it to her—and yet, he was also worrying. He knew what that meant, knew how difficult it was for a Harpy to let down her guard and sleep in front of another. It meant she trusted him to protect her, to keep her safe. And he was glad. He *wanted* to protect her. Even from herself.

But could he? He didn't know. They were so different.

Until they got into bed, that is.

He could not believe what had just happened. He had become a creature of sensation, his baser urges all that mattered. The pleasure…unlike anything he'd ever experienced. Her taste was like honey, her skin so soft he wanted it against him for the rest of eternity. Her breathy moans—even her screams—had been a caress inside his ears. He'd loved every moment of it.

Had he been called to battle, he wasn't sure he would have been able to leave her.

Why her, though? Why had *she* been the one to captivate him?

She lied to him at every opportunity. She embodied everything he despised. Yet he did not despise her. For every moment with her, he only wanted more. Everything she did excited him. The pleasure she'd found in his arms…she had been unashamed, uninhibited, demanding everything he had to give.

Would he have been as enthralled by her if she had led a blameless life? If she had been more demure? He didn't think so. He liked her exactly as she was.

Why? he wondered again.

By the time she stretched lazily, sensually against him, he still did not have the answers. Nor did he know what to do with her. He'd already proven he could not leave her alone. And now that he knew all of her, she would be even more impossible to resist.

"Lysander," she said, voice husky from her rest.

"I am here."

She blinked open her eyes, jolted upright. "I fell asleep."

"I know."

"Yeah, but I feel asleep." She scrubbed a hand down her beautiful face, twisted and peered down at him with vulnerable astonishment. "I should be ashamed of myself, but I'm not. What's wrong with me?"

He reached up and traced a fingertip over her swollen lips. How hard had he kissed her? "I'm…sorry," he said. "I lost control for a moment. I shouldn't have taken you so—"

She nipped at his finger, her self-recrimination seeming to melt away in favor of amusement. "Do you hear me complaining about that?"

He relaxed. No, he did not hear her complaining. In fact, she appeared utterly sated. And he had done that. He had given her pleasure. Pride filled him. Pride—a foolish emotion that often led to a man's downfall. Was that how Bianka would make him fall? For as his temptation, she *would* make him fall.

With a sigh, she flopped back against him. "You turned serious all of the sudden. Want to talk about it?"

"No."

"Do you want to talk about *anything?*"

"No."

"Well, too bad," she grumbled, but he heard a layer of satisfaction in her tone. Did she enjoy making him do things he didn't want to do—or didn't think he wanted to do? "Because you're going to talk. A lot. You can start with why you first abducted me. I know you wanted to change me, but why me? I still don't know."

He shouldn't tell her; she already had enough power over him, and knowing the truth would only increase that power. But he also wanted her to understand how desperate he'd been. Was. "At the heart of my duties, I am a peacekeeper, and as such, I must peek into the lives of the Lords of the Underworld every so often, making sure they are obeying heavenly laws. I...saw you with them. And as I have proven with my actions this day, I realized you are my one temptation. The one thing that can tear me from my righteous path."

She sat up again, faced him again. Her eyes were wide with...pleasure? "Really? I alone can ruin you?"

He frowned. "That does not mean you should try and do so."

Laughing, she leaned down and kissed him. Her breasts pressed against his chest, once again heating his blood in that way only she could do. But he was done fighting it, done resisting it. "That's not what I meant. I just like being important to you, I guess." Her cheeks suddenly bloomed with color. "Wait. That's not what I meant, either. What I'm trying to say is that you're forgiven for whisking me to your palace in the sky. I would have done the same thing to you had the situation been reversed."

He had not expected forgiveness to come so easily. Not from her. Frown intensifying, he cupped her cheeks and forced her to meet his gaze. "Why were *you* with *me?* I know I am not what your kind views as acceptable."

She shrugged, the action a little stiff. "I guess you're my temptation."

Now he understood why she'd grinned over his proclamation. He wanted to whoop with satisfied laughter.

"If we're going to be together—" She stopped, waiting. When he nodded, she relaxed and continued, "Then I guess I could only steal from the wicked. Or not at all. I don't know. Argh! I need to think about this some more."

It was a concession. A concession he'd never thought she would make. She truly must like him. Must want more time with him.

"So listen," she said. "My sister is getting married in a week, as I told you before. Do you want to, like, come with me? As my guest? I know, I know. It's short notice. But I didn't intend to invite you. I mean, you're a Sent One." There was disgust in her voice. "But you make love like a pro so I guess I should, I don't know, show you off or something."

He opened his mouth to reply. What he would say, he didn't know. They could not tell others of their relationship. Ever. But a voice stopped him.

"Lysander. Are you home?"

Lysander recognized the speaker immediately. Raphael, the warrior. Panic nearly choked him. He couldn't let the man see him like this. Couldn't let any of his kind see him with the Harpy.

"We must discuss Olivia," Raphael called. "May I enter your abode? There is some sort of block preventing me from doing so."

"Not yet," he called. Was his panic in his voice? He'd never experienced it before, so didn't know how to combat it. "Wait for me. I will emerge." He sat up and slipped from the bed, from Bianka. He grabbed his robe, or rather, the pieces of it, from the floor and wrapped it around himself. Immediately it wove back together to fit his frame. The material even cleaned him, wiping away Bianka's scent.

The latter, he inwardly cursed. *For the best.*

"Let him in," Bianka said, fitting the sheet around her, oblivious. "I don't mind."

Lysander kept his back to her. "I do not want him to see you."

"Don't worry. I've covered my naughty nakedness."

He gave no reply. Unlike her, he would not lie. And if he did not lie to her, he would hurt her. He did not want to do that either.

"So call him in already," she said with a laugh. "I want to see if all Sent Ones look like sin but act like saints."

"No. I don't want him inside right now. I will go out to meet him. You will stay here," he said. Still he couldn't face her.

"Wait. Are you jealous?"

He gave no reply.

"Lysander?"

"Stay silent. Please. Cloud walls are thin."

"Stay...silent?" A moment passed in the very silence he'd requested. Only, he didn't like it. He heard the rustle of fabric, a sharp intake of breath. "You don't want him to know I'm here, do you? You're ashamed of me," she said, clearly shocked. "You don't want your friend to know you've been with me."

"Bianka."

"No. You don't get to speak right now." With every word, her voice rose. "I was willing to take you to my sister's wedding. Even though I knew my family would laugh at me or view me with disgust. I was willing to give you a chance. Give us a chance. But not you. You were going to hide me away. As if *I'm* something shameful."

He whirled on her, fury burning through him. At her, at himself. "You *are* something shameful. I kill beings like you. I do not fall in love with them."

She didn't say anything. Just looked up at him with wide hurt-filled eyes. So much hurt he actually stumbled back. A sharp pain lanced *his* chest. But as he watched, her hurt mutated into a fury that far surpassed his.

"Kill me, then," she growled.

"You know I will not."

"Why?"

"Because!"

"Let me guess. Because deep down you still think you can change me. You think that I will become the pure virtuous woman you want me to be. Well, who are you to say what's virtuous and what isn't?"

He merely arched a brow. The answer was obvious and didn't need to be stated.

"I told you that from now on I'd only hurt the wicked, right? Well, surprise! That's what I've done since the beginning. The pie you watched me eat? The owner of that restaurant cheats at cards, takes money that doesn't belong to him. The wallet I stole? I took it from a man cheating on his wife."

He blinked down at her, unsure he'd heard correctly. "Why would you have kept that from me?"

"Why should it change how you feel about me?" She tossed back the cover and stood, glorious in her nakedness. Her skin was still aglow, multihued light reflecting off it—he'd touched that skin. Dark hair cascaded around her—he'd fisted that hair.

"I want to be with you," he said. "I do. But it has to be in secret."

"I thought the same. Until what we just did," she said as she hastily dressed. Her clothes were not like his, did not repair on their own, and so that ripped shirt revealed more than it hid.

He tried again. Tried to make her understand. "You are everything my kind stands against, Bianka. I train warriors to hunt and kill demons. What would it say to them were I to take you as my companion?"

"Here's a better question. What does it say to them that you hide your sin? Because that's how you view me, isn't it? Your sin. You are such a hypocrite." She stormed past him, careful not to touch him. "And I will not be with a hypocrite. That's worse than being an angel."

He thought she meant to race to Raphael and flaunt her presence. Shockingly enough, she didn't. And because he hadn't commanded her to stay, when she said, "I want to leave," the cloud opened up at her feet.

She disappeared, falling through the sky.

"Bianka," he shouted. Lysander spread his wings and jumped after her. He passed Raphael, but at that point, he didn't care. He only wanted Bianka safe—and that hurt and fury wiped away from her expression.

She'd turned facedown to increase her momentum. He had to tuck his wings into his back to increase his own. Finally, he caught her halfway and wrapped his arms around her, her back pressed into his stomach. She didn't flail, didn't order him to release her, which he'd been prepared for.

When they reached her cabin, he straightened them, spread his wings and slowed. Snow still covered the ground and crunched when they landed. She didn't pull away. Didn't run. Something else he'd been prepared for.

Clearly he knew very little about her.

"It's probably best this way, you know," she said flatly, keeping her back to him. The wind slapped her hair against his cheeks. "That was my afterglow talking earlier, anyway. I never should have invited you to the wedding. We're too different to make anything work."

"I was willing to try," he said through gritted teeth. *Don't do this,* he projected. *Don't end us.*

She laughed without humor, and he marveled at the difference between this laugh and the one she'd given inside his cloud. Marveled and mourned. "No, you were willing to hide me away."

"Yes. Therefore I was *trying* to make something work. I want to be with you, Bianka. Otherwise I would not have followed you. I would have left you alone from the first. I would not have tried to show you the light."

"You are so arrogant," she spat. "You're still in darkness yourself and you want to show me the light? Please! You claim to do good, but your actions don't fit your words. You took something that belonged to me."

"What?"

"My hea—freedom. And you know what else? You're rigid. I will never live up to the person you want me to be. No one can."

"You could try."

She laughed again, this one bleaker, grim. "The scarves I took were made by child laborers. So I haven't really done anything too terrible yet. But I will. And you know what? If you were to do something nauseatingly righteous, I wouldn't have cared. I would still have wanted to take you to the wedding. That's the difference between us. Evil or not, good or not, I wanted you."

"I want you, too. But the way you feel now was not always the case, and you know it. You *would* care." He tightened his grip on her. "Bianka. We can work this out."

"No, we can't." Finally, she twisted to face him. "That

would require giving you a second chance, and I don't do second chances."

"I don't need a second chance. I just need you to think about this. To realize our relationship must stay hidden."

"I'm not going to be your secret shame, Lysander."

His eyes narrowed. She was trying to force his hand, and he didn't like it. "You steal in secret. You sleep in secret. Why not this?"

"That you don't know the answer proves you aren't the warrior I thought you were. Have a nice life, Lysander," she said, jerking from his hold and walking away without a backward glance.

CHAPTER 12

Lysander sat in the back of the Budapest chapel, undetectable, watching Bianka help her sisters and their friends decorate for the wedding. She was currently hanging flowers from the vaulted ceiling. Without a ladder.

He'd been following her for days, unable to stay away. One thing he'd noticed: she talked and laughed as if she was fine, normal, but the sparkle was gone from her eyes, her skin.

And he had done that to her. Worse, not once had she cursed, lied or stolen. Again, his fault. He'd told her she was unworthy of him. He'd been—*was,* right?—too embarrassed of her to tell his people about her.

But he couldn't deny that he missed her. Missed everything about her. That much he knew. She excited him, challenged him, frustrated him, consumed him, drew him, made him *feel.* He did not want to be without her.

Something soft brushed his shoulder. He barely managed to tear his gaze from Bianka to turn and see that Olivia was now sitting beside him.

What was wrong with him? He hadn't heard her arrive. Normally his senses were tuned, alert.

"Why did you summon me here?" she asked. She glanced

around nervously. Her dark curls framed her face, rosebuds dripping from a few of the strands.

"To Budapest? Because you are always here, anyway."

"As are you these days," she replied dryly.

He shrugged. "Did you just come from Aeron's room?"

She gave a reluctant nod.

"Raphael came to me," he said. The day he'd lost Bianka. The worst day of his existence.

"Those flowers aren't centered, B," the redheaded Kaia called, claiming his attention and stopping the rest of his speech to his charge. "Shift them a little to the left."

Bianka expelled a frustrated sigh. "Like this?"

"No. *My* left, dummy."

Grumbling, Bianka obeyed.

"Perfect." Kaia beamed up at her. "For an amateur."

Bianka raised a fist at her.

Perhaps she had not lost her spirit, after all, he thought with a small grin.

"I think they're perfect, too," her youngest sister, Gwendolyn, said.

Bianka released the ceiling panels and dropped to the floor. When she landed, she straightened as if the jolt had not affected her in any way. "Glad the princess is finally happy with something," she muttered. Then, more loudly, "I don't understand why you can't get married in a tree like a civilized Harpy."

Gwen anchored her hands on her fists. "Because my dream has always been to be wed in a chapel like any other normal person. Now, will someone please remove the naked portraits of Sabin from the walls? Please."

"Why would you want to get rid of them when I just spent all that time hanging them?" Anya, goddess of Anarchy and companion to Lucien, keeper of Death, asked, clearly offended. "They add a little something extra to what would otherwise be very boring proceedings. *My* wedding will have strippers. Live ones."

"Boring? Boring!" Fury passed over Gwen's features, black bleeding into her eyes, her teeth sharpening.

Lysander had watched this same change overtake her multiple times already. In the past hour alone.

"It won't be boring," Ashlyn, companion to Maddox, the keeper of Violence, said soothingly. "It'll be beautiful."

The pregnant woman rubbed her rounded belly. That belly was larger than it should have been, given the early state of her pregnancy. No one seemed to realize it, though. They would soon enough, he supposed. He just hoped they were ready for what she carried.

What would a child of Bianka's be like? he suddenly wondered. Harpy, like her? Sent One, like him? Or a mix of both?

A pang took root and flourished in his chest.

"Boring?" Gwen snarled again, clearly not ready to let the insult slide.

"Great!" Bianka threw up her arms. "Someone get Sabin before Gwennie kills us all in a rage."

A Harpy in a rage could hurt even other Harpies, Lysander knew. As Gwen's consort, Sabin, keeper of Doubt, was the only one who could calm her.

With that thought, Lysander's head tilted to the side. He had never seen Bianka erupt, he realized. She'd viewed everything as a game. Well, not true. Once, she had gotten mad. The time Paris had punched him. Lysander had been her enemy, but she'd still gotten mad over his mistreatment.

Lysander had calmed her.

The pang grew in intensity, and he rubbed his breastbone. Was he Bianka's consort? Did he want to be?

"No need to search me out. I'm here." Sabin strode through the double doors. "As if I'd be more than a few feet away when she's so sensitiv—uh, just in case she needed my help. Gwen, baby." There at the end, his tone had lowered, gentled. He reached her and pulled her into his arms; she snuggled against him. "The most important thing tomorrow is that we'll be together. Right?"

"Lysander," Olivia said, drawing his attention from the now-cooing couple. "The wait is difficult. Raphael came to you and...what?"

Lysander sighed, forcing himself to concentrate. "Answer a few questions for me first."

"All right," she said after a brief hesitation.

"Why do you like Aeron when he is so different from you?"

She twisted the fabric of her robe. "I think I like him *because* he is so different from me. He has thrived amid darkness, managing to retain a spark of light in his soul. He is not perfect, is not blameless, but he could have given in to his demon long ago and yet still he fights. He protects those he loves. His passion for life is..." She shivered.

Bianka fought, too, he just hadn't realized it until too late. Yet Lysander had tried to make her ashamed of herself. Ashamed when she should only be proud of what she had accomplished, thriving amid darkness, as Olivia had said. "And you are not embarrassed for our kind to know of your affection for him?"

"Embarrassed of Aeron?" Olivia laughed. "When he is stronger, fiercer, more alive than anyone I know? Of course not. I would be proud to be called his woman. Not that it could ever happen," she added sadly.

Proud. There was that word again. And this time, something clicked in his mind. *I'm not going to be your secret shame, Lysander,* Bianka had said. He'd reminded her that she committed all her other sins in secret. Why not him? She hadn't told him the answer, but it came to him now. Because she'd been proud of him. Because she'd wanted to show him off.

As he should have wanted to show *her* off.

Any other man would have been proud to stand beside her. She was beautiful, intelligent, witty, passionate and lived by her own moral code. Her laughter was more lovely than the song of a harp, her kiss as sweet as a prayer.

He'd considered her beneath him, evil, yet she was a gift from above. They made each other want to be and to better.

"Have I answered your questions sufficiently?" Olivia asked.

"Yes." He was surprised by the rawness of his voice. Had he ruined things irreparably between them?

"So answer a few now for me."

Unable to find his voice, he nodded. He had to make this right. Had to try, at least.

"Bianka. The Harpy you watch. Do you love her?"

Love. He found her among the crowd and the pang in his chest grew unbearable. She was currently adding a magic marker mustache to one of Sabin's portraits while Kaia added… other things down below. Kaia was giggling; Bianka looked like she was just going through the motions, taking no joy.

He wanted her happy. Wanted her the way she'd been.

"You think you are embarrassed of her," Olivia continued when he gave no response.

"How do you know?" He forced the words to leave him.

"I am—or was—a joy-bringer, Lysander. It was my job to know what people were feeling and then help them see the truth. Because only in truth can one find real joy. You were never embarrassed of her. I know you. You are embarrassed by nothing. You were simply scared. Scared that *you* were not what *she* needs."

His eyes widened. Could that be true? He'd tried to change her. Had tried to make her what he was so that she, in turn, would *like* what he was? Yes. Yes, that made sense, and for the second time in his existence, he hated himself.

He had let Bianka get away from him. When he should have sung her praises to everyone he knew, he had cast her aside. No man was more foolish. Irreparable damage or not, he had to try and win her back.

He jumped to his feet. "I do," he said. "I love her." He wanted to throw his arms around her. Wanted to shout to all the world that she belonged to him. That she had chosen him as her man.

His shoulders slumped. Chosen. Key word. Past tense. She would not choose him again. She did not give second chances, she'd said.

She often lies...

For the first time, the thought that his woman liked to lie caused him to smile. Perhaps she had lied about that. Perhaps she would give him a second chance. A chance to prove his love.

If he had to grovel, he would. She was his temptation, but that did not have to be a bad thing. That could be his salvation. After all, his life would mean nothing without her. Same for her. She had told him that he was her own temptation. He could be *her* salvation.

"Thank you," he told Olivia. "Thank you for showing me the truth."

"Always my pleasure."

How should he approach Bianka? When? Urgency flooded him. He wanted to do so now. As a warrior, though, he knew some battles required planning. And as this was the most important battle of his existence, plan his attack he would.

If she forgave him and decided to be with him, they would still have a tough road ahead. Where would they live? His duties were in the heavens. She thrived on earth, with her family nearby. Plus, Olivia was destined to kill Aeron, who would essentially be Bianka's brother-in-law after tomorrow. And if Olivia decided not to, another angel would be chosen to do the job.

Most likely, that would be Lysander.

One thing Germanus had taught him, however, was that love truly could conquer all. Nothing was stronger. They could make this work.

"I've lost you again," Olivia said with a laugh. "Before you rush off, you must tell me why you summoned me. What Raphael said to you."

Some of his good mood evaporated. While Olivia had just given him hope and helped him find the right path, he was about to dash any hopes of a happily-ever-after for her.

"Raphael came to me," he repeated. *Just do it; just say it.* "He told me of the council's unhappiness with you. He told me they grow weary of your continued defiance."

Her smile fell away. "I know," she whispered. "I just...I haven't been able to bring myself to hurt him. Watching him gives me joy. And I deserve to experience joy after so many centuries of devoted service, do I not?"

"Of course."

"And if he is dead, I will never be able to do the things I now dream about."

His brow furrowed. "What things?"

"Touching him. Curling into his arms." A pause. "Kissing him."

Dangerous desires indeed. Oh, did he know their power. "If you never experience them," he offered, "they are easier to resist." But he hated to think of this wonderful female being without something she wanted.

He could petition the council for Aeron's forgiveness, but that would do no good. A decree was a decree. A law had been broken and someone had to pay. "Very soon, the council will be forced to offer you a choice. Your duty or your downfall."

She gazed down at her hands, once again twisting the fabric of her robe. "I know. I don't know why I hesitate. He would never desire me, anyway. The women here, they are exciting, dangerous. As fierce as he is. And I am—"

"Precious," he said. "You are precious. Never think otherwise."

She offered him a shaky smile.

"I have always loved you, Olivia. I would hate to see you give up everything you are for a man who has threatened to kill you. You do know what you would be losing, yes?"

That smile fell away as she nodded.

"You would fall straight into hell. The demons there will go for your wings. They always go for the wings first. No longer will you be impervious to pain. You will hurt, yet you will have to dig your way free of the underground—or die there. Your strength will be depleted. Your body will not regenerate on its own. You will be more fragile than a human because you were not raised among them."

While he thought he could survive such a thing, he did not think Olivia would. She was too delicate. Too…sheltered. Until this point, every facet of her life had dealt with joy and happiness. She had known nothing else.

The demons of hell would be crueler to her than they would be even to him, the man they feared more than any other. She was all they despised. Wholly good. Destroying such innocence and purity would delight them.

"Why are you telling me this?" Her voice trembled. Tears streaked down her cheeks.

"Because I do not want you to make the wrong decision. Because I want you to know what you're up against."

A moment passed in silence, then she jumped up and threw her arms around his neck. "I love you, you know."

He squeezed her tightly, sensing that this was her way of saying goodbye. Sensing that this would be the last time they were offered such a reprieve. But he would not stop her, whatever path she chose.

She pulled back and smoothed her trembling hands down her glistening white robe. "You have given me much to consider. So now I will leave you to your female. May love always follow you, Lysander." As she spoke, her wings expanded. Up, up she flew, misting through the ceiling—and Bianka's flowers—before disappearing.

He hoped she'd choose her faith, her immortality, over the keeper of Wrath, but feared she would not. His gaze strayed to Bianka, now walking down the aisle toward the exit. She paused at his row, frowned, before shaking her head and leaving. If he'd been forced to pick between her and his reputation and lifestyle, he would have picked her, he realized.

And now it was time to prove it to her.

CHAPTER 13

I've got to pull myself from this funk, Bianka thought. This was her youngest sister's wedding day. She should be happy. Delighted. If she were honest, though, she was a tiny bit—aka a *lot*—jealous. Gwen's man loved her. Was proud of her.

Lysander considered Bianka unworthy.

She'd thought about proving herself to him, but had quickly discarded the idea. Proving herself worthy—his idea of worthy, that is—would entail nothing more than a lie. And Lysander hated lies. So, according to him, she would never be good enough for him. Which meant he was stupid, and she didn't date stupid men. Plus, he didn't deserve her.

He deserved to rot in his unhappiness. And that's what he'd be without her. Unhappy. Or so she hoped.

"So much for our plan to go naked," Kaia muttered beside her. "Gwen saw me leave my room that way and almost sliced my throat."

"Did not," the bride in question said from behind them.

They turned in unison. Bianka's breath caught as it had every time she'd seen her youngest sister in her gown. It was a princess cut, which was fitting, the straps thin, the beautiful white lace cinching just under her breasts before flowing to her ankles. The material covering her legs was sheer, allowing glimpses of thigh and those gorgeous red heels.

Her strawberry curls were half up, half down, diamonds glittering through the strands. There was so much love and excitement in her gold-gray eyes it was almost blinding.

"I almost pushed you out a window," Gwen added.

They laughed. Even stoic Taliyah, their oldest sister, who had her arm wrapped through Gwen's. Since it turned out Gwen's father was the Lords' greatest enemy, and Gwen's mom had disowned her years ago, Taliyah was escorting Gwen down the aisle.

"Hence the reason I'm now wearing this." Kaia motioned to her own gown, an exact match to Bianka's. A buttercup-yellow creation with more ribbons, bows and sequined rose appliqués than anyone should wear in an entire lifetime. They even wore hats with orange streamers.

Gwen shrugged, unrepentant. "I didn't want you looking prettier than me, so sue me."

"Weddings suck," Bianka said. "You should have just had Sabin tattoo your name on his butt and called it good." That's what she would have done. Not that Lysander ever would have agreed to such a thing. Whether they were together or not.

Which they never would be. Jerk.

"I did. Have him tattoo my name on his butt," Gwen said. "And his arm. And his chest. And his back. But then I casually mentioned how much I'd always wanted a big wedding, and well, he told me I had four weeks to plan it or he'd take over and do it himself. And everyone knows men can't plan anything worth attending. So…" She shrugged again, though the excitement and love on her face had intensified. "Are they ready for us yet?"

Bianka and Kaia turned back to the chapel, peeking through the crack in the closed doors.

"Not yet," Bianka said. "Paris is missing."

Paris, who had gotten ordained over the internet, would be presiding over the nuptials.

"He better hurry," she added grumpily. "Or I'll find a way to make him oil-wrestle again."

"You've been so depressed lately. Missing your Sent One?" Kaia asked her, pinkie-waving to Amun, who stood in the line of groomsmen beside Sabin at the altar.

Amun shouldn't have been able to see her, but somehow he did. He nodded, a smile twitching at the corners of his lips.

"Of course not. I hate him." A lie. She hadn't told her sisters why she and Lysander had parted, only that they had. Forever. If they knew the truth, they'd want to kill him. And as all but Gwen were paid killers, immensely good at their job, she'd find herself the proud owner of Lysander's head.

Which she didn't want.

She just wanted him. Stupid girl.

"I only would have teased you for a few years, you know," Kaia said. "You should have kept him around. It might have been fun to corrupt him."

He didn't want to be corrupted any more than she wanted to be purified—fine, she did. Still. They were too different. Could never make anything work. Their separation was for the best. So why couldn't she get over it? Why did she feel his gaze on her, every minute of every day? Even now, when she looked like a Southern belle on crack?

"So Sabin doesn't have a last name," she said to Gwen, drawing attention away from herself. "Are you going to call yourself Gwen Sabin?"

"No, nothing like that. I'm going to call myself Gwen Lord."

"What's Anya plan to call herself? Anya Underworld?" Kaia asked with a laugh.

"Knowing our goddess, she'll demand Lucien take *her* last name. Trouble. Or is that her middle name?"

"I here, I here," a voice suddenly screeched. Legion pushed her way in front of Bianka and Kaia. She was wearing a yellow dress, as well. Only hers had more ribbons, bows and sequins. A basket of flowers was clutched in her hands, her too-long nails curling around the handle. Best of all, she wore a tiara. Because she didn't have hair, it had had to be glued to her scaled head. "We begin now."

She didn't wait for permission but shouldered her way through the door. The crowd—which consisted of the Lords of the Underworld, their companions and some gods and goddesses Anya knew—turned and gasped when they saw her. Well, except for Gideon. He'd recently been captured and tortured by Hunters, the Lords' nemeses, and was currently missing his hands. (His feet weren't in the best of shape, either.) Because of his injuries, he was beyond weak, so he lay in his gurney, barely conscious. He'd insisted on coming, though.

From his pew, Aeron smiled indulgently as Legion tossed pink petals in every direction. Just as she reached the front, Paris raced to the podium. He looked harried, pale, and Sabin punched him in the shoulder.

Sabin looked amazing. He wore a black tux, his hair slicked back, and when he turned to face the door, watching for Gwen, his entire face lit. With love. With pride. Bianka's jealousy increased. She wanted that. Wanted her man to find her perfect in every way.

Was that too much to ask?

Apparently so. Stupid Lysander.

"Go, go, go," Gwen ordered, giving them a little push.

Bianka kicked into motion, heading toward Strider, her appointed groomsman. He smiled at her when she reached him. He would be proud to call her his woman, she thought. She tried to make herself return the gesture, but her eyes were too busy filling with tears. She looked around, trying to distract herself.

The chapel really was beautiful. The glittery white flowers she'd hung from the ceiling were thick and lush and offered a canopy, a haven. They were the best part of the decor, if you asked her. Candles flickered with golden light, twining with shadows.

Kaia approached her side, and everyone except for Gideon stood. The music changed, slowing down to the bridal march. Gwen and Taliyah appeared. Sabin's breath caught. Yes, that was the way a man should react to the sight of his woman.

What makes you think you were ever Lysander's woman?

Because she was his one temptation. Because of the reverent way he had touched her. Because she liked how he made her feel. Because they balanced each other. Because he completed her in a way she hadn't known she needed. He was the light to her darkness.

He was willing to show you that light. Over and over again.

Perhaps she should have fought for him. That's what she was, after all. A fighter. Yet she'd given in as if he meant nothing to her when he had somehow become the most important thing in her life.

Bianka didn't mean to, but she tuned out as Paris gave his speech and the happy couple recited their vows, her thoughts remaining focused on Lysander. Should she try and fight for him now? If so, how would she go about it?

Only when the crowd cheered did she snap out of her haze, watching as Sabin and Gwen kissed. Then they were marching down the aisle and out the doors together. The rest of the bridal party made their way out, as well.

"Shall we?" Strider asked, holding out his arm for her.

"She can't." Paris grabbed her arm. "You're needed in that room." With his free hand, he pointed.

"Why?" Was he planning revenge against her for forcing him to oil-wrestle Lysander? He hadn't mentioned it in the days since her return to Buda, but he couldn't be happy with her. He should be thanking her, for freaks' sake. He'd gotten to touch all of Lysander's hawtness.

Paris rolled his eyes. "Just go before your boyfriend decides he's tired of waiting and comes out here."

Her boyfriend. Lysander? Couldn't be. Could it? But why would he have come? Heart drumming in her chest, she walked forward. She didn't allow herself to run, though she wanted to soooo badly. She reached the door. Her hand shook as she turned the knob.

Hinges creaked. Then she was staring into—an empty room. Her teeth ground together. Paris's revenge, just as she'd figured. Of course. That rat jerk turd was going to pay. She wasn't just going to make him oil-wrestle. She was going to—

"Hello, Bianka."

Lysander.

Gasping, she whipped around. Her eyes widened. In an instant, the chapel had been transformed. No longer were her sisters and friends inside. Lysander and his kind occupied every spare inch. Sent Ones were everywhere, light surrounding them and putting Gwen's candles to shame.

"What are you doing here?" she demanded, not daring to hope.

"I came to beg your forgiveness." His arms spread. "I came to tell you that I am proud to be your man. I brought my friends and brethren to bear witness to my proclamation."

She swallowed, still not letting hope take over. "But you think I'm evil, and what if I am? What if I can never change? I'm your temptation. You could, I don't know, lose everything by being with me." The thought hit her, and she wanted to wilt. He could lose everything. No wonder he had wanted to destroy her. No wonder he had wanted to hide her.

"I do not think you are evil, and I was wrong to judge you. I was meant to be no one's judge. And we are both changing. Everything does. But we are changing for the better, helping each other."

She gulped. "What if I get you into trouble?"

"We will deal with it together. That's the way I want things to be from now on. You and me. Together."

Okay. A small kernel of hope managed to seep inside her. But no way would she would let him get into trouble. He meant more to her than, well, her pride. And she had to face facts. Pride was the only reason she'd lasted against his appeal—and what they could have—this long. "What brought this on?"

"I finally pulled my head out of my posterior," he said dryly.

He'd said posterior. How cute was that. More hope beat its way inside and she had to press her lips together to keep from smiling. And crying! Tears were springing in her eyes, burning.

Could they actually make their relationship work? Just a little bit ago, she'd been grateful—or pretending to be grateful—that they were apart, since so many obstacles existed.

"I only hope you can love so foolish a man. I am willing to live wherever you desire. I am willing to do anything you need to win you back." He dropped to his knees. "I love you, Bianka Skyhawk. I would be proud to be yours."

He was proud of her. He wanted her. He loved her. It was everything she'd secretly dreamed about this past week. Yes, they could make this work. They would be together, and that was the most important thing. But she told him none of that.

"Now?" she screeched instead. "You decided to introduce me to your friends now? When I look like this?" Scowling, she peeked over his shoulder at them and saw their stunned expressions. "I usually look better than this, you know. You should have seen me the other day. When I was naked."

Lysander stood. "That's all you have to say to me?"

She focused back on him. His eyes were as wide as hers had been, his arms crossed over his middle. "No. There's more," she grumbled. "But I will never live this yellow gown thing down, you know."

"Bianka."

"Yes, I love you, too. But if you ever decide I'm unworthy again, I'll finally show you my mean side."

"Deal. But you don't have to worry, love," he said, a slow smile lifting those delectable lips. "It is I who am unworthy. I only pray you never learn of this."

"Oh, I know it already," she said, and his grin spread. "Now c'mere, you." She cupped the back of his neck and jerked him down for a kiss.

His arms banded around her, holding her close. She'd never thought to be paired with an angelic type, but she couldn't regret it now. Not when Lysander was the angelic type in question.

"Are you sure you're ready for me?" she asked him when they came up for air.

He nipped at her chin. "I've been ready for you my entire life. I just didn't know it until now."

"Good." With a whoop, she jumped up and wound her legs around his waist. A wave of gasps circled the room. They were still here? "Ditch your friends, I'll blow off my sister's reception and we'll go oil-wrestle."

"Funny," he said, wings enveloping her as he flew her up, up and into his cloud. "That's exactly what I was thinking."

★ ★ ★ ★ ★

SHADOW HUNTER

KAIT BALLENGER

Dear Reader,

In the upcoming pages you'll find a prequel to my paranormal romance series, The Execution Underground, about an international organization of elite men, hunters of the supernatural who fight to protect humanity from the evil lurking after dark. This prequel, *Shadow Hunter,* is the story of Damon Brock, vampire hunter and founder of the Rochester, New York, division of the clandestine organization. When the hunters of the Rochester division first came to me, the attitude I received from Damon's character simply said, "Piss off, lady," so it's not surprising that he became the last member on my roster to get his own book.

In September 2013 *Twilight Hunter* debuts. It's the first full-length novel in the series and features werewolf hunter Jace McCannon. I intended it to be the beginning of the series, but when the Harlequin HQN line approached me with the offer to fill the remaining section of this two-in-one with a prequel I jumped at the chance, and the story of Damon, the elusive badass we briefly glimpse in Jace's novel, came immediately to mind. Though I never intended to showcase Damon's soft side, the more I told of his origin story, the more his character opened up. Now I can't wait to tell the rest of his story, and I hope once you finish reading his prequel, you'll be equally excited.

Though his full novel will still be the last in the series, Damon's metamorphosis is intertwined with the stories of his fellow hunters, and it all starts here, in *Shadow Hunter.* I hope his story brings you all the smiles, laughs, gasps and tears it brought me.

Thanks so much for reading. I'm blessed to be able to share this with you.

Sincerely,

Kait Ballenger

For my husband, Jon. No hero will ever compare. I'll love you always.

CHAPTER 1

Damon Brock clutched the neck of the guard and twisted. The crack of broken bone pierced the silence in the alleyway as the spine snapped beneath his fingers. The wind whistled in a large gush of freezing air, so cold that Damon's breath swirled in front of his face. The guard's pulse beat several feeble times against his hands before fading.

Not a single scream. Damon released the guard, and the body crumpled to the cold winter ground. He nudged the corpse with the steel toe of his boot.

No movement. Only deadweight. A quick kill.

Not even 9:00 p.m. and already he'd taken out one blood-sucker. Rochester seemed promising.

He stepped over the corpse and slipped through the back entrance of Club Fantasy. A silver dagger under the sleeve of his leather trench coat, a Desert Eagle .44 caliber semi-automatic tucked into the back of his jeans, one silver throwing knife in each boot and a smooth, lacquered wooden stake inside his coat—you could never be too prepared when it came to vampires. The leeches were nearly impossible to kill. While bullets and silver would give them pause, only a severed spine, decapitation or a stake through the heart destroyed the undead.

Like a neon sign in a red-light district, the establishment's name flashed over the door: Club Fantasy.

He shook his head. Club Fantasy? More like club hell. If only the patrons knew the monster vampire who owned it. The man sitting at the top of Damon's hit list.

He pushed through a second door and into the main level of the club. If the night went well, he would gladly up the body count to at least four.

The thick smell of liquor, cigarettes and sweat from one too many dancing bodies assaulted his nose as he scanned the crowd. Bright red lighting flashed over the floor, and the bass of the heavy dance music pounded in his ears. The most difficult thing about hunting vamps: they were damn near indistinguishable from humans. After nightfall, the pulses of the undead beat with the same intensity as any human civilian, but their craving for blood, their inhuman strength and their drive to drain life from unsuspecting victims lingered. If only humanity knew what they were up against.

Damon strode across the dance floor, navigating between writhing bodies before he slid onto the black leather bench of one of the club's booths. His hands ran across the smooth, newly lacquered black tabletop. Despite the underlying seediness, the atmosphere of Club Fantasy came out on top compared to most of Rochester's low-scale raves. With western New York prices and Manhattan quality, Club Fantasy had young twenty-somethings flocking to it like drunken sheep led to a bloodlust-fueled slaughter. High quality aside, Club Fantasy was twice as dangerous as any New York City club. At least, the City offered ample backup.

He'd admitted one disadvantage to himself: navigating the supernatural scene of a city with no hunting division would be damn hard. But he was up to the challenge. He'd tracked his target to Mark's hometown, Rochester, and he wouldn't stop until he avenged his friend. He'd requested assignment to Rochester for that purpose—even if it meant a chance of running into *her*. He let out a long sigh. He couldn't think about that now.

His gaze jumped from face to face, searching for his target: blond hair, blue eyes, medium build, a strong, slightly crooked nose and a small but noticeable scar beneath his left eye. He dreamed of that face every night.

An ancient piece of Roman shit, Caius Argyros Dermokaites ruled over the Rochester vamp nests with an iron fist, more because he was old as dirt, rather than because of some great attribute of his own. The older the vampire, the more deadly he—or she—became, and Caius was the highest on Damon's hit list.

Damon was going to kill him. He would make sure of it this time.

His eyes locked on to the vampire. Though the swaying limbs of the dancing patrons skewed his view, he could see Caius sitting on the other side of the club. Anger bubbled up inside his chest, and pure rage filled every inch of his body. It took all he had not to pull his Desert Eagle and shoot Caius point-blank before driving a stake straight through his heart.

His hands clenched into fists. It was his fault. His fault that Caius sat there laughing while Mark's ashes had gone unburied. His fault the only woman he'd ever opened his heart to wished him dead. He'd failed Mark—his closest friend—and he had failed *her,* too.

A grin crossed Caius's face as he wrapped his arm around the skimpy-leather-and-fake-silver-chain-clad woman next to him. He was surrounded by women. Not surprising. Few things were larger than a male vampire's ego, and Caius overcompensated like a pair of tricked-out rims on an already overpriced car. Damon observed the vampire's interactions.

If there was one thing he'd learned during his field training, it was how to be a quick judge of character. Vanity was no doubt Caius's number one weakness, and striking that vein would make him bleed.

A sexed-up raspy voice purred right next to Damon's ear. "You gonna order a drink, hot stuff, or just stare into the crowd all night?" A cheap pair of too-tight latex pants blocked his view.

The bottle-blonde waitress smacked her lips together as she chewed on a piece of gum. She leaned down and rested her elbows on the table in front of him, treating him to a prime-time view of her fake chest. Her breasts squeezed into a top smaller than some women's panties. Her breath reeked of over-chewed bubble gum and the sharp smell of cheap gin.

She licked her lips. "You look like a vodka-on-the-rocks kind of man to me—strong, bold, served on ice but easily warmed."

Damon barely glanced at the woman. He leaned back in his seat, aligning his vision with Caius again. "I don't drink."

The waitress sighed and peeled herself off the table. "Well, if you're not gonna order anything, you can't take up an entire booth."

A slender redhead ran her fingers through Caius's hair and pushed closer to his body. The women surrounding Caius literally threw themselves at him, practically begging to be drained, but Caius's stare was fixed on something out of Damon's line of sight. If he could just see where…

The waitress huffed. "Uh, hello? Did you hear me?"

Moving about the club for different views was a better option than staying put, Damon decided, and stood, then brushed past the now pissed-off waitress. Nothing was going to distract him. A drive to fulfill his quest pulsed through him. With six human women missing from Caius's inner circle and a growing number of gruesome, fatal street attacks, neglect was not an option.

When he'd joined the Execution Underground, he'd sworn an oath to protect innocent humans from the dangerous creatures lurking out of their unsuspecting sight. An international elite group of men, the Execution Underground trained hunters to annihilate everything from vampires to werewolves, demons, shifters and more.

Though trained extensively in combat and packing loads of hard-earned muscle, no plain man could fight the supernatural alone. Upon swearing in, each hunter received a serum injection, and while the resulting longer lifespan, increased strength to battle the supernatural and extra healing capabilities were perks, putting their lives on the line every day was one hell of a sacrifice. Even with the serum, they still couldn't match the supernaturals' strength completely. That was where the training came in, to ensure they weren't easily annihilated. They swore to protect their fellow humans no matter the personal cost, swore to keep the supernatural world hidden from view and away from the vulnerable. They promised to give everything, even their lives, if needed.

Mark had given his life for the safety of others, and Damon wouldn't dishonor his memory. He'd meant every word of that promise he'd made.

Damon followed the line of Caius's gaze and strode to the bar. He found a seat in the far corner, right where he could see Caius. He followed the ancient vampire's eyes and found their target.

A woman. No surprise.

Her back was turned toward Damon, revealing nothing but a thick mane of dark brown waves cascading over her shoulders. The bartender handed her two glasses of red wine. Slowly, she sashayed to Caius's side, his gaze never leaving her body. Her gender didn't matter. He intended to hurt Caius and his minions in any way he could, but even to avenge his fellow hunter, Damon refused to endanger the innocent human patrons around him. Mark wouldn't have wanted it any other way. He would need to lure Caius away from the crowd.

Damon's outrage simmered at the thought of all the innocent lives lost.

The instinctive fight-or-flight response forced most people away from supernatural predators. But used, beaten, downtrodden and abused humans swarmed the undead like flies on a half-eaten corpse, and they were the most susceptible to supernatural manipulation. Somebody needed to protect them. Somebody needed to give a damn about their lives when no one else ever had.

Damon's cell phone vibrated inside his jacket pocket. Headquarters.

But he couldn't return the call out in the open. He slipped away from the bar and headed toward one of the private club rooms. He ducked through the curtained door and into the empty space. Scanning the room, his eyes adjusted to the darkness, revealing nothing more than the outlines of assorted couches, throw pillows and other ordinary furniture. He was alone.

He pulled the phone from his pocket and flipped it open, quickly glancing at the message.

The all-capitalized text glared across the screen. New information from his contact at headquarters. UPDATE. CALL BACK.

Damon's jaw clenched. Damn. An update meant another dead body. Another death piled on to his conscience. If he hadn't failed Mark that night three months ago...

He cursed under his breath and quickly hit Redial.

Chris answered on the second ring. "You're not going to like what I have to tell you."

Damon rested his free hand on his head and ran his fingers through what little hair remained after his buzz cut. "Get on with it."

Chris let out a long sigh. "You're not going to like any of this. You want the shitty news or the straight-up awful news first?"

Damon shook his head and paced the room. "Out with it."

Chris sighed again. "Well, first matter of business—there's another dead body."

Damon dug the fingernails of his left hand into his palm. His fist itched to punch through the plaster wall. Someone might as well have stabbed him in the back and twisted the knife. Knowing the news before he called didn't make it any easier.

"Damon, you still there, man?"

Damon unclenched his fist and tried to focus. He would not let his emotions distract him. Not again. "Yeah, I'm here." He shook his head. The Rochester P.D. would jump all over this. Already they deemed the murders the work of a serial killer with vampiric delusions. Another victim with fang marks would fuel the fire.

What kind of bloodsucker didn't seal up the damn fang holes after he sank his teeth in? Even the dumbest vamps knew to keep themselves hidden from the public eye. Was one small lick to close the wound too much to ask?

"Victim is a Caucasian female. Only sixteen. Found four blocks away from Manhattan Square Park. A connection with the police force called it in to us. Body's in the morgue of the Golisano Children's Hospital at the University of Rochester Medical Center. As of now, she's listed as Jane Doe. No ID on her and, well…from the crime scene photos we've been sent, it won't be easy to identify her. You better get over there soon."

Damon leaned against the nearest wall and rested his head on his forearm. "What's the other news?"

A moment of silence passed on the other end of the line before Chris cleared his throat. "There's, uh…there's been a new development in Mark's case."

Damon snapped upright, his whole body rigid. All his senses peaked, and adrenaline raced through his bloodstream. "What do you mean 'a new development'? He's dead, Chris. His body burned in the fire. I saw him lying on the ground, bled out and dead, before the building exploded, and we know exactly who killed him. What kind of 'new development' can there be?" Desperation and anxiety hit him hard, and he knew his voice wavered. His hands were shaking.

"I'm so sorry, Damon."

All the wind rushed from Damon's lungs and bile rose in the back of his throat as he realized what Chris was saying. "No. No. He can't…no…." He lost the ability to speak. His stomach churned.

"Another hunter spotted him in New York City a few days ago. The information just made it into the system. He's not dead, Damon. He turned."

The phone fell from Damon's hand. His heart pounded in his ears, and red clouded his vision. A sharp pain flamed in his chest as if someone had driven a blade straight through his heart. Mark had turned. He wasn't dead. No…

A loud angry battle cry ripped from Damon's throat, and tears ran down his face. He gave in and punched his fist into the wall. A large chunk of plaster crumbled to the floor, but no one heard over the loud thumping of the music.

Mark was worse than dead. He was a bloodsucking leech, and the fault fell on Damon's shoulders. Images of him and his best friend, his comrade, flashed through his mind.

"There's nothing worse than becoming a vamp." Mark sharpened the end of his silver blade as he sat next to Damon.

The training room smelled of male sweat, blood and heavy artillery. After a full day of training, all the muscles in Damon's body ached. He nodded. "Nothing worse."

"At the very least, I'm glad my family didn't turn. In that respect, I'm glad they're dead." Mark glanced down at the blade in his hand. "Promise me that if I ever get turned, you'll stake me straight in the chest."

Damon shook his head. "That'll never happen."

Mark thumped him hard on the back. "I mean it, D. Promise me."

Damon let out a long huff. He clapped Mark on the back in return. "I promise."

Damon threw another punch at the wall, then started pounding the plaster with his fists and praying the images in his head would disappear. Mark's body lying on the pavement with puncture wounds in his neck. The blood. Oh, God, the blood and the stillness of his body as he lay across the concrete. Dust clouded the air, and Damon's knuckles bled as he released every ounce of rage coursing through his bones.

If he'd been a weaker man, he would have eaten his gun right then.

CHAPTER 2

Rage surged inside Tiffany Solow as she handed the ancient vampire his Bordeaux. She wished she could smash the delicate glass on the table and plunge the leftover shards into his neck. Waiting hand and foot on Caius Argyros Dermokaites sent waves of anger and hate through every inch of her body. As if rubbing shoulders with the creatures she hated most wasn't enough, Caius was the worthless bloodsucking piece of crap who'd murdered her brother and the definition of arrogance. She would kill him. It was only a matter of time, and when she did, she would enjoy every single second of it.

"Thank you, my precious," he purred.

My precious? Gross. I hope you choke on it, you undead piece of crap.

Tiffany forced a smile on her face and slid into the booth beside him. Caius snaked his arm around her. The rank smell of his skin mixed with the aged Bordeaux and a faint hint of blood. The stench hit her nose full force, and she fought to keep from gagging. Thank God she was an amazing actress. If she didn't have such a rock-solid poker face, infiltrating Caius's inner circle would have been damn near impossible.

But every time he made her skin crawl was well worth it if it gave her the chance of murdering the son of a bitch. There was no such thing as a decent bloodsucker. They'd proved that the day she'd first become a hunter—the day her family had been stolen from her.

Caius would be tough to kill. Everything in her craved to stab him right then, get it over with. But if she even made a quick move at him, he would crush her before she blinked. She had to catch him with his back turned. His trust was key to his death. And she'd baited him perfectly into wanting her as a Host.

Serving their purpose for a short time, Hosts fed the vampires and sated their blood thirst, but once the anemia set in, the vamps had no more use for their weakened prey. Humans with knowledge of vampires were too high a risk to keep around. Hosts always ended up dead or undead. And despite the Hosts' presence, vampires weren't only leeches, they were greedy; feeding regularly on Hosts didn't stop them from massacring innocent civilians for sport; it only delayed the actions on occasion.

Tiffany had found ways to warn multiple women and men during the time she'd spent with Caius, but it was no use. They were too entranced, nearly hypnotized, by the charm of the bloodsuckers to listen to reason. Tiffany had to admit, that charm was hard to ignore. But every time she thought of the deaths of her parents and brother, not to mention the loss of a deep friendship, her disgust snapped into place and she remembered exactly why she lived to drive stakes through vampires' hearts. She thanked her lucky stars that Caius was still trying his persuasive skills on her, practically begging her to be his.

He could tell she was healthy and strong. To keep her iron high and appealing, she ate enough red meat and spinach to last her a whole lifetime—the thought of one more piece of spanakopita or rare steak made her stomach churn. Hell, every spare cent she possessed went toward that. Steak wasn't exactly in the usual budget for a flat-broke college senior with four years of med school and then several more years of residency ahead of her. But it worked in her favor. Caius knew from her scent that she would provide a long Host relationship with all the expected sexual benefits, ensuring that she was too tempting for him to kill her in one quick meal. Caius wanted her for the long term.

Little did he know his efforts would have been more effective on a piece of broccoli. She almost snorted. Was she hungry or what?

He interrupted her thought. "Darling, do you see that private room over there?" Caius gestured toward the far side of the bar.

Tiffany nodded. "Yes."

Caius sipped his Bordeaux, his eyes fixated on the closed curtain of the private room. "I believe we have a new visitor. Vampire, it appears. He has the movements of a predator." He set down his wineglass a little more forcefully than necessary. "I won't have an unannounced alpha traipsing around my club. Please go fetch Calvin and see that he's taken care of."

"My pleasure." She smiled and stood to find the bodyguard. As soon as she turned her back on Caius, her smile faded into a frown.

Eat my stake, you nasty leech.

She was really feeling the pure bitchiness tonight. But then again, spending more than five minutes with Caius would turn any sane person into a complete basket case. He would pay for everything he'd done. She would gladly drive a stake into his heart and watch him explode to pieces like the blood bag he was. Vampires were so damn messy to kill, but she didn't care. She wanted nothing more than to make him bleed.

As quickly as possible, she navigated through the crowd toward the back of the club. She exited the first door and stepped into the small area leading back to the offices. She glanced up and down the hall. No Calvin.

An immediate chill ran down her spine. The hairs of her neck and arms stood on end, and goose bumps prickled over her skin. Something was not right. She needed to get out of there, and fast. Pushing through the final exit, a rush of cold winter air hit her hard in the face. She stepped out into the alleyway and fell straight on her ass.

What the hell?

Her eyes widened as she took in the sight of what she'd tripped over: Calvin's dead body. His neck was twisted at a strange angle as he lay lifeless on the pavement. Not a single drop of blood or any evidence of a fight.

Damn. It took a lot of *cojones* to snap the neck of a vampire. Whoever had done this was vicious.

She hopped to her feet and brushed herself off. No skin off her back if Calvin was dead. One less bloodsucker made for a better world. Though Caius would go ballistic at the news, and she didn't want to deal with one hell of a pissed-off vampire, unless...

Her eyes widened again. She knew how to lessen Caius's anger: deliver the new alpha vampire.

She rushed through the back door and reentered the club. If she could move fast enough and deliver the head of the anonymous vamp to Caius, she would be that much closer to gaining his trust. One step closer to destroying the scumbag who'd murdered her family.

Pushing her way through the club patrons, she headed toward the private room. She weaved in and out of the crowd to avoid Caius's gaze. Once she reached the curtained entrance, she pulled her Smith & Wesson from her jacket. Always loaded with silver bullets, her rounds sure wouldn't kill a vampire, but they *would* inflict a serious wound, enough to make the leech pause.

She quickly slipped inside. With her eyes already adjusted to the darkness from being outside, she searched through the dimness, gun aimed.

No one.

She stepped farther into the empty room.

The end of a gun barrel pushed against her skull. The small click of the hammer sent adrenaline pumping through her body. Her heart thumped hard against her chest.

Positioned at the end of a vampire's gun.

Royally screwed didn't even begin to cover it.

Damon held the Desert Eagle without a single ounce of fear in his body. If there was one thing he was excellent at, it was staying detached in intense situations. He wasn't used to dealing with vampiresses, but there was a first time for everything.

He held the gun steady, resting right against her skull. "Drop your weapon."

With slow tentative movements, she spread her arm to her sides, so he could see the firearm. She released the magazine clip, and it fell onto the floor before she dropped the gun.

He increased the pressure on the base of her skull. "Names. All the high-ups in the Rochester nests."

In a risky decision, she spun away from his gun, grabbing hold of his hand and digging her long fingernails into his metacarpals. A very smooth martial arts move. He let her go and released the gun, not from the pain, but from the reassurance of his silver dagger. Giving her a false sense of accomplishment could work in his favor. With quick agility, she threw a roundhouse kick. He blocked the blow from his face, but the force of her attack gave him pause.

She was strong and an impressive fighter, but she was no

match for him. He grabbed hold of her leg and twisted. She lost her balance, toppling toward the ground, but he caught her midfall, holding her.

With precision, he pulled his dagger from his sleeve and forced it against her throat. Not enough to make her bleed, just so she could feel its presence. He had to know for certain if she was a vampire. He couldn't bring himself to harm a woman without being sure.

She stopped struggling. Smart.

He backed her into the corner nearest the light switch. If he got lucky and she was angry or afraid enough, her irises would reveal the answer to him. "Turn around."

She did as she was told. He pushed her body against the wall with his own, the dagger still at her throat. With his free hand, he flipped the switch.

Then wished he hadn't.

Damon's breath rushed from his lungs, and his heart skipped several beats. Adrenaline kicked into his system like a tidal wave. Every inch of his skin electrified. He was a live wire, all senses enhanced and awake from their deadened state. His arousal was instantaneous as the sweet smell of her perfume hit his nose. She smelled like baked cinnamon apples, autumn spices, vanilla and sweet, sweet sex.

He'd never been one to stop and take in the beauty of the world, but he was certain that her face was more gorgeous than anything he'd ever laid eyes on. Her thick dark brown hair fell just past her shoulders, and from that he recognized her as the woman from the bar. His eyes trailed over that gorgeous hair, which stopped just above a pair of ample breasts that pushed against him. Her slender frame felt amazing against his body.

But what completely entranced him was her stare. A pair of large honey-colored eyes rimmed with dark layers of full lashes gazed up at him. A slight hint of fear showed behind her irises, mixed with the drive to fight, and he immediately hated himself for being the one to put that fear there. He cursed silently. What was wrong with him? He never regretted terrifying bloodsuckers, and she wasn't even afraid enough to give him the answer he sought. He cursed himself again. God, she was gorgeous. Vampiresses were impressive beauties, but no woman he'd ever seen, human or vampire, compared to her.

No. He snapped his attention into focus.

He wouldn't be distracted. He clenched his jaw and crushed his own desire. How could he be thinking of sex? Mark was a vampire, and it was his fault. His own neglect had killed his closest friend—more than once. It was his fault Caius had stolen Mark's life. If he'd only staked Mark as an extra precaution before the building exploded, Mark wouldn't...

He pushed all his feelings deep inside himself, where there was no escape. His focus wouldn't be broken, not again. He had three tasks he needed to accomplish: kill Caius to avenge Mark's death, end the gruesome killings plaguing Rochester's streets...and murder his best friend.

He would not let her faze him. His brain fought to concentrate, but his body was saying otherwise. Not once had he ever had this problem. Well, not since *she* refused to answer his letters.

He wished he could end it right then, draw the blade across her throat and free himself from the agony of wanting her. He scowled, disgusted with himself. Wanting a vampire? The thought made his stomach churn. But bloodsucker or not, he'd never laid a hand on a woman, and he hoped he wouldn't have to change that now. Unless an innocent life was in danger, he doubted he could bring himself to do it, and his life was far from innocent.

Still, something in his gut protested that he needed to know for sure what she was, and there was one sure way.

He shook his head. The sight of her Mark of Caine would shock him back to normal. To the version of himself that had little interest in women when there was a job at stake—and there always was, especially now.

"Turn," he said. When she didn't move, he increased the pressure on her neck. "Turn around."

With a glare of pure hate in her eyes, she turned away from him.

Before she could escape, he locked his arms around her, pressing her back against his body. He held the knife to the front of her throat and forced her to bend over. If the mark was there, he wouldn't hesitate to use the necessary force to get answers from her. Then, female or not, he would do what he had to do.

As his gaze trailed the length of her spine, he caught himself admiring the curve of her ass. Her round behind rubbed against him. Holy smokes... Had he ever wanted a woman so badly? He couldn't remember the last time he'd been interested in sex.

No distractions. He was weak, selfish. Stupid.

Need raced through his veins while he lifted the hem of her black tank top. He hooked two fingers beneath the edge of her leather pants, then slid them down an inch. The two cute dimples just above her ass were enough to leave him wanting for days, but her skin was smooth and unmarred.

No mark. A female vampire's Mark of Caine always appeared on her lower back. He blinked several times. He found himself at a loss for words. "Where's your...?"

"My what? My vamp stamp? News flash, buddy, I don't have one."

That she even knew what a "vamp stamp" was gave him pause. He released her shirt and allowed her to stand up straight, but he maintained the knife at her neck. An odd sense of relief washed over him, and he immediately chastised himself. Whether she was human or not, he had a job to do. "Who are you, and why are you wielding a gun in a dark room in a known vampire club?"

She shook her head. "Tell me who you are, and then maybe I'll consider sharing."

He pressed the sharp blade against her skin, reminding her of its presence. He didn't have the patience for this. "I'm the one with the knife," he said.

She stood completely still, nothing but the rise and fall of her chest giving away her agitation. "Touché."

He forced her toward the wall again. She turned around before he even told her to do so. She was trying to show her lack of fear by taking the lead, not waiting for directions. Not surprising, with her overly trigger-happy attitude, but her confidence was her weakness. Her gaze met his in a show of defiance, but he wouldn't let himself be fooled into picking a fight. He was easily twice, if not three, times her size. Though she well trained in fighting, she would never be a match for him.

He held her stare until finally she looked away.

"Tell me your name," he demanded.

She closed her eyes, glanced at the floor and let out a deep breath. Her eyes flickered up to meet his gaze again. "Sandra—"

He pushed her harder against the wall. "Real name."

She gaped at him as if he'd slapped her. "How do you know that's not my real name?"

"Everyone has a poker tell." One of the things he'd learned in his time at the E.U. headquarters was to interpret body language. It came in particularly handy when trying to distinguish vamps from humans, though detecting lies was always advantageous. She glanced down and to the left when she lied—

a classic sign for many people and overly predictable. But he wasn't about to tell her that.

"What's your *real* name?" he asked again.

Her jaw clenched. Her anger at her current position was apparent in her eyes, but her voice was a sexy feminine alto when she finally said, "Tiffany Solow."

The air rushed from Damon's lungs as if a high-speed bullet had hit him straight in the abdomen. His head spun, and it took every ounce of self-control he had not to shake with anger. He couldn't believe the night had actually gotten worse, although he knew he deserved the massive beating the universe had just dished out to him.

Tiffany Solow…Mark's baby sister. His own Achilles' heel.

Rochester was a huge city. Though it was her hometown, when he transferred there in order to hunt Caius, he'd hoped like hell he would never run into her. What the hell were the chances? And what was she doing hunting vampires?

The memories flashed through his head in a nonstop pulse. His training officer's voice rang in his ears. *Brock, see a therapist or find someone to tie yourself to. Pronto!*

With no family to support him, Damon had been deemed at risk of "low morale" by the Execution Underground. They'd thought the pressure of hunting might turn him into some crazed psycho if he didn't have someone to talk to. They covered their asses by insisting on "therapeutic ties."

Rather than see the resident shrink, he'd opted for Choice B: to forge a bond, anonymously, with someone outside the E.U. He'd preferred to write a few BS letters to a stranger than have the E.U. psychiatrist record his every thought. The Execution Underground already rode his ass about everything. He didn't need them inside his head, too. And being his usual giving self, Mark had volunteered to help his best comrade and had contacted his baby sister.

Headquarters was all about "family contacts." In other words, they ensured that their hunters had something to live for besides the hunt alone. It was a numbers game to them. An overwhelmed hunter who committed suicide forced the E.U. to shell out money to train a replacement, not to mention compensation for the family. They were saving their pocket change.

Tiffany was in the same age group as many of the female victims the hunters set out to avenge, so the E.U. found her an appropriate contact. Because she'd known already that vampires existed, because she'd lost her parents to a vampire attack and had a hunter for a brother, there had been no security breaches involved in writing to her. According to the E.U., it also benefited her to know there were other men out there, aside from her brother, keeping her safe at night. Damage control, really.

Headquarters called it personalization and bond forging. He called it a load of crap. Like he'd needed any more incentive to do what he'd been trained to do. He would never forget the first letter he wrote to her.

> Tiffany,
> They say I need to write someone, so here it is.
> Yours truly,
> B

She'd replied with an eight-page letter telling him all about her. Little did he know when he'd signed that first damn letter "yours truly," he really *would* be hers. In a matter of weeks she'd clutched his heart in her hands.

The last picture Mark had shown him of Tiffany, she'd been only seventeen, long before Mark's death...before everything fell to shit...before she grew to hate Damon. Now she was twenty-two. He met her gaze and took in the breathtaking woman standing before him.

Mark had loved her more than anything in the world. She had been the only family he had left, and he would have wanted her cared for, protected. Not in the line of fire of the same vampire who had killed him. Damon lowered his eyes. How could he look her in the face when he held the blame for her brother's death? And if she knew Mark had turned…

No. She would never know. Damon had sworn to Mark that if he were ever turned, he would drive the stake through Mark's heart himself. A small part of him would die as he did it, but his promise stood firm. But she couldn't know any of that, which meant he needed to get her out of Club Fantasy, away from Caius. An overwhelming need to protect her surged through him, accompanied by the desire to claim her as his own.

No.

Without a doubt, he could not seduce her. Not only for the sake of his job, but because he owed that much to the memory of his fellow hunter and best friend. Taking Mark's sister into his bed? He might as well spit on his grave. Her eyes showed she didn't know who he was. She'd never met him in person, never seen his face. There was no way she would recognize him, and it needed to stay that way. Not even his name would give him away. He was thankful revealing his full identity had been against the rules during their correspondence. He would protect her anonymously and nothing more.

He inhaled a deep breath to cool his head. He tried not to think of how sweet her voice would sound saying his name as he drove himself into her. *No.* He wouldn't get attached to anyone again, then he couldn't fail anyone, then protocol couldn't get in the way of relationships. Hunting, protection. Nothing more. "What are you doing here?"

She scoffed. "Shouldn't I be asking *you* that? I'm here every night. You're the new vamp on the block."

He growled, low in his throat like an animal. Anger boiled inside him at the accusation. "I am *not* one of those worthless leeches."

She froze. Her eyes widened. "You're too strong to be human." She scanned his body, her eyes stopping on the muscles of his arms, chest and abs. "Prove it, then."

Tiffany stared at the stranger before her, her eyes locked on to his icy gaze. A shiver ran down her spine, but heat pooled between her legs. That alone made him dangerous.

"Go on. Prove you're human." Her pulse began to race from excitement instead of fear as she challenged him. Her gut screamed not to fight him, that he was no threat to her, but the knife at her throat and the ferocity in his eyes said otherwise.

"Just trust me on this," he said.

Not a chance. "Well, unfortunately for you, I don't trust people easily." With as much force as she could muster, she stomped on his instep.

He didn't cry out, but the move surprised him enough that the knife shifted slightly away from her throat. She seized the advantage and grabbed hold of his arm, pushed his sleeve up and dug her fingernails into his skin. She wasn't against fighting dirty. Not if it saved her sorry ass.

Her assailant didn't even curse at the pain, only grunted in response as her sharp acrylics dug into the flesh of his arm. Blood pooled around the edges of her nails before she released him. She lunged forward, knocking into his midsection like a linebacker. Damn, that had been a stupid idea. The man was built, and running into his abdomen was like hitting her head on a solid concrete wall. That would really hurt in the morning.

He tucked his knife up his sleeve instead of using the weapon against her. What was that about? He grabbed at her as she stumbled back, but she was short enough that she managed to duck out of his reach. He towered over her and was probably twice her weight with all the sexy muscle he was packing.

Regaining her footing, she threw a spinning roundhouse kick. He blocked it with ease as if he often fought third-degree black belts without blinking an eye. He was fierce, no denying it. She continued going at him, throwing nonstop kicks and punches, but he blocked every one, and she was running out of options. Wait! Her gun. Her gun was lying on the floor.

She rushed to reach the weapon. Seconds later, he loomed over her, trying to grab her. Why wasn't he fighting back? She was sure that if he really wanted to, he could kick the living shit out of her.

She snatched the gun from the floor, but she had no time to aim. She threw a sidekick, but he caught it, then swept her other foot out from under her. She toppled to the floor, landing with an audible *oof* as the wind rushed from her lungs.

Before he could make his next move, she spun around and kicked his ankles. Pain shot through the edge of her big toe, despite her high-heeled boots; even his legs were pure muscle.

Without thinking, she lunged into his legs, wrapping her body around his knees. He started to fall, but he caught himself and landed prepared to kick out, except that…oh, snap… she was attached to his leg!

She scrambled backward, but he was too fast. Within seconds he was on top of her, straddling her hips and holding her hands against the ground.

He let out a long deep growl and leaned in near her face. "Next time, I won't hold back from hurting you."

The ice-cold look in his eyes showed he meant it, and she

vowed to herself that there would be no next time. The man was pure unadulterated muscle and no matter how good a fighter she was, she knew when to call it quits.

As she stared up into his eyes, she wished she hadn't charged him, because damn it, her head hurt and her brain was sending all sorts of crazy mixed signals into parts of her body that had never been lit up before. Though he was on top of her and she was clearly in a vulnerable position, he wasn't threatening her, just pinning her down and, oh, man, what on earth was wrong with her, because she didn't mind one bit.

Her gaze traveled over his rock-hard body. His chest heaved in and out from the adrenaline. Through his shirt she could see a nicely defined pair of pecs, and she knew from the pain in her head that washboard abs hid beneath.

Even his forearms, which she'd dug her fingernails into, were well defined. She could tell from the fluid way he moved that he wasn't some steroidal bodybuilder. No, his muscles were honed from serious training. The thought of his nearly naked body covered in a sheen of sweat as he worked out flooded her mind.

Whooaaaa, Nelly. Back up for two seconds. She *never* fantasized about men. Ever.

A small pang hit her heart, equal parts pain and anger. Her thoughts traveled to B, the nameless hunter who'd stolen her heart, only to break it to pieces with his betrayal. She could admit a teenage girl had her needs, and she'd fantasized about meeting B in the flesh so many times that real men need not apply. She'd been solo since she was fifteen, when her brother had left home to hunt monsters, and without B in the picture, she intended to keep it that way. She didn't need any distractions. Her one goal in life was to avenge her family, not snuggle up all lovey-dovey with some sweet guy, get married and have loads of chubby-faced cherubic babies. Not that Mr. Tall,

Dark and Scary would ever fit that scenario, anyway. From the looks of things, he was a grade-A badass.

What was wrong with her? She needed to get back to Caius. If she disappeared for long enough, someone would come searching for her. Wasting time ogling a hot man wasn't in the cards for tonight—for any night. Not while Caius lived and breathed. Besides which, she chastised herself, she didn't know anything about this man. He'd held a knife to her throat, for God's sake.

But when she met his cold ice-blue eyes she thought she could drown in their intensity. She wanted to run her hands over his black buzz-cut hair as he pushed inside her. The thought alone sent a wave of heat rushing between her legs and a jolt of electricity shooting down her spine.

A long silence passed between them as he watched her, those haunting blue eyes boring into her.

"I guess I'm not really in a position to bargain now, am I?" She tried to make it sound lighthearted in hopes that maybe he would release her.

He glared at her. His stare alone was enough to make her want to talk.

Clearly he wasn't a vampire or he would have sunk his fangs into her throat by now. All her instincts said he didn't intend to harm her, and no vampire would ever take a no-harm approach against someone who'd attacked him.

She cleared her throat. "One of us has to go first, and from your stiff upper lip, I can tell it's not going to be you." She sighed. "If I start talking, will you at least let me go?"

He didn't reply. But the intensity of his gaze compelled her to confess.

She sighed again. "My name is Tiffany Solow, and I'm a vampire hunter."

His brow furrowed, as if the words *vampire hunter* confused him. "A female hunter?"

She frowned. Nothing annoyed her more than men who thought women were incapable. She was certainly capable of taking care of herself and of killing supernaturally strong vampires to boot.

"Yeah, buddy. You have a problem with a little girl power?" She wasn't weak. But this guy had the strength of a vampire and the training of an extremely professional hunter, not someone self-taught.

Could he be from…?

No. What were the chances of *that?*

His eyes widened before they narrowed again. "You're alone? No one trained you?"

She nodded. "No one but my brother taught me, so, yeah, I'm solo. You know, Solow—like my last name."

Usually that got at least a little bit of a chuckle out of people, but Mr. Tall, Dark and Scary didn't so much as crack a grin.

He released her hands, still pinning her to the ground with the weight of his body. She tried not to think of the way his hips pushed against hers and the obvious thickness she felt beneath his belt buckle.

He shook his head. "You're no hunter."

She frowned. "Oh, yeah? And what qualifies you to make that judgment? I could say the same thing of you, after all."

He shot her a look that said *Don't make me laugh.* "Why are you here? Are you a Host?" A look of disgust crossed his face.

"Hell, no! I would never let those leeches feed off me. Don't insult me."

The side of his mouth twitched slightly at that. The closest he'd come thus far to a smile. Apparently he appreciated a hate for the undead.

"Caius wants me as a Host, but he's not going to get me.

Other than that, the reason I'm here is none of your damn business."

He didn't respond, only scanned the length of her body. Watching his irises as he drank her in was like watching fire flicker and blaze beneath crystals of ice. Breathtaking.

He wrenched his eyes away from her figure and met her gaze. "You're right. It isn't."

She sucked in a deep breath and balled up the courage in her chest. She needed to push him, to challenge him, even though he had the advantage. "Why are you hunting on my turf?"

He ignored her question. His spine straightened, and she could practically see him training his senses on something like a lethal animal.

"What is this room usually used for?" he asked.

"What?"

He lowered his voice. "What is this room used for?"

She gaped. What the hell was he getting at? "Uh...I don't know. I think people come in here to have sex and drink from their Hosts in private. But why—"

"Shhh."

"Why are you hushing me? What the—"

He shoved his hand over her mouth to silence her, but with her hands now free she quickly wrenched it off. "No way are you shutting me up, buddy. I'm—"

Before she could comprehend what was going on, they were nose to nose. With gentle but strong movements, he cupped his hand behind her head and his soft lips met hers. All her thoughts came to a screeching halt as the force of his kiss overwhelmed her. His tongue moved against hers in a slow sensual rhythm as his warm body pressed against hers.

The sweet scent of his skin filled her nose like expensive aftershave and amazing, mind-blowing sex. Another wave of heat rushed to her core, and she felt herself buck against him.

She didn't even know his name, but her body was screaming in need for him. She'd never wanted anything, anyone, so badly in her life. Every inch of her skin was electrified as wave after wave of arousal rushed through her.

With soft smooth movements he lifted her so her torso was cradled in his arms while her hips were still pinned beneath his. The hard length of him pressed between her hips, and she felt herself slicken. No man had ever had such a powerful effect on her.

Somewhere in the distance, she was vaguely aware of the sound of an opening curtain.

"Oh, shit. Sorry," an unknown voice said. "Didn't know the room was taken."

Within an instant, his lips were gone.

She gasped for air. The world spun, though he still held her in his arms. Cold air hit her lips, and her heart thumped hard as she longed for the warmth of his kiss to return. He lingered over her, his face barely inches away.

Slowly he released her and stood, walking to the other side of the room. Her head cleared. A distraction. He'd kissed her as a distraction. She'd said people had sex in the room, and someone had come in, so he'd deliberately given the impression that they were having sex. She exhaled a long breath to collect herself. Without his weight on her body, she felt strange and uneasy. Though she knew she shouldn't, she wished the moment hadn't ended.

Once she caught her breath she didn't quite know what to say. Finally she managed to whisper the only words she could manage. "What's your name?"

"Damon Brock." His voice was cold and distant, no different from before.

Tiffany sat on the floor, completely stunned. Just like that, she'd had her first kiss ever, and from a tall handsome stranger.

CHAPTER 3

Damon didn't know what the hell had happened or why the fuck he'd chosen to kiss her....

He glanced down at Tiffany as she sat on the crimson carpeting, and his heart jumped. Her gorgeous hair was slightly ruffled from where his hand had cradled her head, and her bottom lip was flushed a brighter shade of pink where he'd gently suckled it. Shit, he had never intended the night to go this way.

When he'd heard the approaching footsteps and covering her mouth wouldn't shut her up, well...he'd done the first thing that had come to mind. And damn if that hadn't been a huge freaking mistake. If he'd wanted her before, now he wanted her tenfold. His body was begging for him to take her, to press her up against the wall and make love to her until she screamed. His thoughts raced. What the hell was wrong with him? He'd never lost his head like this before. This was Mark's baby sister!

He fought the temptation to curse under his breath. He needed to knock some sense into himself. But he wouldn't lose his cool. Before he'd sworn himself to the Execution Underground, if there was one thing his father had taught him about being a hunter it was not to lose his cool. And he'd never had a hard time with that until tonight.

He hadn't even been with Tiffany more than half an hour and she was already unraveling him, but he sure as hell wouldn't let that get in the way of his job. He couldn't.

He closed his eyes and rubbed his fingers in slow circles over his temples. There were six missing women out there, all probably dead, and who knew how many murdered and drained of their blood on the streets. It was *his* job to protect the future victims. The weight fell on his shoulders alone. He wouldn't neglect his job, his sworn oath, for any woman, even Tiffany.

Not sure of what he was doing, he picked up his Desert Eagle and holstered the piece behind his back again.

Tiffany grabbed her Smith & Wesson from the floor, reloaded the magazine clip and stood.

He glanced at her, and his heart jumped into his throat. He had to get out of here, but he sure as hell couldn't leave her behind.

She opened her mouth to speak. "I—"

He shook his head and cut her off. "You shouldn't be dealing with these vampires. I won't allow you to place yourself in danger like this."

Her jaw dropped. She crossed her arms and fixed him with a hard stare. "Who do you think you are? Last time I checked, I didn't wake up in the morning with the goal of pleasing random strangers. I'll do whatever I damn well please."

He should have expected her reaction. He just wasn't used to dealing with women.

Damon fought the urge to throw her over his shoulder; he didn't care if she kicked and screamed the whole way, nothing would stop him from protecting her. He exhaled a long breath. "This city isn't safe for you. Six women are missing, and more have been murdered. I won't have another death on my conscience because I let you waltz back into that club and play with murderers."

Tiffany strode across the room to stand straight in front of him. The top of her head barely reached his pecs, but she glared at him as if she were seven foot two. She jabbed a finger into his chest. "Look, buddy, I've handled myself perfectly well for twenty-two years without any help from you, so I don't care who you are, I'm not taking orders from you unless I damn well choose." She jabbed at him with her finger again. "I'm a vampire hunter, not some tutu-wearing princess who needs to be rescued."

Pushing past him, she stomped off toward the dance floor.

Just as stubborn as her older brother. Mark had always refused help when he'd needed it most.

Damon followed her. His eyes locked on to her figure as she nudged her way through the sweat-covered bodies on the dance floor. The pulsing red lights cast shadows on her hair, tinting it gorgeous shades of red and purple. Even from behind she was gorgeous. He pushed through the crowd until he reached her.

Before she knew he was there, he grabbed her around the waist and pulled her against his body. Using his leather jacket as a cover, he placed the Desert Eagle against her spine, leaned down and growled into her ear, "Walk toward the back door quietly and we won't have a problem."

"This is how you try to protect me?" she seethed.

Damon nudged her with his gun, and she walked forward. He battled the urge to suck on the delicate skin of her earlobe, to kiss his way down the length of her neck and collarbone. The smell of her skin was intoxicating. "I'd rather take you to the E.R. for a bullet wound than scrape your insides off the pavement because some demented vampire attacked you. At least with the gun you'd have a chance of survival."

He forced her to march ahead of them until they reached the back of the club. He pushed open the door and corralled her into the dimly lit street alley. A burst of cold air hit his face, giving him the wake-up call he needed.

"Are you going to take the gun off me now?"

Without a word, Damon patted down the sides of her jacket and confiscated her Smith & Wesson. His hand slid over the stake inside her coat pocket.

"What the hell do you think you're doing? I thought you wanted to protect me." The pitch of her voice dropped as her impatience rose.

He tucked the gun into his inside coat pocket. "I'll let you keep the stake for protection, but I can't have you wielding a gun at me." He patted down her jacket again. "Any other weapons I should know about, or can I trust you?"

She didn't answer. Her jaw clenched, and he could tell from her body language that she was seriously ticked off. Her expression made it very clear that she didn't like being stripped of her weapons.

Damon lowered his gun.

She spun to face him. "You know—"

Before she could finish speaking he slung her over his shoulder as if she weighed no more than a feather from a very pissed-off eagle and jogged toward his gunmetal colored BMW Z4.

She kicked her feet and slammed her fists into his back, but he barely noticed. She yelled profanities at him the entire way to the car, but he didn't care. He just needed to get her out of there. With the way Caius had been fixated on her, it wouldn't be long before he questioned where she was, and he wasn't going to be too happy about his dead bodyguard, either.

When they reached the Z4, Damon quickly hit the unlock button on his remote, wrenched open the door and dropped Tiffany, still kicking and screaming, into the passenger seat. He slammed the door. She shoved herself against it and beat against the window as he slid into the driver's seat. Thank God for automatic locks and bulletproof glass. Standard issue from headquarters.

Within seconds he was shifting into Drive and stomping on the pedal. They zipped out of the alley at sixty miles per hour.

"What's wrong with you?" Tiffany yelled. "Stripping me of my weapon and then throwing me over your shoulder like a sack of potatoes? What are you? A caveman?"

He tried to tune her out, but it was no use. Damn him, he'd just sucked face with Mark's little sister. But if he admitted it to himself, how many times had his thoughts wandered in that direction as he'd read Tiffany's letters? Not while she'd been a teenager, but later, once she entered college, when the handful of years separating them hadn't been as big a deal. Yeah, he'd wondered, all right.

"Hello!" She banged her fist on the dashboard. "This is the twenty-first century. This is called abduction, and in case you didn't know, it's illegal in every state!"

Damon growled, so low and throaty he surprised even himself. "Don't."

The tone of that one word shut her up.

He let out another grumble. "I'm trying to keep you safe, whether you like it or not. Sit back and put your seat belt on."

Slowly she relaxed into her seat and clipped the seat belt into place. Damon sped toward the Golisano Hospital at full speed. The city lights and few people roaming the streets blurred as they sped by. There was no way of knowing the next best move without seeing the victim. Crime scene photos never did the actual carnage justice, and now that he was on the scene he needed to see the details firsthand.

After several minutes of silence, Tiffany finally broke. "Why are you doing this? Why do you care about me?" She fixed him with a hard stare. "Why do you care if I die?"

Damon bit his tongue and concentrated on keeping his expression flat, distant. He couldn't let her know who he was. If he did, she would hate him and never trust him to keep her safe. But he couldn't avoid her questions for long.

"It's my job," he said.

She shook her head, clearly not buying that for a single minute. "What about the other humans in there? Isn't it your job to keep them safe, too?"

He gritted his teeth. She'd hit him right where it hurt, but he would never let her know that. "I can't save everyone."

She crossed her arms over her chest. "So you save the one person in the entire building who needs the least amount of saving?" He didn't respond. She huffed. "That makes total sense."

He shot her an icy stare. "That sort of attitude is exactly why you need saving. You're not invincible."

She scoffed. "Neither are you." She yanked up the sleeve of his leather coat. "See, I jabbed you right..." Her voice trailed off as she ran her fingers over his skin.

Electricity shot through his limbs. One small caress and she could bring him to his knees. He clenched his teeth. Everything in him fought against that knowledge. He couldn't grant her power over him.

She stared at his forearm. The wounds had already begun to heal. The only remaining signs were several pink crescent-shaped scars, which at this rate would soon disappear.

Her eyes widened. "What *are* you?"

★ ★ ★

Tiffany stared at Damon's arm. Her fingernails had dug deep into his skin not even half an hour earlier, and already the healed wounds were nothing but faint pink lines and some residual dried blood. She ran her fingers over the skin once more. Desire pulsed through her every time her skin connected with his. Her nipples hardened into taut peaks as she brushed the muscles of his forearms. She wanted to touch him all over. Run her hands up his thick biceps and onto his chest, down to places where she'd never touched a man before. The thought of their kiss lingered in her mind. She didn't care that he'd only done it out of necessity. Her lips burned with the need to touch his again.

She drew in a sharp breath. She needed to calm herself. She barely knew this man. How could she want him, need him, so desperately? "What are you?" she repeated.

He didn't look at her, just continued to stare at the road. "A vampire slayer, a hunter."

"My brother, Mark, was a vampire slayer before he died." She held back a small smile. "He's the one who taught me how to kill vampires."

Damon's whole body stiffened like a rigid board. His hands squeezed the steering wheel tighter. The ice behind his eyes blazed a captivating blue.

Tiffany wished those eyes were hovering over her as his muscled body slammed into hers. She cleared her throat and blinked several times. She needed to get the image of him naked out of her head, no matter how delicious she was sure he would be. She knew nothing about him. She snapped her wits back into place.

"Look, I get that most hunters have this overwhelming sense of duty to protect the innocent. My brother was the same way, always spouting at me about what to do if a vampire ever attacked me and feeding me horror stories so I wouldn't stay out too late at night. But I don't need protecting. I may be a woman, but you seem to forget that I hunt vampires, too."

Damon stared straight ahead at the road, his face unmoving and cold. "Not in my sanctioned territory, you don't."

Hot as he might be, the man had some serious control issues, and she would only take so much bossing around. "And who gave you the authority to claim this territory?"

He didn't respond.

Realization washed over Tiffany like a tidal wave. She stopped her jaw from falling open. She deserved a good whap upside the head. How could she be such a moron? The thought crossed her mind briefly before, but it had seemed so unlikely.

"You're a member of the Execution Underground," she said. "Just like my brother."

And B…

His hands tightened on the wheel. She didn't need his confirmation to know she was right.

"You probably knew him."

While she didn't know many specifics about the clandestine organization, she did know that they trained men to be elite hunters of the supernatural and dispatched them across the globe to protect humanity. The Execution Underground had recruited her brother once they'd gotten wind of their parents' brutal deaths. During the attack, he'd managed to save her from the monster, though he was totally untrained. The Execution Underground had been interested in him from that point on. They'd whisked him away to a private facility to train, while she'd stayed with their aunt Cecelia.

Whenever Mark had visited, he'd never shared much about the Execution Underground with her. She'd always gotten the impression that she wasn't meant to know, and at the time she didn't have the courage to ask.

To this day, she still didn't know which vampire led the attack that killed her family, but she was determined to find out. Mark worked every day after their deaths to find their killer and to destroy the monsters that had stolen their parents' lives, but Caius had taken his life before he could avenge their family. Now she wouldn't rest until both Caius and the murderous vampire who destroyed their parents exploded like the overstuffed blood bags they were. She would never forget the moment when she discovered who Caius was. All the Execution Underground disclosed to her was the location of the nest Mark had raided. Their letter said he died "valiantly fighting the leaders of the nest." It didn't take much snooping around the vamp world to find out who that leader had been. Once she'd put two and two together, hunting Caius had consumed almost all her waking thoughts.

Without a word, Damon pulled the car to a stop outside Golisano Hospital.

She raised a brow. "What are we doing here?"

He turned to face her. "Would you cooperate more if I said I'm working a case and you could help me as long as you listen to my instructions?"

"I'd be more inclined than when you're ordering me around for no reason."

He fixed her with a hard stare before he exited the car. Once he pressed the unlock button, she scrambled after him, eager for more information. She'd never been part of an official case before. She'd only worked to avenge her family's deaths, and always alone. Sure, she'd killed other vamps in the process, helping one innocent soul or another, but she had never worked a case.

Apparently there was a first time for everything.

CHAPTER 4

Dead was an awful smell to get used to. The scent of formaldehyde hit Damon's nose as he and Tiffany walked into the morgue. After a few calls to the E.U. in order to clear things with security, they were able to enter the room with ease. The reflective silver surfaces and sharp sterilized instruments laid out on tray tables made the room as cold as the chilled air around them. She coughed and covered her face with her sleeve. Though Damon was new to working on his own, he'd shadowed some of the world's most elite vampire slayers for the past several years. The smell of dead bodies no longer churned his stomach.

But the thought of all the children in the silver drawers lining the walls *did*.

There was nothing worse than working on a case involving children. The fact that Jane Doe was on the older side of childhood didn't make it any easier. So much for sweet sixteen.

He walked to the small coroner's desk in the corner and riffled through the files. There was bound to be more than one Jane Doe in the morgue, but only one with the type of extensive damage they were looking for.

Tiffany cleared her throat, still wiping desperately at her

nose as if she were trying to erase the smell. "Do you know who we're looking for?"

He continued searching through the stacks of papers without answering. She had to be somewhere near the top. He noticed a freshly printed page sticking out of a manila folder. He pulled at the edge. The header of the report identified Jane Doe by her extensive mutilation. This was not going to be pleasant.

"Damon," she said again.

He turned toward her with the paper in hand. "Yeah, I know."

Reading over the IDs, he matched the number on the report to the corresponding label on a drawer. He placed his hand on the cold metal handle as Tiffany walked to his side.

He nodded toward the drawer. "Don't watch this."

She shook her head. "I'm fine. I don't have a weak stomach."

"There are some things nobody should have to see."

She crossed her arms over her chest and planted her feet firmly.

He let out a long sigh. "Suit yourself." He pulled open the drawer and fought not to gag.

Immediately Tiffany ran to the small wastebasket near the coroner's desk and hurled. Damon didn't blame her one bit. He stared down at the unidentifiable body as anger built inside him. Even if they'd found an ID, it would have been next to impossible to identify this girl, and no parent deserved to see their child like this. A large, gaping hole took the place of her face. The lips, eyes and mouth were gone, like some gruesome figure in a haunted house or a B horror film.

As if the facial mutilation wasn't enough, several sets of fang-size holes marred her neck and collarbone. From the heavy purpled bruising, they were evidence of the M.O.D.—

method of death: exsanguinations. Damon had stopped hoping for the existence of a higher power long ago, but, damn, he prayed the mutilation had occurred after she'd already been drained. The thought of her suffering from the injuries to her face as a vampire slowly bled her out was more than even he could handle. Every inch of his being longed to kill the sick bastard who'd done this. The worthless piece of shit deserved to die a slow, painful and torturous death. And he intended to make sure that happened.

He carefully examined the holes on her neck. There was no mistaking it. Her wounds were definitely fang marks, the exact shape and width of the average vampire's canine teeth. Walking to the coroner's cabinet, he searched until he found three cotton swabs and the containers used for sending away samples for DNA analysis. He traced one around the edge of her fang bites, another near the edges of her facial wounds and the third over a small speck of dried blood on her cheek. He capped all three samples and glanced down at the body.

A feeling of disgust hit him. Desecrating the poor girl's corpse was the last thing he wanted to do at that moment, but he couldn't risk her turning into a vampire within one month's time. He needed to take preemptive measures to ensure she wouldn't turn, the measures he should have taken with Mark. Pulling his stake from inside his coat, he placed it over her heart. He closed his eyes, inhaled a deep breath and thrust the stake downward.

He opened his eyes again. Dry bloodless flesh, but otherwise there was no reaction. He let out a long sigh of relief. It was bad enough she'd been murdered by a vampire, but thank God she hadn't turned in the process. Bile rose in his throat as he thought of Mark being one of those bloodsuckers. Of Mark killing humans to fuel his own immortality. Because once turned, there was no fighting the change, and for the first year a vampire's blood thirst raged so hard that all the self-control in the world wouldn't aid him.

Removing the stake from her heart, he pulled his cleaning rag from his pocket, wiped off the lacquered wood and placed the stake inside his jacket again, then closed the drawer, sealing the corpse inside, and walked to Tiffany's side.

Tiffany lifted her head from the trash bin. Shoving her hair away from her face, she inclined her head toward the drawer. "Is it closed now?"

Damon nodded. "Yeah, let's go."

She shot out of the morgue and toward the car as if someone had lit a fire under her ass. Judging by her pale white face, she was more than a little spooked. She didn't speak again until she slid into the passenger seat.

"I thought you had a strong stomach," he said as he slid behind the wheel.

She shook her head. "I thought so, too."

Damon wasn't surprised. Regular people thought being immune to motion sickness constituted a strong stomach. Dealing with the dead was different. She would need to toughen up for med school, if that was still her goal. She'd been prepping for her studies when they'd last communicated, several months ago. He opened his mouth to comment, but caught himself.

Do not go there, Damon.

He shifted the car into Drive and paused to plan out his next move. Getting the samples into the headquarters database via his personal analysis equipment before the evidence could be comprised needed to be his first priority.

Within a few seconds they were back on the street, and he sped away from the hospital.

She slumped against the headrest and closed her eyes. "Where are we going now?"

He held back a string of profanities. Sending off the samples meant taking her to his place. What the hell would Mark say if he knew he was taking Tiffany home with him? His hands tightened on the steering wheel. The image of her lying across the black Egyptian cotton sheets of his bed sent his sexual imagination into overdrive.

No. Nothing would result from her being in his home, near his bed. He owed Mark that respect. "To my apartment."

She let out a long sigh. "What for?"

Damon shifted into gear. "To analyze the samples."

When they reached the Temple Building on Franklin Street, Tiffany's eyes widened.

"Holy guacamole! You live in the Temple Lofts?" Her eyes scanned the tall brick building. "Very nice."

He didn't respond.

She gave a slight laugh. "That's definitely not where I expected you to live. I mean, obviously, driving this Beamer, I'd be stupid to think you didn't have some dough, but dang. My little hellhole of a college apartment is nothing compared to this."

Damon slid out of the car and slammed the door. Tiffany followed suit.

He led the way to the entrance as she trailed behind him. Several minutes later they were on the third floor. He unlocked his door and flipped on the lights.

Tiffany followed him into the two-story loft apartment. Her face lit up. She glanced at the twenty-five-foot-high ceiling, clearly admiring the open staircase and the high quality furniture. Mostly black, white and tan. He'd gone for muted but classy, not to mention that he prided himself on keeping his apartment virtually spotless.

"Wow. Very impressive." She walked to the skyline window and studied the lights of the city.

Damon closed the door behind him and locked the dead-bolt. "What were you expecting?"

She spun to face him. "Huh?"

"You said this wasn't what you expected from me. What *did* you expect?" He stripped his jacket off and laid it on the kitchen island.

She shrugged. "I don't know. I guess something a little bit... rougher around the edges."

He removed the Desert Eagle from the back of his pants and placed it on the counter.

The large silver gun thunked as it hit the countertop. Rough around the edges? Try jagged on every corner.

He watched as Tiffany ran her hand over the banister of the wooden staircase.

"If you're a member of the Execution Underground, what are you doing in Rochester?"

Damon froze for a moment, but then forced himself to relax. He kept his back to her and managed to speak evenly. If she knew he was responsible for her brother's death, she'd never trust him. Sure, there were other reasons for hunting Caius, but he knew how sharp Tiffany was. He would need a damn good excuse to make her think he had absolutely no connection to her brother, much less any knowledge of his death. Keeping his mouth shut was the best option.

He walked to the refrigerator and pretended to search for something to drink. "Who said I was a member of anything?" He grabbed a bottle of water and closed the fridge. After chugging down the water in a few quick swigs, he turned to her again.

She rolled her eyes. "Look, my brother was one of you, okay? I understand how you guys are with keeping your secrets, never admitting your true occupation to anyone, blah,

blah, blah, but there's nothing to hide here." She shrugged as if secret international networks of lethal hunters chasing the supernatural were no big deal. "I already know the Execution Underground exists, so why the tight lip?"

He recapped the now-empty plastic bottle and placed it on his countertop. "Organization or not, I don't make a habit of sharing my personal life—with anyone."

She gestured to the large open space around them. "Uh… I'm in your apartment. How's that for *personal?*"

He smashed the empty water bottle with his palm. Man, she drove him up a wall with the nonstop questions. But what wouldn't he give to throw her over his shoulder and carry her up to his bedroom. Maybe in another life.

Another life where he wasn't a worthless excuse for a hunting partner, where his mistakes didn't cause innocent people to get killed and where the deaths of more than one person didn't rest on his shoulders. Mark could have gone after Caius without the need for a transfer, closing in much sooner than Damon could. And any extra time meant bodies piling higher.

"There's no division of the Execution Underground in Rochester. I know that because otherwise my brother would have worked here. So why are you here?"

He took the samples from his coat pocket and walked toward the tech room. It had been meant as nothing more than a bedroom, but it hadn't even taken him two days to hardwire everything in place. His own personal contact with headquarters.

"Stay here."

She shot him a scathing look before she marched to the other side of the room and flopped on to the white leather couch.

Certain she was firmly planted in place, he slipped down the short hall to the tech room. He punched in several series of codes to unlock the door and stepped inside. The wall was lined with monitors of all shapes and sizes. The highest-end technology headquarters could supply him with was all contained within this one room. It was a tech nerd's wet dream.

Damon dropped into the desk chair and typed several numbers on the keyboard. The monitor rang like a telephone until a small beep confirmed that Chris had answered the other line. Seconds later his face appeared on one of the monitors.

Chris's expression was one of concern. "Hey, Damon. How you holding up?"

Damon held up the three samples. "I need these processed as fast as possible. If I load them into the DNA analysis machine, can you connect with my database and look them over?"

"Yeah, sure. Though…want to trade jobs? I'd rather be an assassin."

Damon fought back a small smirk as he rolled his chair to the opposite wall and carefully loaded the specimens into the scanner, which processed the data instantly, locking the genetic code into Damon's control system. Only the technological abilities of the Pentagon and the CIA rivaled those of the Execution Underground, and even they sometimes fell short.

"The samples are from the latest victim. One blood culture, one saliva analysis and one unknown." He fixed Chris with a hard look. "Looked like the killer *ate* the body. Ate it. If I didn't know any better, I'd say the bloodsucker ate it."

Chris raised an eyebrow. "Like a zombie?"

"Sure, whatever you want to call it. But vampire, zombie or who knows what, I don't care what it is. I just want to know who and where it is so I can stake it straight through the heart."

Chris focused on one of his monitors and typed at full speed. "The blood looks normal, nothing unusual about it.

But the saliva and the unknown, I'm going to have to get back to you on those. There's something off about them."

"Off like how?"

"Like there's a different genetic marker that's screwing up the whole code. They don't look anything like normal." Chris pounded away at his keys. "Are all these from the victim on the far side of Franklin Street?"

Damon gripped the arms of his chair like a vice. "What do you mean, the far side of Franklin Street?"

Chris stopped typing and looked at Damon through the screen. "The most recent killing ten minutes ago on the far side of Franklin Street. A P.D. informant tipped us off. He said he'd call you. He saw it on patrol, and he's been holding off on calling the cops. I thought you said this was the most recent one? I—"

"I have to go." Damon stood and jabbed at the keys, beginning to shut down his system. "Chris, I didn't know about the newest killing and F.Y.I., I live on Franklin Street."

Tiffany pressed her ear against the door. She strained to hear even the smallest sound, but the door was apparently soundproofed. She sighed. She missed her brother every second of every day, and, as pathetic as she knew it was, she needed to know if Damon was in the Execution Underground, regardless of whether he'd fought alongside her brother or not. Anything that would help her hold on to Mark's memory was worth fighting for. And she had lost B, too....

Part of her hated him for the role he'd played in Mark's death. The other part missed him like hell. She could have used a friend these past three months.

The steel-reinforced door was yanked out from under her ear, and she toppled into Damon's chest. "What the hell?"

Holy guacamole!

Looking past him, she spotted what he was hiding: a control room that wouldn't have been out of place at NASA.

Damon slammed the door shut behind him, helped her regain her balance and then hurried past her in a full-on jog. She heard his steel-toed boots clomp up the staircase. What in the world was going on?

She raced after him.

When she reached the top of the stairs, she watched as he threw open the doors of a walk-in closet lined with weapons.

Whoa. Mr. Tall, Dark and Scary sure packed a whole lot of heat.

He shoved various weapons into the military loops on his belt before he slammed the closet doors shut and thundered down the stairs again as if she weren't even there.

She followed. "What's going on?"

He grabbed his jacket and gun from the counter, slipping the jacket on and tucking the gun into place before she could blink.

He wrenched open his front door. "If you're coming, then haul ass. If not, stay here and keep this door locked no matter what."

He nearly closed the door on her as she rushed after him.

She stayed at his heels as he ran out to the street. She grabbed his shoulder. "What's going on?"

"Dead body nearby. The vamp probably ghosted it by now, but to be safe, hold your stake at the ready and follow my lead."

A shot of adrenaline raced through her, and her brain switched to hunting mode.

They jogged to the nearest alleyway, but stopped before moving forward. Tiffany's eyes widened as she caught sight of the uniformed police officer on the ground. He slumped against the wall behind him. A trickle of blood ran from the crest of his hair. The man groaned.

Damon knelt beside him. "You the informant?"

The cop nodded. Man, the poor guy had taken a beating. "Were you bitten?"

The officer coughed, blood spewing from his mouth. He spit out a tooth, and then shook his head.

Damon placed a hand on his shoulder. "Good. Are you alright?"

The cop gulped as if trying not to spit more blood, before he managed to say, "Yeah. Hurry. Called patrol, thought I'd lose consciousness. Fifteen minutes till they're here." His last several words came out in a slurred mess. Slowly, he lifted his hand and pointed toward the alleyway. "Go."

Damon gave his shoulder a light, reassuring squeeze. "Thank you."

Standing, Damon slipped into the alleyway and blended into the shadows at its mouth. Tiffany remained close at his heels. Moving at a slow steady pace, she snaked around the corner right behind Damon. She followed each careful step he took with equal care.

Halfway through she bumped into his shoulders as he came to a sudden halt.

In the middle of the alley, half-hidden by shadows, lay a limp and bloodied body. A pool of dark blood, black against the barely lit pavement, formed in the shape of a halo around... *his* head?

Tiffany covered her mouth. Her head spun, and she steadied herself on the brick wall of the building that formed one side of the alley. Most vampires preyed on the weak, on those they thought were the easiest targets—not because they couldn't handle it, but because they liked an easy snack. The only exception was the most ancient bloodsuckers, whose strength was legendary. They barely had to lift a finger. Nausea hit her stomach. The last time she'd seen a young, strong, capable man killed by a vampire was when she and Mark found their father lifeless on their living room floor as their mother clawed uselessly at the monster's arms. He'd sucked the life from her throat, deaf to Mark's and Tiffany's screams. Though she hadn't yet found him, she would never forget his face.

"He's not drained completely," Damon said, his words barely above a whisper.

Tiffany shuddered. There was something not right about this.

Vamps didn't leave leftovers, yet a puddle of blood surrounded the man's head. A newborn vamp wasn't capable of that kind of self-control, but an ancient vamp would lick his dinner plate clean and leave. Near invincible or not, vampires chowed down, drank every last drop of their victim, then they beat feet. They weren't about to make themselves known to the human population. They were greedy arrogant bastards, but they weren't stupid. Modern man packed an arsenal of weapons, and an all-out attack from the human race would lead to their demise. Tiffany often wondered if the world would be better off knowing what monsters crawled out after dark. But humanity couldn't cope with the existence of anything "other," anything different. They couldn't handle the truth. They would panic.

Numb, Tiffany stepped out of the shadows and slowly walked over to stand near the corpse, a young guy of around thirty-five who looked as if he'd been healthy and fit before the vamp got him. Now the man's arm was detached from his body, gnawed to shreds. Exactly the way the young girl's face had been. His eyes were wide-open, staring toward the night sky, the stars drowned by the lights of the city. Bending down, she carefully brushed her hand over his eyelids, closing them for the final time. She stood.

"Tiffany!" Damon roared.

Before she could comprehend what was going on, he tackled her full force and knocked her to the ground. A loud hiss pierced the darkness, and her mind snapped to attention. A fierce, red-eyed vampire stepped forward from the shadows, its fangs already extended and blood ringing its mouth.

Damon crouched in front of her, blocking her from the vampire's attack. As the creature lunged, Damon ripped the Desert Eagle from his waistband and fired a round into the bloodsucker's gut. With such a high-caliber bullet, the vamp's midsection blew to pieces. Blood and guts splattered over the alleyway, but that wasn't enough to kill it. Only a severed spine, decapitation or a stake straight through the heart would destroy a bloodsucker for good. The vampire screeched and staggered. It held its internal organs in as the damaged flesh knitted over, healing the bullet wound. It lifted its head. Glowing red eyes pierced through the darkness.

"You will die, hunter." It crouched in front of the body, guarding the corpse as a lion guards its prey.

Suddenly it ran at Damon, barely visible thanks to its intense speed. It clawed at Damon's throat, but he kicked his steel-toed boot straight into its still-healing wound. A feral growl escaped the monster's throat. Damon fought the vampire blow for blow, matching its supernatural strength with a power she'd never seen in a human being before.

For several seconds she stared, completely frozen. She watched their killing dance as the vampire's blood spilled in all directions, yet each time it lunged, Damon emerged unscathed.

Holy hell. She couldn't sit there. She had to help. She ripped her own stake from her belt and rushed into the fight.

She lunged at the vampire from behind and stabbed the meaty flesh of his shoulder. Not enough to kill, but enough to injure. In an angry fury, the vampire spun and grabbed at her. She dropped to her knees and sucker punched the blood-sucker straight in the groin.

Take that, sucker.

Human or vampire, getting hit in the crotch hurt like hell.

The creature doubled over in pain, falling on top of her. They rolled across the pavement, each trying to gain the upper hand. Though she was stronger than the average man, the vampire's supernatural strength overpowered hers. With all its weight it pinned her to the ground. If it sank its fangs into her neck she would be done for. Like a snake, it hissed and threw back its head to attack. A growl, deep and full of anger, sounded in her ears.

It wasn't the vampire.

CHAPTER 5

Suddenly the weight of the vampire's body disappeared. Tiffany's chest heaved from adrenaline and fear. She stared upward and saw the vampire's feet dangling above her as the creature struggled helplessly. Damon clenched the monster by the throat. His whole body shook with uncontrollable rage as he crushed the bloodsucker's esophagus.

"Stake it before I tear its head from its neck," he growled.

She scrambled to her feet and with both hands drove the lacquered wood of her stake into the vampire's heart. One last batlike screech ripped through the night before the monster exploded like a bursting sack. Blood splattered over her face and torso, and she thanked God she'd remembered to close her mouth.

Damon lowered his hands and unclenched his fists, and the last remnants of the creature's flesh fell to the ground.

With her one semi-clean hand Tiffany wiped the vile liquid from her face. "I hate when they do that."

Damon fixed his stare on her. The raw power that surged from him hit her full force. He was fierce, terrifying and beautiful all at once.

"You are *not* leaving my sight," he said. "Understood?"

She nodded, at a total loss for words.

Drenched in vampire blood, he walked over to the dead man and hoisted him into his arms.

He resettled the weight of the dead man's body over his shoulder before nodding for her to follow him. They needed to get out of there before the cops showed up, and fast. As they snaked down the back of the alley, the distant sound of sirens, followed by the red-and-blue lights casting into the alleyway, lit a fire under their feet. They moved faster. Tiffany sighed. Thank goodness help for the wounded officer had arrived.

They kept to the shadows all the way to the Temple Building before slipping up the fire escape. Two people soaking wet with blood, holding a mutilated corpse, was not a sight for civilian eyes. Damon hit a keypad beside the fire escape window and they climbed into the loft. Wow. Keypad on the fire escape? How paranoid *was* he?

Once they were safely inside the apartment, they positioned the body on the kitchen island. She stripped off her leather jacket, and Damon followed suit. He held out his arm, and she laid her coat across it. He placed both coats in his laundry room before returning to the kitchen. They both used the sink and washed the caked-on blood from their faces and hands.

Tiffany stared at the body as she used a dishrag to dry her face. "What the hell was wrong with that vampire?" They were the first words either of them had spoken since the alley.

Damon shook his head. "I don't know. I've never seen a vampire guard a dead body, or leave so much leftover blood in its victim like that. And I've *definitely* never seen a baby vamp capable of stopping in the middle of a feeding to take a breather, and strong as it was, from the sloppy movements of that thing that was a baby vamp as sure as I live and breath."

She attempted to wipe some of the blood off her shirt and failed miserably. "It was like it was an animal with a piece of food. Vampires are chickenshits. Every peon vamp feeding off the street runs like hell if their victim is already dead and someone approaches. And you're right, what kind of blood-sucker leaves blood like that? I've learned at least that much from hunting."

Damon shot her a look. "You shouldn't be hunting vampires alone."

She glared at him. "Oh, yeah, why's that? I've been hunting vampires for years."

"You're not trained. If I hadn't been there, that bloodsucker would have drained you."

She turned away from him. Her jaw clenched, and frustration built up inside her.

"How many times have you come that close to death?" he asked.

She stared at the floor.

"How many times, Tiffany?"

"Lots, okay?" She spun to face him. "You're just like my brother, acting as if I can't handle myself. Just because I'm a woman doesn't mean I'm incapable of fighting. Why do you act like I can't hold my own?"

Something sparked behind Damon's eyes, something she couldn't interpret. "Because you can't."

"I am not weak. I'm not a victim." Her hands balled into fists.

Damon walked toward her, his boots clomping against the hardwood floor. He towered over her, staring down into her eyes. If she'd been a weaker woman, she might have been in-timidated, but she refused to back down.

His tone remained calm and even despite the clear frustra-tion behind his words. "Vampires are stronger and faster than even the most powerful human. Being a woman has noth-ing to do with it. Being untrained on top of being a normal human is what makes you incapable of fighting, not your gender. The vampire in that alleyway was nothing compared to a vampire who has lived even twenty years, let alone thousands. The bloodsucker we fought tonight couldn't have been a vampire for more than a few days, and still he would have bested you..."

She looked away from him.

He let out a long sigh and held her chin gently in his hands, forcing her to face him. Even when he was covered in blood and dirt, his touch sent electrifying waves through her, and as mad as she was, she wished she could kiss him again. She cursed herself. She didn't know this man. She still wasn't even sure why he was so intent on protecting her.

"Tiffany, look at me."

She did as he asked, studying the contours of his face. He seemed so familiar, but she couldn't place where she'd seen him before. Though she knew he wasn't, it was as if he was an old friend she hadn't seen in years. His presence was both tantalizing and comforting.

"Stop flirting with death. I can tell by looking at you that that's why you're doing this. Only someone with a suicide wish would try to fight something they know they can't win."

A lump blocked her throat, and she fought hard to keep her eyes from watering. She blinked to hold back the tears and prayed he wouldn't notice. Damon cupped her cheek, his touch gentle for a man so gruff and strong. She swallowed the lump in her throat and turned away from him.

No one had ever said something so blunt to her. No one had ever seen straight through her before, been so right about her motivations—not even her brother. No one...

...except B.

Even though she'd never met him. She'd been asked to correspond with B to give him something to hold on to in tough times, but in those letters, he'd been *her* savior. Now, with no more letters cluttering her mailbox, B seemed like a distant dream.

Damon watched Tiffany step away from him. His fingers buzzed with electricity where their skin had connected. He bit his lower lip. He hadn't meant to put her on the slab and expose her like that. The last thing he wanted was to make her uncomfortable. The look in her eyes said he'd seen right through her.

She cleared her throat, acting as if he hadn't nearly made her cry, which seemed very *her*. From what he'd gathered, she wasn't the type of person to show weakness.

"Tell me why you brought him back here." She gestured toward the dead man.

"To examine him." Time to focus. He ducked into the downstairs bathroom and returned with his scalpel. It had saved him a time or two, letting him avoid unnecessary trips to the emergency room. Nothing like explaining why you had a bullet wound in your shoulder to open up the kind of investigation he didn't need.

She raised an eyebrow at him. "Do I even want to ask why you keep a scalpel in your bathroom?"

"Useful if you get something lodged in you. Glass, bullets, whatever."

"That happens to you a lot?"

"Comes with the job." He ran the scalpel from the dead man's sternum to his navel before he glanced at Tiffany.

All the color drained from her face, leaving her skin with a slight greenish tinge. She gulped.

He nodded over his shoulder, trying to hide a smile. "Bathroom, if you need it."

She frowned. "Don't get haughty. It's different seeing it for real, that's all."

He tugged back the skin.

"Ugh." She gagged. "Do you have to do it so...forcefully?"

"Yes."

She turned away and walked to the other side of the apartment. His eyes locked on to the sway of her hips, but he forced himself to look away. She would need to get used to dealing with gore if she was going to stick around for long. Damon paused.

Shit. She would *not* be sticking around for long. Only long enough for him to ensure that she wasn't chasing vamps anymore, that she was safe.

He'd already done enough to Tiffany. If she stuck around, things would only end with him ruining her life even more.

He glanced in her direction. She was staring out the window at the city lights. Her lips had tasted like warm brown sugar when they'd kissed. His gaze lowered to her sweet behind, and the thought of cupping her ass in his hands before he trailed kisses over the porcelain skin of her neck sent a shiver down his spine.

Damn. He ripped his eyes away from her. He would not think about her no matter how deliciously round her ass was or how perfectly ample her breasts were.

Dead body. Dead body. Dead body.

He looked at the corpse lying on his counter. That was enough to act as a cold bucket of water for anyone. Pushing Tiffany from his mind, he stared down at the dead man's insides. What was it about the latest victims that caused vampires to act like zombies, going for flesh and not just blood? Why were they eating these people? And the way the new vampire in the alley had guarded this man's body screamed of a predator protecting its prey.

No. Leeches were leeches.

Once a human was drained, they moved on. Wham, bam, thank you, human. Aside from Hosts, leeches didn't stick around and play with their food. As much as he hated the relationship, at least Hosts served a purpose. Better a couple pints low than dead, though most Hosts drove themselves to that, anyway. But in all his years of hunting them, he'd never seen a single vampire interested in anything but blood—until now.

From the look of the man's insides, there was nothing unusual about his blood or his organs. Damon pulled latex gloves from one of the kitchen drawers and slipped them over his hands. He reached inside the open cavity of the man's midsection and moved around several organs, searching for anything even remotely unusual that would cause a vampire to behave uncharacteristically.

Nothing. No tumors or anything out of the ordinary.

Damon removed his hands from the chest cavity. He pulled at the edge of his glove, ready to be done with his examination, then paused. Something in his gut told him it was worth checking *inside* the man's organs, as well.

He reached deep into the man's body and began to palpate the organs. He bit his lip as his hands squished against the soft tissue. How the hell did morticians and coroners manage to do this for a living? Then again, how did he manage to kill for his?

When he finally reached the man's kidneys he used the scalpel to extract one. The organ was already cold. Carefully, he slid the scalpel through the spongy tissue.

A loud hiss filled the room. Something vile poured from the kidney, and heat like liquid fire washed over his hand. He ripped the glove off just in time for the greenish liquid to eat through the latex like acid. A putrid smell hit his nose, and bile burned at the back of his throat. Drawn by the noise and the stink, Tiffany came running over from the window.

The damn mess was like a sixth grade science fair project gone wrong, one of those spewing volcanoes every kid built at least once. He hardly noticed Tiffany running off and rummaging in the fridge. A second later, white powder clouded the air as she dumped an entire box of baking soda on top of the acid.

"What the hell *was* that?" she demanded.

Coughing from the soda cloud, he tossed his gloves in the kitchen garbage can, chuckling. "Overkill on the baking soda much?"

She frowned. "For all you know that could have exploded and I saved your sorry ass. Now, what the hell happened?"

He dusted baking soda from his clothing, not that it did much good with all the blood already there. "There's something wrong with the kidney fluids."

"Ya think?" She stared at the rest of the green acid oozing from the dead man's kidney.

A smile crossed his face. He had to give her credit. Even though he knew she was probably fighting not to toss her cookies, she was standing there like a champ.

He appreciated a strong woman.

She wrinkled her nose. "That's just disgusting. What *is* that? Maybe you should check the other organs, too."

Putting on a new pair of gloves, he held the man's heart carefully, preparing to jab it with the scalpel. Just as he got ready to slice, the corpse lurched.

Shit!

Damon jumped back as the now newly turned vampire sat upright, hissing and reaching for Damon's neck. How the hell had the thing changed so quickly? Before he could respond, Tiffany plunged her stake deep into the monster's exposed heart. One high-pitched screech pierced his ears before the vampire exploded like the blood sack it was.

Blood splashed onto his face and throughout his kitchen.

He looked at Tiffany, who smiled despite all the blood she was covered in. "I told you I could hold my own."

Damon narrowed his stare. "Sometimes." He pointed to the stairs. "You can use the shower upstairs. Toss your clothes over the balcony and I'll throw them in the washer."

"You don't need to ask me twice."

Stake still in hand, she trudged up the stairs. A minute later a large pile of bloody clothes flew over the balcony rail and landed on his hardwood floor with a splat. He quickly threw them in the washer, trying not to think about how deliciously naked she was, about the hot shower water running over the curves of her body. He pushed the thoughts aside.

Down, boy. Focus.

With any luck, he would at least be able to get most of the blood out of their clothes. He glanced down at his own threads. He was covered in blood and dirt, but there was no point in changing before he finished cleaning up.

He reached under his kitchen sink and removed a mop and bucket, a sponge and a gallon of bleach. It was times like these when he wished he wasn't too paranoid to employ a maid.

Not that your average housecleaner could handle a kitchen resembling a horror movie.

CHAPTER 6

An hour later he'd thoroughly scrubbed down the kitchen, returning it to a near sparkling clean. He would give it another going over later. Right now he needed a shower. Using the downstairs bathroom, he scrubbed all the blood, guts and debris from his body. When he finished, he wrapped his hips in a towel, threw his own clothes in the washer and padded up the stairs to his bedroom.

Water from the shower pummeled the tiled floor, sounding like heavy rain. He didn't blame Tiffany for the extra-long shower. When you washed the blood off, no matter how clean you got, sometimes you still felt dirty.

He finished drying off and threw the white towel into the laundry bin. He slipped on a pair of old loose-fitting jeans, zipped and buttoned the fly, then reached into the top of his closet for a black shirt. Tiffany cleared her throat from behind him.

Still shirtless, he turned around. The breath caught in his throat, and every inch of him stiffened. His erection was immediate. She was standing in the middle of his bedroom, still slightly damp from the shower, one of his towels wrapped around her. It took all the strength in him not to rip the towel from her body and take her on top of his bed. Thinking about what was underneath that towel would be the death of him.

He watched as Tiffany scanned the length of his body and a look of hunger filled her eyes. She inhaled a deep breath, and he admired the rise and fall of her chest. Her every movement exuded raw sexuality. If she looked at him that way much longer…

Her gaze dropped to the floor. "I *knew* you were with the Execution Underground."

He nearly swore. Damn. She'd seen the E.U. brand on his shoulders, a variation of the symbol Mark and every other hunter had. It marked them as humans with something more—their incredible strength, their speed, their fighting abilities. Each member was branded with his own unique symbol upon graduating the Execution Underground training.

A sad smile crept across her lips. "I like your design more than the one my brother, Mark, had." She continued to stare at the floor. "The first time he came home after he got his, he flaunted it as if it were a badge of honor. The purple heart of tattoolike brandings."

Damon froze at the sound of his best friend's name. He let out a long breath through his nose. She couldn't know he was responsible for her brother's death—and worse. His jaw clenched. She couldn't know that he was going to have to kill Mark all over again.

She shifted from one foot to the other nervously. He admired the sway of her hips and immediately cursed himself. She was Mark's baby sister. It didn't matter if she was twenty-two, or that she was her own independent woman, that he'd known her for years—he owed it to her brother's memory to stay away, to keep his hands off. Not to mention that he needed to stay objective, detached from his mission if he was going to complete it successfully. And how could he be detached while sexing up the sister of the man he was avenging?

The sound of a car horn down in the street brought him back to reality. He would have to gouge out his eyes and break his eardrums to avoid wanting her. Her looks, the sound of her voice, her scent… She drew him in like a siren.

She broke the silence. "Sorry, I didn't mean to make it awkward, like I was being creepy and sneaking a peek at your emblem. I know your vow to the Execution Underground is kind of a personal thing, so it's none of my business. Anyway, uh…do you have a blow-dryer?"

If he hadn't been too busy raking his eyes over the gorgeous hourglass figure beneath the towel, he would have chuckled. He ran his fingers over his buzz cut. "I don't have much hair to dry."

She met his eyes quickly, then lowered her own gaze to the floor again. "Do you have any more towels, then?"

He pointed to the bathroom. "Under the sink."

She hunched her shoulders, curling in on herself as if she were embarrassed to stand before him, barely covered. "I didn't see any."

Exercising every bit of self-control possible, he walked past her to the bathroom. He reached under the sink, feeling for the stray towels. Finally he found one tucked far in the back corner. He pulled it out, stood and turned, ready to take it to her, only to find her standing directly behind him. Her large amber eyes examined his torso again, lingering on the line of highly defined muscles leading from his chest to his hips.

He couldn't resist. "Like what you see?" he said playfully.

The deep red blush that bloomed across her face sent his heart racing into overdrive, and he knew that if she dropped her gaze she would see his excitement.

"Sorry," she said, starting to turn away.

He held the towel out toward her. "Don't be."

She reached for the towel, and her soft, delicate fingers brushed against his hand. She met his eyes and stared up at him, her expression innocent and perfect. She bit her lower lip. He thought of the perfect taste of her mouth on his own. Being honest with himself, he had to admit that she'd tasted delicious when he'd kissed her, just like he'd always dreamed she would.

Another blush crossed her cheeks. She glanced toward the floor before she met his gaze again. Her desire was palpable. He hated himself for it, but he couldn't hold back any longer.

The fiery look in Damon's normally icy-blue eyes sent Tiffany's heart thumping hard against her chest. He stepped toward her. She didn't care if she didn't know him. He was handsome, strong, intelligent—and dangerous. Dangerous to the monsters they hunted. Dangerous to her. Her mind, her heart. And worse, he was hell-bent on protecting her. For a woman who'd been on her own for so long, been alone for so long, here, finally, was a man who knew her secrets. Understood her on a level no one else ever had. No one except B.

And, boy, did that spark a fire inside her.

He reached out and toyed with the edge of her towel. She wanted him, and from the look in his eyes, he wanted her, too.

She balled up her courage and dropped the towel to the floor.

Within seconds he was pressing her against the tiling of the shower as his lips met hers. The delicious masculine taste of him flooded her mouth as he kissed her deeply. No one else had ever kissed her, but there was no doubt that Damon's abilities were mind-blowing. His tongue danced with hers in sensual, soft movements.

Gently, he suckled on her lower lip. She moaned and bucked

her hips against him. Heat rushed to her center. Every inch of her body longed for a man's touch, for Damon's touch. She ran her hands over his shoulders and onto his strong muscled chest. Her fingers crossed the hard ridges of his abs before her hand slipped into his jeans.

A growl rumbled in his throat as she stroked the length of him, feeling the power that came from touching him, knowing she was pleasuring him. His lips trailed from her mouth, and he nestled his head beside her neck so he could kiss the sensitive skin of her collarbone. Shivers rolled down her spine.

His hands slipped behind her back and cupped her ass, then lifted her with ease so her hips were up against him. He pulled back from her neck, taking in the view of her naked form. Supporting her with one arm, he trailed his hand along her skin and down to the juncture of her thighs. A wave of excitement rushed over her. No one had ever touched her there before. Should she tell him?

His warm hand nestled between her legs, and he rubbed his fingers in slow circles over her most sensitive flesh. She moaned, and a fresh wave of heat flooded her. His fingers were covered with her sweetness. She was so wet. Should she be embarrassed? He met her eyes and slipped his fingers into his mouth, licking off her nectar. A deep moan escaped his lips. She nearly moaned herself, to know he liked that....

He lowered his hand between her legs again and massaged her. Fire coursed through her body, warming her in a way she hadn't known was possible. The last of the water drops from her shower dripped onto her skin. The coolness sizzled against her in an amazing sensation.

He placed his cheek against hers, his mouth trailing sweet kisses up to her ear. The heat of his breath sent waves of electricity rolling through her body.

He gently nipped at her earlobe. "You taste so sweet."

Still supporting her with one arm, he captured her hand in his and led her fingers down to the button of his jeans. She knew what he wanted. She inhaled a deep breath. She wanted him more than anything imaginable. She was ready for this. Leaning forward, she undid his jeans and his pants fell to his ankles, revealing the hard strong length of him.

She fought back a gasp. He was enormous, and the thought of him plunging deep inside her sent both chills and fear racing through her body. Kissing her deeply again, he placed himself just outside the entrance to her body. Adrenaline and excitement overwhelmed her as the pressure increased.

She pulled back from his kiss. "Damon, wait," she whispered.

He stopped immediately and met her eyes.

"I...I..." she stammered. As tough as she was, she was no tigress in the bedroom—not yet.

"It's all right, Tiffany, we can stop. I don't want to pressure you if you don't want—"

"No," she interrupted. "I want to." Her eyes trailed over the length of his body again. Her desire for him surged and built the courage inside her. She inhaled a deep breath, then let it out in a rush. "I'm a virgin."

Damon's eyes widened.

She bit back a groan. Did he not want her now that he knew she was so inexperienced? She could tell from his raw sexuality and strong confidence that he'd known his fair share of women. A large lump rose in her throat, and her eyes welled with tears.

With his thumb he wiped away the tears from her eyes. Then he stroked his knuckles over her jawline, and a slight purr sounded from his throat. His sweet smile told her that he was sincere. "I'll be gentle with you."

Before she could respond, he scooped her into his arms and carried her into his bedroom. He laid her out on the bed. The soft mattress engulfed her in a sea of black sheets. His eyes drank her in. She marveled at the sight of him kneeling over her.

He ran his fingers over her thighs, and she shivered. "So, you've never been with anyone before?"

She shook her head.

For a brief moment, she worried what he thought of her. Twenty-two wasn't too old to still be a virgin, was it? But all her nerves subsided and were replaced with excitement when she saw the ravenous hunger in his eyes.

"I promise you, I'll be gentle, and I'll make certain it won't hurt." He slid off her and knelt near her feet. He pushed her legs open, and his lips trailed kisses and soft caresses up the insides of her thighs. Her heart quickened.

Before she could prepare herself, he ran the length of his tongue over her lower lips. He massaged and sucked the sensitive flesh.

Tiffany threw her head back and moaned. Electricity radiated from her center, sending waves of pleasure throughout her body. She bucked against him. Her spine arched as heat pulsed through her core.

He teased her with his mouth until she reached the brink of ecstasy, faster than she'd ever expected. With one more hard pull from his lips, sweet release hit her hard and fast. She clasped her hands around his head, riding his face as he tasted her.

She gasped for air when he released her. He smiled from between her legs and licked his lips. The look in his eyes was enough to make any woman want him between her bedsheets.

White hot need crashed over her. She wanted more. She moaned. Oh, she wanted so much more.

"Damon, can you do that a—"

A grin crossed his face, and he chuckled. "You don't need to ask me twice."

★ ★ ★

Damon latched his mouth onto her and savored the moment. He could drown in the taste of her, the scent of her. She was divine. He hardened with need as he pleasured her with his mouth. He wanted to be inside her, losing himself in the softness of her.

No, not want...need. He *needed* to be inside her.

But his desire to make her first time magical and painless was more important than his own desire. He intended to make her come until she was so soft, so wet, that the width and length of him would be a welcome relief to her overwhelming desire.

She moaned. The sound of her pleasure intoxicated him.

How many women had he turned down over the years because they weren't his Tiffany? It didn't matter that he only vaguely knew what she looked like, that he'd never heard the sound of her voice, never felt her touch until now. Despite all that, he knew her, and not one of those women ever measured up to the one woman who cradled his heart in her hands. Hell, she didn't even know what she did to him. The ache in his chest built. The ache that brutally reminded him that she was so much more than a one-night stand.

He ran his hands over the sweet creamy skin of her thighs. No matter where or how he touched her, energy raced through every ounce of him. He increased the pull of his mouth as her muscles tightened in pleasure. She was so close to climax again, and he could taste it.

She cried out. Her orgasm gripped her hard, and she bucked her hips against his face from the sweet feeling of release. But he couldn't let her go yet; he needed to work her until she was begging for him inside her, needing every inch of him.

Without stopping, he continued to suck her sweetness into his mouth. He angled his chin slightly upward, making enough room so he could position two fingers outside her entrance. Her wetness coated him as he rubbed her slick flesh.

Slowly, with gently increasing pressure, he slid his fingers inside her. She moaned in pleasure. He curled his fingertips up to the top wall of her core to tickle against her G-spot. He fought back a grin as he continued sucking her. The deep throaty cry that escaped her lips as he fingered her didn't sound like the cry of a meek virgin.

"Damon…Damon…"

The sound of her whispering his name sent power and adrenaline through him. Another release crashed over her, and he felt the bed beneath him rock with the force of her straining and pushing against his mouth.

"I want you," she panted.

He released her and licked his lips. He grinned. "What was that you said?" he teased.

"I…mmmhhh…I…" She attempted to catch her breath. She kept her eyes closed. All the muscles in her body visibly relaxed from enjoyment. "I can't say it."

He chuckled. "Yes, you can." He crawled up the bed, lingering over her body, only inches separating them.

She opened her eyes and met his gaze.

He leaned down and kissed her deeply, digging a hand into the damp tresses of her gorgeous hair. He pulled away, but only far enough to speak. His lips brushed against hers as he said, "I'll do anything you want. Never be too shy to ask."

She lifted her hand to his face and ran her fingertips across his cheek.

"Anything," he repeated.

A blush colored her cheeks, but fire filled her amber eyes. "I want you inside me."

He growled, nipping at the soft skin of her neck before he took her breast into his mouth. His tongue circled over one sweet hard nipple, then the other. He took care to pay equal attention to both her delicious breasts. She sighed, relaxing against him.

When he released her nipple from his mouth, he positioned himself outside her entrance. Her eyes widened, and a mixture of emotions crossed her face.

"Don't be nervous." He smiled down at her. "I'll take good care of you."

He eased himself inside her, and she whimpered with pleasure. Damon moaned. She was so tight. So unbelievably tight. He'd never wanted anything more than he wanted this. He wanted to drive himself deep inside her, pounding hard into her until she pulsed against him. Being inside her, being so close to taking her hard and aggressively, was like sweet torture. The thought of her screaming his name nearly drove him over the edge.

With slow movements he rocked into her as gently as he could, careful not to penetrate too deeply. But she caught him off guard. Her walls clenched around him, and she was already teetering on the brink of climax.

Damn. His whole body shook as he fought to hold himself back.

White-hot moisture flooded her tight opening. She threw back her head and moaned, eagerly meeting his every thrust as she peaked.

He gripped the headboard with one hand to brace himself. In all his time hunting and training, nothing he'd faced could compare to the difficulty of holding back from ravishing her.

Keep your cool. This is about her.

He whispered against her ear. "How are you feeling?"

"Like I'm in heaven." She let out another moan and pushed against him. "Like I want every inch of you deep inside me. Like I want you hard and deep."

He clenched his teeth. Everything in him wanted the same. "If you keep teasing me, I might not be able to hold myself back, and I don't want to hurt you." He kissed her forehead.

With a devious grin, she ground her hips into him.

Damn and double damn!

He nearly lost it right then and there. Couldn't she see how hard he was trying to exercise restraint?

He stroked his fingers over her cheek and pushed into her. "You're playing with fire. I don't think you know what you're getting yourself into."

She bit her lower lip in a "come and take me" look and ground into him again.

"Tiffany...!" All the muscles in his body strained, and he gasped for air.

Before he could stop her, she kissed him hard and ran her hands over the muscles of his chest. When she pulled away, she smiled and shot him a seductively playful look. "I *do* know what I'm getting myself into, and I want you deep inside me. Hard and fast."

If she really wanted it, he would give it to her. He lightly bit her ear. She whimpered, and goose bumps prickled across her skin. "Anything you ask."

Within seconds, Tiffany found herself flipped and lying on her stomach, and she marveled at Damon's strength and power. He gripped her by the hips and pulled her up toward him. Her ass ground against his hips as he positioned himself outside her slick hot entrance he had withdrawn from only seconds before.

He thrust into her, harder than she expected. She cried out. The pressure as he filled her was amazing. She'd been scared of her first time. She'd been scared of the pain, the bleeding and the embarrassment of lying naked beneath someone's eyes.

But Damon had destroyed all those fears with the intense hunger behind his eyes.

He wanted her, but he was man enough to take his time with her, preparing her for his possession. As she'd expected, there had been a flash of pain, but she'd been prepared for it. What she hadn't anticipated was so much pleasure.

"How deep do you want me, Tiffany?"

She shivered. The sound of him saying her name sent every nerve in her body into spasms of arousal.

"However deep you want me."

The pressure of his fingers on her hips tightened, exciting her.

He ran a hand down the length of her spine. "Don't tempt me. I might not be able to hold back."

She inhaled a deep breath. She wanted to hear his pleasure. Wanted him to cry out her name. She was ready. She turned her head to look at him, narrowed her eyes and challenged him. "Try me."

The fire in Damon's eyes blazed, gorgeous and intimidating in its intensity. He let out a dark chuckle. The grin that crossed his face was devious, and sexy as hell. "You asked for it."

He thrust into her so deeply that her whole body lurched forward. She cried out and moaned, bracing her hands against the headboard as he pounded into her. His strength was incredible. Her core stretched wide to take the full length of him. Wave after wave of white-hot need pulsed through her.

"Damon!" she screamed. Her legs shook, and she fought not to collapse beneath him. Her core slickened with wetness and heat. Holy smokes. The man was a sex god—she was sure of it.

Damon palmed her breasts as he continued to thrust deep inside her. Her walls pulsed against him, clenching. The pressure inside her built until she teetered on the brink of ecstasy, the pleasure so intense it was almost too much.

Damon rolled her right nipple between his fingers. The tips of both breasts tightened into taut peaks, tingling beneath his touch. "Tell me what you want," he demanded.

"You," she said. "I want you." The words came out as a breathless whisper.

"Louder."

She raised her voice. "I want you."

Pulling harder, he thrust into her with every ounce of his strength. Her whole body shook as he brought her to the brink.

"Louder," he growled.

"I want you!"

She screamed and Damon let out a harsh groan. With another massive thrust, she clenched against him as wave after wave of ecstasy crushed her. He pumped into her. There was nothing but Damon. His touch, his scent, the feeling of him buried deep within her. She wanted to drown in him and never resurface. She fell onto the bed, unable to hold herself up against the weight of him any longer. He collapsed next to her and pulled her into his arms. She snuggled into his chest and he kissed her forehead, before stroking his fingers through her hair.

She'd never known such sweet bliss.

Her body relaxed into his and within moments she was drifting into sleep.

CHAPTER 7

Damon lay on his bed wide-awake as Tiffany slept peacefully with her head nestled against his chest. She was the most beautiful thing he'd ever laid eyes on.

And his best friend's baby sister.... God help him.

What had he done? He'd told himself he wasn't going to get emotionally involved in this mission, but sleeping with a woman under your protection was one hell of a way to keep work separate from pleasure. He'd told himself he wouldn't touch Mark's baby sister. Well, he'd done a lot more than touch her.

He let out a long sigh. What was wrong with him?

He glanced down again at the beautiful woman lying against him. He knew what was wrong with him. She was everything he wanted in a woman. She was strong, fierce, intelligent, passionate and beautiful. Any man would be lucky to have her, yet here she was in bed with him—a killer. He made his living off destroying things. Granted, he fought monsters and sometimes that saved lives, but it didn't change the fact that being successful at his job meant being ruthless, cold and bloodthirsty. When emotions entered the mix, that was when missteps crept in and innocents died. That was when good men like Mark died.

What kind of a lowlife was he that he'd gone to bed with Mark's sister? Mark had trusted him to write to her with no idea of the consequences. No matter which way he looked at it, there was no justification for what he'd done. Even as they'd made love he'd tried to convince himself that Mark would have wanted Tiffany to be protected. That he would have wanted her to find a man who could defend her and care for her to stand at her side. Maybe at one point that man *could* have been him. But after all he'd done, everything that had happened, it certainly wasn't him now.

He stroked the soft tresses of her hair and watched the rise and fall of her chest.

Stunning.

He shook his head. What was she doing with someone like him?

A lump lodged in his throat as he thought of the last words in the final letter she'd sent him. They were burned permanently into his mind and his heart.

I don't know how you can miss a person you've never met, but somehow, I miss you every day.
With love,
Tiffany xoxox

He knew that after Mark's death the Execution Underground had given her as many details as they could, to help her achieve closure, which meant she knew he could've saved Mark, but he failed. There was no way she didn't know. She'd never answered a single one of his letters after that.

Careful not to wake her, he slipped out from beneath her and rested her head on one of his pillows. He made quick work of throwing on some clothes before he headed downstairs. They'd slept most of the day away, and now, with sundown not far away, his work day was about to start.

He thought of the time he'd spent with Tiffany last night. Already he'd been neglecting his job, making love to her instead of closing in on Caius or searching for the vampire who was killing innocent women. There were so many things wrong with this situation. Images of partially devoured corpses, the awakening bloodsucker's kidney exploding with green acid and the way the vamp in the alley had guarded the body, flooded his mind.

He punched in the security code for his tech room, and the heavily reinforced door unlocked. He shoved it open, stepped into the room, flopped into his chair and dialed Chris's number. The monitor beeped on, and Chris stepped in front of the camera.

"Hey, man—"

Damon interrupted him. "Green acid came out of his kidney."

Chris's eyes widened. "What? Whose—"

"After you told me about the killing I went and located the body. The guy was in his thirties, fit, already drunk from, and chewed up like the girl was, only his arm this time. Then a vamp jumped from the shadows and started guarding the body like it was a three-course meal."

Chris shook his head. "This is fucked up, Damon."

Damon nodded. "It gets worse—and stranger, too. There was an abnormal amount of blood left at the scene, wasted, which a newly turned vampire wouldn't even be capable of leaving. They'd be way too hungry. The vamp that attacked us was newly turned, which means it wasn't the one who took the guy out. Baby bloodsuckers don't have that much strength."

Chris ran a hand through his short blond hair. "What do we do next?"

Damon held up a hand. "There's more. After the vamp was dead, I brought the victim's corpse back here to examine. His kidney had green acid in it, too. It nearly burned my damn hand off."

Chris started pounding at his keyboard. "That's not normal, Damon. That's bad, really bad."

"That's not all."

Immediately Chris stopped typing and looked at Damon.

"The dead guy turned into a vamp an hour later. Had to stab him in the heart. He exploded like a blood bag."

Chris's mouth fell open. "Only an hour later? That's barely a fraction of the normal transformation period. You've got to be kidding me."

Damon leaned forward. "Wish I was."

Chris buried his face in his hands. "And to add fuel to the fire, I got in five new reports for your area last night."

Five? Rage filled Damon's chest, and his hands clenched into fists. "What?"

Chris raised his head. "It's not what you think. Not vamp news."

Damon sat in silence, waiting for Chris to elaborate.

Chris let out a long sigh and swore. "I hate to tell you this, but Rochester is swamped with supernatural predators. There are reported werewolf sightings, possibly a full-on pack, there are demons lodged so deep the people they've possessed are pretty much done for, there are several small witch covens, loads of non-werewolf shifters—oh, and that's not even including all the poltergeists and ghosts reported in the old abandoned asylum."

They both sat in silence, uncertain what to say. Words couldn't express what deep shit Damon was in. Welcome to Rochester.

Chris cleared his throat and broke the silence. "You know you can't handle all that on your own."

Damon clenched his teeth and slammed his fist onto the desk. He wasn't ready to lead another division, not given the way he'd failed Mark. But the laundry list of supernatural waste Chris had just dished out was far more than any hunter could handle on his own. The Execution Underground trained all their members to deal with a variety of supernatural creatures, but then headquarters assigned each hunter a species and conditioned them into elite specialists. Damon excelled across the board and was one of the few who'd been granted their choice of specialization. But none of that would do him any good in hunting other beasts full-time. There were too many. Per his choice, hunting vampires was his only true purpose.

He clenched his fists, and fought down his frustration and anger. "Send me a list of prospective hunters for every type of monster we have in the city. I'll look through them, pick a team and put in a request to headquarters."

He wanted to bash his fist into a wall. He'd thought coming to Rochester would let him work alone, since there were no other hunters in the area and until now there hadn't been all that much paranormal activity. But not even New York City was drowning in as many supernatural predators as Rochester suddenly was. He'd landed in the exact situation he'd been trying to avoid: being the lead hunter of an entire division.

"You got it," Chris said. "But let's focus on one thing at a time. I ran those samples, but I was only able to determine one thing. Something caused a mutation in the vampire's saliva, which probably means the vampires themselves have morphed into something new. The weird thing is that the mutation has a lot of similarities to a human virus."

If Damon had been a more lighthearted man, he might have laughed. "The vampires are sick?"

"Yes. I think somehow they're passing around some sort of virus, and that's causing the strange behaviors you described. But based on the change in their DNA, I think it's only being passed on to newly turned vamps. Maybe it has to happen at the moment when a new vamp is made, and that's why the old ones can't get it. I have no idea what the original source could be, though. Does any of this fit what you're thinking?"

Damon ran his hand over his hair. "Not sure. If the vampires have a virus, the weird behaviors make sense. But what about the dead guy turning so quickly? It only took an hour for him to turn and regular vampire gestation is at least a month, sometimes longer, when buried in the ground. He shouldn't have changed that quickly."

Chris started typing again. "The virus could be causing a genetic mutation in their makeup and speeding up the transformation process."

Damon rested his head in his hands. "So we have sick vampires running around who are mutating into zombielike monsters. But that doesn't explain why a newborn vampire would leave blood. Once a baby vamp bites, it doesn't detach until the person's drained, and this guy wasn't."

Chris gave a single nod.

Damon finished his thought. "But a stronger vamp could do that."

Chris stared at him. "You're thinking an older vamp is killing these people and then feeding the leftovers to the baby zombie vamps?"

If an older vampire was controlling younger ones within the Rochester city limits, there was a clear culprit. Damon and Chris exchanged knowing looks. They didn't need to say it aloud to know they were on the same page.

Caius Argyros Dermokaites.

★ ★ ★

Tiffany yawned and stretched as her eyes flickered open. She blinked away the sleep from her vision and rolled over. Sitting up in bed, she glanced around the bedroom. No Damon. She flopped back into the pillows and let out a long sigh.

Holy smokes, the things they'd done…

A sweet ache pulsed through her core. The slight soreness was just enough to remind her of every move they'd made between the sheets. She'd never thought she would have been capable of anything even close. A small smile crept over her face.

She'd never thought her first time would be with a strong handsome hunter, though if she'd been the kind of girl to daydream of the perfect man, Damon or someone like him—someone like B—would have been the star of her fantasies. The members of the Execution Underground were brave warriors, the soldiers of the supernatural world, and Damon embodied everything the E.U. stood for. He was strong, intelligent, skilled, ruthless and passionate. Wow. She'd never been one for the sappy stuff, but the thought of the night they'd spent together gave her butterflies.

She stood and stripped one of the sheets from the bed. Wrapping it around herself, she padded down the stairs. She went into the laundry room and pulled her clothes from the dryer, checking them over. Still mildly stained with blood. No surprise there, but it would have to do. She dropped the sheet and threw on her clothes before heading into the living room in search of Damon. Who wasn't there, or in the kitchen.

Where the heck was he?

She heard a heavy door closing, and moments later he emerged from the downstairs hallway with a scowl twisting his face.

"Did someone spit in your coffee?" she said.

Without a word, he flopped down onto the sofa and buried his head in his hands.

Tiffany raised a brow. "Okay, then. No 'hope you slept well after that crazy time we had.'" She dropped her hands to her sides with a slight humph. Was she an idiot to expect a little sweetness? Given how tender he'd been earlier...

"Is this city really overrun with supernaturals?" he asked, lifting his head from his hands.

She blinked several times. "What?"

He let out a long breath. "According to H.Q., this city is overrun with supernatural predators. Way more than just vampires. Is that right?"

She nodded. "Yeah, pretty much. Mark never taught me anything about hunting supernaturals other than vamps, though, so I stay clear of the others." She walked to the couch and sat down beside him.

He glanced toward her. "How do you know they're here, then?"

She grinned. "Once you know of the existence of supernaturals, it doesn't take a trained hunter to spot one. You know how it is. It might be a flash of a wolf eye here or there, or just a strange feeling when you encounter someone. I've learned never to ignore my instincts."

A moment of silence passed between them. She waited for him to speak. When he didn't, she finally cleared her throat and asked, "Why does it matter?"

"I need to assemble a division of hunters."

Her eyes widened. "So you mean there's going to be a whole load of you guys here in Rochester now?"

He nodded. "Five others." He got up off the couch and walked across the room. His demeanor matched his distant tone.

She knew he had a lot on his mind, but after last night she...

well…she wasn't really sure what she'd expected, but more than this, anyway. Damon's skills between the sheets made the guys in the romance novels she read look like bumbling idiots. But out of bed, cold and distant was his default setting.

"What's so bad about that? About bringing in other hunters?"

Damon ignored her question. "We've got worse things to worry about. The results of the samples I sent to headquarters arrived. The bloodsuckers have some sort of virus they're passing between them. That's what's making them act like zombies and causing their victims to turn so quickly."

Tiffany whistled low and long. "That is *not* good. How are they passing it around?"

He shook his head. "No idea. But it seems the vamps contract the disease at transition. Chances are it started from one vamp who turned someone and continued from there. I don't know how or why, much less how to stop it, but I have to find out."

"If it keeps spreading, won't the entire vampire population be overrun with these freak zombie leeches?"

Again Damon didn't respond. His stare was fixed and distant, and she could tell he was lost in thought. Suddenly he snapped back to attention. "If we find the source of the virus and destroy it, then we can go after all the spawn. We think the current existing vamps can't contract it, since they're already turned. I think one of the old ones is behind this, though—creating an army of monsters to destroy, maybe to gain more power in the vamp world, and make hunting humans easier, as well—and I think I know who it is."

She knew exactly what he was thinking. "If you expect to go into Caius's nest with guns blazing, you're out of your mind." She stood up and walked toward him. "I have a better suggestion." Lingering directly in front of him, she wrapped her arms around his neck, stood on her tiptoes and pulled his head toward her for a kiss. Their tongues swirled together, and immediately heat rushed between her legs. She pulled back. "*I'll* kill Caius."

"Over my rotting corpse." Damon wrapped his arms around her waist and raised a single brow at her. "Did you really think kissing me would get me to agree to that?"

She shrugged. "It was worth a shot."

Damon let out a long sigh. "Tiffany, look—"

"Let me finish," she said, cutting him off. "Whether you like it or not, I know a lot more about the dynamics of this city's vampire scene than you do. All the local vamps have their heads so far up Caius's ass they might as well take up permanent residence. They'll do anything he asks of them, and they'll kill to protect him."

"Vampires have no loyalty. Why do you think they're so devoted to him?"

She crossed the room again to sit on the sofa. "Caius is a good leader, I'll give him that. He's good at controlling, even other vamps. He's been here only three months when he fled here from New York City, after he killed my brother. Since Club Fantasy was already his, this was a natural place to relocate, I guess. He'd been an absent club owner before that. In only three months, he's taken a disbanded group of rogue-like vamps and changed them into an organized nest. He must have been some sort of Roman version of Charles Manson in his day. He's a manipulative psychopath. He was only second in command when my brother raided his nest in New York City. With the head honcho dead, Caius is the big fish now, and he takes his position very seriously." She shot Damon a pointed look. "With so many vampires in this city, in order to kill Caius you'd have to get him alone, and in order to do *that* you'd need to gain his trust." She pointed to herself. "I've already done that."

He met her stare. "What are you proposing?"

"I'll get back inside Caius's inner circle. I'll make up some excuse for having run last night, and then I'll let you in to help me fight once I have him alone."

Damon shook his head. "Absolutely not."

She placed her hands on her hips. "Do you have a better idea?"

He grunted in exasperation and fixed her with a hard stare. "Why do you keep trying to tempt death?"

She scoffed. "Would you quit with that? Maybe I just want to avenge my brother, all right? How do you know I can't—"

He interrupted her as he walked to her side. "Even if you were completely capable of handling an ancient vampire on your own—" he narrowed his eyes "—which you're not, I still wouldn't want you anywhere near Caius. I don't know what I'd do if you were hurt or if I was unable to protect you." He placed a hand on her cheek. "Don't try to pull the wool over my eyes. You trying to fight a vampire as ancient as Caius is foolish. We both know why you're willing to risk your life. I can see your pain over your brother, and I can't imagine how painful losing your parents to vampires at such a young age was, but there are few things worth throwing your life away over, and your family wouldn't have wanted you to throw it away over them."

Her heart stopped, and her eyes widened. How did he know about...?

She swatted his hand from her face. He froze as she stepped away. "How did you know that?" she rasped. "How did you know my parents were killed by vampires, too?"

He didn't respond.

No. No. It couldn't be.

Damon Brock. Damon *Brock*. The words fell out of her mouth before she could stop herself. "Has anyone ever called you B?" No. She didn't want to know. She *couldn't* know. It would ruin everything.

Damon flinched as if she'd struck him.

Before she knew what she was doing, she rushed forward and shoved his chest as hard as she could. He didn't even stagger. "Do they call you B?" she yelled.

Tears poured down her face. This wasn't happening. It couldn't. No. She pummeled his chest, but he didn't move, didn't defend himself. "Did *he* call you B?" she screamed.

The muscles in Damon's throat strained as if he could barely choke out the words. "He called me B because my last name is Brock. That's why I signed the letters that way."

All sound, all movement, all feeling...stopped. Her hands shook at her sides, and her heart thumped against her chest, the sound of her own blood throbbing in her ears. Every inch of her body went numb.

Mark had always referred to his partner as B. She never knew it was the letter for a last name. She always assumed it was his first initial.

"B's an amazing fighter, Tiff. I wish you could meet him. I wouldn't trust anyone else to watch my back." He nudged her in the shoulder. *"Good-lookin' guy, too. Maybe you'll find a hunter like him someday and then I won't have to take care of you anymore."* He grinned.

Tiffany rolled her eyes. "Yeah, right. If he's anything like you I'd kick him to the curb."

Mark met her eyes. "Seriously, Tiff. He's a good man."

Mark's voice rang in her ears—the day he'd asked Tiffany to write to B. His fighting partner. The man he'd looked up to when they no longer had a father. Mark had said B had been like an older brother. His best friend.

Something inside Tiffany snapped. No. No. No. No. No. No. She had *not* slept with the man responsible for her brother's death. She *hadn't* lost her virginity to him. She sobbed, sobbed as she hadn't sobbed since she'd buried the last person she ever loved, the last and only person who had ever loved her, only three months earlier.

"How could you abandon him?" She choked on her own tears, barely able to speak. "Why didn't you save him?"

She stumbled backward, and Damon grabbed hold of her wrists, holding her up so she didn't collapse to the floor. Her whole body shook as she looked up at him.

A single tear ran down his cheek, and the pain on his face was staggering.

"No!" She wrenched away from him. How dare he cry on Mark's behalf? As if he hadn't been capable of saving him? "Don't you dare act like you cared about him! He trusted you and you let him down, and now he's dead because of it."

Damon's hands clenched into fists, and his pain was so palpable she felt it in her bones.

Tears continued to roll down her face, drenching her cheeks. "He looked up to you. He loved you, and you let him die in Caius's arms."

Damon's fist collided with the wall so hard plaster fell to the ground, and she felt the force of the blow in her feet. He threw another punch. Dust flew through the air as he released his rage. Then his head snapped toward her.

"You think I don't blame myself for his death every day?" His ice-blue eyes blazed with anger, pain, sadness, remorse. He strode to her and grabbed her shoulders, staring hard into her gaze. "You think I wouldn't give anything, wouldn't give my own life, to bring him back? Nothing I could *ever* possibly do would be enough to pay for how I failed him. I don't deserve forgiveness, but you *have* to know that I will bear the pain and regret of how I hurt him—" he paused and brushed her cheek, wiping her tears away "—of how I hurt *you,* for the rest of my life."

She sucked in a hard breath. "Why?"

His eyes widened as if he couldn't comprehend what she was saying.

"Tell me why you left him there to die, why you didn't save him."

As if unable to face her a moment longer, he turned away from her.

"Tell me why the valiant, brave, courageous *B* left his partner for dead. Tell me why the man I thought I knew turned out to be a coward."

Damon hung his head, his back still turned toward her. "Because I am not, and never was, any of those things."

She marched up to him and forced him to face her. "Don't evade me. Tell me why, damn it!"

He shook his head. "You don't want to know the details, Tiffany. You—"

She jabbed a finger into his chest. "Don't tell me what I do and don't want. You don't know me." She pushed at him again. "Tell me."

He cursed under his breath. "Because I let my feelings for the job cloud my judgment. I let my hatred for vampires fuel me and went by the book instead of saving my friend." He ran his fingers through the short stubble of his hair. His jaw clenched as she forced him to remember the moment, remember what he'd done.

"We'd been planning a raid on the nest for months. They'd killed hundreds, that band. We planned everything out, but it all backfired when one of the new hunters-in-training stepped out too early. The vamps rushed us as soon as they knew we were there. Your brother fought hand to hand with Caius. He was a brave man. Then Caius managed to stab him with his own stake. The bastard left him bleeding and ran. I was in pursuit of Caius's elder, the head of the nest. I was right on his heels."

He put his hand over his mouth as if to hold in the words, then dropped it to his side again. "With all the other vampires battling for their lives against other hunters and Caius gone, I knew none of the bloodsuckers would be hungry enough to go after Mark. His wound didn't look deep, and I was so caught up in the fight, in the adrenaline and anger of the chase, that I left him. I followed protocol to kill the vampires instead of saving my partner. I was seeing red. All I could see, all I could hear, all I could think about, was all the dead people I needed to avenge." He let out a long breath. "By the time I finished off the elder and went back for Mark, he was gone. Dead. I tried to save his body, but the vamps had the nest protected with explosives. The building blew up with Mark's body inside. I barely managed to get out alive."

A fresh round of tears streamed down Tiffany's face.

"I was the leader of that raid, and instead of saving my wounded partner, I was too obsessed with making the kill and following orders." Damon's hands curled into fists. "I will never allow my anger, my emotions to get the better of me during a fight again. Ever. And I swore to myself that I wouldn't get close to anyone again, wouldn't make any personal attachments, so I couldn't fail someone, but I failed at that, too." He met her gaze.

"Well, aren't you the good, obedient soldier." Tiffany walked toward the door. She needed out. She needed fresh air to breathe. She needed to be away from him. She placed her hand on the knob and turned the handle. "I hope you enjoyed the kill."

Without another word, she left the apartment, tears still streaming down her face.

★ ★ ★

Pain stabbed through Damon's heart as if someone had shoved a knife into it and twisted. If words could kill, the pain and sorrow in Tiffany's voice would have destroyed him.

The old feelings of regret rose to their peak. Never had he wished harder that he could have taken Mark's place. That he'd died and Mark had lived. Damon's father had died late in life in the line of duty at an old age, and his mother had passed not even two months later, the grief of her husband's death, of his absence, too much to bear. Both of them had been gone for years, and he'd never had siblings, leaving no one who would have missed him if he'd died in Mark's place. But Tiffany would feel the loneliness from her brother's death for the rest of her life.

And he'd practically stolen her virginity.

Shit.

The pain that had radiated from her floored him. And she still didn't know the worst of it...that Mark had to die again, but this time by Damon's own hand.

It had been a long time since he'd prayed, but it was worth a shot. He wasn't quite sure where to start, so he just closed his eyes. He didn't need any of the formal Catholic rituals he grew up with—he just needed to talk.

"I know I don't deserve it, but I could use some help right about now." He drew in a long breath and waited, expecting no response and receiving exactly that. He hoped for a feeling, just a small indication that someone was out there. Did the Big Man Upstairs even listen to the prayers of a killer?

Damon opened his eyes and let out a long sigh. He stood alone in his apartment, where only a few hours ago he'd autopsied a dead man right on his kitchen counter. And he thought God would want to listen to him? He laughed at his own ignorance before he looked up toward the heavens. "If You're listening, just…just help me make it up to her, all right?" he said into the silence of the apartment.

Then, without even stopping to put on his jacket, he rushed from the apartment and ran after Tiffany.

The cold air of the falling January night nipped at his skin, but it didn't even register in his mind. He needed to find her. He owed it to Mark, and as worthless as he was, the thought of her hurt sent his blood boiling. Nobody would lay a hand on her unless they wanted his knife shoved into their esophagus. *Nothing* would happen to her while he lived and breathed. She was going to get herself killed if she continued going off to fight vampires, but that would *not* happen on his watch.

He jogged for three blocks, eyes constantly scanning the streets for her. Assuming she had a car parked near Club Fantasy, heading toward the club was his best bet. Twenty minutes later, when he still hadn't caught up to her, he sprinted full speed back to the lofts, grabbed his car keys and jacket, and revved up his Z4. She must have taken a cab back to Club Fantasy, which only meant one thing: she was in a hurry…

…because she was going after Caius and she wanted to get to him before morning.

CHAPTER 8

Club Fantasy was nearly as dead as the majority of its patrons when Tiffany strode through the front entrance. It was still too early in the evening for all the vamps to be wide-eyed and awake yet. They could survive sunlight, but they sure didn't like it, and it left one hell of a skin rash.

She made her way through the virtually empty club to where Caius normally perched his overly smug self. He wasn't there yet, and she wondered what he was doing before his club's initial rush came in?

Janette, one of Caius's regular Feeds, strolled by, her hips swaying side to side as her bloodred pumps floated across the carpeting. Tiffany tapped her shoulder. The bleached blonde spun around, her face so pale the contrast with her fire-engine red lips was almost frightening. A fresh pair of fang marks were visible just beneath her golden tresses. She looked more like the walking dead than a human.

Then again, to all intents and purposes she *was* the walking dead.

Not much longer and she would be dead from the malnutrition and combined blood loss of being a Host, or—worse—she'd be drained and be a vamp.

Tiffany met the eyes of the grotesque-looking woman. "Do you know where Caius is?"

Janette scanned her, sizing up how much of a threat Tiffany was to her own position in Caius's bed. She must have thought the answer was "not much," because she said, "He's in his office."

"Thanks," Tiffany muttered. She brushed past the woman and hightailed it toward the main office, then skidded to a stop when she was met by a closed door. Caius either wanted privacy as he banged another helpless Host on top his desk or he was meeting with someone.

She pressed her ear against the door and prayed she didn't hear any hot-and-heavy moaning. She could do without those mental images.

"Yes, I'm very pleased with how it's been spreading." Caius's voice was muffled but made it through the door.

Her eyes widened. *Spreading?*

Caius chuckled. "It's becoming quite widespread in Seattle now. I think we're off to a great start. It's moving faster than I expected."

A moment of silence passed. From the one-sided nature of the conversation, she realized he was on the phone.

"Absolutely not. I'll ensure it continues to spread here. No newly transitioned vampire will escape its reach. The hunters won't know what hit them."

Tiffany gaped as she backed away from the door. That son of a bitch. He *was* helping to spread the virus. Anger hit her like a kick to the gut. The cosmos really had it in for her today. First losing her virginity to the man responsible for her brother's death, and now her brother's killer was creating flesh-eating zombies. Just. Friggin'. Peachy.

She cursed under her breath. She'd been foolish to run off. As much as she wanted to hate Damon for what he'd done to her brother, for not saving Mark when he needed it, for what he'd done to *her,* she needed his help to pull this off. An empty feeling balled in her stomach. For a moment, as she'd lain in Damon's arms last night, she'd actually thought she might not be alone anymore. So much for that.

As quickly as she'd come in the front a few minutes earlier, Tiffany rushed out the back entrance of the club. She jumped and pulled her stake as she almost ran headfirst into Damon.

Their eyes locked, and a pained look crossed his face. It took everything she had not to brush past him, telling him he could kiss her overly round white ass. Despite everything he'd done, meeting his fiery ice-blue eyes sent shivers down her spine and heat tingling between her legs. She hated herself for it, but her anger at him almost made her want him more.

"What are you doing here?" she snapped, ignoring the fact that a minute ago she'd been hoping for his help. "Why are you following me?"

He let out a sigh and stepped even closer to her. She stepped back.

"I'm making sure you don't get yourself killed. Nothing is going to happen to you on my watch," he said

"On your watch?" That was it. The hell with his help. "Look, just because I'm not a member of the Execution Underground and I don't have your strength, that doesn't mean I'm not a good hunter. You've seen me in action, so you know I'm good. Now step back and let me handle this myself."

He reached out to touch her cheek, but she turned away. He sighed. "I don't deserve a single ounce of your forgiveness. I know that. But I won't let you out of my sight. I have to protect you. For Mark's sake."

Her hands clenched into fists. If she didn't think his jaw was as rock-hard as the rest of him, she would have punched him right then and there. "For Mark's sake?" Who the hell was he kidding? If he thought she was going to buy into that, he was a few Froot Loops short of a bowl. "Cut the 'I'm sorry' crap, Damon. Sorry doesn't cut it when you're standing right here and Mark's dead."

He winced, and she crossed her arms over her chest, hoping she'd hit him where it hurt.

He lowered his eyes to the ground. "I told you I wish I'd been in his place. I'd give anything to go back in time and fix what I did, to save him, but I can't. I cared for Mark like he was my own brother. I know you don't see that. All you see is the worthless excuse for a hunter who failed his partner, who might as well have killed your brother himself, but I cared for Mark then, and I still do. Allow me to make it up to him, Tiffany. I've never begged for anything, but please, let me do this one thing."

Without a word, she turned on her heel and marched down the alleyway, leaving him in her dust.

Why would she want to grant him closure? A sharp pang hit her heart. Because, despite all he'd done, a small part of her still cared for him, still wanted him. After their night together, she felt as if she'd known him her whole life, and in some ways she had. She'd heard so many stories about him from her brother, exchanged so many letters with him. The courageous, valiant B.

Damon didn't follow her. His feet stayed firmly planted on the cold, wet ground. "I know you want to kill Caius as much as I do."

She stopped in her tracks.

His voice echoed off the walls of the alley. "And we both know you can't do that without me."

If looks could kill, Tiffany's expression would have massacred an army.

She spun around to face him with her lips pursed tight and her eyes blazing. She stomped toward him, her hands balled into fists as she stared him down—sexy and angry as all hell. Despite the negative emotions swarming him, he fought back a smile. He couldn't help it. This felt like a Texas standoff with an angry kitten. But as innocent as she seemed, she was pissed, and that kitten had sharp claws ready to rip him to shreds.

"Who says I need your help to kill Caius?" she demanded.

"Just let me protect you. For Mark's sake. For your sake." And, if he admitted it to himself, for his own selfish reasons, as well. No other woman could make him so angry and so turned on at the same time.

Shit, what was wrong with him? He could *not* continue to think about her like that. Once he'd found out who she was, she hadn't needed to tell him she didn't want him—he already knew. Nevertheless, he wouldn't let Mark down again. Whether Tiffany wanted to admit it or not, she needed protection.

"We work together to kill Caius, then you leave me in peace." She jabbed a finger into his chest. "No following me. No protecting me. None of it."

He let out a long breath. "You'll stop hunting after that?"

Pausing for a moment, she glanced at the night sky, as if she were weighing all the possibilities. Finally she met his gaze again. "Fine. We kill Caius, and then I retire from hunting vamps. I'll leave Rochester's bloodsuckers to you. But if I keep my end of the deal, you agree to leave me alone and never bother me again."

A large lump lodged in his throat. Though it killed him inside, he nodded.

She was right. Once they murdered Caius, Mark's death would be avenged. She could stop hunting vampires, and her life would no longer be in danger. His own next task—a task she would never know anything about—would be killing Mark again, exactly as Mark had asked him to. After that there would be no way for him to fulfill Mark's wishes and honor his memory besides continuing to be a good hunter. He would never forgive himself for the past, but there would be nothing more he could do, and Tiffany could move on with her life, put him and the entire supernatural world behind her.

It was for the best.

They locked eyes. An emotion he couldn't interpret crossed her face before she quickly looked away.

"All right, then. Let's get this over with as quickly as possible," she said.

Damon suppressed a wince. Yeah, that hurt.

For the best, he repeated silently to himself.

She gestured for him to follow her. "We can't be hanging out in this alley. Show me where you parked the Z4 while I fill you in."

He walked ahead of her, leading the way. "Fill me in?"

"While you were out stalking women fully capable of taking care of themselves…"

Shit. How could she have so much power to hurt him? How the hell had he gotten himself into this damn mess?

"…I was going after Caius."

Damon stopped walking and shot her a glare. "Why do you keep going after Caius alone?"

She frowned. "Because I know he won't hurt me, at least not for now. There's nothing to worry about."

"What do you mean, he won't hurt you *for now?* What good are you to him if he's not feeding from you? You said you weren't a Host."

She twirled a swath of her perfectly curled hair. "Not exactly."

His eyes widened. "What do you mean 'not exactly'?" The thought of Caius feeding off Tiffany, piercing his filthy fangs into the sweet creamy flesh of her throat, draining her of her life force, shoved him into a state of unparalleled rage. "You let that disgusting bloodsucker feed from you?"

She shot him a pissed-off glare. "Don't insult me. He's never drunk from me and he never will." She paused, as if she wasn't certain she wanted to share. Sucking in a deep breath, she continued. "He *thinks* he'll get to feed from me, but he won't. He wants me as a long-term Host, not a quick feed."

Damon's hands shook at his sides. It would be so easy to lose his temper and release his rage onto one of the brick walls of the alley, but he would *not* forget his head. He'd buried himself in enough emotions for a lifetime, thanks to Tiffany; allowing any more would be a mistake. She didn't want him. She wasn't his to protect. He was protecting her for Mark's sake. Strictly business.

Forcing his breathing to remain even, he spoke through clenched teeth. "How do you know he won't change his mind and drain you immediately, or take you without your consent?"

She stared at the ground, refusing to look at him. "I make sure my iron is high. I'm too valuable in the long-term for him to drain me immediately. As for the lack of consent, that's a risk I'm willing to take."

He pressed his lips together. "I don't think I need to tell you how st—"

Tiffany glared. "Don't call me stupid! I—"

Without thinking, Damon stalked forward and grabbed her hands, pinning her hard against the brick wall. They were nose to nose. "I'm not calling you stupid, but your behavior *is* reckless. Don't try to deny that fact. Now, I'll let you hunt Caius with me, but that doesn't mean I'll allow you to dangle yourself like a piece of succulent meat in front of a ferocious bloodsucking beast. Do you understand?"

She nodded, and he quickly released her. The nearness to

her made his stomach churn. It was pure torture, knowing exactly how amazing she felt beneath him, how soft her lips were against his, how sweet she tasted, what a deep and caring heart she had—and knowing he could never have that, never have *her*.

"Caius is the one spreading the virus," she said, breaking the momentary silence. "I don't know how, but I heard him speaking on the phone before I stormed out of the club. He was talking about the virus spreading, and saying that no new vampire would escape its reach."

Damon stood in silence, calculating all his possible moves. As much as he would like to, he couldn't just rush in and kill Caius. If he killed the bastard, which he would, all Caius's loyal vamp friends would swarm him, and even in the unlikely event that he survived, he would be revealed as a hunter in two seconds flat, not to the vamps alone, but to every supernatural in the city. He needed to get Caius alone, where he could destroy him in private. Then he could figure out how to deal with containing the vamp infection without Caius further aiding its progress.

He opened his mouth to speak, but she beat him to it. "You need to get Caius alone, but you're never going to manage that unless I lead him to a secluded spot and you rush in."

Shaking his head, Damon kneaded the base of his neck to ease the tension. "That won't work. What happens if he attacks you during your meeting? I won't be there to see it, and I won't be there to save you."

Tiffany let out a long breath and placed a hand on her hip. "The Execution Underground can equip you with pretty much any electronic device you need, right?"

He raised an eyebrow. He didn't think he liked where she was going with this.

A small smile curved her lips. "Have them make me a panic

button. One I can keep somewhere Caius won't see it. Then, if anything happens, I'll hit it. You'll have the receiver and you can trail us, so you'll be able to rush in if I need you."

Narrowing his eyes, Damon analyzed her expression. She couldn't be cocky about this. But from the look on her face, she was serious and focused. It killed him to agree to put her in harm's way for even a moment, but he would be right there to save her. Nothing would happen to her. Nothing.

"I'll set up a meeting with Caius, and then we'll go from there. If all goes well, I'll hit the button when I get him where we want him, danger or not. I'll make sure it's completely private. Somewhere no other vamps should be."

He gave a single nod. She had to know he didn't like it one bit, but they had no other choice.

Whipping out her cell phone, Tiffany pressed the number two and then hit Send.

Damon buried his face in his hands. What in the world would he ever do with her? He sighed. "Tiffany Solow, only you would place an ancient vampire on speed dial."

CHAPTER 9

Nothing like a master vampire to go with your brand-new stiletto heels. Tiffany balanced on one lone shoe, her other braced against the Dumpster outside the club. She patted the panic button one more time to make sure it was securely in place before she handed her weapons over to Damon and re-arranged her light shawl.

Without a word, they walked to the entrance of the alley-way. Around the corner was the entrance to Château Blanc, the newest restaurant in town. With her budget, she had never eaten there, but she'd heard the place was primo. Thank God Damon—and the E.U.—had loads of cash to buy her a nice dress for the occasion.

"You look ravishing," he whispered from behind her. The heat of his breath on her neck hardened her nipples to taut peaks. Screw him and the sexual dominion he had over her. "But try not to entice the monster too much, okay?"

She inhaled a deep breath, then glanced over her shoulder one last time, expecting to see Damon encouraging her on, but he'd already disappeared into the night. She swallowed the lump in her throat. She felt naked without her weapons hanging by her sides.

Damon was right. Facing a vampire without weapons was

light-years different from having a stake at your side. Even if she wanted to, there was nothing she could fight with now. But Caius had never scared her before, and she wasn't about to allow him to scare her now. And all emotions aside, she knew Damon would protect her.

He would be there when she hit the panic button.

She exhaled the breath she didn't realize she'd been holding. There wasn't any time to waste. A master vampire was waiting for her.

She wrapped her shawl more tightly around her shoulders and entered the restaurant. The soft sounds of melodic piano music carried to her ears amidst the murmurs of the demure dining couples. The dim lighting hit her cocktail dress at the perfect angle, and the midnight-blue material glittered like the clear night sky.

Her stomach growled as the smells of lobster bisque, freshly baked bread and fresh herbs filled her nose. For a college student who subsisted on a diet mainly made up PB&J sandwiches, microwave macaroni and cheese, and chicken-flavored ramen noodles, *divine* didn't even begin to cover the nosegasm she was having.

A handsome restaurant host in a nicely pressed suit cleared his throat. "Are you meeting someone, miss?"

She eyed the layout of the restaurant.

Well, damn.

The only entrance was the door she'd just come through, not even a single emergency exit visible. There had to be a way out, though. The law required it. She searched and saw the Emergency Exit sign right above the kitchen door. Inconvenient, but not worth abandoning the opportunity. Come hell or high water, Damon would figure out how to slip inside the building undetected if necessary.

And where was Caius? She had just started to look for him when the host cleared his throat again. "Miss?"

She snapped to attention. "I'm sorry. Yes, I'm meeting Mr. Dermokai—"

The name hadn't even escaped her lips before the host's eyes widened, and he swept his arm out in a welcoming gesture. "My apologies, madam. Right this way." He hopped to as if someone had lit a fire under his ass and poured gasoline on it. She glided across the restaurant behind him. At least she hoped she was gliding. Heels were not her thing.

Her heart beat hard as the host led her toward the far corner of the restaurant.

Shit.

Privacy was not what she wanted with Caius—at least, not at the moment. She had agreed to have dinner with him before he escorted her to a private location for feeding.

Caius's ill temper and inflated ego needed stroking, and removing himself from the public eye clashed with that deep-seated need. This was not his usual style. She hoped he hadn't sensed something, wasn't intending to change their plans, and she was unable to contact Damon to even give him a heads-up. She focused on the friction of the button strapped to the top of her thigh. She reminded herself that it was a weapon in its own right. All she had to do was hit it.

The host led her to a secluded room, opened the door and ushered her inside.

"Someone will be right with you," the host said before closing the door behind her.

Tiffany's eyes locked with Caius's, and a wide devious grin spread across his face. He was waiting for her at a table set for two, the only table in a room clearly intended to host multiple diners, even large private parties. A pure white cloth was draped across the table, and the lights from a tiered crystal chandelier reflected off the flawless marble flooring.

She was a not-so-helpless romantic, but even if she'd been with someone she *wanted* to be with—she refused to think about the man whose name immediately came to mind—this was a little over the top. Then again, Caius came from an era of overindulgence.

"Good evening." He stood and gestured her forward. "Won't you join me, Tiffany?"

Her gut clenched. She hated the way her name rolled off his tongue with the slightest trace of an accent from thousands of years ago.

She forced a grin across her face. "Gladly."

Crossing the room, she allowed Caius to pull her chair out for her. She slid onto the comfortable cushions, far from relaxed as he squeezed her shoulder and leaned in to speak. His hot breath brushed against her ear, and goose bumps covered her whole body. The small hairs on the back of her neck stood on end.

"You look good enough to eat," he purred before he returned to his side of the table.

How sweet: a bloodsucker who enjoyed toying with his food. She wanted to roll her eyes. *As if I try to marinate myself to an edible state each day.* The battle between the words that came from her mouth versus what she really thought commenced.

She batted her eyelashes. "I'm glad you're pleased, but I'm nothing compared to how you look. Dashing and handsome." *More like disgusting and vomit-worthy.* "As always."

Caius soaked in the B.S. of her ego stroking as if it were the heat of a rose-scented hot tub on a freezing cold night. "I'm pleased you recognize that."

A moment of silence passed between them. An unreadable smile crossed Caius's face. "Let's eat. Shall we?"

As if on cue, there was a knock at the door, and on Caius's command a waiter entered with two menus in hand. He approached their table with a smile. "Good evening. My name is Joshua, and I'll be taking care of you this evening. May I interest you in something to drink? Perhaps a bottle from our wine list?" He glanced toward Tiffany. Ladies first.

"I'll just have some wat—"

Caius interjected. "If you could bring two wineglasses and a bottle of Pétrus, it would be greatly appreciated."

The waiter nodded. "I'll return in a moment to take your ord—"

Eyes locked on Tiffany, Caius held up his hand. "I think we're ready to order now."

Joshua paused midstride and returned to the table.

Tiffany blinked. *Control freak much?* "I haven't looked at the menu yet," she said.

Caius reached across the table and placed a hand over hers. "Trust me. You'll love this." Releasing her hand, he unfolded his napkin as he spoke. "We'll have a starter of spinach and sea-urchin ravioli in a white-wine reggiano broth, and chèvre-stuffed smoked dates wrapped in prosciutto with aged balsamic saba on a bed of arugula. For our meal we'll have fresh herb-crusted Kobe filet mignon, cooked rare, and Maine crab cakes with a micro-green and lobster remoulade served on a plate of pure pink Himalayan sea salt, and the apricot crème brûlée for dessert."

Joshua's eyes grew to the size of saucers as he scrambled to write down every detail of the order. Scribbling on his notepad, he nodded vigorously. "Right away, sir." He rushed out of the room to fill their order.

Tiffany removed her napkin from the table and unfolded it across her lap. "You really know how to order your food. Very specific."

Caius ran his fingers through his golden-blond hair. If she hadn't known he was a vampire and a major douchebag to boot, maybe she could have found him handsome—at least before she'd met a certain dark-haired vampire hunter.

"I make it a habit to eat nothing but the finest foods." He grinned. "You only live once."

Tiffany swallowed hard and fought not to clench her hands into fists, ready to protect herself. Was that statement intended to be as threatening as she thought? She returned his smile. "I suppose that's true."

Joshua returned with a bottle of wine, opened it tableside and gave Caius a sip to taste, then poured the red liquid into two sparkling glasses. "Your appetizers will be out shortly." He removed the extra plates from the table before exiting.

Tiffany sipped her glass of Bordeaux. The wine slid down her throat, already warming her cheeks. "Very nice. It has quite a complex flavor to it."

Caius smiled and sipped from his own glass. "Let's get to the point, shall we? We both know what we're here to discuss."

She nearly spat the wine back into the glass. Shit. This was happening much more quickly than she'd expected.

He inhaled deeply. "I can tell by your scent that you'll be a perfect Host. My main Feed." He ran his tongue over his teeth, and she prayed his fangs stayed in place. Leaning back in his seat, he fixed his ice-cold stare on her. "You'll reap all the benefits, of course. I hear the human sensation as we feed is phenomenal."

She nearly choked on her own tongue, then reminded herself that no fangs would mar her throat. Never. As for phenomenal… Yeah, right. Maybe if you were into pain.

She ran her hand over her thigh, reminding herself of the panic button. And she would wager that the flatware lying before her was at least part silver—an extra protection. Once it penetrated the skin, silver was like acid to a vampire's insides. Her hand itched to hold her stake. When it was strapped to her side, she felt power surging through her in the face of vampires.

Now, she wasn't as certain.

Joshua and a second waiter paraded into the room, balancing their starter plates on trays. Fast service. One of many bonuses of shelling out ridiculous amounts of money for a meal.

They set down the plates in front of Tiffany and Caius. Joshua flashed a respectful smile. "We hope everything is to your liking." Then he and his shadow exited.

Tiffany eyed the plate before her. Artistic foodie explosion or delicious high-class meal? She wasn't quite sure which, but the overcompensating extravagance was certain.

Caius leaned forward in his seat and fixed his stare on her. "Where did I leave off?" He paused, then, grinning, pushed his seat away from the table. "Ah, yes, the advantages." He stood and crossed to her side of the table, looming behind her. "As I said, you'll reap every benefit. I'll make sure you have the finest of everything, and, of course, there are always—" he squeezed her shoulders and whispered in her ear "—the sexual benefits."

She froze beneath his touch. Her mouth went dry, and sweat gathered on her palms. "In other words, I'll be your high-end call girl." She slid away from his hold and rose from her chair to face him.

The ancient vampire frowned. "Call it what you like, but I assure you that you will be receiving the better end of the deal."

He leaned closer, and a feeling of dread crashed hard in her chest, turning her breathing labored. This was going south, and fast. She wouldn't show her fear, but she wouldn't allow him to have any more of a physical advantage, either.

She held her voice steady. "What exactly would those benefits be?"

He stepped closer, and she took a matching step back. Slowly, they circled the table, and the frown on Caius's face became a smile. He thought she was being playful, she realized. Better that than have him realize what she was really being.

"You're the one who asked me to meet you tonight, Tiffany, so don't play coy. You know *exactly* what those benefits are. Don't you?" His gaze narrowed, staggering in its intensity.

She glanced at the floor and up again, praying she looked flirtatious instead of terrified. "I'm really not sure. You may have to spell things out for—"

Before she knew what was going on, Caius had pinned her between her chair and his body. He moved so fast she barely saw him.

He grasped her throat. With one squeeze, he could crush her windpipe. "Don't get cute with me," he snapped. "We both know what I want, and I intend to get it whether you're willing or not."

Her eyes widened. Heat rushed to her face as she fought to breathe. She strained for the panic button and gasped for air as Caius's grip tightened. With the tiniest snap, his fangs descended. His canines glistened in the light of the chandelier. He reared his head and prepared to sink his fangs into the delicate skin of her throat.

Damon stormed through the kitchen, shoving his way into the restaurant. The smells of simmering white wine and melted cheeses invaded his nose. Shouts echoed behind him. An angry cook yelled as he passed, "You can't come in here!"

Not a surprising reaction to a man in a ski mask. He ignored them all and kept going.

At the sight of him, a woman in his path spilled a large vat of what appeared to be pea soup. The liquid splashed over the steel toes of his boots.

But he didn't care—nothing would stop him from finding Tiffany. When he heard the panic button sound, her safety became his sole mission.

He burst into the restaurant. His eyes darted across the room. Shit. Where was she? His line of vision followed a waiter as he walked past a back hallway. She had to be in a private room. Damon slipped through the crowded room as fast as he could, before he bolted down the hallway. A faint whimpering sound carried through the only door. Something inside him snapped.

Pulling his gun from his belt, he wrenched the door open, stepped to the side and aimed, making sure Tiffany wasn't in the line of fire. He squeezed the trigger. The mix of music and voices from the main dining room drowned out the muffled shot. Silencers were a hunter's blessing.

Caius's body jolted before he spun to face Damon. Tiffany fell to the floor, gasping for air. A small trickle of blood ran down her neck from where Caius's fingernails had dug into her skin as he choked her. Rage coursed through Damon at the sight. A loud snarl ripped from his throat. Caius would die.

He fired another shot straight into the ancient bloodsucker's chest, blowing a massive hole in Caius's body, but at Caius's age, the skin and organs knitted together again in seconds. Damon tucked his gun away, and ripped a silver dagger and his wooden stake from his jacket.

Fangs already down, Caius hissed, and the two of them charged each other. They collided at full speed, meeting each other blow for blow. A normal man stood no chance against a vampire as old as Caius, but gifted with the speed and strength of his Execution Underground training, Damon held his own. Anger and rage fueled his every move.

No vampire hurt Tiffany and lived. None.

Raising his dagger overhead, Damon slashed the knife across Caius's face. The leech hissed in pain. Blood gushed down his cheeks, and the wound smoked as if Damon had poured acid into it, but that didn't deter Caius. He blocked the swing of Damon's stake and punched Damon in the solar plexus. Gasping for air, Damon rushed the vampire, hitting him straight in the midsection. They toppled to the ground. Caius grabbed for Damon's stake, but Damon held tight. No way in hell was that vamp getting it.

Rolling his body overtop Caius, Damon plunged his knife downward and nicked Caius's arm, but the vampire managed to roll out of his grasp. Caius jumped to his feet and gripped Damon's throat, lifting him into the air. Damon was over six feet, but Caius dangled him above the ground.

Tiffany screamed. Shit. She was unarmed.

She lunged for a piece of flatware.

Damon gaped. "Tiff—" he choked out.

With both hands, she jabbed a fork into the back of Caius's neck, and he whipped his head around to address the distraction. Exactly the opportunity Damon needed.

He twisted and kicked his foot straight into Caius's gut. Caius's grip faltered. Seizing the vampire's arm, Damon drove the blade of his silver dagger straight through the bone. A loud roar ripped through the empty room, Caius grasped at the dagger, pulling the blade out so his wound could heal. Blood spurted from his forearm as he threw the blade with expert precision straight into Damon's shoulder.

Pain exploded through Damon's flesh, and adrenaline raced through him. He fell to his knees. Warm blood gushed down his chest, and he faintly registered the sound of Tiffany yelling his name. Clutching the dagger by the hilt, he ripped the blade from his wound. His vision spun from the pain, but he would *not* falter.

A fresh wave of adrenaline-fueled energy pumped into his veins. Caius rushed forward, but Damon swept the vampire's legs out from under him. The bloodsucker toppled over, and they rolled in a heap on the ground, both fighting to gain the upper hand. Caius's fist slammed into Damon's face.

Damon hit the bastard with an uppercut to the jaw, sending him flying backward. Caius scrambled across the floor as Damon jumped to his feet. Using every ounce of strength he possessed, he gripped Caius by the throat, lifting him into the air and slamming him down onto the dinner table. Shattered plate shards flew through the air.

Damon lifted his stake over his head, then brought the wood down. Caius clamped both hands around Damon's wrist, struggling to hold off death. Blood dripped across Caius from Damon's injured shoulder, but Damon fought through the pain.

The image of Mark's face contorted with pain flashed through his mind. This leech had killed his fellow hunter, his closest friend. The filthy beast lying beneath him had robbed Tiffany of her brother.

He would pay. He *would* die.

Damon shook as he shoved against Caius. Losing blood, and fast, he felt the wooden stake being raised as Caius gained the upper hand.

No.

Damon's vision blurred. Blood spurted from his wound, and he felt the color drain from his face, but he refused to give in.

Caius. Would. Die.

He released one of his hands from the stake and saw Caius grin. The dumbass thought Damon was losing the fight. No chance in hell. With his free hand Damon pulled his gun from his belt. A bullet to the chest wouldn't deter Caius, but he knew what would. Looking up, he aimed his gun straight for the fragile hook that held the chandelier in place. He squeezed the trigger.

The bullet blasted into the plaster of the ceiling, and the chandelier teetered before plunging toward the ground. Damon jumped back. The gold bars and crystals of the chandelier exploded on top of Caius's body.

Writhing beneath them, Caius squirmed to release himself from their weight.

Now.

A loud battle cry ripped from Damon's throat. Running forward, he lifted his weapon over his head and stabbed the stake straight through Caius's heart.

The ancient vampire burst to pieces. Blood splattered in all directions, coating Damon in the thick crimson liquid.

"Damon!" Tiffany ran to his side.

Damon crumpled to his knees, wiping the blood off his face. Tiffany fell to her own knees beside him. Specks of blood covered her face and her sparkling dress. Dots of black clouded his vision. Tiffany examined his wound.

"Shit." She pressed her hand onto the hole to gauge its depth. He let out a low hiss from the pain.

She grabbed her now blood-covered shawl from the chair and wrapped the material tight around his shoulder to slow the bleeding. Man, she looked like an angel as she cared for him. His heart thudded against his rib cage. He couldn't be sure whether it was Tiffany or the blood he'd lost that was making him delirious.

"Damon, we have to get out of here. All you have to do is make it to the car. All right?"

He clenched his teeth and nodded. With her help, he stumbled to his feet and hobbled from the room as fast as he could, though he was teetering on the brink of passing out. Loud gasps and shrieks filled the restaurant as Tiffany led him out the front door, holding his arm around her shoulder to help steady him.

The sweet smells of food faded from his nose, and the fresh air of the cold Rochester night blasted him in the face. He coughed, fighting to breathe. "S-s-sorry I ruined your dinner." He was trying to joke even as his vision spun. He wanted to be strong for her, show her it was okay.

Tiffany joked back. "Oh, yeah, I was really looking forward to some of that pink Himalayan crap." She forced a small smile.

But hard as she tried, even in his fading consciousness, she couldn't fool him. Her eyes told him everything. He knew how she felt…and she was terrified.

CHAPTER 10

A large mountain of sailor-level profanities wouldn't have been enough to express the deep shit Tiffany was in. Damon slumped against her shoulders more heavily each minute, quickly losing blood. He needed to get to a hospital as soon as possible. The bleeding wasn't slowing, despite the make-shift pressure bandage she'd placed on it.

As if that wasn't enough, pure horror clutched her hard as she stared at the familiar face looking at her from inside Caius's Bugatti Veyron, the metallic finish of the limited edition Pur Sang glaring beneath the orange streetlights. Damn it all to hell.

Caius had brought his vampire chauffeur.

Carl looked at her and Damon, taking in all the blood. His eyes widened, and she could practically see the light-bulb flicker on inside his head. Once an average man who'd served as Caius's Host back in N.Y.C., Carl flashed his elon-gated fangs. He'd been a vampire for two years, and there was nothing average about him any longer. A fiery blaze lit behind his eyes. His master was dead, and he knew it.

If Carl reported Caius's murder to the local nest, the death would infuriate the local vamps. With every vampire in the city on their tail, Tiffany and Damon would be dead within hours. And apparently Carl knew that, as well, because he ripped his gaze away from them and shifted the Bugatti into Drive.

Shit.

Damon groaned and swayed, barely holding himself upright as Tiffany released his weight. Pushing aside his leather trench coat, she snatched the Desert Eagle and her stake from his belt. She wasn't bad with guns, but she sure as hell wasn't a sharpshooter.

Still, she had to try.

Carefully but quickly aiming, she shot at the passenger-side rear tire. Her bullet hit the diamond-cut finish of the hubcap and ricocheted

Damn.

She squeezed the trigger again, hitting closer to the hubcap. *Come on, just a little closer.*

She held her arms steady as the Bugatti rounded a corner. Last chance.

One eye closed for a more accurate aim, she pulled the trigger for a third time.

The rear tire of the Bugatti exploded. Rubber flew in all directions. The awful scrape of metal against concrete hit her ears, more nerve-racking than nails on a chalkboard. She gripped Damon's elbow and pulled him forward.

"Come on, Damon. You have to run."

She kicked off her heels and bolted full speed toward the damaged car. Like a champ, Damon jogged behind her despite his bleeding wound. Carl threw open the door, briefly locked eyes with her then ran full speed down the nearest alley. A grin crossed Tiffany's face. He was fast, but not fast enough. He might be strong compared to what he'd been like as a human, but he wasn't nearly as strong and fast as an ancient master like Caius. Having been the star of her high school track team never failed to be useful when hunting.

A loud groan echoed from behind her. She glanced over her shoulder and saw Damon crumple to his knees. All the color had drained from his face, leaving his lips a pale white. He gasped for air. Tiffany skidded to a stop. Should she give up the chase?

The image of the victims' mauled flesh seared its way to the surface of her mind. If she didn't stop Carl, the news of Caius's death would race through Rochester like wildfire, and there would be no way in hell she and Damon could ever destroy the viral bloodsuckers before the virus spread out of control.

Damon was a hunter, a member of the Execution Underground. His wounds would heal.

She ran after Carl.

Bursting into the alley, she spotted the vamp racing along the far side, in the shadow of an office building. She launched herself into a full-on sprint. The muscles of her legs burned in protest, and the freezing concrete tore through the bottoms of her feet.

But she had an advantage: Carl didn't think she could take him.

When the leech reached the end of the alley, instead of rounding the corner onto the next block, he halted. Spinning to face her, he bared his fangs and hissed. The bastard was fooling himself if he thought she was scared. Two minutes of sitting with Caius across the dinner table was scarier than this guy threatening to kill her. The man couldn't weigh more than one-seventy soaking wet. It wasn't him she was scared of, it was what his words could do.

Before she stopped running, the vampire lunged. He knocked her to the ground, snapping viciously at her neck as he writhed on top of her. Really? That was all he could do?

She jammed her elbow upward and clocked him straight in the jaw. His head flew backward, and before he could return to attack she pulled the Desert Eagle and fired a shot straight into his forehead. The kick from the larger-than-average gun slammed her shoulder against the pavement. The wind rushed from her lungs. That was going to hurt in the morning. The monster screamed, falling onto the ground in pain as blood and brain fluid seeped from his head. Though the wound sealed itself within seconds, he clearly wasn't used to being shot in the head.

Wimp.

As he clutched his healing skull, she threw her body weight forward and landed on top of him, her stake held tight. He gripped her neck, cutting off her breath and holding her off him, but not before she positioned the stake between her breasts. With all the strength she possessed, she contracted her abs and shoved the weight of her chest downward. The sharp end of the stake pierced his skin and into his flesh.

He released her throat and grabbed her shoulders in an attempt to push her off, but it was too late. One more good shove and her weapon sank through to his heart. His undead body shattered in a burst of blood, and she flopped onto the concrete. Her elbows scraped the asphalt, and fresh blood coated her hair, face and dress.

For a moment she lay sprawled on the pavement. She squeezed her eyes shut. Her heart thumped, and she felt a slight soreness in her chest where she'd braced her weapon as she stabbed Carl. There was sure to be one hell of a bruise there later. The skin of her elbows burned, and she let out a small groan.

Her lids shot open.

Damon.

She scrambled up from the pavement and ran back down the

alley. A small cry ripped from her lips as she rounded the corner. Damon was lying on the cold winter ground, unmoving. She rushed to his side. Her heart stopped, and bile rose in the back of her throat. She couldn't tell if he was even breathing.

Dislodging his arm from beneath the dead weight of his body, she fingered his wrist, searching for a pulse. A faint beat still remained, though she could tell it was quickly fading.

Somewhere in her mind, she was vaguely aware of the sound of her own screaming as she pulled his phone from his pocket and dialed 911. She tried desperately to lift him. They needed to get out of there so the cops, who were surely headed to the restaurant already, couldn't find them. All she needed was an ambulance. Tears streamed down her face, clouding her vision. She couldn't think straight. Only one thought held firm in her mind.

She'd left B to die....

An incessant beeping noise echoed in Damon's ears. It sounded in rhythm with every thump of his heart. The pounding in his head matched his pulse.

Man, he felt like shit.

A blinding light hovered overhead, but his vision was so blurred that he couldn't tell what it was. He squeezed his eyes shut. It felt as if there was tubing in his nostrils. Though his arm weighed a thousand pounds, or at least it felt like it, he gripped the thin tube and ripped it away from his face.

"Damon, no!" a panicked voice cried.

The smell of antiseptic assaulted his nose. It smelled as nasty as a...

His eyes shot opened, and he frantically scanned the hospital room. He was wearing an awful white hospital gown, barely long enough to cover his upper thighs. Before he could say anything, the smell of Tiffany's sweet vanilla perfume wafted into his nose and her arms were wrapped around his neck. The smell was comforting, bringing to mind memories of the perfume-scented letters she used to send him.

Her body shook as she cried into his shoulder.

He blinked, taking it all in, before he gripped her by the waist and dragged her from the chair beside him onto the bed. She sat next to him, tears filling her honey-colored eyes.

"What in blazing hell is going on?"

Her lip trembled before she burst into another round of tears.

Damn it.

Pulling her into his arms, he cradled her against his chest. Though she'd obviously washed herself off, her gown was crusted with blood, but damn, the slinky thing still looked good on her. "Shh. Shh. Stop with the waterworks and tell me what happened."

She let out one last sniffle and sat up again.

"Are you all right?" he said.

She stared at him for a long moment, then blurted out, "I almost killed you."

He stared at her as if she'd grown six heads. "What do you mean, you almost killed me?"

He racked his brain, but the last thing he remembered was the pain of his knees hitting the restaurant's marble floor after he'd killed Caius.

He'd killed Caius.

If he hadn't been lying in a hospital bed, he might have done a victory dance. Hell, yes. The bloodsucking bastard was dead.

Tiffany wiped her eyes. "After you killed Caius, you'd lost so much blood. I managed to get you out of the restaurant, but then Carl was there."

"Who the hell is Carl?"

"He is—was—a vampire. He was Caius's chauffeur."

"What kind of a vampire name is Carl?" Damon scoffed. He tugged the edges of the hospital gown to make certain he didn't expose the family jewels for all the world to see. Not that he minded the gorgeous woman next to him getting a full-frontal view.

She gaped. "Who cares how stupid a vampire name Carl is? You almost died!"

Given the pounding in his head, Damon didn't feel in the mood to bicker. "But I'm not dead, so that's all that matters."

Swearing under her breath, Tiffany stood and paced to the other side of the room. Immediately, he wished she hadn't. The warmth she'd provided slipped away fast, replaced by the coldness of her absence. Why did she have to be so stubborn? He wanted her with him.

He grumbled, "If you want to make up for almost killing me, get back over here where you belong and lie down with me."

Her whole body stiffened, but she crossed the room and sat back down on the bed. Before she could protest, he lifted her legs onto the mattress and tucked her against his side. She nestled there as if they did this every night. Though he knew he would never have that, at that moment he couldn't bring himself to care.

"I think that's the morphine talking," she whispered. The heat of her breath brushed over his chest like a soft caress.

Morphine? So that was what was giving him that relaxed feeling.

"Nope, it's that dress. You're lucky every man in this place hasn't come on to you. *I'm* too much of a gentleman for that."

She giggled, and the swell of her full breasts pushed against his side. Oh, shit. He yanked the covers up to his waist. Whoever thought flimsy hospital gowns were a good idea needed a strong kick in the ass.

"Back to Carl," Tiffany said. "He would have ratted us out. Every vamp in Rochester would have known we were responsible for Caius's death, and then, even if we managed to survive, we never would have been able to stop the virus and the murders. I couldn't let that happen. I was so focused on stopping him that I chased him and left you behind. I staked him, but then, when I came back for you, your heart was barely beating and I had to call an ambulance."

She twirled a single finger to indicate the room around them. "That's how we ended up here." She let out a long sigh. "I thought you would heal quickly—you know, with all the extra Execution Underground abilities—but you didn't. Joseph said when Caius stabbed you he nicked your brachial artery, which is why you lost so much blood."

Damon mulled over the current situation. Him in a hospital with all his extra abilities was *not* good, and that begged the question how Tiffany had explained his injuries, not to mention what she would do about any fallout from what had happened at the restaurant. But most importantly... "Who is Joseph?"

"A guy I knew in undergrad. He's a couple of years older, so he's already doing his residency. He's kind of sweet on me."

Damon frowned. It didn't matter whether or not she was his, whether or not she still hated him for what he'd done to Mark, he didn't want any other man looking at her. He eyed the way she was nuzzling into him. Did she still hate him? He shook his head. The morphine must have hit him harder than he'd thought if he imagined she would ever forgive him for what he'd done.

"Don't worry," she said. "I told him we were mugged, but I asked him not to call the cops until you woke up. I figured if the cops showed, you'd know how to handle them, but I think we might be able to slip out of here unnoticed before they arrive. I don't think Joseph bought the mugging explanation for a second, but he's eager to please me. Plus, I offered him five hundred bucks to keep his mouth shut."

Damon rubbed the base of his neck to ease the tension. "Where are you going to get that kind of money?"

Shrinking in on herself, Tiffany looked away from him. She was flat broke, and he knew it from the way she'd talked in her letters. Now, with Mark dead, all she was living off of was Mark's E.U. accidental death insurance.

She bit her lower lip. "Well…I figured you would pay for it."

He chuckled. "I suppose I can file for reimbursement with the E.U. I'll make sure to list it under bribery."

She frowned. "I was trying to help. If I hadn't brought you here, you would have died. But then…it was my fault you were almost dead to begin with."

He lifted her chin with two fingers. "As you said, if you hadn't brought me here I'd be dead, so I'm thankful for that. The E.U. will pay for your friend's silence *and* the hospital bills. Not much to worry about." He paused. "Aside from getting me out of this hellhole."

She smacked herself in the forehead. "Oh! I forgot you told me you hate hospitals." She scrambled off the bed and pulled out his clothes from the small closet. "I made sure the EMTs didn't cut them off you." She tossed the clothes to him.

"Thanks."

She glanced at the floor, refusing to meet his eyes. "You're welcome."

She wouldn't meet his gaze. What was that all about? He could tell she was upset, but he wasn't sure why, and he wasn't sure how to ask, either. Had he done something awful in his sleep?

He swung his legs off the bed and stood. An IV dangled

from his arm. Ugh. There was nothing worse than the poking and prodding of annoying hospital staff. Without flinching, he pulled out the needle. When he faced front again, Tiffany stood in silence, staring at him as he untied the back of his robe.

A sly grin snaked across his face. "Admiring the show?"

Her embarrassed grin coupled with her deep blush was priceless. Her voice came out in a near squeak. "Sorry." She turned in the opposite direction.

He dropped the hospital robe and examined the bandage across his shoulder. The wound beneath it was probably healing over already. With the extra help from the hospital to keep him breathing, a nick in his artery felt like nothing.

He pulled on his jeans. "You can turn around now. I'm dressed."

Tiffany faced him, and her blush deepened at the sight of his bare chest. "I thought you said you were dressed?"

"Tiff, you've seen a *lot* more of me than this."

She bit her lower lip and stared at the floor again. "I know."

As he pulled on his shirt, he eyed the beautiful woman in front of him. "Do I look anything like you imagined?"

Her head shot up, and she gaped. "Who said I ever imagined you?"

Damon rolled his eyes. "Come on, Tiff. You wrote to me for years. You're telling me you never once wondered what I looked like?"

She shrugged. "Yeah, I guess I imagined a few times."

"And…?"

She shook her head, flustered. "I don't know. I guess I imagined you shorter and with more hair. But I was wrong—wrong in a good way."

He would chop off part of his legs and grow his hair longer if it pleased her. That was the sort of thing he used to say in his letters. As far back as he could remember, he'd always been a quiet person. But over time, when he'd written to Tiffany, he'd begun to confess things to her, to speak to her in ways he'd never spoken to anyone else. In ways he now knew he couldn't speak to her in person. With the morphine no longer dulling his pain and with all that had happened between them…how could he be the man she'd once cared for when he no longer had her faith to support him?

"What about you?" she asked, interrupting his thoughts. "Am I anything like you imagined?"

In his head, he told her she was more gorgeous than he could possibly have imagined, that the soft curls of her hair and the honey color of her eyes rivaled the divine, that when she smiled it was like God raining down blessings from heaven. And on a sexual level? Sir Mix-a-Lot would've drooled over her backside, and he himself would love to hold those sweet cheeks all night long and grab on to them while he—

"Well?"

"I had a vague idea what you looked like. Mark showed me a picture from when you were seventeen."

Tiffany looked as if she were about to be hit by an oncoming train. "Oh, man. You don't mean the one where I'm wearing the Gru—"

"Grumpy Bear Care Bear T-shirt," he finished.

She stuck out her lower lip in a pout. "If Mark were here, I'd smack him upside the head for showing you that. What an awful photo."

He chuckled. "I never thought you looked bad." If he was honest with himself, at twenty-five, when he'd first eyed that picture, the only thought that crossed his mind was that she was total jail-bait. Seventeen-year-old him would have tapped that for sure.

Of course, an overwhelming urge to pound his own head

against a wall had immediately hit him. Even back then, he'd hated himself for thinking about Mark's sister that way.

Tiffany stared around the room, as if she were too uncomfortable to meet his eyes. "So Caius is dead." She met his gaze at last, and something flickered behind her amber irises, something he couldn't identify. "I guess it's time for you to take me home, then. No more stalking me."

Damon's fingers clenched into fists, and he struggled not to throw whatever object was in reach. Why the hell had he ever promised to leave her alone?

Because she's giving up hunting, and because she doesn't want you in her life.

Her safety and her happiness, that was why.

He gave a single nod. "I'll take you home."

CHAPTER 11

Damon trudged up the stairs of the apartment building, following Tiffany. Though Caius was dead and Mark's death avenged, his stomach twisted into knots, dreading what lay before him. Damned if he hadn't sent himself to hell…

He swallowed hard, lifting one foot in front of the other, trying to act as if his one chance at happiness wasn't about to walk right out of his life. His heart pounded in his ears. Whoever the hell had come up with the bright idea that traumatic moments moved in slow motion could eat one of his fists. He would rather climb this stairway for eternity than face the next step—and, man, the climb was going fast.

Their goodbye had only lasted this long because he'd insisted on seeing her to her door.

They reached the final landing. She crossed to lucky apartment number seven. No, there was nothing even remotely lucky about that number. It would be the last trace he would see of her once she closed—or, more likely, slammed—the door in his face. She seemed all too eager to get this over with.

Pulling her keys from her purse, she reached for the knob before turning toward him. "This is it," she said. "Are you satisfied now?"

He bit his lower lip. Hell, no. He would never be satisfied

until she was his, until he knew that every morning when he woke up she would be lying right by his side, her face as peaceful and gorgeous as it had been during their night together.

The night she'd given him her virginity.

He wanted to tell her that, no, he *wasn't* satisfied. He wanted to tell her that she needed to be at his side. A sharp pang hit his heart, but he nodded to say that, yes, he was satisfied.

It couldn't have been further from the truth.

How could he have let this happen to him? How could he have fallen so hard? The thought of her staying with him sent pulses of ecstasy and elation beating through him. But as he stared at her beautiful face, knowing he would never see it again, all he felt was pain the likes of which he'd never known before.

He would willingly have suffered death a thousand times over rather than see her walk away from him.

She let out a long sigh. "I never thought I'd be saying this to the man I thought was responsible for Mark's death, but thank you. Thank you for helping me to kill Caius." She flashed him a weak smile. "I know it's probably not much consolation, but after what happened in the alleyway, when I left you behind, I understood why you left Mark. I got caught up in the hunt exactly like you did, and if I'd been in your place the night Mark died, I can't say I would have done any differently."

Damon exhaled a long breath. He wasn't sure what to say. All he managed to choke out was, "Thanks for telling me that."

Another weak smile crossed her full lips. Then she slid her key into the doorknob and twisted until it unlocked.

His mind raced, and every function in his body seemed to shut down and come alive all at the same time. Was he really going to let her walk away?

Say something, asshole!

Finally he forced her name out. "Tiffany?"

Turning toward him, she met his gaze, a slight look of happiness and hope in her sparkling honey eyes. "Yeah?"

Say something. Say something. Say something—anything. "Uh… you should get a stronger lock than that. I'll send someone over to install some extra enforcement. Don't worry about the cost, it's on me."

Fuck! That was all he could say?

Within an instant the spark in her eyes faded. "Oh, okay." Pausing, she met his eyes one last time. "Well, thanks again. Good luck with your hunting. I trust you'll destroy all the viral vamps." She turned away from him and opened the door.

He was a weak man. The woman he loved, his one chance at happiness, was about to leave him and he was going to let her. His heart stopped.

The woman he loved… His breath caught. Did he really love her?

Who was he kidding?

Stepping over the threshold, she began to pull the door closed behind her.

He raced across the hall and pushed through the doorway.

Tiffany spun around. "Da—"

Lifting her into his arms, he kissed her before she could utter another syllable. Her tongue met his, and they crashed together hard as he held her in his arms. Her hands snaked over his shoulders. Her touch sent pulses of energy through him. His body stiffened to attention and pushed against her soft stomach as he pressed her against him.

Quickly, he slammed the door behind them and pushed her up against the door frame. She gasped as he lifted her and wrapped her legs around his hips. He longed to feel her hot and tight around him. She was beautiful. She was intelligent. She was driven, kind, forgiving—and he couldn't think of a single reason not to love her. Never before had any woman driven him to his knees, but he would willingly have begged her not to leave if he'd had to. Nothing could keep her from him.

He shoved his hips harder against hers, and she let out a small cry. Her lips brushed against his before he pulled his mouth away from hers to trail soft but desperate kisses across her collarbone. A moan escaped her lips. The delicious scent of her warm vanilla and cinnamon-scented skin filled his nose, and she tasted just as sweet.

He kissed her neck one last time before whispering softly against her lips, "You didn't think I'd let you walk away that easily, did you?" Cupping her cheek with one hand, he captured her lips again.

Several small tears trailed down her cheeks, and he prayed they were happy ones. He pulled away and whispered in her ear again. "Will you let me make love to you?"

She nodded, and a rush of adrenaline flooded every inch of his body. She giggled softly as he carried her toward the bedroom. A more angelic noise had never graced his ears.

Walking into Tiffany's bedroom was like stepping back into a dorm. Then again, despite all her maturity, she *was* still a college student. He chuckled as he laid her down on her pale green comforter. From the brightly colored lamp shades lined with small fake crystals to the bookcases stocked with textbooks to the fluffy white carpet beneath his boots, Tiffany's room shouted her spirit from the hilltops.

Damn.

He was pushing thirty, and here he was with his best friend's baby sister. He stared down at her. The swell of her ample breasts lifted with her quick breaths. He ran his hand over the soft curve of her hips, admiring every feminine detail. For someone who tried so hard to appear tough and callous, beneath the surface she was anything but. And right now she was staring up at him with pure sexual hunger.

Without a word, he dragged her dress off over her head, unhooked her bra with one hand and drew the pink tip of one nipple into his mouth. She moaned beneath him as he teased her breasts with his mouth and hands. She rocked her hips against his, eager for him to take her.

He released her from his grasp and stood before her. He shrugged his coat off and threw it onto the nearby desk chair before kicking off his boots. She pulled herself up and knelt on the bed in front of him, then toyed with the hem of his shirt before slowly lifting it over his head. She tossed it to the side and unbuttoned his jeans.

Pausing, she leaned her head back and gazed into his eyes. She wrapped her arms around him, hugging his middle. "My heroic B." A small smile crossed her lips. Then she unzipped his pants and thrust them down around his ankles.

He was on top of her within seconds, straining with need as he positioned himself outside her entrance. She was already so wet for him.

She ran her fingers over his naked chest, then wrapped her arms and legs around him. "You have no idea how many times I dreamed of this," she whispered.

A lump filled Tiffany's throat, and she fought back tears. She hadn't exaggerated. She'd dreamed of lying beneath B, beneath Damon, countless times. He was even more handsome, even more incredible, than she had imagined. A shiver ran down her spine.

Their first time turned out to be nothing compared to the intimacy she discovered in his touch now. She didn't wish it any different. This time there would be no pain, no fear or reluctance.

In one quick push, he penetrated her. Her warmth wrapped around him as he slid deep inside. He filled every inch of her core, and she cried out. With strong but sensitive movements, he thrust into her, the rhythm sending waves of pleasure through her. Every nerve, every inch of her skin, was alive and on fire.

The scent of his skin filled her nose. He was everywhere. His hands, his mouth, his tongue reached every part of her, leaving no spot untouched, as if he was discovering her body for the very first time.

But the faint scent of antiseptic from the hospital still lingered on his skin, a crude reminder of his still-healing shoulder. A tense knot gathered in her chest. How could she have been so stupid? She ran her hands over the muscles of his shoulders. Because of her negligence, she'd nearly lost him.

Propping himself up on one arm, he suckled on her lower lip, then kissed her long and deep. The sweetness of his tongue sent a rush of heat straight to her core. A gruff moan escaped his lips as she slickened against him. His pleasure empowered her. The man holding her was a fierce warrior who fought against the strongest supernatural beings in the world. He could massacre monsters with his bare hands, but she longed to be the one to make him as weak in the knees as he made her.

Slipping his hand between them, Damon fingered the soft flesh between her legs. She cried out as he rubbed against her soft, sensitive folds. Pressure built inside her until she teetered on the brink of ecstasy.

He ran his lips over her ear, his hot breath sending shivers down her spine as he whispered to her, "Come for me, Tiffany."

He drove into her in a hard thrust that launched her climax.

She cried, "Damon!" Heat rushed to her core. She bucked against him as wave after wave of pleasure rolled over her.

Grabbing his face with both hands, she met his eyes. "Kiss me, damn it."

He smiled and playfully nipped at her neck. "Only if you come for me again."

She gasped. He didn't have to ask twice. He continued to pump into her as he kissed her so hard her head spun with desire. Another pulse of heat flooded through her, igniting a blazing fire.

As she finished riding the last remnants of her climax, she pushed hard against Damon's chest, fighting to roll him over onto his back. He grinned at her feeble attempt before wrapping a single arm around her waist and rolling her on top of him. He lay back as she straddled his stomach.

Her eyes widened as she drank in the sight of him. The toned muscles of his arms and chest flexed as he reached out to cup her behind. She squealed and wiggled against him as he tickled her. She fell forward, her breasts pressing against his pecs before she moved up and gave him a short kiss on the lips that was so intimate in its familiarity it made her breath catch.

Slowly she drew herself down the length of his body, her skin sliding over the hard ridges of his abs. Resting her head on his stomach, she snaked her fingers over his mouthwatering hips and belly, a delicious triangle of muscle with a small trail of dark hair leading down to his erection.

A low growl escaped his lips as she continued to move downward. "What mischief are you up to?" he purred.

He groaned as she brushed her lips against his arousal. "You pleasured me," she said. "Now it's my turn to pleasure you." She ran her tongue over the length of him, and the sound of his deep moans filled her ears.

Crawling up the length of his body, she left tender, soft kisses around his bandage. But a tinge of pain filled her heart. The image of his pained face, his unmoving chest and the paleness of his cold lips were seared into her mind forever. His pain had shattered her. Something inside her crumbled to pieces at the thought of losing him.

Not again.

Twice she'd nearly shoved him from her life forever, but now, after seeing him so close to death, she knew she would never be able to live without him. She would show him pleasure and entice him to stay. Though deep down, she knew she shouldn't worry. B would never abandon her.

After trailing kisses across his collarbone, she followed the line of his chest to the muscular curves of his abdomen. Her mouth practically watered at the sight of his abs. She imagined all the hard work, the training, the dedication it had taken to tone his body. He was perfect, like a piece of art.

He moaned as she massaged and caressed every inch of his body, from the crook of his neck and the bulk of his shoulders, all the way to his legs, hips and feet. He melted beneath her touch, and the look of ecstasy that crossed his face sent a rush of heat between her legs. She snuggled her body against him, her head resting on the tightness of his belly.

She whispered to him, allowing the heat of her breath to brush against his skin. "What can I do to please you? I'll do whatever you wish."

Tangling his fingers in her hair, he played with her long curls. "Your pleasure is more than enough." His ice-blue irises blazed in the dim light of her bedroom. That fire told her exactly what he wanted, though he refused to ask. He was too sweet, too much of a gentleman, to express desire for anything but *her* pleasure.

Another moan escaped his throat as she stroked her hand over his shaft. "Tiffany…"

She placed a finger over her lips and hushed him. "Shh. No

protests." She placed her lips on him, and it was his turn to buck beneath her mouth. "I want to make you come," she whispered.

Damon groaned as Tiffany's lips wrapped around him. The warmth and wetness of her mouth enveloped him despite his considerable size. She slid her lips up and down the length of him, her hands working in tandem with her sweet, sweet mouth. When she finally released him, he was so close to finishing that the delay was pure torture.

She straddled his hips, rubbing her soft flesh against him. He ran his hands over her porcelain skin from her breasts to her narrow waist, all the way down to the delicious expanse of her hips.

The perfect hourglass.

A low feral growl grumbled deep in his throat. One single curl fell into her face, highlighting her gorgeous smile. She looked so good it hurt. He couldn't take it anymore.

"I need to be inside of you."

She flashed him a coy smile and bit her lower lip. That was all the answer he needed. He spread her legs to reveal her sweet pink center, then wasted no time. He filled her, and she threw back her head and cried out. She rocked her hips against him as he continued to pummel into her. A shiver shuddered through his body as he neared his finish.

Tiffany ran her hands over his arms. Her glowing honey eyes locked with his. She was barely able to speak through her labored panting. Her chest heaved in and out, and she moaned as she neared her own peak.

But a mischievous grin crossed her lips as she mimicked his words. "Come for me, Damon." The sound of her whisper drove him wild.

In one final thrust, he emptied himself into her. They both cried out; ecstasy the likes of which Damon had never felt before billowed through him in a mind-blowing release. She collapsed on top of him, and he wrapped his arms around her and pulled the coverlet over him. Elation filled him as she nuzzled her head into the crook of his neck.

Gently, he kissed her forehead before he buried his nose in her hair. They lay there in silence as the energy subsided. His heart thumped hard against his chest. Several times he opened his mouth to speak, but no words came as she relaxed into sleep.

If he'd told her then that he loved her, that he wanted to spend the rest of his life with her in his arms, he wouldn't have been lying....

CHAPTER 12

If bones could talk, Tiffany's would have groaned and said, That. Was. Amazing. She stretched and twisted herself out of the tangle of bed linens, grinning like a fool as she mentally replayed the passion she had shared with Damon. She inhaled deeply, the scent of his skin filling her nose. He lay on his stomach next to her, mouth cracked open and arms spread, one over his head, the other dangling off the side of the mattress as he slept. She listened to the sound of his breathing, and watched his chest rise and fall.

Her fingers itched to run over the brand across his shoulders. The dark black ink contrasted with his lightly tanned skin. Watching him sleep, seeing him so totally relaxed, sent her heart racing faster. He was so sexy, so perfect. She bit her lower lip and fought to restrain herself from waking him, from pushing herself against him, kissing him deeply and seeing if what she'd heard about a man's sex drive upon first waking was true.

Before she could stop herself, she brushed the smooth skin of his face with her thumb. The sharp chiseled lines of his cheekbones and face stunned her. Even while he slept, he was breathtaking, beautiful in his intensity. But when he was awake, nothing gripped her more than the icy-blue depths of his eyes. They pierced through her, wild and ferocious, and sent chills down her spine. Like an angered Siberian tiger, both hypnotic and terrifying.

Still dead to the world, he responded with a low grumble. He leaned into her touch, then settled into sound sleep again. She smiled. Being with him for a second time had been so different from the first. When she'd given him her virginity, the pain had been minimal, and he had impressed her with how quickly he'd assuaged her fears. But the second time had blown her away with how familiar it had been in its intimacy. And unlike the first time, this time she'd known that the man she lay with was her B, the man she'd dreamed of for years.

Rolling to her side of the bed again, she stared up at the ceiling. For someone so distant, calculating and sometimes downright cold, Damon's capacity for tenderness had touched her, revealing the man behind the mask, the man she'd come to know through letters. There was no doubt in her mind that he cared for her. The same feelings coursed through her when they touched.

Whether he knew that or not, she wasn't certain.

She clenched her jaw. Anger built inside her as she thought of how stupid she'd been. How could she have been such an idiot? She should have known that the man she knew, her B, wouldn't intentionally have left Mark for dead. Damon still blamed himself, but after nearly losing him in the same way, *she* didn't blame him anymore.

Her mind wandered to all the letters she'd never answered. How deeply had she hurt him?

Swinging her legs over the edge of the bed, she stood and padded across the room to her desk. She slid the bottom drawer open and dug underneath the piles of school papers until she found what she was looking for. She pulled out the large stack of envelopes—not a single one opened.

She set the letters down, then quickly cleaned herself up and got dressed, then pulled on a black pea coat. Finally she grabbed the letters, walked through to the living room and stepped out onto the fire escape.

The cold winter air stung her cheeks. She sat down on the top step, her favorite quiet place. She glanced at the sky. Not a single star in sight thanks to the overwhelming lights of the city. She exhaled a long breath.

She had to know.

After removing the rubber band holding the letters together, she shuffled through them, reading the dates. One letter each day for over a month. A large lump caught in her throat. Her breath swirled around her face as she held the last letter Damon had ever sent her.

Tucking the rest of the pile under one knee, she opened the envelope. The paper made only a small ripping noise as it tore, but in her ears the sound was amplified by a factor of ten, a noise nearly as painful as a blaring alarm clock during an awful hangover.

Her hands trembled as she removed the single piece of paper, and pain filled her heart at the sight of B's familiar handwriting. She paused. For a moment she almost released the paper into the wind. It would be so much easier not to know.

But she had to.

Hands still trembling, she unfolded the letter and slowly read the scrawled words.

Dear Tiffany,
I have so much to say, but little time to say it as I start to search for Mark's killer. I doubt you will even read this letter, since there's been no response to the others I've sent for the last month.

But I have to write this in the hopes that maybe someday you'll open this envelope.

No matter how much you may hate me, no matter how much you may wish me dead, you will always hold a place in this cold heart of mine. I never intended to care for you, but I do. We both know I do, and for that I have no regrets.

Losing Mark, and now you, has driven me to the brink of insanity, and the pain is more than I can bear. You know how difficult it is for me to admit this to you, but I'm not okay.

I can never be okay.

Nothing I can say or do will ever express to you how sorry I am. I'll bear the guilt of what I've done for the rest of my life.

This isn't something I can just get off my chest, and as much of a relief as it would be for all the pain of what's happened to be taken away, I don't deserve any relief. I wish there were something I could confess to you that would turn this around, something that would make this better. I wish I knew the perfect lie.

Tiff, I'm begging you.

Tell me what it is you want to hear and I'll make sure you hear it. I'd say and do anything to have you back in my life again. I've got no family to fall back on, and my heart is so rooted in our friendship that even if I did, their love would never be enough to heal me without you in my life.

It's amazing how we got this far, how a one-line letter could turn into these feelings I have for you. Maybe it's meant to be this way, because Lord knows I don't deserve a woman like you in my life.

We both know what I want to say. It's always been on the tip of my pen, waiting for me to write it. But I'm too much of a coward.

You know how I feel, and if I could just say it to you in person one time...I could die knowing I'd had something meaningful in my life.

Yours always,

B

With still shaking hands, Tiffany attempted to refold the letter, but it was no use. Tears blurred her vision and spilled over onto the paper. She trembled at the thought of what she had to do.

He has to know.

Damon sat straight up in bed, heart racing as he gasped for air in the aftermath of the dream. His pulse beat in a heated rhythm, and he clutched the sheets in his hands. His eyes darted around the room. Tiffany. Where was Tiffany?

He launched himself from the bed and threw on his jeans. Rushing into the living room, he spotted a hunched-over figure on the fire escape. He ran back into the bedroom and threw on his shirt and boots before he strode to the living room window.

In his dream, Tiffany had changed her mind and decided that she *did* blame him for Mark's death. She'd said she'd been wrong to forgive him.

He wrenched open the window and climbed onto the fire escape. A blowing northern wind hit his arms like hundreds of small needles pricking his skin. Damn, it was cold outside. Tiffany was sitting on the top step, completely still.

"Tiff?" he said.

When she didn't respond, he walked up behind her. His heart stopped as he saw what she held in her hands. His letters. He brought his hand to his mouth and lightly bit his thumb so a string of profanities wouldn't fall from his lips. One letter lay open on her lap, and it was *the* letter, his final letter.

The letter that told her he loved her.

Shit.

He opened his mouth several times to speak but couldn't find any words.

He was *still* too much of a coward. Every time he tried to find the right thing to say, his mouth went dry and the words dissipated. What the hell was wrong with him? Why couldn't he tell her? For fuck's sake, he knew exactly why. Because admitting he loved her would make him vulnerable. Though he'd often refused to admit it to himself, he'd been in love with her for years. They both knew it. She already held his heart.

But if he said he loved her, he would be defenseless and exposed. She would have even more power to hurt him than she did now, and damn if that wasn't the scariest thing he could ever imagine.

Tiffany patted the spot next to her, motioning for him to sit. He sat down, resting his elbows on his knees, completely unable to speak. The pain in his chest overwhelmed him. Everything inside him wanted to grab her, tell her that he loved her and kiss her senseless, but he just couldn't do it.

She let out a long sigh. "I don't think I need to tell you that I was wrong. I think you already know it."

Damon's stomach churned. Suddenly nothing else mattered but the words that had just left her lips. The cold weather ceased to chill him, and the wind stopped burning his cheeks. She wasn't saying what he thought she was…was she?

"Here." She pushed an overstuffed, unstamped envelope toward him.

"What is this?" he choked out.

She bit her lower lip and stared straight ahead, refusing to meet his eyes. "The letters I wrote you. I never sent them."

He watched her in disbelief. She'd written to him?

She turned toward him. Tears streamed down her face, staining her porcelain cheeks. Her voice cracked as she spoke. "You need to know—I need you to know—that I never stopped loving you, not for one second."

Damon tangled his fingers into her hair and encircled her waist with his arm. He pulled her into him so fast that he barely realized what he was doing before his lips crashed against hers. He kissed her deep. Their tongues swirled against each other, the heated passion radiating over both of them. The feel of her body pressed against his sent his heart racing into overdrive.

Slowly he released her hair but never stopped cradling her head. His lips brushed against hers as he spoke. "I never stopped dreaming of you," he whispered.

A single warm tear slid onto his cheek, falling from her face as he kissed her again. He scooped her into his arms and carried her into the warmth of the apartment toward the bedroom. If he couldn't say he loved her, he could at least try his damnedest to show her in whatever way he could.

Damon couldn't have been more content. Tiffany lay against him with her head nestled into the crook of his arm. His eyes ran over her naked form. She was so damn beautiful. Angels couldn't compare.

He allowed his head to sink into the softness of the pillow. He closed his eyes and pinched himself, but when he opened his lids again he was lying in the same exact spot. Was this really happening? Was this what lay in his future? His nights spent protecting the innocent, with Tiffany there to lie in his arms when he arrived home at the crack of dawn?

For once in his life he hoped for the best. He prayed God wasn't playing some cruel, sick joke on him. After they'd returned to the bedroom, he'd tucked her letters inside the pocket of his jacket. He was still in a state of disbelief. She'd written him letters. He couldn't decide whether he was looking forward to reading them...or dreading it.

A sharp buzz sounded from the bedside table as his cell phone vibrated. Tiffany stirred, blinking lazily as her eyes opened. The phone continued to buzz.

He looked at the caller ID. Shit. The E.U. calling never meant news about flowers and rainbows.

He snatched the phone from the table, flipped it open and placed it to his ear. "Hello?"

Chris's voice on the other end of the line sounded desperate. "Have you seen it already?"

Tiffany met his eyes, listening to Chris, whose voice was loud enough to carry.

"Seen what?" Damon asked.

Chris swore. "You'd better get to the nearest computer."

Without hesitation, Tiffany darted to her desk, where her too-old laptop sat closed and asleep. She opened the screen and hit the power button.

"What's going on, Chris?" Damon asked. He pressed the button to switch the phone to speaker.

Chris spoke at the speed of light, his nerves clearly getting the better of him. "There is a viral video online. You need to see it before H.Q. gets it taken down. Search for 'zombie apocalypse Rochester.'"

Damon gestured to Tiffany. She typed in the search terms and hit Enter.

Damon shook his head, trying to wrap his mind around what seemed to be happening. "Please tell me this isn't what it sounds like." He could hear the sound of Chris's fingers flying across his keyboard in the background.

"If by 'what it sounds like' you mean dumbass teenagers getting video footage of the bloodsucker who's orchestrating your virus transitioning a dead guy into a viral vamp, then, yes, it's exactly what it sounds like."

Adrenaline shot through Damon's veins. "What are you talking about, Chris? We killed Caius last night."

"We? Who's we?" Chris rasped. "Who do you have working with you? And whoever you killed last night clearly wasn't the right vampire."

"Never mind who—"

Tiffany beckoned Damon. "Found it." She clicked Play.

The rustling sound of movement near an unsteady camera echoed from the speakers. The shaky video phone pointed down a dimly lit alleyway. A hooded man with his back to the camera over an unmoving form. A disgusting slurping sound carried through the video. Damon's heart raced.

After nearly a minute of continuous slurping, the figure pulled away.

"Fuck!" Damon roared.

The camera showed what was clearly a freshly dead corpse. Fang marks marred the victim's throat, plain as day.

"Holy sh—" The whispering of a teenage boy's voice was cut off as, judging by the sounds, one of his friends clapped a hand over his mouth.

Shit. Shit. Shit.

Damn teens these days and their freaking video phones.

A trickle of blood ran from the man's neck before the shadowed figure hunched over the body again. Reaching into his pocket, the faceless vamp removed a small syringe.

Tiffany mumbled under her breath. "Holy crap."

The shrouded figure lifted the arm of the corpse and injected the serum into the deadened vein. When it finished, the figure stood and stepped away, looming over the body. The corpse twitched, jerking to life. The dead man's eyes snapped open. The irises glowed a pulsing red.

The hooded figure disappeared into the night.

One of the teenage boys swore. The newly turned leech's head snapped in their direction. It opened its mouth and bared its fangs. A loud hiss ripped from its throat, and with unnatural jerky movements it scrambled into a crouched position, ready to pounce.

"Fuck! Run!" one of the boys yelled. The video blurred and jerked as footsteps pounded the ground. Seconds later the video cut abruptly to black.

Chris cleared his throat. "We are in some deep shit."

CHAPTER 13

An hour later Damon sat facing the rows of monitors in his home control room. Tiffany lingered outside the doorway, pacing. Sweat gathered on his palms, and a dry feeling filled his mouth. The last time he'd spoken with the Sergeant had been directly after Mark's death. The E.U. designated all accidental deaths as "under investigation," and Damon had been the Sergeant's lead witness.

One of the highest-ranking officers in the Execution Underground, Sergeant James Winfield took shit from no one and commanded respect without even batting an eye. He was one of only a handful of men in the Execution Underground who Damon absolutely refused to spar with, because he was *not* about to embarrass himself by having his hind end handed to him on a platter. With years of experience, age was nothing but a number to the Sergeant. Fifty-six years old and he could still kick some serious trainee and field operative ass. Aside from his salt-and-pepper hair, the gruff bastard didn't look a day over forty, and he didn't fight like an old man, either.

The green light on Damon's switchboard flashed, and the alert alarm sounded throughout the apartment. Tiffany jumped at the sound. On first moving in, Damon had rigged the sound system to blare in case of emergencies, and the Sergeant calling him definitely qualified. With a deep breath, Damon pressed the button to accept the call.

A small beep sounded, and then the Sergeant's stern face appeared on the nearest monitor, with Damon's own image boxed in the lower left corner of the screen.

The Sergeant's lips made a tight line, and he cast a frustrated glare at Damon. "What the hell sort of trouble have you gotten yourself into now, operative?" he barked. "Your town's little vampire-turned-zombie video bullshit is raising holy hell, operative. Do you know how much damage control that cost the security department?"

When Damon didn't respond, the Sergeant yelled, "Answer the damn question, operative!"

"No, sir. I don't know how much damage control it cost."

The Sergeant eyed Damon up and down. "A hell of a lot. That's how much. I don't give a flying shit if the video had nothing to do with you. It originated from your division area, so therefore you're responsible for it. Understood?"

Damon nodded. "Yes, sir."

The Sergeant glanced down at a stack of papers lying in front of him. "Your nerdy tech tells me you believed you killed the son of a bitch who was injecting these bastards, but it appears you were wrong. Is that correct, operative?"

"Yes, sir," Damon replied.

Sergeant James frowned. "You want to explain to me how the hell that happened, operative?"

Damon dug his fingers into the armrests of his chair. At the moment, there were very few things he wanted less to tell the Sergeant about than his failure to follow code and his misconceptions. He really hoped it was a rhetorical question.

No such luck.

The Sergeant banged his fist on his desk and glared at Damon. "Answer me, operative."

Damon inhaled a deep breath. "I received misleading information, sir. I was under the impression that the vampire at large, Caius Argyros Dermokaites, was responsible for the spread of the virus, and as a result I sought his death. I was mistaken."

The Sergeant shook his head as if Damon blew it on a regular basis when it came to protocol. In truth, never once had Damon been admonished for a protocol infraction. If there was one thing he knew how to do, it was play by the E.U. rules.

"From whom did you receive this faulty information, operative?"

Damon fought to keep his face impassive. "An outside informant, sir."

"And who is this outside informant, operative?"

"A family member of a former E.U. operative who is highly knowledgeable about the current vampire situation in Rochester, sir."

The Sergeant let out a long sigh. "Dear God, Brock. This doesn't have anything to do with Operative Solow's sister, the one you always daydreamed over, does it?"

Damon didn't respond. There was no point. The Sergeant had busted him more than once for reading Tiffany's letters over and over when he should have had his mind on his training.

Damon heard steps behind him.

Oh, no.

Tiffany stood behind his chair, posture perfectly straight and confident as she smiled at the Sergeant through the screen. "That would be me you're talking about, sir, and yes, Operative Solow was my older brother."

The Sergeant appraised Tiffany. "Your brother was a good hunter, Miss Solow, and from what I hear you seem to be following in his footsteps, becoming quite the freelance huntress yourself. Perhaps if the Execution Underground ever allows women to join I'll contact you."

Tiffany grinned from ear to ear. "Thank you, sir. I'd like that very much."

"Brock!" the Sergeant barked. "What is the fine young woman doing with your sorry ass?"

Damon opened his mouth, but Tiffany spoke first. "With all due respect, sir, the misconception was my mistake. I overheard Caius speaking on the phone about something spreading throughout the vampires in Washington State and how it was following suit here. I assumed it to be the virus."

The Sergeant paused and looked over his paperwork. "From what we've heard from our division in Seattle, there appears to be some sort of vampire governmental organization forming, a whole separate can of worms from this viral issue. The shit is about to hit the fan with these bloodsuckers. We need to get this under control as soon as possible." He folded his hands and leaned toward the camera. "This is what's going to happen, Operative Brock. With her consent, and since her place in Caius Argyros Dermokaites's inner circle means that she will be expected to maintain contact with his subordinates, Miss Solow will wear a tracking device that will lead us to the local vampire nest. Our best plan of action is to learn from the inside who is responsible for the spread of this virus, destroy as many of these monsters as we can and scatter their organization. I'm rushing in a team of hunters who will be under your command in this mission. Is that understood?"

Damon nodded. "Yes, sir."

The Sergeant looked at Tiffany. "Miss Solow, do you agree to act as an extension of the Execution Underground on this occasion and uphold all the same oaths as a true member of the organization agrees to, including putting your life on the line to save those of innocent civilians?"

"I do," she replied.

The Sergeant gave a single nod. "That is all, then. Operative Brock, your team will be there in three hours." He pointed a finger at Damon. "Don't fuck this up, Brock. And hurry up and build your permanent division. I want to get in the request to create your division before the shit hits the fan with all these supernaturals crawling around your city. If anything goes wrong with this vampire raid, H.Q. will blow off the request until these damn bloodsuckers are taken care of, and I don't want to risk innocent lives because you didn't do your job. So choose your permanent team and then prep for the raid." Without another word, the Sergeant logged off.

Damon released the breath he hadn't realized he'd been holding and slumped into his chair. Really? Pick his team *now?* A video had gone viral—bringing *way* too much attention to his city—somewhere out there a rogue vampire was hell-bent on spreading an infectious bloodsucker disease, he was expected to use Tiffany as a means of locating said psycho vamp, and yet the Sergeant wanted him to waste valuable time scanning résumés?

He let out a groan. Whether it made sense to him or not, an order was an order.

Tiffany placed her hands on his shoulders. "Are they all like that?"

Damon shook his head. "No, that's just the Sergeant. He's an ex-Navy SEAL commander turned E.U. hunter after his granddaughter got killed by werewolves."

"Oh, wow." Tiffany released him and stepped toward the door. She paused. "And what's this about you daydreaming of me?"

Leaning his elbows onto his knees, Damon rested his face in his hands. "I can't believe he mentioned that."

Tiffany laughed as she leaned against the door frame. "Well, since you have very little time before a group of vampire hunters starts knocking on your door..." She stood as straight as possible and pointed an accusing finger at Damon. Twisting her face into a scowl, she mimicked the Sergeant. "I suggest you get your worthless behind to work, operative!" she yelled.

Damon leaned back in his seat and closed his eyes. "Fine. But I'll never get any work done with you in here taunting me."

Tiffany crossed her arms over her chest and shrugged. "All right. I can take a hint, but get to work."

She left the room, and Damon watched as her deliciously round behind and hips swayed down the hall. He got up and closed the door so he wouldn't go chasing after her, slam her against the nearest wall and take her hard. Clenching his hands on the desk, he thought about what lay ahead of him. Another raid with him as leader? Was he prepared to do that again, so soon after Mark's death?

So many things could backfire. Though they did have one advantage this time, which they hadn't had previously: an informant inside the nest.

He didn't like the idea of Tiffany going into a nest of vampires alone, but what other choice did they have? There was no other way for them to track the nest, and the vamps weren't stupid enough to allow her to bring an outsider with her. It was the only way.

As much as he could, he pushed his worries aside. There were too many things he needed to do.

He typed in his security codes, and within seconds Chris's face greeted him from the monitor.

"Hey, Damon. How's it go—"

Damon met Chris's eyes. "Do you have the résumés the Sergeant asked me to go over?"

Chris spoke while he typed nonstop on his keyboard, the

clicking sound of the keys forming a strange robotic rhythm. He paused and emphatically jabbed the enter key. "Done."

Damon's side monitor flashed as dozens of images loaded. The faces of the finest hunters the Execution Underground offered filled the screen. "You've got to be kidding me. That's even more than I expected." With everything else on his plate, narrowing down this list was going to demand hours of work he couldn't afford to spare.

Chris cleared his throat. "And lucky for you, you have a contact at H.Q. who, despite your often grouchy demeanor, has taken the liberty of assembling a program for you, so you can refine the search and avoid having to read every single profile. What would normally be two or three hours' work has been narrowed down to less than an hour." He pointed at himself. "And that amazing contact to whom you owe your undying gratitude is me."

Damon glared at Chris. "Remind me the next time I see you in person to give you a nice big kiss on the lips."

"Considering the mood you're in, I'll take that as a thank-you." He reached forward to press the off button on his web camera. "Get to work."

In seconds the monitor transitioned to black.

Utilizing his touch screen, Damon slid the images onto his main monitor and started his search. It appeared his best option was to organize the candidates by hunting specialty first, before narrowing his search in each category. He glanced over the list of supernatural groups in Rochester and their current status. He needed a lot of manpower.

With the E.U. efforts intensely focused on N.Y.C. for years, Rochester had slipped under the radar. But now, with the N.Y.C. division finally gaining control of all their unruly boroughs, focus was shifting. Damon's division would not only secure the city, it would do it quickly. He would make certain of it.

First things first. Unrest in the Were community due to a possible change in packmaster.

He typed "werewolf" into the search box and roughly twenty profiles surfaced. He started mentally listing the attributes he wanted on his team. Young, able-bodied men, either fresh out of the academy but with lots of field training or only several years seasoned.

Though older hunters held the advantage of being wiser and more precise, he wanted to assemble a team that wouldn't disband anytime soon. Men near his age who possessed a drive, a fire, that too often faded over the years.

He typed in an age range and came up with three profiles, complete with photos. The emerald eyes of the hunter in the middle photo blazed with intensity.

He pulled up the man's stats, skimming for the important information.

Name: Jace McCannon

Hometown: Honeoye Falls, New York

Specialty: Werewolf

Experience: Three years field training

Current location: Atlantic City, New Jersey

Interesting. Honeoye Falls sat right outside the city limits. McCannon was practically a Rochester native. Damon's index finger hovered over the mouse. The hunter's burning eyes made him wonder if the man would be resistant to following orders.

After an extended moment of debate, he clicked the button to add the hunter to his roster. If he was unruly, Damon would whip him into shape. After all, he'd dealt with countless unruly trainees while he led raids during his field training. McCannon would listen, or Damon would send him straight back to H.Q.

Next up: demonic possession. There were two types of demon hunters: those who could kill demons and those who could exorcise the demon from a human's body, saving the innocent civilian. Looking at the numbers of possession reports on his sheet, he wanted somebody who could do both. He typed "Demon Hunter/Exorcist" into the system and prayed he would get a hit.

Yes! One hit.

Name: David Aronowitz

Ethnic Origin: Jewish

Hometown: Rochester, New York

Current location: Brooklyn, New York

*Requesting transfer near hometown for family issues

Perfect. Damon clicked the "add to roster" button without a second thought. No way would he pass up having a guy like that on his team.

Next in line: newly discovered occult activity and the possible formation of a Dark Wiccan coven.

Witches were extremely intelligent and cunning, and their relationships between covens could be immensely complex. Handling the occult wasn't black-and-white. It required someone with a level head. Figuring out the complex dichotomies of the witching world demanded patience. He tapped his fingers on the desk. He needed someone smart.

He narrowed the search to people with B.A. degrees or higher. The highest on the list was Shane Grey, Ph.D.

Bingo.

Three down, two more to go.

An increase in hauntings.

For the most part ghosts, while terrifying to humans, were

nonconfrontational. But an angry Poltergeist wreaked havoc and terror. Damon wagered that the many abandoned asylums of Rochester contained a shit-ton of pissed-off Polters.

He typed in "ghosts and poltergeists."

A lone profile popped onto the screen. The haunted gray eyes of the hunter stared at him from the monitor. Damon could tell that some seriously traumatizing shit had passed in front of that man's eyes. A small red flag flashed near the profile picture.

He clicked on the flag and the screen flashed "Post-Traumatic Stress Disorder." Damon raised a brow. Damaged goods weren't generally listed. Why the hell were there so few ghost hunters? He widened the search.

Damn. The majority of them were already assigned to the Florida Keys and Saint Augustine.

He hit the return button to the single profile.

Name: Ashley (Ash) Devereaux

Current location: New Orleans, Louisiana

*Transfer required (Post P.T.S.D.)

New Orleans? Now there was a city with one hell of a ghost population. He hit the add button, and hoped the guy wouldn't freak out on him. If he was still listed after a P.T.S.D. diagnosis, then the E.U. saw something in him that went beyond his stats.

Last one.

Several new species of non-werewolf shifters reported.

After entering "non-were shifters" into the search engine, he pulled up roughly ten profiles. His gaze shot to the profile of one hunter immediately. Two different colored eyes, not a common trait in anyone. Intrigued, he opened the stats.

Name: Trent Garrison

Experience: One year field training, two years full-time off-site operative

Current Location: Jersey City, New Jersey

★Transfer requested (Post-facial injury)

He eyed the man's features. The E.U. had yet to update his profile shot. He respected someone who fought post-injury, and since non-werewolf shifters had been rising in population over the past two years, this man had been a pioneer in the field.

A muffled knocking sounded from the other side of the door. "Damon?" Tiffany called.

He punched in the door code, and the latch clicked open.

Tiffany stepped inside. "You'd better get a move on. We have to prepare."

In his mind, the walls he erected during every hunt snapped into place. A level head would be the key to the success of this raid. He would *not* have a repeat of Mark's death. Come hell or high water, every member of the team the E.U. provided him with would come home safe. But his main concern, far and away more important than anything else, was ensuring Tiffany's safety.

He nodded. "Okay, I'm ready."

Her eyes darted to the main monitor. "Are these the hunters you're picking for your team?"

He didn't respond. Was that really what was sitting in front of him? His future team that he'd handpicked? A surreal feeling washed over him. He should have felt honored to lead an entire division, but the tight knotted feeling in his gut refused to subside. After what had happened with Mark, did he deserve to lead?

A low whistle escaped Tiffany's lips. "Daaannng. Are all the guys in the Execution Underground hot or what? Is that a requirement? Every single one of these dudes is frickin' gorgeous."

Damon grumbled in response. What was so fantastic about the men pictured on the screen? He didn't see it.

Tiffany grinned as if she were picking out her favorite Mr. February calendar pin-up. "They're all easy on the eyes, though I'm kind of partial to that one. He has awesome hair." She pointed at the golden-blonde from Louisiana with the haunting eyes, and then to the werewolf hunter. "But he's definitely my favorite."

He scratched his head and looked away. He tried to ignore her comments.

"Jace McCannon," Tiffany read from the hunter's statistics. She bit her lower lip. "He is one fine piece of—"

Damon hit Power-off on the monitor. The men's faces were gone in a second. Damn. It bothered him when she even looked at other men.

Tiffany hmphed, but a small grin crossed her face. "Jealous, much?"

Damn right he was jealous. He was jealous of any man she found attractive, and he would shove his fist straight down the throat of any man who made a move on her. He wasn't about to confess that, though.

"We'd better prepare for the raid," he said.

He stood to leave. Before the other hunters arrived, she needed to arrange the meet-up with the vampires, and he needed to prep his weapons. Preparing their plan of entry would have to wait until she led them to the location via the tracking device.

She crossed her arms over her chest and smiled. "If it's any consolation, I think you're sexier than all of them. You've got the whole tortured-soul thing going on. It's in your eyes. Women love that." Without another word, she brushed past him and walked out of the control room.

He raised a single brow. Tortured soul?

CHAPTER 14

After mulling over the plan with Tiffany, Damon stood in his room, arranging his array of weapons. Tiffany was downstairs, preparing to make her call. Everything was planned to the full extent it could be.

The incoming hunters would provide the tracking device for Tiffany to wear. His contact in the police department had ensured that word of Caius's and Carl's deaths and the abandoned and—much to Tiffany's chagrin—now-impounded Bugatti was never released to the press, and somehow the mess at the restaurant had been entirely hushed up. Without evidence of Caius's and Carl's deaths, the other vamps would be confused as to their sudden absence. Everyone knew of Caius's obsession with her, and luckily, it gave her a higher standing in the hierarchy. She was going to request a private meeting at the nest to discuss his disappearance. She'd prepped to play the role of the grieving, overly attached human.

Once she met up with her contact, she would be escorted to the nest. Damon and the other hunters would monitor her movements from a safe distance and follow her to the location. Damon had instructed her to play it cool once she was inside and not draw too much attention to herself. Caius's subordinates would undoubtedly engage in a power struggle if they assumed he was dead. She needed to encourage them in the direction of declaring him missing, instead. Ideally she would also find out who was behind the zombie virus.

While Tiffany distracted the vamps, the tech specialists would map a layout of the building and use a high-powered heat sensor to detect where all the beings in the residence resided. It was Damon's job to make the call on when to enter and to direct their routes of entry.

Tiffany promised him that once the hunters were inside, she would seek safety in the van with the tech team.

The hunters' objective was simple: annihilate as many vamps as possible, particularly the ones showing any signs of viral infection. With luck all the Rochester vamps would be in attendance, including the bloodsucker orchestrating the spread of the disease.

No matter what, they hoped to effectively control the situation by destroying the source of infection, even if they were unable to identify him, which would free Damon to hunt down any remaining infected vamps—should there be any left—as quickly as possible.

He finished tucking his weapons into place, with one last piece to go. With care, he removed a long black case from the top shelf of his weapons closet and laid it across his bed. Damn, it had been a long time since he'd opened this thing.

He unhooked the latches and opened the lid to reveal his father's pure silver slaying sword. The sword had passed through the past ten generations of Damon's family, a treasured possession even before the Execution Underground's formation in the late 1600s, uniting freelancing hunters who were newly settled in the Americas into one central group, a group which would later become international. The beautifully crafted piece of weaponry had served his ancestors in slaying thousands of vampires over the years, and now he intended to use it for the very first time.

He strapped the custom scabbard on his back and slipped the sword in. Assessing his mental check list, he made certain he'd prepared. He glanced at his watch. Ten minutes before the Sergeant's chosen hunters arrived.

He grabbed his jacket from the bed, felt something in a pocket and realized what it was. Tiffany's letters.

A tight feeling constricted his chest.

Before he could change his mind, he snatched the letters from the pocket and opened the single envelope holding them.

Tiffany was right. He needed to know.

He had ten minutes. He sat down on his bed and opened the pages. The first letter was dated three weeks after Mark's death.

> Dear B,
> Your letters are piling up. I've received one every day for a week now. I haven't read a single one.

Damon stopped breathing. Deep down, he wasn't surprised she'd never read them, but it still hurt.

But she *had* read his letters now. One, anyway.

The letter.

He flipped to the next letter.

> Dear B,
> I wish you'd stop sending letters. Every time I see the return address of the Execution Underground, my stomach churns because I know it's either a check that's meant to pay me off for the brother I lost, a check I have

to cash if I don't want to be homeless...or a letter from you. I don't know which makes me feel worse.

He bit his lip. Shit. That one stung.

Dear B,
Why?
All I can think is why...?

A sharp pain stabbed at his heart as he read the words. The next was merely a single sentence.

I feel nothing...

God help him. He had to keep reading. He couldn't pause to think. It hurt too much.

Dear B,
I tried believing this today.
Everything is normal. Mark is not dead. You are not the cause of any pain in my life. Life is the way it used to be. I'm a happy college student, preparing for med school.
Yeah...it didn't fool me for a second, either.

And the next:

If you were here, I'd stab a knife straight into your back, just like you did to Mark. What worthless excuse for a man betrays

his friends? What kind of pathetic human being leaves the ones they love to die?
You do.

Next:

I wish I hated you. Things would be less complicated if I hated you.

He hated to keep reading, but he had to.

Dear B,
I'm addressing this to you, because though I know I'll never send it, I don't know who else to write to. It's strange that the only person left in this world who I feel a strong connection to is the man responsible for the death of my brother.
  I'm all alone now. I have no family left. My grandparents are dead. Aunt Cecelia's dead. My parents are dead. Mark is dead. And now you might as well be dead, too.
  I must be next....
Tiffany

He had to force himself to keep going.

Dear B,
I realize now that not only is my brother really dead, but so is the friendship you and I had. I've run through endless possibilities of ways to fix this, ways we could reconcile, but there is no way.
Tiffany

He wanted to stop, but he couldn't.

Dear B,
I need to move on, to forget about you and put the past behind me, but your letters just keep coming.

I tried to burn them. I built a small fire out behind my apartment building last night. As I watched the flames, I held your letters—all of them, the ones I've read and the ones I haven't—over the fire. But even though I will never read them again, no matter how hard I tried, I couldn't burn a single one.
Tiffany

And finally...

Dear B,
This is the last letter I will ever write to you. I'm moving forward with my life.

I wish I could say what we once had between us was good, but I question whether a relationship built entirely on letters is really a relationship at all. The bitter, cynical side of me says it was never really anything. The nostalgic side disagrees and insists that at one point in time we did have something good, but that the goodness was just lost.

On most days, it feels as if I'm at war with myself about what to make of what we once were and what we are now. Was it good?

Bad? Worth it? Not worth it? I don't know if I'll ever fully come to terms with either feeling. Perhaps that's because it's a little of both.

All I can hope for is that in the future I'll be able to go a day, maybe a week, maybe even a month or, finally, years without thinking about you, because at the current moment...

You occupy my mind every second, and without you, life doesn't feel worth living.
Yours truly,
Tiff

Damon folded the letters and placed them back inside the envelope. Mechanically, he tucked them inside his pocket again. A knock sounded at the front door. The team had arrived.

Tiffany called out to him from downstairs. "Damon?"

For a long moment he couldn't breathe, couldn't speak. His heart pounded, and adrenaline pierced through him. He could feel her pain, her grief within every word, but...

Damn. Despite everything she'd said, her feelings had never faltered. They were back to where they'd been prior to Mark's death. He sucked in a deep breath. A massive weight lifted off his shoulders. They were back to where they'd started, as if they'd continued writing all along. Back to both of them knowing but never speaking it aloud.

She loved him...and God help him, he loved her, too.

Tiffany stood stock-still as Damon attached the tracking device to the clasp of her bra. Despite all her nerves, the feeling of his fingertips brushing her skin sent chills racing down her spine, and heat rushed between her legs. The last time she'd felt that feeling, he'd been on top of her, pushing inside her. Pure ecstasy.

She barely noticed the small device rubbing against her skin as Damon lowered the hem of her shirt. With gentle movements he moved her long hair to hang free down her spine. She bit her lower lip. She didn't know why, but since right before they left his apartment with the E.U. team, he'd been more tender with her than ever, similar to how he'd been in bed, but...different.

Not that she was complaining.

"Are you ready?" he whispered in her ear.

She nodded. "Yeah, as ready as a girl can be for playing in a vampire nest." Nerves built inside her again. A light sheen of sweat covered her palms. She always felt a little clammy before meeting vamps, even when fully armed, with her gun hidden beneath her jacket as it was now. But the feeling always subsided when she encountered them and her hatred for what they'd done to her family rose to the top.

It was the anticipation that raked her nerves, not the mission itself.

"Repeat to me what you're going to do again. I want to be completely certain we're on the same page," Damon said.

She let out a long sigh and faced him. "I've already repeated this to you twenty times, but all right. I'm driving to Club Fantasy and meeting up with Janette. I'm riding with her to the nest, and when we enter, I'll stall the discussion of Caius's disappearance for as long as I can. When you guys burst in, I'll hightail it out of there to the van."

He gave her a single nod. "Good." He met her eyes as he placed his hands on her shoulders. "We'll be close by the whole time. Nothing will happen to you. I swear it."

She smiled as much as she could, considering her nerves. "I trust you to keep me safe."

He circled his arms around her waist and pulled her flush against him. Pressing his lips against hers, he kissed her deep. A small round of catcalls and whistles echoed from his fellow hunters.

He released her and shot a glare in their direction. "All you morons shut your gaping mouths and get back in position before I put you there," he commanded.

The other operatives snapped to attention. Their mouths slammed shut.

Tiffany planted a kiss on her palm, before pressing it against his lips. She grinned. "For you to keep."

She longed to hear him utter three words to her. But she knew how hard that would be for him. For a man who'd been taught to bottle up his emotions, to be distant for the sake of the job, telling her how he felt would be torture. He wasn't prepared for that yet, not while he still bore the guilt of Mark's death.

He opened his mouth, trying to force words out, but she placed a single finger over his lips.

"You don't have to say it. I already know." She ran her hand over his arm before she sighed. "Let's go massacre some leeches." She turned away and walked toward the door.

Fifteen minutes later she sat in the passenger seat of Janette's silver sedan, cruising away from the city. She had no idea where they were going. She assured herself that there was nothing for her to be afraid of; Damon and the rest of the Execution Underground team were right behind her.

Once the vamps had accepted her suggestion of a meeting, entering the nest should have been a piece of blood pudding, but a mounting feeling of dread crept through her. She couldn't shake the feeling that the night wasn't going to go as smoothly as planned.

After thirty minutes of silence, Janette parked her car outside what appeared to be an abandoned warehouse. Tiffany nearly scoffed. What a cliché. Was it just her, or did all drug dealers, gangsters, monsters and the general underbelly of the population operate from inside old warehouses?

She and Janette exited the vehicle and slipped inside the freezing cold building. Tiffany almost choked on her own tongue. The inside held more vampires than she had ever imagined resided in Rochester. Nearly thirty bloodsuckers filled the room, along with only a small scattering of the humans she knew to be Hosts.

With twenty members of the Execution Underground at Damon's side, the vampires outnumbered them. She tried not to think about that. Few of the vampires were very old, of that she was certain. She prayed the E.U. hunters could handle the extra monsters.

All eyes turned to her and Janette as they entered the room. Tiffany scanned the crowd and recognized several faces. The closest in rank to Caius was Lucas. The regular bartender at Club Fantasy, Lucas had been on this earth since the mid-1800s, when he'd been working as a scientist, or so Caius had told her. The vamp wasn't nearly as ancient as his egotistical Roman superior had been, but in age he trumped all the other vamps in the room. Caius had told her that Lucas was the second-eldest vampire in the city, another migrant from N.Y.C.

"Finally our absent leader's pet is here," Lucas said with a grin.

From the look on his face, she already knew he couldn't have been happier about Caius's disappearance. With Caius gone, it was highly likely power would fall to him. Others might try to battle him for the position, but considering his age, his defeat would be highly unlikely.

He eyed her up and down. "You don't look to be grieving very deeply over the death of your master."

Master, my ass. In her head, Tiffany pulled her gun and shot Lucas point-blank solely for the disgustingly smug grin painted across his face. She fixed him with a hard glare. "I'm not grieving because Caius is not dead," she said.

A murmur of whispers ignited throughout the small crowd. So much for not drawing attention to herself.

Lucas raised a brow. "That's quite an assertive claim. Do you know something we don't?"

She shrugged. "Perhaps. It depends on what you know. Gentlemen first."

Lucas frowned. He didn't like being sassed by a lowly human. His lips remained shut.

Janette answered instead. Her ghostly face reminded Tiffany of a skeleton. And, man, was the red lipstick freaky against that pale skin. Janette glanced in her direction. "All we know is that Caius, Carl and the car have disappeared. Perhaps you know something more than we do?"

Tiffany continued to stare straight at Lucas. "Actually, I don't. But why Caius going missing would cause all of you to believe he is dead is beyond me." She scanned the crowd, meeting several pairs of eyes along the way. "There is nothing pointing to Caius's death, and knowing him as I do—as we all do—it seems quite likely to me that he's putting a plan in motion, something he doesn't want anyone to know about until he's ready to reveal it. It sounds to me—" her gaze locked with Lucas's again "—that some may be all too eager to declare him dead."

His jaw clenched. "Don't get too cocky, human," he spat.

She feigned an innocent look. "Too cocky? I'm just trying

to protect Caius's interests…exactly like everyone else here who is loyal to him."

Many vampires and Hosts alike nodded.

She cleared her throat. She had to keep this situation under control. "Rather than bickering about whether or not Caius is dead, I think it would benefit all of us to come up with a strategy to search for him. Until it's proven otherwise, we should proceed as if Caius is alive and well. I'm quite certain he left to attend to pressing business."

Lucas chuckled. "Without informing you or any of his fellow vampires?"

Tiffany shrugged innocently. "Who am I to question the motivations of my master?" Her stomach churned. The word tasted disgusting on her tongue.

He crossed his arms over his chest. "Perhaps you're correct."

What? Tiffany's eyes widened. Where was he going with this? Why was he agreeing with a human?

A devious grin spread across Lucas's face. "May I have a word, Tiffany? While the others create possible action plans, you and I can discuss the finer details of Caius's disappearance in private."

Damn it all to hell. With everyone standing there watching, she couldn't refuse or she would appear insubordinate, a deadly sin for a human, as if she had something to hide or a reason to fear. And as Caius's favorite, she was somewhat safe—hurting her would be as blatant as attacking Caius himself. So if she wanted to appear as if she truly believed he was still alive, she couldn't act as if she feared Lucas in any way. But she wouldn't put it past him—or any powerful vampire, for that matter—to attack her in Caius's absence, if only to strike a blow at Caius if he sought the elder's position.

She flashed a fake smile. "Of course."

Lucas gestured for her to follow him down a nearby hall.

Voices erupted in open discussion behind them, heatedly debating Caius's disappearance, as she walked toward what felt like her doom.

She followed Lucas to the end of the hall, where he held open a door to what had probably once been an office. She walked inside, and he followed suit. Adrenaline raced through her. When he closed the door behind them, the distinct sound of a dead bolt clicking into place sounded in her ears.

Shit-tastic sign number one.

Damon rode in the first of four E.U. vans. He sat next to the tech team leader, staring at the tracking screen. From what they could tell using their maps, a few minutes ago Janette had parked outside an abandoned warehouse near Brighton, a nearby suburb.

Courtesy of the silent hybrid engines, they surrounded the warehouse undetected. Though Damon's feelings regarding the raid remained steady and focused, his nerves circled around the thought of Tiffany in danger. He couldn't push their earlier moment from his mind. She'd known exactly what he'd been struggling to say, and despite that the words had still refused to leave his mouth, she cared for him, anyway.

Damn his stupid emotional inhibitions. If something happened and he'd never told her he loved her, he would never forgive himself. His failure would haunt him for the rest of his days.

No.

He couldn't allow himself to think like that. Nothing would happen to her. Her safety was his highest priority.

"All units secured," a muffled voice sounded over Damon's handheld radio.

Damon pressed down the button for confirmation. "Copy. Tech unit establishing ground layout."

Careful to not make any sound, one of his tech hunters slid open the side door of the van. He and two other hunters hopped out, the high-powered heat sensors in their hands. The three of them rushed around the building, hooking their equipment into place.

"Operative," a voice whispered from outside the van.

Damon turned.

Shit.

The Sergeant was standing outside the van, dressed in full gear and—from the bulges underneath his short leather jacket—fully armed. He climbed into the vehicle and crouched next to Damon.

Damon gave a single nod to his commanding officer. "Good evening, Sergeant. With all due respect, sir, may I ask why you're here?"

The Sergeant fixed Damon with a look that was half annoyance, half "What do you think I'm here for, idiot?" After a long moment, he said, "To make sure this goes smoothly, operative."

Damon met his eyes. "With all due respect, sir, I can—"

The Sergeant jabbed his finger into Damon's chest. If he'd been speaking above a whisper, he would have been barking at Damon, as usual. "Don't tell me what you can and can't do, Brock. I know you can do this or I wouldn't have put you in charge, would I? I'm here to make sure you don't call 'go' too soon. I can't have you getting trigger-happy. I'm no imbecile. You think I'm forgetting this is your first raid since we lost Operative Solow? Not to mention Operative Solow's sister is inside there. That's the woman you love, Brock. Don't think I don't know that."

Damon frowned. Damn. The Sergeant had always been so friggin' perceptive. It pissed Damon the hell off, but at the same time he respected the man for it. The Sergeant grated on his every nerve, but he was the man who'd made Damon into the hunter he was, and for that he looked on the Sergeant almost as if he were a second father—and the Sergeant acted is if Damon were a surrogate son, always giving him a hard time because he expected more of him.

Static crackled over the radio. "All secure."

Damon flipped three switches connected to the second monitor. A shadowy green layout of the building appeared on the screen. Damon's eyes widened.

"Damn. Don't know if I've ever seen more bloodsuckers in one place," the Sergeant said as he shook his head.

Damon scanned the screen. There had to be nearly thirty vamps in the main area and…

He paused. Three on the far side of the building? His breath caught. Shit. This was not good.

"Prep your team, operative, and remain calm. We'll get her out of there safely," the Sergeant said.

Tiffany's heart raced as she faced Lucas. Her pulse thumped in her blood, and she could feel the rhythm all through her body. Standing tall, she glared at the bloodsucker. She wouldn't show her fear. "What is this about, Lucas?"

An evil grin twisted his face. "That worthless hunter of yours, Damon Brock." The way he said Damon's name sounded as if he considered Damon the scourge of the earth.

Tiffany froze. It took everything she had to hold her face completely still. How did he know about Damon? She met his eyes and decided to bluff. "I don't know what you're talking about."

Lucas snarled. "Don't be cute with me, human. You know exactly what I'm talking about. Your vampire slayer lover and his brigade of Execution Underground cronies positioned outside this building." He stepped closer. "Lie and pretend you don't know again, and I'll sink my fangs into your throat."

She held her breath, holding her face still and stern.

He walked toward the wall and leaned against it. "I know you killed Caius."

All the neurons in Tiffany's brain fired. How the hell was she going to get herself out of this? She tried to steady her breathing. Damon and the other E.U. members would rush in soon, and when Damon saw she wasn't in the main room, he would come looking for her. Could she hold Lucas off until then?

Lucas went on. "But it's not Caius's life I care about. It's my master, Apophis."

Tiffany stared at him as calmly as she could. "If you expect the name to mean something to me, you're going to be disappointed."

A low growl escaped Lucas's throat and a shiver rushed down her spine. "Apophis, named for the Egyptian God of chaos and war, my master—the ancient vampire your hunter murdered."

She held her position. "Damon has destroyed hundreds of vampires, and you expect me to know the name of one in particular?"

Lucas chuckled. Moving faster than she could comprehend, he came to stand behind her, grasping her throat in one hand and her hair in the other. He led her toward a closed door that she assumed led into another room. "Perhaps you'll put two and two together when you see what I've saved as a surprise for the two of you."

Still gripping her hair, he wrenched the door open. A dark form loomed in the shadows. Lucas shoved her forward. She stumbled inside, and he flipped on the light. Her eyes locked onto the sight before her, and her heart stopped. Her stomach churned, and her whole body shook violently. Tears welled in her eyes as she choked down a scream.

Chained against the wall by his wrists stood her brother. At the sight of her, his irises flashed red and he hissed. His fangs descended as he fought against his restraints.

Bile rose in her throat. Unable to scream, she doubled over and vomited the entire contents of her stomach onto the floor. She panted, attempting to catch her breath, but to no avail. Her brain refused to process what stood directly in front of her.

Mark wasn't dead. He was a vampire.

And he was infected...

"No doubt that hunter of yours told you that your brother's body burned in the fire from the raid, and believe me, until this day he still thinks that to be true. But there's one problem with fires...." He stepped up behind her, and the warmth of his disgusting breath brushed against her neck. "There are no bodies to be found."

As fast as she could, Tiffany withdrew her stake from its hiding place and lunged toward Mark. But Lucas grabbed her midmovement. He dug his fingers into her hand, and the stake fell from her grasp as she felt the bones of her hand crushed beneath his fingertips. She crumpled to the ground.

Lucas kicked her spine, knocking the wind from her, then put his foot between her shoulder blades, holding her down. She prayed he wouldn't move his foot low enough on her back to find her gun. "See, here's what happened. That hunter of yours murdered my master, Apophis. Caius, being the coward he is, stabbed your brother with his own stake, then left to save his own skin. When I saw your brother lying there on the cold ground, bleeding, I saw my window of opportunity."

He stomped harder on her spine. She reached for her stake, but the lacquered wood had landed just beyond her reach.

Lucas continued. "To make your hunter suffer, I turned

your brother. I knew that to a vampire slayer of the Execution Underground, the only thing worse than death is being transitioned into one of the creatures they hunt."

Foot still on her spine, he bent and picked up her stake, then released her. She gasped for air.

"At first your brother was a normal vampire—under my direction, of course, seeing as I'm his master. But, well...a little experiment backfired on us. As Caius may have told you, other than the master I lost, science is the one love of my life. When the new vampire movement asked me to create a serum that would allow us to walk by day without weakening, I decided to use your brother as a test subject."

He paused to break her stake in two as if it were nothing more than a twig. "Turns out because it's been tampered with, the DNA of the hunters of the Execution Underground doesn't mix well with my vaccine, and, well, you know the virus that resulted."

Tiffany stared up at her older brother. Mark hissed and spat like an animal, fighting to be freed. If he hadn't been restrained, he would have torn into her flesh without hesitation.

"With the help of your brother, we were able to spread the virus and create a new strain of vampires by letting the newly turned feed on the humans he devoured."

Tiffany's stomach churned. If she'd had anything else there, she would have been sick again.

"Now I've combined the Execution Underground serum and my anti-sun vaccine into a single shot, and one injection can turn a new vampire into a flesh-eating monster. But for one special dose—" he pulled a syringe from his jacket pocket and held it up for Tiffany to see "—I've reversed the effect. Injected into the arm of an Execution Underground hunter, this will turn him into a ravenous flesh-hungry monster in minutes." A smirked crossed his face. "And guess which hunter I've saved it for."

Her eyes widened. Adrenaline raced through her body. Tears poured down her face. Dear Lord, no.

No, not Damon. She couldn't lose him, too.

"When the hunters storm in here any minute, your hunter will come straight here, looking for you. One injection." He grinned and raised the syringe into the light. "Or I can crush it now, and you won't have to go through the horror of seeing the man you love murdered, like I did. I'll give you a chance to save him—if you agree to sacrifice yourself."

Tiffany lay on the cold concrete of the warehouse floor, her whole body trembling. All the warmth drained from her face. "Only if you get rid of the injection first." She fixed him with a hard stare. Nothing was more important to her than Damon and his safety. She couldn't take risks.

Lucas placed the syringe on the ground and positioned his foot overtop it.

Then she nodded. She would do anything to save Damon. Anything.

"What do you want from me?"

He crouched and prepared to lunge for her. "Don't hold back." He met her eyes. "I like it when my victims put up a fight."

Happy to oblige, she pulled her Smith & Wesson from her lower back, aimed and fired.

The sound of a shot from somewhere inside the building rang in Damon's ears. His heart stopped. "Go!" he yelled into his radio. He and the Sergeant lunged from the van, hitting the pavement at full speed.

The hunters rushed from their positions and burst into the warehouse. Shots were fired, the sounds echoing off the metal walls, followed by the clatter of ricocheting bullets. Damon unsheathed his sword and launched himself through the main entry. He didn't think twice. He swung the heavy weight of the silver sword in front of him, slicing the head of the vampire in front of him clean off.

The vampire exploded in a burst of blood. Shrieks and cries of pain filled the room, but a steady constant buzz filled Damon's ears.

Tiffany.

Nothing would stop him from getting to her.

Brandishing his weapon, he cut savagely into vampire after vampire, destroying any and all of the monsters standing in his path. A male leech rushed him from behind. Spinning, Damon brought down his sword and chopped through the monster's skull. Blood splattered his face.

He drew his sword back, only to have the weapon wrenched from his grasp as something huge tackled him from behind.

Spinning to face his attacker, Damon snatched his stake from his side and plunged the sharpened weapon downward. Huge hands caught his wrist, and he locked eyes with his opponent. His breath caught in his throat as he stood nose to nose with the shell of what had once been his best friend.

A blazing red pulsed in Mark's eyes. He hissed and twisted Damon's arm, trying to get him to release the stake. Damon gritted his teeth and pushed forward. He would not allow the pain constricting his chest to deter him. He would kill Mark, releasing his friend from the fate he'd always dreaded.

The two men met each other punch for punch and kick for kick. It was just like sparring class, where they'd always partnered to fight against each other. Being older and stronger, Damon had always won. He intended to win this time, too.

Mark stepped closer, and his fist collided with Damon's gut. It was the one move Damon always caught him on. It was as if Mark was handing him the fight. Damon stepped into him, clutching Mark's arm and using the weight of his body against him.

With the help of his hip, he dropped Mark onto his back, but Mark quickly shifted to his knees.

Damon brought the stake down with all his might. Mark grabbed Damon's wrist, but he was at a clear disadvantage, on his knees with Damon standing over him. A loud yell ripped from Damon's throat, releasing a fresh wave of adrenaline. He channeled all his energy into his biceps, struggling until he positioned the stake directly in front of Mark's heart.

The vampire bared his teeth, battling with all his strength, but Damon held firm. One small shove and he could end this. He would keep his promise to his best friend, his fellow hunter. His whole body shook as he tried to force himself to do what he needed to.

Sweet Lord, help him. He had to murder his friend.

The pulsating red in Mark's eyes flickered and for a quick moment his face slackened. The rage and fight disappeared from his expression completely.

"D-do it, Damon," he stammered, before his eyes blazed crimson again.

Damon gritted his teeth and didn't think twice. He plunged the wood of his stake straight into Mark's heart. The blood of his only friend, his fellow hunter, of Tiffany's brother, covered his face.

"Everybody out!" he heard someone scream.

A loud explosion sounded from his right, and a wave of heat washed over him. The force of the explosion knocked him to the ground. Fire spilled through the building.

With shaking hands, he wiped the crimson liquid from his eyes.

"Brock!" The Sergeant's muffled yell carried from behind him.

Damon looked up and everything stopped.

For one long second he couldn't move, couldn't breathe, couldn't function.

Amid the smoke and flames, a large vampire stood silhouetted on the opposite side of the room, his arm around Tiffany's neck in a choke hold. She writhed against the bloodsucker's grip, struggling fruitlessly against him.

Damon launched himself from the ground and sprinted full speed toward her. Several of his fellow hunters and the Sergeant hooked their arms through his and tugged him back. Damon fought against them with every ounce of strength he possessed. They struggled to hold him back.

"No! Let it go, Brock! No!" the Sergeant yelled in his ear.

As the vampire disappeared into the smoke of the building, carrying Tiffany with him, her head snapped in Damon's direction.

No!

A loud cry ripped from Damon's throat as Tiffany's eyes flashed crimson and she bared her fangs.

★ ★ ★ ★ ★

To find out the fates of
Damon Brock and Tiffany Solow,
you won't want to miss a single volume of
THE EXECUTION UNDERGROUND
the new miniseries by Kait Ballenger.
Look for volume one,
TWILIGHT HUNTER,
coming in September, available wherever
Harlequin HQN Books are sold.
Now turn the page for a special sneak peek!

TWILIGHT HUNTER

THE
EXECUTION
UNDERGROUND

From the moment he pulled his gun on her, Frankie Amato knew what he was. A hunter. She'd stumbled onto a hunter. Still in wolf form, she stared down the barrel of his gun with fear and adrenaline pumping through her veins. A large lump filled her throat.

The rumors are true.

What had she gotten herself into? Humans—and hunters—had murdered her kind for centuries, but she hadn't expected this. A hunter in Rochester—on her turf. How could she have been so oblivious?

In the past few months several lone wolves who'd refused to join her pack had been murdered. As Alpha to the Rochester Pack, it was her job to protect her people and keep them out of harm's way. But the protection she guaranteed didn't extend to the Rogue wolves, so she hadn't given more than a fleeting thought to the rumors that they'd died at the hands of a hunter. Now the voices of gossip and the murmurs of trouble that had spread like wildfire through her clan smacked her in the face like a major reality check.

And son of a bitch, he'd backed her into a dead end. She'd let her guard down, and the bastard had cornered her.

She bared her canines, growling from deep within her

throat. The hunter strode closer. Shadows covered his face, but she could see his gun pointed at her head. The silver dagger he'd pulled from his coat flashed in the streetlights. Her heart pounded in fear, knowing the fate she would be subjected to if she didn't fight fast.

Frankie's tail bumped the wall, surprising herself; she hadn't realized she'd backed away in the first place. The hunter maintained the upper ground, holding the fighting advantage. Even if she lunged for him, his dagger would pierce right through her chest. Anger and rage filled her, and she snarled, dying to rip his throat out. But her sense of logic prevailed. She would wait until the right moment, when he thought she was weak, then speed-shift—her specialty.

A shiver ran down her spine as her limbs and muscles contorted. Pleading wasn't her style, but it was worth a chance. A loud howl escaped her lips, slowly transitioning into the cry of a pained woman as she shifted. She fell back against the brick wall behind her, bare flesh scraping the pavement.

The hunter stepped closer, his gun barrel held steady. A streak of rage rushed through her.

On the average day she could handle this, but now she was knee-deep in trouble and shit out of luck. Damn estrus always clouded her judgment. Hell, she'd even warned her pack against doing anything stupid. And on the list of stupid things to do, hunting a supernatural serial killer on her own while in estrus ranked number one by far.

And now he clearly thought she herself was that same killer, who he'd obviously been hunting himself.

She scanned the alley. Sheer brick walls, a couple of Dumpsters too far away to offer protection and nothing in the garbage lying around that she could use as a weapon. Nothing that would help her escape, and there was no way in hell she could dodge around him when she was cornered like this.

She lifted her hands and held them up, palms out. She wasn't below milking the helpless female card. Not if it saved her ass.

Draw him in. Pretend you're weak. Then finish him off and get the hell outta Dodge.

He hovered in the near shadows, a massive black silhouette, nothing visible but the width of his body and the gun still trained on her. Yeah, there was no missing that.

★ ★ ★ ★ ★

To see what happens next,
don't miss Kait Ballenger's
TWILIGHT HUNTER,
available in September
wherever Harlequin HQN Books are sold.

ACKNOWLEDGMENTS

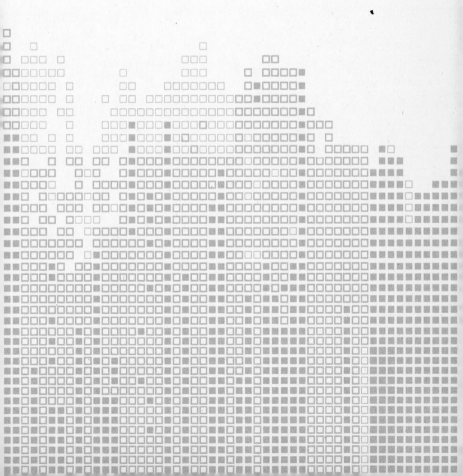

A huge thanks to all of the following people:

To my super agent, Nicole Resciniti, for dealing with all my neurotic tendencies and having the most awesome agent editorial chops I've ever encountered. Nic, thanks for taking a chance on this young, inexperienced writer and being my greatest cheerleader every step of the way. Having you for an agent has been a true blessing, and has changed my life for the better. You are both a great business partner and a great friend. I know we're both in this for the long haul. I couldn't have done any of this without you. I'll be forever grateful.

To my lovely editor, Leslie Wainger, and to the head of the HQN imprint, Tara Parsons, thank you for championing my work and for believing in the heroes of the Execution Underground. Leslie, thank you for giving me the final polishing touches on my manuscripts and for being my guide through the crazy publishing process. I couldn't ask for a kinder editor to help me through my journey.

To my first writing mentor, Mark Powell, for telling me I was good enough to build a writing career and for making me believe it. Mark, I may not be writing literary fiction, but I hope you're proud of me and enjoy this book all the same.

To my writing friends and mentors at Spalding University:

you all rock! Special thanks to Rebekah Harris for reading this before it was polished. Rebekah, you're a fantastic friend and hopefully I will find myself in the acknowledgments of your debut YA novel in the near future.

To Dr. Thebaud and Dr. Romain, thank you for restoring my health when I needed it most and for always keeping my well-being in mind. You've seen me at my worst but lifted me to my best. My family and I are beyond thankful.

To the best author girlfriends I could ever ask for, Cecy Robson and Kate SeRine. Thank you for holding me up every time I need it. I hope to always call you both my friends. And to my good friend and dance guru, Hollie Ruiz, for being such an enthusiastic fan and cheering for me: shimmying equals happiness. You're a great friend and a beautiful person. You inspire me.

To one of my best friends on the planet and the most awesome critique partner ever, Britt Marczak. Thank you for being there for me every step of the way. You read about Jace and the E.U. heroes when they weren't decent to see the light of day, but you loved them nonetheless. I don't know if I would have pushed through Jace's book without you.

To my pets: Sookie, Olivia and Elliot, for keeping me company in my office and being my favorite lazy editors—writing isn't the same without you interrupting me every five seconds and walking across my keyboard.

To my family (both immediate and extended) for supporting me in every single endeavor, I know that at the end of every day, no matter what has happened, you will all always love me and continue to support me. Mama, you believed in me. You believed in my writing way before it was any good, from that first butterfly book we made when I was little, to my sixth grade stories, through the first drafts of my first novels, all the way to where I am now and beyond. You're my best friend. You brought me into this world, and you've been the one to hold me up ever since. I love you.

To my husband, Jon, for sticking with me through all the ups and downs of the deadline for this book, for cooking dinner and cleaning the house when I'm too stressed out to do so, even in the face of a forty-hour work week. More importantly, honey, thank you for teaching me what it's really like to fall in love. I'm looking forward to spending our lives together, for better and for worse, until we are old and gray. I love you more with each passing day.

And greatest thanks be to God with Whom anything is possible. You rain down blessings on me every day, Lord.